S0-ASH-765

MISSING

Also available from MIRA Books and
JASMINE CRESSWELL

FINAL JUSTICE
FULL PURSUIT
DECOY
DEAD RINGER
THE THIRD WIFE
THE CONSPIRACY
THE REFUGE
THE INHERITANCE
THE DISAPPEARANCE
THE DAUGHTER
SECRET SINS
NO SIN TOO GREAT
DESIRES & DECEPTIONS

Watch for the newest novels from
JASMINE CRESSWELL

SUSPECT
Coming October 2007

PAYBACK
Coming November 2007

JASMINE CRESSWELL

MISSING

DOUBLEDAY LARGE PRINT HOME LIBRARY EDITION

This Large Print Edition, prepared especially for Doubleday Large Print Home Library, contains the complete, unabridged text of the original Publisher's Edition.

ISBN-13: 978-0-7394-8963-5

MISSING

Printed in U.S.A.

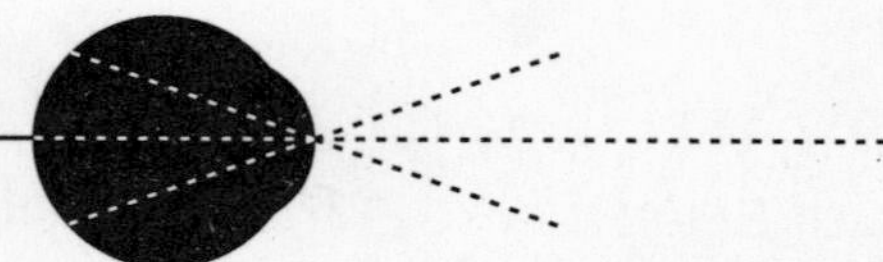

This Large Print Book carries the Seal of Approval of N.A.V.H.

ACKNOWLEDGMENTS

The author gratefully acknowledges the contributions of four outstanding storytellers: Diane Mott Davidson, Constance Laux, Emilie Richards and Karen Young.

For Maggie Osborne, who first decided
Ron Raven should be a bigamist,
and for Marsha Zinberg, editor extraordinaire,
who always loved this story.

Prologue

June 8, 2004, Fairfax, Georgia

Adam Fairfax stepped out from behind his desk and greeted his brother-in-law with a smile, a warm handshake and a friendly thump on the shoulder. "Ron, it's good to see you. How was your flight?"

"No major problems for once, but I travel too much and the flying's getting real old, if you want to know the truth." Ron Raven clapped the younger man on the back and pumped his hand. "You're looking fitter than ever, Adam, damn you. Still running those marathon races of yours?"

"Half marathons these days. It's all I have time to train for. But I guess I can't complain. My work schedule's a stroll in the park compared to yours. Every time I speak to Avery or Paul they tell me you're on a plane or just getting off one."

Ron sighed. "Seems that way to me, too, and flying's no fun these days, that's for sure. Shuffling through those security lines in your socks is about as enjoyable as watching mold grow on the shower wall."

Adam reached into his top desk drawer and pulled out the loan agreement that had been ready for his brother-in-law's signature for the past week. "It must be stressful, too, even when you've learned all the insider tips for making the process a bit easier."

"You're right, it's very stressful. My blood pressure's through the roof." Ron looked momentarily gloomy, then chuckled. "But that sister of yours is something else. A tyrant who looks like an angel. Avery's determined to keep me healthy even if we both die in the attempt. She tells me I've gotta eat lots of fish and green leafy vegetables and then I'll live to be a hundred. I told her that if all I can eat is fish and vegetables, why the hell would I want to live that long?"

Adam laughed in sympathy. "But Avery doesn't listen, of course."

"Of course not. Just keeps serving the damn spinach. And salmon. That's her other biggie. I'm surprised you didn't tell me my skin's turned orange from all the salmon she makes me eat."

"That's my sister for you." Adam gestured for Ron to sit down. "Beneath the Southern charm, she's just like our mother—as stubborn as a mule."

"Well, that's not unique to Avery, or even your mother! I swear stubborn is built into the female DNA." Ron chuckled. "Still, I wouldn't be without 'em, not for all the tea in China. You should try getting married, Adam. Workaholics like us need women to keep us in line."

"The hell we do." Adam smiled. "Listening to you always reminds me of all the reasons I'm happy to be a bachelor."

"You just haven't met the right woman," Ron said. "Trust me, you're gonna fall hard one of these days and then you'll wonder how you held out so long."

Adam pulled a wry face. "Has my sister deputized you as her front man? You're parroting her lines."

"Well, shoot, Adam, you caught me out. But what do you expect? I'm just a western cowboy. I'm no match for a steel magnolia like your sister. When she gives me orders, I salute and say, *Yes, ma'am,*" Ron replied. "I'm a brave man, but I'm not stupid."

Adam sighed. "I've learned there are few things in this life harder to resist than the genteel nagging of a Southern lady. I should just give up and marry the next woman Avery parades in front of me."

"Don't." Ron was suddenly serious. "Ignore the nagging, genteel or otherwise." He stabbed his forefinger into the desk for emphasis. "Despite what I said earlier, don't marry to satisfy anyone except yourself. I've seen what happens when a man marries to please his family and it isn't pretty."

"At the moment, I'm in no danger of marrying, period. Running the bank hasn't left much time for socializing this past year. And speaking of socializing, I hope you have time to stay for lunch today."

"I was planning on it. Thanks."

"We'll go to the Oak Room." Adam gave a conspiratorial glance. "Their beef is the best in town—and I promise not to report back to Avery if you order French fries."

"You're a mighty fine brother-in-law, Adam. Knew I could count on you for more than money." Ron grinned as he drew out a stack of papers from his briefcase, and Adam grinned back, appreciating his brother-in-law's camaraderie. Both men were perfectly well aware that Ronald Howatch Raven, founder and senior partner of Raven Enterprises, Inc., could raise money wherever the hell he wanted and that Adam, in fact, was very much the junior partner in this deal, even though he was the man handing over the money.

As the president of the First Bank of Fairfax, a once-rural farm community now located on the far southern rim of Atlanta's commuter belt, Adam was more accustomed to loaning a few thousand bucks to open a beauty salon or family restaurant than three million dollars to help transform a vast Wyoming cattle ranch into an upscale vacation resort. He was well aware that he would never have been given the opportunity to participate in Ron's latest real estate venture if not for the fact that his older sister happened to be Ron's wife.

Adam was honest enough to admit that there were certain ironies involved in authorizing this loan to his brother-in-law. He'd taken over the presidency of the bank from his great-uncle fifteen months ago, a few days after his thirty-first birthday. He recognized that he'd been given the job chiefly because of his name and heritage and was considered a foolish whippersnapper by a significant minority of the board. He'd spent a lot of the past year persuading managers and shareholders that the First Bank of Fairfax was only going to survive if they stopped making loans to friends and relatives and started making loans to entrepreneurs with a decent business plan. Adam hadn't counted on the fact that the most exciting business plan to cross his desk would come from his brother-in-law.

"Here are the latest architectural drawings for the Flying W project," Ron said, pushing a stack of papers across Adam's desk. "Thought you'd like to see them, just to keep abreast of what's going on. And here are some photos I took myself of the precise area where we're going to build the lodge. We can look at the plans in more detail over lunch, and you'll see how we're going to use the Silver River to define the footprint of the main lodge. As I mentioned before, the river's perfect for fly fishing."

"And makes for great views, too, for the visitors who don't care to fish." Adam picked up a picture of the river, foaming with white water, from the many calendar-worthy snapshots Ron had spread out on the desk. "Damn, but this is beautiful country."

"Between the river and the Tetons, I'd say we're going to wow the tourists. This is a can't-fail project, in my opinion."

"I agree. The development potential of this location is fantastic."

Ron pulled a face. "Fact is, the ranching operation should have been shut down years ago, but I've been too busy to take care of the arrangements. To be honest, I don't get back to Wyoming as often as I should."

"You've always said that your ranch manager is excellent. That must make it easier to keep everything ticking."

"You're exactly right." Ron nodded reflectively. "If the Flying W ranch manager hadn't been so good, I'd have been forced to move forward with the redevelopment years ago."

"Has your manager found a new job? Ranching isn't exactly a growing industry these days."

"He's going to be fine." Ron didn't elaborate on the fate of his ranch manager. "Anyway, you'll be pleased to hear I've had no trouble raising the rest of the capital we need to fully fund the project. I anticipate that we'll be breaking ground within the next couple of weeks. Unfortunately, the building season isn't long, but I'm optimistic that we'll have at least the main building under roof before winter sets in."

Adam stacked the photos into a neat pile. "I'm delighted that the First Bank of Fairfax can share in the development of the resort and I appreciate your willingness to include us among your investors. I'm convinced that, over the next decade, luxury accommodation with access to surrounding wilderness will become more and more popular as a vacation destination."

"You're singing my song," Ron said. "I'm real happy to have this chance to work with you, Adam. Hope it's the first venture among many. You have the paperwork on the loan ready to go, I take it?"

"Yes, I have everything waiting for you to sign." Adam twisted the file folder around on his desk.

Ron held up his elegant Mont Blanc pen. "If you have the papers, I have the pen." He put on a pair of reading glasses and flipped through the five double-spaced pages, skimming. "I assume this is a duplicate of the agreement you couriered to me last week?"

"Yes. The only changes are the two you suggested." Adam referred to his notes. "They're both on page three. We've substituted the revised wording you requested regarding precisely when and how the loan can be called." He smiled. "As long as you don't die, we're being very generous."

"Give me a minute to check through this one more time." Ron hadn't turned an inheritance of a hardscrabble ranch and less than fifty thousand dollars into a fortune of several million by being careless about the documents he signed.

He read in silence for ten full minutes, concentrating fiercely, and then glanced up, his friendly expression returning. "Everything looks to be in order." He extracted another sheet of paper from his briefcase and pushed it across the desk. "Here are the instructions as to where you should wire the three million. You'll see that I've provided you with both my personal account number and the wire-routing number for my bank."

"Thanks." Adam slipped the instruction sheet into the Flying W Development loan file. "The funds will be transferred Monday, and they'll be available immediately. Let me call in our notary public and we'll get these documents signed." Adam pressed his intercom button and spoke to his assistant. "Gayle, could you step into my office to witness Mr. Raven's signature, please?"

Gayle Tummins came into the office in less than thirty seconds, her official record book tucked under her arm. Ron initialed each page of the loan agreement in triplicate, signing with a flourish. Adam added his signature to each copy and Gayle completed the formalities with her notary seal, her license number and her own signature.

Ron thanked the clerk and then turned to Adam with a big smile. "Okay, now that's taken care of, we can move on to the fun stuff. Let's go to the Oak Room and order ourselves a couple of prime steaks and some honest-to-God, artery-clogging French fries."

Adam reached for his sunglasses. "Sounds like a great plan to me. Shall we walk? It's less than three blocks and it's not too hot today."

"Lead the way, since you're the man who knows where we're going." Ron was happy to let Adam precede him. He needed a few seconds to conceal the adrenaline rush that always accompanied a successful scam. Not that this was a scam, exactly. He fully intended to pay back the money, as soon as Las Criandas started to generate some profits and he had access to funds that wouldn't be scrutinized either in Chicago or Wyoming. It was damn annoying to have so much money and not to be able to access any of it when you really needed to. He should never have taken on Paul Fairfax as his partner. True, the guy was a moron—which helped—but even a moron would notice three million bucks missing from the partnership accounts.

Ron followed Adam across the marble-floored bank lobby, giving a friendly nod to various clerks and tellers, his amiable expression concealing the intensity of his focus. He always tried to create the impression that he'd succeeded in business more by good luck and fortunate friendships than because of a sky-high IQ and a bone-deep instinct for profitable deals. He was not in the least averse to having his brother-in-law underestimate him. Adam Fairfax was acquiring quite a reputation in Atlanta banking circles as an outstanding manager and a fine, intuitive judge of character. In Ron's opinion, Adam was the smart one in his family. Paul was all showmanship and no brains. Adam, it seemed, was going to be a very different sort of businessman—which wasn't good news, from Ron's point of view. He had to make sure there wasn't a single note in his pitch that was off-key. God forbid if Adam should ever become suspicious. Lately, there'd been altogether too much suspicion going around.

Ron always appreciated the feeling of power that came from deceiving people, and after a bad start, this project to raise three million bucks was turning out to be one of his more satisfying ventures. He loved the symmetry of it: Ted Horn needed to be paid off, and he was using Ellie's land and Avery's brother to rustle up the necessary funds. Playing off one end against the other and both ends against the middle. What you might call a real satisfying game plan.

None of which, of course, had anything to do with development plans for the Flying W. Although one of these years he might even get around to building the resort, if he could ever manage to talk Ellie into giving up the ranching life. Now that he'd written up the business plan, the idea of a wilderness-vacation resort struck him as potentially a hell of a lot more profitable than raising cattle. The location of the Flying W, reasonably close to Jackson Hole, was a huge factor in its favor.

"You're looking very pleased with yourself," Adam commented as they exited the bank.

"I'm thinking about the steak I'm going to order," Ron said. "Medium rare, with horseradish on the side. Hell, what red-blooded American male wouldn't be looking happy?"

Adam laughed.

Sometimes pulling off a scam was almost too easy, Ron decided, blinking as they emerged into the full glare of the midday sun. Especially when your mark was somebody as honest as Adam Fairfax. He'd discovered over the years that it was the honest folk who were far and away the easiest to deceive. Ellie, for example. And Avery, too, despite her superficial sophistication. Pity he couldn't tell anyone what a brilliantly smart deal he'd just put in place.

Adam Fairfax might not know it, but he'd just saved his brother-in-law's cheating ass. Ron was duly grateful.

One

May 2, 2006, Thatch, Stark County, Wyoming

Harold J. Ford, Sheriff of Stark County, wished like hell that he were somewhere else. Almost anywhere other than here would feel pretty good to him right now. Despite the spring sunshine and budding wildflowers, the familiar road leading to the Flying W ranch struck him as slightly less appealing than the frozen tundra of Alaska in midwinter. Unfortunately, there had been no stray cows or broken tractors to slow him down and he'd made the journey out from town in record time. He was now less than half a mile from Ellie Raven's front porch and he still had no clue what he was going to say to her.

He braked to give a couple of white-tailed prairie dogs time to scurry across the rutted gravel driveway, then drew his official Jeep

Cherokee to an unusually quiet and sober stop on the patch of blacktop in front of the Flying W's machine-storage shed.

A pair of quarter horses were munching grass in the side pasture and he gave them an envious stare. One of the horses stared back, new spring grass dangling from the side of its mouth, the picture of equine contentment. Lucky damn horse. Harry sighed. Some days it really sucked to be the sheriff of Stark County.

Ellie, thank God, must be working in the kitchen out back, as she didn't come to the door to greet him. Another brief reprieve. Harry threw a frustrated punch at the steering wheel. Unfortunately, bruising his knuckles did nothing to sharpen his brain function. He rubbed his sore hands, mentally rehearsing a couple of possible opening lines before giving up with a disgusted exclamation. Jesus, how was he going to find the words to tell Ellie about her husband? Everything he'd come up with since he got the call from the cops in Miami seemed insulting, patronizing or just plain heartless.

Megan, Ellie's daughter, came to the front door and whistled for the dogs, waving when she saw him. Harry waved back, finally forcing himself to step out of the car. He gave the dogs an absentminded pat as they bounded past him.

It was a big relief to discover that Megan was at the ranch. Harry had called her apartment in Jackson Hole before he left town, but he'd reached her answering machine. Then he'd called the fancy ski lodge where she worked. They'd told him she wasn't scheduled to come in again until Wednesday, which wasn't surprising since this was the off-season: too late for skiing and too early for the summer crowd. Harry had been afraid Megan might have left for a minivacation in Denver or Salt Lake City. Unless you were fascinated by watching cows swat flies, Stark County didn't provide much in the way of entertainment for a young, single woman. But Megan, thank God, was here and he'd count that as a blessing. At least Ellie would have her daughter right beside her when he delivered the news.

"Hi, Harry. What's up?" Megan greeted him with a smile, not waiting for an answer to her own question as she butted the front door open with her hip and shooed the dogs inside. She was a dynamo of energy, packed into a curvaceous five-foot-two-inch package. Conversations with Megan tended to be conducted at warp speed. "How is it that every time Mom bakes one of her chocolate-fudge cakes, all the neighbors know to come calling?"

Harry didn't joke as he usually would. "I'm here on official business, Megan. May I come in?"

"Of course." Megan shot him a glance that was still more surprised than worried. She gestured him inside. "Official business, huh? Has there been another report about wolves in the area?"

"Plenty up near Yellowstone, but nothing in this county, or I'd have heard about it. We're hoping the one Jerry Hotchkiss spotted last month was the proverbial lone wolf." Harry realized he was babbling and clamped his mouth shut. Tucking his uniform hat under his arm, he followed Megan into the living room. Ellie had told him about the new sofa and chairs she'd ordered online—her first Internet purchase—and they had been delivered since the last time he stopped by the ranch. The sofa loomed big and golden in the middle of the room, and the copper-colored armchairs flanked the massive brick fireplace where before there had been empty space. Maybe that was why the familiar room suddenly looked so alien.

"If it's not wolves, what's going on?" This time Megan clearly expected an answer. "You look upset, Harry."

"Yeah, I'm upset. This is going to be very difficult. Fact is, I've been given some bad news to pass on." There was nothing for it but to say what had to be said. "Could you ask your mother to come in here, please?"

"You're scaring me, Harry." Megan finally looked alarmed. She drew in a shallow, nervous breath. "Has something happened to my father? Or my brother?"

Her spectacular green eyes darkened with foreboding when he didn't interrupt to reassure her. "Oh my God. There's been an accident, hasn't there? Is it Liam? Or Dad?"

"Something like that." Before he had time to say more, Ellie pushed open the swinging door that led from the kitchen straight into the living room. Harry found himself thinking that nowadays builders would consider a door like that a lawsuit waiting to happen. Then he realized he couldn't avoid looking at Ellie for the rest of the afternoon, so he shifted his gaze to meet with hers.

Her green eyes, slightly more hazel than Megan's, were warm, friendly and unreservedly happy to see him. "Hi, Harry. What's up? I didn't expect to see you this week."

He cleared his throat. "Hi, Ellie." He didn't ask how she was doing or make a comment about the weather, and she immediately responded to his somber mood. Her smile switched off with the abruptness of a snuffed candle.

Her hand went to her throat. "Harry, what is it?"

"I'm sorry, Ellie, but I'm not here on a social visit. Truth is, I just finished a long phone call with a detective sergeant in Miami."

"Miami?" She tilted her head in a frightened question. "That's where Ron was going on Sunday morning."

"Yeah, I know." Now that the moment couldn't be delayed any longer, Harry spoke crisply, standing straight, draping himself in the mantle of his professional obligations. He needed to handle this like the sheriff of Stark County, not like a friend who'd known Ellie since the eighth grade. And he definitely shouldn't handle it like a man who had always thought Ellie deserved a better husband than Ron Raven.

"I'm sorry, Ellie, but there's no easy way to say this, so I'll give it to you straight. The police in Miami called me because they think that Ron has met with an accident. There's signs of a struggle in his hotel room." The sheriff breathed deeply. "Fact is, the police believe there's a chance that he's dead."

"No! That's impossible! Not Dad!" Megan's protest was harsh with shock, but Ellie said nothing. She stood rock still, except for her forefinger, which tapped in a quick, erratic rhythm against her throat. Harry had expected her to sob uncontrollably and he'd been terrified he'd have to comfort her, which almost guaranteed he'd end up saying all the wrong things. Like, *I hope he is dead. You're better off without the bastard.* Or, *you could have married me and saved both of us from choosing the wrong person.* Her unnaturally restrained reaction struck him as even worse than his imaginings.

Megan wasn't anywhere near as controlled as her mother. Tears running down her cheeks, she put her arm protectively around Ellie's shoulders and hugged her close, ignoring her mother's unyielding stiffness. She rocked her gently back and forth and Ellie didn't resist, although she didn't respond, either. But the fact that Megan was comforting her mother at least made it easier for Harry to resist the urge to walk over and hug Ellie at the same time as he yelled insults at Ron. Goddammit, Ellie was a good woman, one of the best, and she didn't deserve what was coming down the pike.

Unlike her mother, Megan soon recovered her wits enough to ask the obvious question. "What do you mean, the police in Miami *think* my father is dead? Don't they know? How can you be confused about whether a person is alive or dead, for God's sake?"

"The police haven't found Ron's body—" Harry corrected himself out of deference to the fragile hope that Ron might still be alive. "I mean, they haven't found Ron yet, so they can't be a hundred percent sure what's happened to him. He's definitely missing from his hotel. The cops are pretty sure he must be either seriously injured or dead, but they've checked all the hospitals in southeastern Florida and he's not a patient anywhere—"

Ellie spoke for the first time. "Ron was staying at the Doral Beach Hotel. He called me from there on Sunday night."

Harry's heart skipped a beat. "What time was that, Ellie?"

"I don't recall exactly. I was reading when the phone rang and I didn't pay much attention. Maybe nine o'clock my time? Ron mentioned he was about to go to bed."

"That would make sense. Nine here is already eleven o'clock in Miami." Harry reached automatically for his pen, then decided this wasn't the moment to be scratching down notes.

"Ron was fine when we spoke," Ellie said. "I'm sure he's still fine." Her tone of voice dared Harry to contradict her.

Harry cleared his throat, which seemed to have developed a permanent frog. "Apart from you, Ellie, the Miami police haven't been able to find anyone who spoke to Ron after eight-thirty eastern time on Sunday night."

"Why is that such a big deal?" Megan's petite frame vibrated with the force of her frustration. "If there wasn't an accident—if there's no body—why do the police believe Dad might be dead? I thought adults could go missing for weeks without law enforcement taking any interest. Dad's been out of touch for less than thirty-six hours. Why are the cops making a mystery out of something so trivial?"

There was no way to avoid describing the gruesome crime scene, so Harry did his best to lead them there gently. "Your father checked into the Doral Beach Hotel around seven on Sunday night. I guess he called down to room service and ordered breakfast for six-thirty the next morning—"

"That would be for yesterday morning," Megan clarified. "Monday, right?"

"Right." Harry nodded. "Ron also made arrangements with the hotel parking valet to bring up his rental car at seven-fifteen on Monday morning. He told the valet he needed to be at the airport by eight because he was taking the ten-thirty flight to Mexico City and security clearance for international flights eats up so much time these days—"

"Did Dad tell you he was going to Mexico City?" Megan asked her mother, cutting across Harry's painstaking explanation. "You didn't mention to me that he was leaving the country."

Ellie blinked. "What? Oh, yes. Ron told

me he had important meetings arranged in Mexico City. He expected them to last four or five days. I have the name of his Mexican hotel written down somewhere...." Her gaze wandered around the room, as if she expected the note about Ron's hotel to materialize out of the ether.

"Did Dad say when he would be coming home from Mexico?" Megan asked.

Ellie focused her attention on her daughter with visible effort. "No, he didn't specify an exact time. He said he had to stop off in Chicago to report on his meetings and check in with his business partners, but he hoped to get back here by the end of next week and he'd confirm later. I never expected to hear from him yesterday when he was traveling."

Megan's forehead wrinkled in puzzlement. "Why would Dad go to Mexico on business? He always claims there are so many opportunities within the States that there's no need for him to go overseas."

"This was something new," Ellie said. "He's looking into an investment opportunity for an old friend from college. Something like that. I don't know the details."

"We never know the details," Megan

muttered. "Dad's great on sticking to the big picture and leaving everyone to guess about the rest."

I'll just bet the bastard left them to guess, Harry thought angrily. As for Ron's excuse that he'd be stopping off in Chicago to brief his business partners—what a load of bullshit. Talk about the wisdom of hindsight! If only people around here had known earlier what the son of a bitch was really up to.

Ellie ignored her daughter's comment. She turned her gaze toward Harry, but her eyes were blind, as if she looked inward to some unshared memory. "I expect Ron will be calling any minute now. He probably changed his plans at the last minute. You know how he does that." Ellie subsided into silence again, her finger still tapping against her throat.

Megan bit her lip, visibly choking back the urge to crush her mother's hope that the two of them could expect to hear from Ron at any minute. "Did my father actually catch the flight to Mexico?" she asked. "Is that why there's so much confusion? Maybe Dad has gone missing in Mexico and there's a communications problem with the police there?"

The poor kid looked so damn hopeful. Harry shifted from one foot to the other, easing the stress. None of them had thought to sit down, as if shock had deprived them of the ability to make ordinary movements. "No, that's not it, I'm afraid. The police down in Florida are sure Ron never left the country. Screening is intense on international flights these days and the cops are one hundred percent confident your dad hasn't flown out of the country."

"Then maybe he was delayed in Miami," Megan suggested. "Or he might have been called to an urgent meeting somewhere in the States—"

"That seems real unlikely. Let me explain why the cops in Miami are worried." Harry gulped in much-needed air. "Here's what happened. The room-service waiter arrived with Ron's breakfast at six-thirty yesterday morning as requested but nobody answered the door. Eventually, the waiter got one of the maids to open up your dad's room. They immediately realized something was wrong."

"Why?" Megan demanded.

"One glance was all it took to see that there had been a struggle," Harry said, deciding they needed to know the unpleasant truth. "The phone was ripped out of the wall and smashed. The TV was damaged. Several pieces of furniture had been overturned and there was blood in several places. Most of it smears near the bed."

"A...lot of blood?" Megan asked. The hostility had vanished from her voice, replaced by stark fear.

"Enough blood that everyone was immediately worried for your dad's safety," Harry admitted. He chose not to tell either of the women that a quick preliminary test showed the blood had come from at least three different people, suggesting a minimum of two attackers and a brutal fight. Or it was possible that the blood might have come from one attacker and two victims, raising the embarrassing possibility that Ron Raven hadn't been sleeping alone.

That was an avenue Harry definitely didn't want to explore with Ron's wife and daughter. He hurried on with his explanation. "Even before the hotel security staff could initiate a search of the premises, they had word from the parking valet that your father's rental car had gone missing. The valet was afraid the car had been stolen since they still had possession of the keys, but the car itself was nowhere to be found."

"Why did they assume the car had been stolen?" Megan asked. "My father could easily have had a second set of keys."

"But he didn't," Harry said flatly. "The Miami police have checked with the rental company. They only gave your father one set of keys. Besides, the car has already been found. It was abandoned in a restaurant parking lot close to the ocean, about ten miles from the hotel. There was a set of keys left in the ignition." Keys that had been polished to a high gloss, obliterating any possibility of fingerprints. Keys that were so shiny it seemed likely they'd been cut within the past twenty-four hours.

"There were more blood traces in the trunk of the car," Harry said when neither woman spoke. "The evidence suggests pretty clearly that a body had been lying in there."

"In the trunk of the car?" Megan asked, her voice very small. "Oh my God."

Harry gave her hand a quick squeeze. "I'm sorry, Meg. Real sorry."

"It's okay." Except that it clearly wasn't okay. Struggling to regain control of herself,

Megan cast a quick glance toward her mother. Ellie's face was paler than the first snow in winter, but she met her daughter's eyes and delivered a ghastly caricature of a smile.

Realizing that her daughter was temporarily silenced, Ellie finally managed to look Harry right in the eyes and issue a challenge. "Just because there was a body in the trunk of Ron's rental car doesn't mean the body was Ron's."

"That's true," Harry said with admirable restraint. He didn't point out that if the blood wasn't Ron's, then he was soon likely to be considered the fugitive suspect in a murder case.

"It could be anyone's blood in that car," Ellie persisted. "Miami has a big problem with drugs, doesn't it? I just read an article the other day about all the cocaine that's still coming in from South America, despite the millions of dollars our government is spending in an effort to stop the drug runners. It could have been some drug lord who got shoved in the trunk of Ron's car, for all we know."

Harry didn't bother to comment on the improbability of Ron Raven disappearing at the precise moment as drug dealers stuffed somebody else's dead body into the trunk of his rental car. "The investigators in Miami have sent blood samples to the crime lab for testing," he said diplomatically. "They've ascertained that the blood in the hotel room and in the car trunk is from the same person, so we do know that much. But they plan to run more tests, of course. Unfortunately, the labs are always overworked and understaffed and the forensics will take time, even though the Miami cops have put a rush on it."

Megan was a smart woman and would normally have wanted to know how the crime lab was going to identify the blood as belonging to her father given that he wasn't available, alive or dead, to provide a sample for comparison. Since neither of the women picked up on the problem, Harry decided he could wait another few hours before mentioning that he would need a DNA-test swab from Megan, or from her brother, Liam. With that, the lab would eventually be able to determine with near hundred percent certainty whether or not some of the blood in the Miami hotel room belonged to her father.

Harry finally crossed to Ellie's side and did

what he'd been wanting to do from the moment she walked into the room—touch her. He took her hands and rubbed his callused thumbs gently over her knuckles. They were very small hands and he felt a sharp tug in his gut.

He drew in a breath that was embarrassingly shaky. "I'm sorry, Ellie, but it's not looking good for Ron. I have to be honest with you, the cops in Miami have listed Ron missing, but it sounded to me as if they were searching for a body. We can hope, of course, but the state of Ron's hotel room suggests that he is either injured or…dead."

And if the bastard turned up alive, he'd better not come into Stark County or Harry would personally kill him.

Ellie made a small, choked sound of distress and the tears finally began to flow. She fumbled in the pocket of her jeans for a tissue and wiped fiercely, but the tears kept coming back.

Megan, her own eyes brimming with tears, tried once again to comfort her mother. "Come and sit down," she said. "Mom, your hands are freezing. Do you want me to light the fire?"

"No, that's not necessary." Ellie blew determinedly. “I’ll be all right, Megan, but don’t fuss. I can’t…handle people hovering over me right now.”

“Why don’t we leave your mother alone for a couple of minutes,” Harry suggested to Megan, relieved that Ellie had given him such a perfect opening. He’d been wondering how the hell he was going to separate the two women long enough for him to tell Megan the rest of what needed to be said.

Megan shook her head. “I don’t think it’s a good idea to leave Mom—”

“Yes, it is,” Harry insisted. “I expect Ellie would like some tea. It’ll warm her up. Help me make some, Megan. I’m a coffee man myself and I do a lousy job with tea bags.” Harry knew he was babbling again, but he was desperate enough to grab Megan’s hand and almost drag her toward the kitchen.

“Harry, no! Whatever she says, Mom shouldn’t be alone—”

“Come with me,” he said, speaking into Megan’s ear, his voice low but his tone leaving no doubt that he was giving an order, not making a suggestion.

Megan finally realized that there was more bad news to come and her resistance ended. As soon as they were safely in the kitchen, she swung around to confront him.

"What is it?" she asked. "What is it you don't want Mom to hear?" She swallowed. "Do the cops suspect Dad was with another woman? Is that what you're trying to tell me?"

She was on the right lines, but still miles away from the scummy truth. Here goes, Harry thought. Now, dammit, I have to tell her the rest of it.

Two

May 2, 2006, the Windemere, Lake Shore Drive, Chicago, Illinois

Detective Sergeant Franklin Chomsky had been with the Chicago police for twenty-two years, which gave him enough seniority that he rarely got called on to do the crap stuff anymore. It must have been at least six years since he'd last been dispatched to deliver a notification of death. However, this particular notification was a doozy, and the people involved were sufficiently prominent that he'd been fingered for the job.

"I need somebody who isn't going to screw up," the captain had said. "You're it, Frank, so get going. You need to haul ass if you're going to get to the Windemere before the TV crews arrive.

"The cops in Miami are sure the guy is dead, right?"

"He's either dead or badly injured. If he's injured, he ought to have turned up at a hospital by now, or been spotted by cops bleeding in an alley. There was one hell of a lot of blood in the hotel room. On the whole, the cops in Miami seem to believe he's dead, but you can allow the wife to hope if you like."

"I'll give it to her straight. Lots of blood. Trashed hotel room. Luggage still in the room. No body. Prospects for finding a live Ron Raven not too great."

"Yeah, sounds about right. And don't forget it's always possible that the wife is the person who offed him. God knows, she has a motive. Check out her alibi for Sunday night."

Frank had changed his street clothes for a clean uniform and hauled ass as instructed. So here he was at the twin towers of the Windemere, one of the most upscale residential buildings in the city. The view of the lake from the higher floors must be spectacular, he thought, parking his squad car neatly between the No Parking signs. A million bucks for a one-bedroom on the ground floor and eight million for the penthouse, he figured. No wonder the captain didn't want this death notification screwed up.

Frank made his way into the lobby and flashed his badge at the security guard who sat behind the reception desk. The guy wore a braided uniform that looked as if it had been dreamed up by a gay designer for a *Princess Diaries* knockoff.

"I'm here to see Mrs. Avery Raven," Frank said, flashing his badge. "Official business. What number is her apartment?"

"Mrs. Raven's *residence* is on the twenty-second floor, in our west tower." The security guard peered down his long nose, not happy to have a lowly cop polluting his lobby, much less demanding admission to the inner sanctum.

"Great. How do I get to the west tower and Mrs. Raven's *residence?*"

"The elevator lobby is to your right, over there. I'll unlock the elevator so you can go up." The guard looked pained at the need to make this major concession.

Frank checked the guy's name tag. "Thanks, Steve." He had dealt with humanity in too many different stripes, shades and indignities to be anything more than mildly irritated by a security guard with a poker up his ass and a bad smell under his nose. "You still didn't tell me the number of Mrs. Raven's apartment. I need it."

"There isn't a number," the guard informed him. "Take the elevator marked West Tower to the penthouse floor. It opens straight into the vestibule of Mrs. Raven's residence."

Frank had seen apartments with their own private-elevator entrances on TV and in the movies, but he'd never actually visited such a place in person. This was going to be a new experience for him, in more ways than one. He hadn't heard of Ron Raven or Raven Enterprises until today, but the captain claimed the company was some big-ass deal, generating a ton of tax dollars for the state of Illinois. Judging by the fancy place where the guy had lived, the captain was right. The property-tax dollars gushing out of this building probably paid the salaries of at least a couple of dozen cops.

Frank nodded goodbye to the security guard and crossed the gleaming floor to the gilt-trimmed alcove that housed the elevators. You could decorate a medium-size cathedral with the amount of gold leaf on the walls and ceiling, he thought, impressed against his better judgment. There were no buttons to summon the elevators, only a slot for key cards, but thanks to the security guard, the doors to the west tower elevator glided open within seconds of Frank standing in front of it.

"I'll let Mrs. Raven know you're coming up," Steve said. "Can I tell her what this is about?"

"Nope. Just that it's official business." Even if the pompous little prick hadn't pissed him off, Frank wouldn't have humiliated Avery Fairfax Raven by broadcasting her personal business to the security guard. Although he wouldn't be able to protect her privacy for long. Somebody in the Miami Police Department would have talked by now. There hadn't been a juicy celebrity murder for at least a year, and this was so much better than a run-of-the-mill killing—a perfect story to whet the voracious appetites of the tabloids and cable news. He figured the Ravens had another hour or two at most before the media were all over the story.

The family-values talk-show hosts were going to have a field day, Frank thought cynically. As for the cable news outlets, they ought to be able to milk at least a week's worth of moral indignation and high ratings out of this. Especially if the cops down in Florida didn't manage to find the body. Then all the conspiracy theorists would ooze out of the woodwork, suggesting that Ron Raven wasn't really dead, or that he'd been involved in some shady deal with the government, and the CIA or the FBI had eliminated him when he threatened to talk. Frank wondered why left-wingers always obsessed about conspiracies and right-wingers always obsessed about public morals. You'd think that every once in a while, something would come up that would cause them to switch obsessions, but it never seemed to happen.

Frank stepped into the elevator and pressed the button for the penthouse. The doors closed with a discreetly muffled thud. Very nice, he thought as the dark mirrors reflected back a flattering image of him in his dress uniform. Even the elevator was designed to make the residents feel good about themselves. He felt a twinge of sympathy for Avery Raven when he realized it was quite likely she would soon find herself with no money and no home. He hoped she turned out to be a real bitch, so that he didn't need to feel sorry for her.

He stepped out on the twenty-second

floor and was greeted by a tall, slender, blond woman with huge blue eyes and boobs that were either a generous reminder from God of what he intended women's breasts to look like or else a gift from one of the best plastic surgeons in the business.

Frank found himself momentarily speechless. Damn, but she was the sexiest woman he'd ever seen outside the pages of a magazine. She was also not a day over thirty, most likely younger. For some reason, he hadn't considered the fact that Avery Raven might be in her twenties.

He swallowed over the bad taste in his mouth. Fifty-six-year-old Ron Raven had apparently been getting it off with a woman almost three decades his junior, but that didn't make a jot of difference to what he needed to do.

Concealing his distaste, Frank took off his uniform hat and tucked it under his arm. "Mrs. Raven? I'm Detective Sergeant Franklin Chomsky with the Chicago Police Department. I'm afraid I'm bringing you some bad news about Mr. Raven."

The young woman's polite smile vanished. "What is it?" Her hands tightened around the magazine she was holding—*Gourmet Today,* he noticed automatically. “Has something happened to my father? Has he been in an accident?”

Her father. Of course! This gorgeous woman must be Ron Raven’s daughter, not a snatched-from-the-cradle trophy wife. Jeez, he’d been on the job so long that his opinion of humanity had apparently sunk even further into the sewers than he’d realized.

Frank didn’t answer her questions. “May I come inside, Ms. Raven? That is your name, I assume?”

“Yes, I’m Kate Raven.”

“Is your mother home, Ms. Raven? I need to speak with her, if she is.”

“My mother got home a few minutes ago, as it happens.” She started to gesture him inside, then suddenly stopped. “Wait a minute. Show me your badge, please.”

He showed her his police ID and she read it carefully before standing to one side and letting him in. “I’ll get my mother, if you’ll wait here.”

Frank nodded to acknowledge the instruction to wait. Kate had conducted him into what he guessed must be the formal living room, a vast space defined by a vaulted ceiling, a marble floor and fancy columns that lined a hallway and hinted at more rooms fading off into the recesses of the apartment. A grand piano, a wall filled with books and a dozen pieces of antique furniture still left enough space to permit twenty or thirty guests to circulate around the room with no danger of knocking priceless knickknacks onto the ground. And as he'd guessed, the floor-to-ceiling windows on the east side did look straight out over Lake Michigan. The view was every bit as spectacular as he'd imagined.

How the other half lives, Frank thought, more amused than envious. Personally, he'd swap all these damn spindly legged antiques for a flat-screen TV and a couch where you could put your feet up in comfort to watch the ball game. Not to mention a table where you could stash a can of beer without wondering if you just destroyed five hundred years of polish.

He heard the sounds of two sets of footsteps approaching and he turned away from the view of the lake, focusing his attention on what lay ahead. Kate Raven came back into sight, followed by a woman who was equally tall and attractive, and looked no more than forty. This must be Avery Fairfax Raven. Clearly, since Kate was her daughter, Avery was older than she appeared—late forties at the very least—but she'd aged real well. From what he'd observed on the job, the rich nearly always did.

In her youth, Avery must have been as stunning as her daughter. She was still a beautiful woman, with light brown hair, smooth cheeks, sensuously full lips and a forehead devoid of wrinkles. She either had fabulous genes or generous injections of Botox and lip collagen kept her blooming. She was wearing a cream silk blouse, tailored chocolate-brown slacks and a single strand of pearls—presumably her definition of a casual outfit for an afternoon at home. His wife wouldn't get that fancy for a funeral, Frank thought wryly.

"Detective?" Avery Raven's voice was low and musical with a charming hint of a Southern accent. Everything about her appearance and manner breathed *aristocrat.* She paused a few feet away from him, outwardly composed. If he hadn't been a cop for so many years, Frank would never have caught on to the fact that she was clasping her hands to prevent them from shaking.

"I'm Avery Raven," she said. "My daughter indicated you need to speak with me, Mr. Chomsky."

Frank wasn't surprised that she had remembered his name. In the movies and on TV, the rich rarely noticed the little people. But in his experience, the classier and more educated a person was, the more likely that they had the ability to file away personal details with a precision that rivaled his computer on one of its good days.

"I'm real sorry to intrude, but I'm afraid I have bad news to report." No point in beating about the bush.

Avery's cheeks lost a little color but she exhibited no other sign of alarm. "Kate said you have information about…my husband."

"It's about Ronald Howatch Raven," he agreed. "Mr. Raven's Illinois driver's license showed this as his home address." His Wyoming license, of course, told a different story, but Avery wouldn't pick up on the subtle distinction. Not unless she knew the truth about Ron Raven, which seemed unlikely. Frank was keeping in mind his captain's warning that this woman had motives to kill Ron Raven, but if she was the murderer, he'd eat his best uniform hat.

"Yes, this is Ron's home," Avery said,

betraying a first hint of impatience. “What’s happened? Why are you here?”

“I’m sorry to tell you, ma’am, that the police in Miami believe Mr. Raven may have come to harm. He’s missing from his hotel room, and the indications are that he has met with foul play.”

“Foul play?” It was Kate who asked the question. “Do you mean—he’s dead?”

“It’s a possibility, miss. I’m sorry.”

“Oh my God, no! Dad can’t be dead! Mom, didn’t you speak to him last night?”

“No, not last night.” Avery stared straight ahead as she answered her daughter’s question. “We spoke on Sunday. Ron called as soon as he arrived in Miami because he knew I was meeting friends for dinner.” Avery relapsed into silence. She fixed her gaze on Lake Michigan, her classically faultless profile containing no hint of what she was feeling.

Frank addressed himself to Kate. “According to the police in Miami, your father hasn’t been heard from since eight-thirty on Sunday night.”

Avery said nothing in response to this information and her face remained a blank mask. Kate, on the other hand, didn’t seem to have perfected the upper-class skill of hiding her emotions. Her cheeks paled before heating to a fiery red and her eyes filled with tears.

"My father was supposed to fly into Mexico City yesterday morning and there haven't been any reports of a plane crash. He's probably in Mexico—"

"I don't believe so." Frank spoke quietly but firmly. It was best not to leave these women with false hopes. "The police in Miami are quite sure Mr. Raven didn't catch his flight. Whatever happened to your father seems to have happened here in the United States."

Avery Raven brought her gaze back from the lake. "How can you be so sure he didn't catch his scheduled flight, Officer?"

"The police in Miami have liaised with Homeland Security, ma'am. Controls are tight these days, and the authorities are confident that Mr. Raven didn't board a flight out of the Miami airport anytime in the past forty-eight hours."

Kate started to protest again, so Frank quickly provided them with details of the wrecked hotel room, the search of local hospitals and the ominous trails of blood, indicating that at least three people had lost traces of blood in Ron Raven's hotel room. He ended up telling them about the rental car that had been found abandoned in a restaurant parking lot close to a busy marina, the Blue Lagoon, in Coral Gables.

"What's the significance of that?" Kate demanded. She sounded hostile, which Frank understood. She was keeping her fear and grief at bay by refusing to accept the official explanation for her father's disappearance.

"The police in Miami believe that whoever attacked your father may have disposed of his body in the ocean, miss, which would be a very convenient way to insure that we never find it. There are forty-eight boats docked at the marina, and several of them were taken out either late last night or early this morning. It seems likely that somebody at the marina will have seen something."

"Only if my father really was taken out to sea," Kate pointed out. "What if he never went anywhere near the marina? What if the rental car location is just a red herring?"

"Then we'll find that out, too, eventually. Right now, the investigative team is checking on any preexisting links between your father and the people who dock boats at the marina. They also need to check whether any of the boats were taken out last night without the owner's permission—"

"If the owner didn't give permission, then there's no way to find out who actually did take the boat out to sea and we'll be no further forward," Kate interjected.

Frank was impressed with her logic. Apparently she was one of those rare people able to reason through a problem even when she was stressed. "You'd be surprised at what trained investigators can discover once they generate a few initial leads. For example, there are security cameras at the marina and in the parking lot where the rental car was abandoned, and the tapes from those cameras are already in police custody. That should help a lot. Unfortunately, there's no magic shortcut for any of us. The detectives in Miami have to follow each line of inquiry until it runs out. It's going to take a while for them to have an accurate picture of what really happened but we'll get there in the end."

Or not. No point in mentioning the percentage of homicides and missing persons cases that went unsolved despite the best efforts of law enforcement.

"Perhaps my father's been kidnapped,"

Kate suggested. Anything, it seemed, was preferable to believing that her father was already dead.

"It's possible, miss. But kidnappers usually make a ransom demand soon after the abduction. I assume you haven't received any such demand?"

Reluctantly, Kate shook her head. "No. Nobody's called. We had no idea my father was...missing."

Avery drew in an audible breath and swallowed a sob, her first overt sign of distress. "Excuse me. I have to leave you for a minute." She turned and walked blindly in the direction from which she'd appeared earlier.

Kate followed her mother, turning to speak to Frank over her shoulder. "I can't leave her alone right now, but please don't go. I have so many questions for you still."

"I'll wait, miss." *You don't know the half of it yet.*

"Thank you." Tears poured down Kate's cheeks. Fighting a losing battle to stanch her crying, she gestured toward the hallway where her mother had just been. "Oh God, I don't know how she's going to bear it if he's really dead. Dad is her whole life."

She turned abruptly and hurried after her mother.

Just what he hadn't wanted to hear, Frank thought grimly, pacing the luxurious living room. He suspected that accepting Ron Raven was dead would prove easier for Avery and Kate than hearing the truth about how the bastard had screwed them over. Now that he'd actually met the two women, his sympathies were engaged. He definitely wasn't looking forward to the next fifteen minutes or so. If only Avery Raven had turned out to be the bitch he'd hoped for. Instead, she seemed like a real classy woman who deserved something better than the piece of crap she'd married. The daughter seemed nice, too. Smart as well as beautiful, which made for a hell of a combination, especially when you considered that the enticing package came wrapped in a comfortable supply of money.

Well, the kid had been rich until now, Frank corrected himself. Perhaps she would be rich again when Ron Raven's estate finally finished winding its way through the probate courts—except that probating Ron's estate was likely to take half a lifetime once the opposing sets of lawyers started battling in court. Two things you could say for sure about Ron Raven's messy death: his family was screwed and disposing of his assets was going to make several members of the legal profession rich.

Frank paced for another three or four minutes. If the two women didn't put in an appearance soon, he'd have to go get them. The Bulls were up against the Detroit Pistons tonight in a playoff game and he had plans to watch with his son. Besides, cooling his heels in this too-fancy living room was giving him a major case of the creeps. Hopefully Kate would return without her mother. He'd much prefer to deliver the bad news to the daughter and let her pass it on.

Frank caught a break when Kate returned a couple of minutes later, alone. "I wasn't sure if you would still be here," she said. Her belligerence had gone, replaced by a control that was visibly fragile.

"I couldn't leave, miss. I still have important information to pass on to you."

"I'm sorry to have kept you waiting. My mother is… We're both upset, as you can imagine. She'll be with us in just a little while. Could you give me a phone number so that we can call you later with all the questions we forget? My mother… We're neither of us thinking too clearly right now."

"Here's my card." Frank had one ready and handed it to her. Kate was likely to have more questions than she could possibly imagine, he reflected wryly.

"Thank you." Kate tucked the card into the pocket of her jeans. Unlike her mother, she was dressed like a regular person, not as if she expected to share afternoon tea with the First Lady. "Tell me, Detective, exactly how much hope do the police have that my father might still be alive?"

"Not very much," Frank admitted. "The trouble is, if your father is alive, the state of his hotel room suggests that he's badly injured. So where is he? Why didn't he call 911? Or if he's unconscious, why have none of the hospitals reported a John Doe?"

She nodded, reluctantly acknowledging the logic of his analysis. "On the other hand, if my father's dead, how did the murderers dispose of his body?"

"As I mentioned, the ocean seems like a real good bet."

"No, I didn't mean that. I was wondering how they got Dad out of the hotel without anyone seeing them."

Frank couldn't see any harm in telling her the truth. "When the Miami police searched the hotel, they found a big steel-framed laundry hamper near one of the service elevators. There's blood on the canvas bag and the blood matches some of the stains found in your father's hotel room. For now, the police are assuming the killers used the laundry hamper to wheel your father down to the parking garage."

"They dumped Dad's body in a canvas laundry hamper?" Kate's breath caught and her mouth twisted downward. "That's like something out of a really bad movie."

Frank could have pointed out that murderers watched the same movies and TV shows as everyone else and usually demonstrated no originality or creative thinking. Instead, he answered mildly enough. "It might be corny, but it seems to have worked. Nobody saw your father or anyone else leave his room. Unfortunately, guests in a hotel don't pay much attention to a cleaner pushing a laundry cart."

"If my father really is dead, the person who killed him must have planned ahead," Kate said. "He couldn't just hope to find a laundry cart conveniently left in the right place. And how did he know which car my dad had rented, or where it was parked?"

Frank nodded his agreement. "That's true. The Miami police are working on the theory that your father's murder was premeditated."

Although, in Frank's opinion, that theory raised almost as many questions as it answered. If the murder had been planned in advance, why had it required so much brute force to kill Ron Raven? Why hadn't he just been shot with a single bullet to his head while he slept? The police had retrieved blood samples from three different people. Presumably at least one sample belonged to the killer. If that was the case, the killer—already injured?—had risked a lot to move Ron's body. Why? Would an autopsy have revealed clues to the killer's identity? Frank could only thank God that he didn't have to find answers to these questions. The cops down in Miami had his sincere sympathy. This case was a mess—and that was before anyone addressed the possibility that Ron had been the killer, not the victim.

Kate gulped in air. "I don't understand why anyone would want to kill my father." She leaned toward him, her hands clenched tightly enough for her knuckles to gleam white in the late-afternoon sun. “Who in the world would have a motive for killing him?”

Frank shook his head. “I’m sorry, miss, we’re still waiting for details of the case to come through from Florida. But your father was a businessman who spent the past thirty years making highly profitable deals. Where there’s a lot of money, there’s always the chance of corruption and double-crosses.”

“Not my father,” Kate protested. “Raven Enterprises is renowned for the integrity of its deals. And as far as the personal side of my father’s life is concerned, he leads a boringly normal life—”

“Not quite.” Frank had to stop her there, although the detective in him was intrigued to see how completely Ron Raven had fooled this branch of his family. He wondered if the folks in Wyoming were equally clueless.

“As I mentioned, there’s more information I need to pass on to you, miss. I’ve been sitting here trying to think of a tactful way to deliver the news, and I’ve decided there isn’t one. So I’m going to be blunt. Here goes. We have reason to believe your father was a bigamist."

"A bigamist?"

"Yes, miss."

"As in having two wives? *My dad?*" Kate stared at him, eyes wide with disbelief. She gave an uncertain laugh. "You're joking, right?"

"I'm afraid not. Your father seems to have had two wives and two sets of children. You and your mother here in Chicago and another wife and two more children living in Thatch—apparently that's a small ranching town in Stark County, Wyoming."

"My father has two more children as well as another wife?" Kate's voice spiraled into an incredulous squeak. "Of course he doesn't! That's absolutely crazy."

"Having two wives at the same time is criminal, miss. It's not necessarily crazy."

"My father isn't a *criminal.*" The realization that her father might have committed a crime seemed to stun Kate even more than the suggestion he had another wife and two more kids. She shook her head vehemently. "No, it's impossible. Apart from the craziness of committing bigamy in this day and age, how could Dad have kept a second wife and family secret? He couldn't possibly have spent time with them without my mother finding out."

She had a good point, Frank thought ruefully, although he'd seen plenty of situations where seemingly upright citizens got away with living secret lives for years. Ron Raven had apparently been one of those talented deceivers who could lie with the ease of an accomplished con artist. Although, come to think of it, what was a bigamist if not a con artist supreme?

"You would know better than I do how your father managed to keep you and your mother in the dark. Perhaps all those business trips he took weren't actually for business. I couldn't say. But he has two other children, that I know for sure. A son and a daughter, according to the sheriff of Stark County."

Kate made little pushing motions with her hand, as if to hold the astonishing news at bay until she could assimilate it. "What are their names? How old are they? Are they little kids?"

"No, they're grown-up, but I don't have any more details. I'm sorry. We're waiting for the sheriff in Wyoming to fax us documentation. Normally, we'd have held off notifying you until we had more complete information, but in this case we decided it was important to warn your mother before reporters get wind of the story. We didn't want your mother to turn on the TV and hear the news of Ron Raven's death that way. Especially the part about him having two wives."

Kate's expression darkened from incredulity into horror. "Oh my God. You think there are going to be news reports about this?"

"I'd say it's a certainty. You'd better be prepared for the media to make a circus out of your family's private business."

Kate sent him a pleading look. "There has to be some way to stop journalists from reporting that my father's a bigamist. That would be slander, wouldn't it?"

"No, miss. It's not slanderous to report true facts that emerge in connection with an official investigation of a crime."

"But you're assuming my father has another wife and I'm telling you that's not possible! There's been a mistake. He adores my mother and she adores him right back. I'd have a hard time believing he'd ever been unfaithful to her, much less that he was *married* to another woman."

Frank didn't attempt to argue with Kate, just reached into his pocket and removed a carefully folded fax. "I don't have birth records for your father's other children, but I do have this copy of your father's marriage certificate. It was sent to us by the sheriff of Stark County. You'll see the name and the date. Eleanor Mary Horn and Ronald Howatch Raven."

She took the fax, her hand visibly shaking. He stood in silence, letting the marriage certificate speak for itself.

"Maybe this is a forgery."

"I doubt it, miss. Like I said, it was the sheriff himself who sent it to us. Besides, there's other evidence. When the police searched Mr. Raven's hotel room they discovered two wallets locked in the room safe, and both wallets belonged to your father."

"The fact that my father owns two wallets doesn't seem grounds for leaping to the conclusion that he's a bigamist."

"The two wallets didn't cause the police to leap to any conclusions at all, although he did have two completely different sets of family pictures and credit cards in each wallet. Still, the cops in Miami just followed procedure. The driver's license in each billfold provided a different address, one in Wyoming and the other one here in Chicago. Therefore the detective sergeant in charge of the investigation contacted law enforcement authorities in both locations to ascertain if Mr. Raven had family either in Stark County or in the Chicago area. It was routine police procedure at that point, since there are plenty of law-abiding citizens with two homes. When the request came in to us, we ran the information we were given through our state data systems and reported back to Miami that our records showed that Mr. Raven lived here in downtown Chicago with his wife, Avery Fairfax Raven. Only thing is, Wyoming reported back similar information, except with a different wife."

"My father owns a ranch in Wyoming." Kate ignored Frank's comment about the second wife. "The ranch is an old family property, first bought by my great-great-grandfather, and now run by a professional manager—"

"You've been there?"

"Of course I have! I went there two or

three times in the summer when I was a kid."

Frank wondered how Ron Raven had pulled those visits off. There must have been a good bit of juggling and sleight of hand to make sure nobody ever mentioned the other wife and kids. Still, it wasn't his business to find out how Ron Raven had worked his scam. He just needed to get Kate to accept the truth about her father.

"How about more recently, miss? Have you been to the ranch since you grew up? And how about your mother? Has she visited the ranch recently?"

"We've neither of us visited Wyoming in at least ten years." Kate subsided into a tense silence.

I'll just bet you haven't, Frank thought. "Doesn't that strike you as a bit strange?"

"My mother isn't the type of person who enjoys spending time on a ranch. She's not a rural sort." Kate rushed on, before Frank could make a comment to the effect that her mother's tastes had nothing to do with the fact that Ron Raven's *daughter* had almost never visited a ranch that had been in the family for three generations.

"The point is, I'm not surprised Dad has

two separate IDs. Probably it was easier for him to keep his accounts for the ranch separate from the rest of his expenses—"

"Ms. Raven, your father didn't simply have two separate sets of credit cards and two different driver's licenses and two different sets of family photos. I'm telling you he had two separate families, as well. And the ranch isn't run by a professional manager, by the way. It's run by your father's wife. His legal wife."

"His *legal* wife?" Kate's voice cracked. "What do you mean?"

Frank grimaced. "Look at the marriage certificate, miss. Your father married Eleanor Horn fifteen years before he married your mother."

Kate looked again at the marriage certificate and her cheeks lost color. "There must have been a divorce."

"I doubt it, miss. My precinct captain heard from the sheriff of Stark County just a few minutes before I came to see your mother. It turns out the sheriff knows Ron Raven personally. He's an old friend of the family, in fact, and he was as shocked to learn about you and your mother as you are to learn about the wife and children in Wyoming. The sheriff personally confirmed that your father has been married to a woman called Eleanor Horn for thirty-six years. The sheriff was at their wedding, which took place at the local community church in Thatch in front of at least a hundred witnesses and there's never been a divorce. As far as everyone in Wyoming is concerned, Ron Raven lived at the Flying W with his wife Eleanor, and the only reason he traveled to Chicago was on business for Raven Enterprises."

"If you're right, that would mean my mother is just my dad's…mistress."

Frank was surprised by the old-fashioned word. But in the rarefied world where Kate and her mother lived, perhaps it wasn't such an outdated concept. "I'm afraid that's what seems to be the case," he acknowledged. "Although I'd advise you to check with a lawyer to find out what your legal rights might be. If your mother genuinely believed she was married, she might have a legal claim to some portion of Mr. Raven's estate. Not that I'm qualified to be making statements like that."

Kate stared at him in silence. Clearly, until that moment she hadn't considered the possibility that there might be financial consequences from her father's bigamy. Then she laughed, although there wasn't a trace of amusement in the sound. "Well, I guess that makes the perfect icing on the cake, doesn't it? You're saying my mother is going to find herself penniless, along with all her other problems."

"Hopefully Mr. Raven made provisions, miss."

Kate gave another short laugh. "Right. Why wouldn't he, when he's behaved impeccably in every other detail of his relationship with us?" She bit off another angry comment and walked to the window, staring out over the vast expanse of water, although Frank had a suspicion she wasn't registering much about the magnificent view.

She finally swung around to look at him again. "How am I going to tell my mother? My God, how in the world am I going to tell her?" She asked the question as much of herself as of Frank.

"How are you going to tell me what?" Avery paused at the entrance to the living room, her hand resting on the back of a silk-covered chair. "Is it more bad news? Have they found Frank's body?"

"No, nothing like that," Kate said, hurrying over to her mother.

You had to give the girl credit, Frank reflected. She might flinch, but she didn't shirk. She took Avery's hands into a protective clasp and he could see the rise and fall of her chest as she drew in a deep breath to steady her voice.

"Mom, there's absolutely no way to make this sound less awful than it is, so I'll give you the straight-up, no-frills version. Detective Chomsky claims that in the course of their investigation into Dad's disappearance, the police have discovered that he's a bigamist."

"A...bigamist?" Avery said the word as if she didn't quite understand its meaning.

"Yes. They claim Dad has another wife and two children who live in Wyoming."

"Another wife?" Avery pressed her hand against her chest. "Another wife *and two children?*"

"Yes. But that's not all. Apparently Dad married this other woman thirty-six years ago and never divorced her. That means...that means she's his legal wife. Here's a copy of their marriage certificate. It seems you and Dad were never really married."

Avery's hands tightened their grip on the silk chair back. She glanced down at the fax Kate held out to her but didn't touch it. "I can't take it in. Are you telling me that Ron already had a wife when he married me? That my parents invited two hundred guests to witness a fake wedding ceremony?"

"I'm afraid it seems that way."

The blood drained from Avery's face, leaving her so pale Frank was sure she would faint. But she was tougher than she looked. He could see the effort she exerted not to pass out.

"Of course the police have made a dreadful mistake," Avery said, echoing her daughter's earlier statement. "They've confused his name with another Ron Raven, or something like that." Her eyes made a silent plea for Kate to agree.

"Maybe they have. I hope so. We'll get our lawyers to check it out, but Detective Chomsky seems quite certain of his facts. He says Dad was definitely married to...to the woman in Thatch thirty-six years ago. It's a small town...well, you know that already...and the sheriff out there is a personal friend of the family. He was at Dad's wedding to this woman. The sheriff knows the children, too, and he seems certain that there was never any question of a divorce."

"Thirty-six years?" Avery's lips were bloodless. "Ron was married to another woman for *thirty-six years?*"

"It seems that way."

"How could he?" Avery asked, her voice low but shaking with anger. "How could Ron do this to us? And where was this woman when Ron took us to visit the ranch?"

"I don't know. I can't even begin to guess at his motives. Most of all, I can't wrap my mind around the sheer *stupidity* of it. This isn't the Victorian era. Why in the world didn't he get a divorce before he married you?"

"I have no idea." Avery was still alarmingly white, but her voice was stronger. "However, it's fortunate for all of us that he appears to be dead, because otherwise I'd kill him."

Three

May 4, 2006, Thatch, Stark County, Wyoming

Megan heard the sound of a car braking to a halt alongside the porch and the pounding inside her head instantly grew worse. She peeked through a crack in the living-room blinds, her stomach knotting at the prospect of seeing yet another reporter parked on the driveway.

The car was a red Ford Freestyle, not one of the roaming TV-satellite vans that had been tormenting her for the past day and a half. Unfortunately, the absence of a broadcast antenna wasn't necessarily good news. She'd discovered that print journalists could be every bit as aggressive as their on-air counterparts.

Tucking her gingham shirt into her jeans, Megan prepared herself to walk outside and repeat for the umpteenth time that she had no comment. The trick, she'd found, was to head off the journalists before they could bang on the door and disturb her mother. The next trick—even more difficult—was to get rid of them without losing her temper and providing them with juicy copy.

A tall man got out of the car, dressed in a gray business suit, his thick, light brown hair blowing in the late-afternoon breeze and his tie hanging loose around his unbuttoned shirt collar. The sun was shining through the window into Megan's eyes and it took her a second to recognize her brother.

"Liam!" She ran out of the house, flying down the porch steps, the dogs bounding at her heels. "Liam!" She hurled herself into his arms, hugging him as hard as she could, caught off guard by the rush of her own emotions.

Liam wasn't usually what you'd call a warm-and-fuzzy kind of a guy and she felt his split-second hesitation before he hugged her back. But for all his reserve, his voice was deeply affectionate when he spoke. "Hey, squirt. You look great, especially considering everything that's going on."

He patted Bruno and Belle, who thrust

their muzzles against his legs and whimpered ecstatically, tails thumping. "How are you holding up, Meggie?"

"Better now that you're here." Megan not only loved Liam, she'd worshipped him as her hero, ever since she was three and he was the twelve-year-old big brother patiently leading her around on the pony their father had just bought as her birthday present. Still, she didn't know him as well as she would have liked. With their nine-year age difference, Liam had been off to college by the time she was starting fourth grade and he'd almost never visited the ranch over the past few years. He lived in Denver and she'd spent time with him there as often as she could, but she always sensed a barrier that allowed her to get just so close and no further. Despite that, the bond between the two of them was important to her. She suspected it was equally important to Liam, for all that he was so emotionally guarded.

"It's really good to see you." Her voice, embarrassingly, was thick with emotion. "I didn't realize how much I needed you until I saw you getting out of the car."

Liam ruffled her hair, then uncharacteristically dropped a kiss on the top of her head, an easy spot for him to reach since he was a good ten inches taller than her five foot three. "I never expected to live long enough to hear my kid sister admit that she needed me."

"It's been a rough couple of days," Megan acknowledged.

"I can imagine." Liam's words sounded more ironic than sympathetic, but he crooked his finger under her chin and tilted her face up, using his thumb to brush away the tears that kept welling up in her eyes despite her best efforts to contain them. Unlike her brother, she was cursed with emotions that bubbled over at the slightest provocation.

He knew how much she despised her own easy tears and, with welcome tact, he bent down and gave the dogs his full attention, allowing her a moment to regain control. "Hey, Bruno. Hey, Belle. Hate to tell you guys this, but you're getting fat."

The dogs ignored the insult and licked his hands in slobbery friendship, clearly remembering him fondly, although it was at least two years since they'd last seen him.

"Okay, you're great dogs, both of you, and now I'd like my hands back." He snapped his fingers and pointed to the ground. The dogs, who considered Megan's commands no more than playful suggestions, instantly quieted. They seated themselves with their front paws on top of Liam's shoes, tongues lolling out of the side of their mouths as they panted their enthusiasm for his return.

Liam turned his attention back to Megan. "I'm sorry I couldn't get here sooner, squirt."

"That's okay—"

"No, it's not. As usual, I was unavailable when you needed me." He took off his tie and shoved it in the pocket of his suit jacket. "I wasn't ignoring you, Meg."

"It never occurred to me that you were. When I didn't hear from you last night, I assumed you weren't home."

"You were right. I didn't get your message until this morning. Then I had to reschedule my court appearances for the next few days before I could leave Denver. I tried to call on my way to the airport, but the ranch phone was constantly busy and your cell number kept switching me to voice mail."

"I took the ranch phones off the hook because I got tired of telling reporters that I had nothing to say, and cell phones still don't work out here so I can't pick up my messages."

Megan asked no questions about Liam's absence the previous night, although she could make a pretty good guess as to why he'd been away from home. If her brother had been running true to recent form, he'd spent the night with some gorgeous woman he would almost certainly never see again.

In high school, Liam had been a jock more interested in football and skiing than girls. During the entire seven years he spent in college and law school, he'd dated no more than half a dozen different women. Then he'd moved to Denver, taken the bar exam and joined a partnership of criminal-defense attorneys. He'd gone out with a fellow lawyer for over a year and Megan had expected to hear at any minute that the two of them were engaged. Instead, their relationship abruptly ended. Overnight, Liam seemed to acquire the ambition to have sex with every attractive single woman in the state of Colorado. Megan wished he could find a woman he liked enough to settle down, but since her own relationships seemed to have all the depth and staying power of wet tissues, she wasn't exactly in a position to criticize.

"I hoped the ranch might be too far off the beaten track for TV crews to waste time driving out here." Liam leaned into the rental car and took out a soft leather duffel bag. With a skill acquired in childhood, he stuck out his foot and blocked the dogs from jumping into the backseat. "Obviously I underestimated the news appeal of Dad's disappearance."

"It's not just the fact that he's disappeared. It's the fact that he was a bigamist. You don't get too many of those nowadays." Megan stopped Bruno from chasing a rabbit by scratching the precise spot behind his ears that guaranteed to make him squirm in ecstasy.

Liam pulled a face. "Just how bad have the reporters been?"

She gave a short, hard laugh. "Somewhere north of rabid. A crew from Channel Six drove down from Jackson Hole within a couple of hours of our hearing the news. The producer demanded an exclusive interview. He informed me that we *owed* him an interview because Channel Six is our local station and the people of Wyoming have a right to know how Mom feels about Dad's other wife and daughter!"

Liam muttered an expletive beneath his

breath. "I trust you told him precisely where he could shove his demands."

"I sure did, for all the good it did me. The crew from Jackson Hole was only the first, and not even the most pushy. I've developed a whole new sympathy for movie stars who punch out paparazzi. Living with these people in your face 24/7 would be enough to drive anyone crazy."

"Since you've been sweeping reporters off the front porch all day long, I guess you won't be too surprised to hear that when I drove into the ranch a roving camera crew was busy setting up shop at the entrance gates."

Megan sighed. "Not surprised, just sick to death of having to deal with them. I finally called Harry a couple of hours ago and asked for help. He came right out, thank God, and ordered them to clear off our land. Unfortunately, I guess there's no way to stop people parking on the public road outside the boundary fences." She shaded her eyes from the sun and stared down the long driveway. "I don't see anyone coming."

"Hopefully we won't. I told the crew I was the family lawyer and threatened to have them arrested for trespassing if they drove so much as their front wheels onto ranch property. They seemed to listen."

"Maybe they'll get bored and go away if there's no activity."

"In your dreams." Liam clearly didn't think there was a chance in hell that the reporters would leave.

"The neighbors might refuse to talk." Megan was more wistful than optimistic. "They're a pretty nice bunch of people and they don't have much patience for big-city folk."

"Yeah, but there's always one neighbor who's dying to see himself on TV and won't care what lies he needs to invent as long as his story gets him on camera."

"You're probably right. Unfortunately."

"Count on it. And even if the reporters can't squeeze any good copy out of our neighbors, you can bet Dad's other family in Chicago will have plenty of so-called friends who are only too willing to gossip for the cameras."

Megan shrugged. "Personally, I'd be thrilled if the media gave up on us and fixated on them. At least Mom would be left in peace."

Liam sent her a sympathetic glance. "They're victims, too, you know."

She sighed. "I know. One day I may start to empathize with them, but right now I can't. There've been too many shocking revelations and too little time to absorb them." Megan was reluctantly fascinated by the idea that she had a half sister, but she wasn't yet ready to cope with the tumultuous emotions precipitated by her existence.

"Have you seen pictures of them?" The question was torn from her against her better judgment. She'd been loath to switch on the TV today not only for fear of seeing herself and the ranch house plastered all over the airwaves but even more for fear of being inundated with images of her father's other family.

Liam nodded. "You can't avoid seeing them. The story of Dad's disappearance was the lead story on every channel when I walked through the airports in Denver and Jackson Hole."

Megan grimaced. "Complete with pictures of the ranch, I suppose?"

" 'Fraid so. Along with endless shots of the penthouse in downtown Chicago where Dad's other wife apparently lives. The media are fascinated by the contrast between the two homes."

Megan drew in a quick breath. "I don't mind being portrayed as a country bumpkin if that means the journalists get bored with us sooner."

"That's good, because they already have you and Mom typecast as exactly that. Apparently Avery Fairfax is big on the social scene in Chicago—she's chaired several important charity events and the TV stations have photos and file footage of her looking incredibly sophisticated and glamorous. Mom comes off sounding as if she's Mrs. Homebody from 1950. It makes for great copy and who cares if there's no truth to the images they're creating?"

"In a way, the distortions protect Mom's privacy, so I'm not sure she'll mind."

"Maybe not. Although the cable news channels keep mentioning the fact that the penthouse where Avery and Kate are living is currently valued at six point five million dollars, whereas Mom's house would probably sell for less than fifty thousand. That might irritate her somewhat."

Megan brushed the information aside. "Thank goodness the journalists don't dig deep with their research. The truth is, some resort-development company offered Mom more than a million dollars for the Flying W land only a couple of months ago."

Liam didn't look impressed. "A million dollars for six thousand acres, as opposed to six point five million dollars for five thousand square feet of Avery's penthouse. That would pretty much piss me off if I were Mom."

She couldn't let herself get caught up in anger over the money, Megan decided. There were so many other things her father had done that were more worthy of her rage.

"What do they look like?" Part of her wanted desperately to know. Another part of her wasn't ready to give substance to her cloudy mental images of her father's second wife and her half sister.

"Tall, blond, very photogenic," Liam said. "Actually, the daughter has facial features that are a lot like Dad's. The same wide-set eyes and high cheekbones."

"Your features are a lot like Dad's, too."

"I know." Liam shrugged. "Unfortunately, I can't change my face short of plastic surgery and I'm not willing to grant Dad that much importance in my life."

"I didn't mean that. I meant if you and...Kate...both look like him—she must look like you. Especially since she's tall." Megan drew in an unsteady breath. "She probably looks more like your real sister than I do."

"Maybe." Liam gave her a quick, reassuring grin. "But she's a stranger despite the biological link, whereas you're the annoying kid that for some crazy reason I've loved since the moment Mom brought you home from the hospital. Looking mighty wrinkled and unappetizing if you must know, although Mom tried to make the best of you with a frilly hat and cute socks."

She answered his smile. "And that's your way of reassuring me? If so, I have to tell you, your charm offensive needs work."

"Hey, I'm your brother. It's the best I can do. Besides, think about what Kate is going through right now. She doesn't even have a sister or brother to share her frustrations with. We're the lucky ones."

"I promise to feel sorry for her sometime soon. Right now, I can't. I'm too busy alternating between feeling betrayed and totally, incredibly *stupid.*"

"You weren't stupid," Liam said. "Dad was criminally deceptive. Don't take his crimes onto your shoulders."

"I'm working on it." Megan managed another smile although she could feel it wobble at the edges. "Let's go inside. You must want to see Mom. She'll be so glad to know you're here—"

Liam put out his arm, preventing her from walking into the house. "Talk to me for a minute longer before we go into the house. Somehow it's easier not to get eaten up with anger out here in the fresh air. How's Mom holding up?"

Megan considered for a moment. "She broke down when she first heard about Dad's other wife, but now I'm not sure what she's feeling. You know how she tends to keep people at arm's length by occupying herself with some chore or other? That's what she's doing right now. She won't let me get close enough to offer real sympathy. Just scurries off insisting she has some vital new task that has to be attended to. Immediately, of course."

"She's always been the queen of busy-work," Liam said, his expression showing his frustration. "It's very effective as a distancing mechanism and it's driven me crazy for years."

"Me, too." Megan gave a rueful smile. "I wish she'd bend her steel spine a little and confess that she needs a friendly shoulder to cry on. Or at least admit that she's angry as hell at Dad."

Liam whistled to call Belle back from chasing a squirrel. "Has she? Admitted that she's angry at Dad, I mean?"

"Not to me, that's for sure. To herself? Who knows."

"Is she in denial? Clinging to the hope that Dad isn't dead?"

Megan shook her head. "She resisted the idea that he was dead for a couple of hours, but she's definitely not in denial anymore. Every report that comes in from Miami seems a bit more conclusive. She spent the morning going through papers, sorting out relevant documents to establish that she's Dad's legal wife and we're his legitimate children. Then this afternoon she started working on organizing a prayer service for Dad—"

"Right after she'd spent hours trying to prove she was actually married to him?"

Liam's voice rose incredulously. He shook his head. "Why am I surprised? It's so typical of Mom to ignore the fact that the son of a bitch totally screwed her over." His mouth tightened. "What she ought to be doing is celebrating the fact that he's met the end he deserved."

Megan flinched at the venom in her brother's tone. "Nobody deserves to be murdered."

"I've reminded myself of that several times since I got your message, but I can't pretend I'm in deep mourning—"

"He was a great dad when we were growing up," Megan protested.

"Yeah, I guess. But anytime I start to feel grief-stricken, I just take another look at the TV images of Avery and Kate. Somehow, that dries all the emotion right up."

Liam's rage at their father was palpable, and Megan could certainly understand why. Oddly, she wasn't angry with their father, at least not yet. She had enjoyed growing up on the ranch and Ron had been a loving parent, despite his frequent absences. Did she have to discard hundreds of happy childhood memories because they were now tainted by the knowledge that her father had been a liar? It was going to take her a while to come to terms with the fact that her idyllic childhood on the ranch had been sustained only at the cost of a series of lies spanning more than twenty-five years.

Megan turned the conversation back to the subject of their mother, which was marginally easier to deal with than her own confused feelings about their father. "Despite the brave facade, I'm pretty sure Mom is devastated. But she's told me in no uncertain terms that she can handle everything herself, including the arrangements for the prayer service. I suggested that maybe since we don't have Dad…since we don't have his body…we could use that as an excuse not to have any sort of memorial service." She raised her shoulders in a frustrated gesture. "Mom told me to butt out."

Liam gave a disbelieving shake of his head. "Has Mom considered that it might be a tad awkward to throw a prayer service for a man who hasn't yet been officially declared dead? Not to mention the even more awkward fact that he was a bigamist when he was alive? What in the world does she expect our neighbors to say when they try to offer their condolences?"

Megan drew in a sharp breath. “I don’t believe she’s allowed herself to think through the practical realities. Part of the problem is that she didn’t sleep last night, so she’s exhausted, and of course you can guess how she reacted when I suggested taking a sleeping pill. The other problem is that she’s walled herself off so completely that she’s getting no input from anyone. She refuses to see anyone except Harry, and although she accepts that Dad is likely dead, she won’t talk about the fact that he seems to have been violently murdered, much less ask at least a few questions as to why. Most especially she won’t talk about the fact that he had another wife and daughter. Last night she cut me off every time I tried to discuss Dad’s bigamy. This morning she flat out told me not to mention *those women in Chicago* again. Almost as if they were the people to blame instead of Dad.”

“The past few hours have obviously been even rougher for you than I imagined.” Liam dumped his duffel bag onto the swing and put his arm around her. “The truth is, I haven’t been pulling my weight for the past several years. You've been left alone to deal with family crises far too often."

"You're giving me way too much credit," Megan said. "I've been nowhere near as close to Mom and Dad as you're assuming. Jackson Hole is only ninety miles from here, but it might as well be on another planet in terms of lifestyle." She sent him a regretful sideways glance. "I had no more trouble burying myself in my work at the hotel than you did burying yourself in becoming Denver's most successful divorce lawyer. Somehow, I've managed to kid myself for the last five years that if I kept my sights fixed on the goal of being promoted to assistant manager at the hotel, all the problems in my life would be resolved."

And now that she'd spelled out what she'd been doing, she realized how pathetic her coping mechanism had been. She could have given an ostrich advanced lessons in head-burying, Megan reflected ruefully.

Liam was quiet for a moment. "I guess we're the poster kids for our dysfunctional family—"

"I guess we are. But until I heard the sheriff say that Dad had another wife and daughter in Chicago, I never even realized we were dysfunctional. How dumb is that?"

"Not dumb necessarily. We were carefully conditioned by our parents—both of them, not just Dad. We were taught not to probe too deeply into the family dynamics and we obeyed our training. You have to keep reminding yourself that Dad's the person who screwed up, not us."

"Why do you think he didn't just divorce Mom?" Megan asked. "As far as I'm concerned, that's a bigger mystery than who killed him."

"Who the hell knows? It can't have been lust, can it? Not for twenty-five years." Liam's voice was harsh. He swiveled around on the porch steps and looked out over the land to the distant pasture where a few heifers grazed. "Do you think Mom knew about Dad's bigamy before he died?" he asked.

"Good heavens, no! Absolutely not!" Megan was shocked by her brother's question.

"Why are you so sure?" he asked. "The two of us grew up accepting what we were told about Dad traveling a lot on business and getting caught at the airport in snowstorms so he couldn't make it home for

Thanksgiving and so on and so on. But Mom was an adult. How could he have scammed her?"

"Well, he worked hard at it, I guess, and he was a really good liar—"

"Twenty-five years of lying and she never twigged? *A quarter of a friggin' century?*"

Megan felt her stomach knot even tighter as she searched for an explanation. "When he was here, he always seemed so happy and committed. There was no reason for us to wonder if he might be leading a double life. Even now, knowing the truth, I have a hard time accepting that he was deceiving us."

"He was definitely deceiving the two of *us.* But Mom? She's a smart woman. How come she never noticed there was something totally screwed up about her marriage? I love Mom, but I can't buy into that level of blindness."

Megan threw the question back at him. "If she'd discovered the truth, why would she have stayed?"

"Maybe for some of the same fucked-up reasons Dad didn't get a divorce."

"Such as?"

"Follow the money," Liam said cynically.

"If there's one lesson being a divorce lawyer drums home, it's that when married couples behave weirdly, there's always money involved. Money—or power that potentially leads right back to money."

Megan rejected that idea at once. "Mom couldn't care less about that. Good grief, Liam, I've never met anyone less motivated by money than Mom!"

"I agree that she doesn't care about cash in the bank or the stock market, but what about the ranch? More than a third of the land that's now part of the Flying W came from her family, remember. That's over two thousand acres of her direct family heritage at stake."

"True, but any divorce settlement would take that into account."

Liam conceded her point. "Yes, Dad would have had a hard time selling the ranch without her consent, however expert his lawyer was in finding loopholes in marital property law. But the ranch has no practical value without money to run it."

"Why do you say that?" Megan shot him a puzzled glance. "Flying W cattle are in huge demand."

"Even so, the cattle operation barely breaks even," Liam said flatly.

"Are you *sure?*"

"I'm positive. And with the threat of mad cow disease cutting into semen exports, the ranch is soaking up money. With a halfway competent divorce lawyer, Dad could have divvied up their assets so that Mom was left without a penny to run the cattle operation. Maybe she kept quiet and pretended not to know anything about his other wife so that she wouldn't be forced to watch the ranch fall back into wilderness."

Her mother loved the Flying W enough that she might have stayed in an unhappy marriage to protect the land, Megan conceded silently. But in a marriage where she knew her husband was married to another woman?

She shook her head, vehement in the strength of her denial. "Mom is way too honest to live in that sort of a sham marriage. She'd never condone bigamy, not for a moment, let alone for almost thirty years. I'm sure Mom had no clue. When Harry and I told her about Dad's wife in Chicago, she was devastated. It took her a good fifteen minutes to get any of her protective barriers back in place even though the sheriff was with us and she clearly hated breaking down in front of him. She didn't know Dad had another wife and daughter. I'd stake my life on it."

Liam still looked doubtful. "I would never have believed a man could pull off that sort of deception without complicity from one wife or the other," he said.

Megan thought for a moment. "Maybe the wife and daughter in Chicago knew."

"Maybe. Although the same question applies. Why would they tolerate it?"

"I can't imagine. But then, we don't know the first thing about them, so we can't possibly guess at their motives."

"The bottom line is that like any other scam artist, Dad exploited the fact that we trusted him." The bitterness was back in Liam's voice. "I dare say he exploited the same thing with his other family."

Megan looked at her brother. "Was that a random question you asked just now, or is there some specific reason why you thought Mom might have known about Dad's bigamy?"

Liam remained silent a moment longer. "I

knew," he said at last. "I figured she must have known, too."

"*You knew?*" Megan gripped the porch railing to steady herself. "You knew that Dad was a bigamist?" Her mouth was so dry that the words seemed to stick to her tongue. She felt betrayed all over again, first by her father and now by her brother. The betrayals were so huge that they annihilated all that was familiar, leaving her without signposts to guide her through the landscape of what had once been her relationship with her family.

"Yeah." Liam gave a terse nod. "I've known for a few years."

Megan's world shattered and re-formed in a different pattern. So many things that had been difficult to understand about her brother suddenly became clear. His decision to leave the practice of criminal law and open his own firm specializing in divorce took on a whole new meaning. Talk about an in-your-face insult hurled at their father! And no wonder Liam had barely visited the ranch over the past few years. Obviously, he had been doing his best to avoid contact with his parents.

"How did you find out about Dad's other

family?" Megan demanded. "Have you seen them? *Met* them?"

"No, I've never met them."

"Talk to me," she said tersely. "Don't retreat into one of your usual damn silences. Why did you keep quiet about something so incredibly important?"

"I was trying to protect Mom. And you."

"Protect me?" Megan's emotions had been in turmoil for forty-eight hours and Liam's crazy excuse was enough to send anger boiling to the surface. "How the hell does it protect me if I'm allowed to go on believing a massive lie?"

She could see her brother retreat even further into himself as he always did when the emotional atmosphere heated up, but he did at least answer her. "You're talking with the advantage of hindsight. I was making decisions and trying to guess the consequences for everyone—"

"In another month, I'll be twenty-seven years old! For heaven's sake, Liam, I'm not a kid sister you're permanently obliged to protect. I'm an *adult.*"

"Sometimes habits die hard—"

"That's a pretty pathetic excuse."

"Cutting you out of the loop was an insulting decision, I see that now." Liam gave an apologetic shrug. "I seem to have made a bunch of bad decisions over the past few years. But I was trying to do what seemed right. At least believe that...."

"You should have told me," she repeated and turned away, still struggling with her anger.

He touched her on the shoulder. "I'm really sorry, Meg."

She moved away from him. "You've been lying to me for years, at least by omission. That's hard to forgive."

"Don't let this force a wedge between the two of us." Liam's voice had lost all trace of its usual ironic edge. "Dammit, that's exactly what I was trying to avoid by remaining silent."

"It's bewildering—make that *infuriating*—to discover that two of the people I trusted most in the world were lying to me." Megan shoved impatiently at her hair, feeling as if her entire body was misaligned and out of sorts. "I *hate* that you kept me in the dark."

"I didn't want to put you in a position where you would have been forced to lie to Mom. It was bad enough for me, and I only saw her a couple of times a year."

"I wouldn't have lied to Mom. I'd have told her the truth."

"Yes, you probably would have done," Liam said. "And that's a big part of why I didn't confide in you."

"Why were you so determined to shield Mom from the truth? I don't understand why you covered for Dad. Or why you felt Mom was in such great need of protection."

"You think of Mom as a pillar of strength...."

"Yes, of course. Because she is."

"She's a pillar of strength here at the ranch, surrounded by everything she loves. Without the ranch, she'd wither away."

Megan gave an impatient shake of her head. "You underestimate her. Just as you underestimated me."

"Maybe. I wasn't willing to put Mom's happiness to the test and Dad exploited that vulnerability. Basically, he blackmailed me into keeping quiet. He warned me not to make him choose between his wives, because he swore that he'd choose Avery."

Each new revelation seemed to bring a little more pain than the last. If Avery had been Ron Raven's favorite wife, had Kate been his favorite daughter?

Megan pushed away the insidious jealousy. “How did you find out about his other family, anyway?”

“By chance. And even then, I practically had to be beaten over the head with the evidence before I put the pieces together.” Liam was visibly relieved to change the subject, even if only slightly. “Six years ago, I went to Atlanta for a business meeting. The night before I was due to fly home I happened to run into Dad at a political fundraiser for one of the local senators—”

“In Atlanta?”

Liam nodded. “Avery’s family is from Georgia, and she was with him at the party. It was obvious that she and Dad knew each other well. It was equally obvious that he was desperate to shepherd her away before I could speak to her. She’s a beautiful woman, a few years younger than Mom, and I assumed they were having an affair.”

“Why didn’t you confront them before Dad could hustle her away?” Megan demanded.

“I was with the senior partner of the law firm where I worked in those days, and we were being hosted by one of our most important clients. I didn’t want to expose my own father in front of a client, so Dad managed to make his escape."

"Did you confront him later?"

Liam nodded. "But only after some internal debate. Naturally, the truth never crossed my mind and I wasn't sure if it was my place to shove my nose into my parents' marriage by accusing Dad of having an affair. In the end, I made a special trip to Chicago, just to talk to him. He assured me the 'affair' was already over. That being caught by me at the fund-raiser had made him realize the risks he was running and how much he cherished his relationship with Mom. And so on and so on, through the laundry list of lies."

"And you believed him?"

"At the time." Liam's smile was bitter. "You won't be surprised to hear that Dad lied very convincingly. It was another two years before I found out that Avery was much more than a passing affair—that our father had actually gone through a formal marriage ceremony with her and that they had a daughter a few months younger than you."

"How did you find out those important details?" Megan heard the shake in her own voice. She wasn't sure if the tremor was caused by anger or something more complicated and even more painful.

"Again, by accident. I was sent unexpectedly to Chicago by my law firm. They needed me to take depositions for a criminal case we were working on. The witness I was sent to interview had offices in Oakbrook—"

"In Oakbrook?" Megan repeated. "That's where the offices of Dad's company are located."

Liam gave a tight, angry smile. "Yeah, that's what I thought, too. In fact, I was working only six or seven blocks away from where I believed R & R Investments was headquartered. So when I finished taking the depositions, I decided to drop in on Dad and invite him to dinner. We'd been estranged since the incident in Atlanta, and I figured it was time to get our relationship back on track."

"I remember the offices," Megan said. "Dad took us there the summer you graduated from high school. I was in fourth grade and I spent at least an hour making Xerox pictures of my hands on the copying machine. Then Mom and I went back for another visit years later when I was about to start college. Dad suggested that we might like to come to Chicago and do some shopping. He said it would be a good opportunity to meet his office staff and his partners."

Liam laughed, the sound harsh. "You have to give the guy credit. He sure had outsized balls. And you met his staff, of course? And his *partners?*" Her brother's questions were heavy with sarcasm.

"Well, yes, we did—"

"No, you didn't," Liam said, his fists clenching. "You met a bunch of actors. Both times. Both visits."

"What?"

"I guarantee that every so-called employee you were introduced to during that visit with Mom was an out-of-work actor, hired for the day. Just like they were the time you went there with me. R & R Investment Partnership isn't even the real name of Dad's corporation."

"What's his company called?" Her dry, cracked lips had to be forced to shape the words.

"The company is called Raven Enterprises, and the head office isn't in Oakbrook. It's miles away, northwest of Chicago, in Schaumburg, near O'Hare airport."

Megan shook her head, which did nothing to clear the fog of befuddlement. "Dad actually set up a fake company and a fake set of offices just to deceive us?" She sat down on the porch bench because her legs suddenly wouldn't hold her up.

"He didn't keep the fake company active on a permanent basis. Just long enough to convince us that we'd visited the headquarters of his company—the mythical R & R Investments."

Megan rubbed her forehead although she'd given up hope of banishing her headache anytime soon. "But even if he hired actors to play his employees, how did he have access to office space?"

"That was easy. He owns the building in Oakbrook and leases it out. He invited us there when he was between tenants. He even had an automated phone service set up so that if Mom or any of us called there, we'd be greeted by a message supposedly from R & R Investments."

A shiver crawled down Megan's spine. She'd learned a lot that she didn't like about her father over the past couple of days, most of it pretty major stuff. It was odd that these relatively trivial deceptions bothered her so much. "It makes his dealings with us seem so calculated. So petty and…cruel."

Liam's eyes glittered, dark with anger. "The extent of his lying takes some getting used to, doesn't it? It was quite a shock for me when I arrived unannounced at the Oakbrook offices and discovered the employees of an import-export firm working at the address I thought was the headquarters of R & R Investments."

"What in the world did you do? Did you assume there was some sort of honest mistake?"

"No. Not for an instant." Liam shrugged. "I guess at some level I'd been suspicious of Dad for a while—"

"You suspected he was a bigamist?" Megan heard the incredulity in her voice.

"Not that, but I was pretty sure he was lying to us about something important. To be honest, I'd begun to worry that maybe his business wasn't a legitimate legal enterprise."

Megan drew in a quick, nervous breath. "Is it?"

"As far as I know, yes, and I've researched the whole setup with a fair degree of intensity. We don't have to worry that Raven Enterprises is a front for organized crime. Which, under the circumstances, has to be considered a major plus."

It was a measure of how far she'd traveled in her view of her father that Megan wasn't entirely reassured. "I hope you're right."

"I have a lot of experience researching criminal business enterprises. I was a criminal lawyer, remember? Last time I ran a check, I can pretty much promise you that Dad's business partnership was clean. He's a shrewd, successful businessman." Liam corrected himself. "He *was* a shrewd, successful businessman."

Megan seized the hope that none of her father's business dealings had taken place on the shady side of the law and clung to it. Given that Ron Raven had been murdered, it struck her as depressingly possible that he'd been involved in at least a few ventures that wouldn't have passed muster with the Better Business Bureau. A criminal deal gone wrong struck her as one of the more likely causes for murder.

She drew in a shaky breath, reverting to their previous topic of conversation. "I don't quite see how you made the leap from realizing that Dad had deceived us about his office address to the fact that he was a bigamist."

"Obviously, from the moment I walked into the Oakbrook offices it became clear that Dad had been doing some heavy-duty lying. I decided not to approach him and ask for an explanation. I figured that was likely to trigger nothing but more lies. Instead I initiated a full-scale investigation, tackling the problem exactly as if he were a suspect in a criminal case."

Megan grimaced. "Which he was, more or less."

Liam nodded. "Yep, he was. Once I got serious, it was only a matter of hours before Dad's entire web of deception started to unravel. For example, it took me two minutes with a Chicago phone book to discover that there was no company called R & R Investments listed, but that a company called Raven Enterprises was headquartered in Schaumburg. A phone call to Raven Enterprises was all it took to discover that Ronald Howatch Raven was the senior partner. Once I knew that, the rest of his lies began to disintegrate. Amazingly fast, in fact. Dad pulled off his twenty-five-year scam basically because none of us questioned him. A couple of inquires, though, and it was all over."

"I guess he could never risk having us visit his real office because of his other wife and daughter. They probably dropped in all the time, given that they live right in Chicago."

Liam nodded. "I'm sure that was one reason he needed to keep us away. The other is that Dad's business partner, Paul Fairfax, is Avery's older brother."

"Oh, no. Oh my God." Megan couldn't say anything more. She gripped Belle's collar so tightly that the dog yelped in protest. Her world, which had seemed totally ordinary only a couple of days earlier, now seemed like a horror movie made by a director who specialized in creating bizarre alternate realities.

"Yeah, that about sums up how I felt when I found out. Speechless, alternating with disbelieving curses. Of course, Dad was deceiving his business partner as well as you and me and Mom. He wanted to keep Paul Fairfax away from us as much as the other way around."

Megan stared at the distant mountain range. For once, the grandeur of the Tetons provided no solace. "I'm starting to get so angry with him that it scares me."

Liam turned toward the mountains, following her gaze. His expression became even more bleak. "Now you understand how I've felt for the past few years."

Megan put her arms around Belle, controlling a sudden shiver. "Probably ninety percent of everything Dad ever told us was at least partly untrue."

"And the other ten percent was a lie by implication."

"I still don't understand why you didn't tell me what you'd found out. And Mom." Megan drew in a shaky breath. "Good grief, Liam! How could you keep this from her? She absolutely deserved to be told."

"When I finally learned the whole truth—especially that Dad had another daughter—I tried to force him to face up to his responsibilities and come clean to both his families." Liam lifted his shoulders, the gesture more despairing than dismissive. "He was very good at applying emotional blackmail. Like I told you, he claimed that if he had to choose between Mom and his other wife, he'd choose Avery. And that he'd not only leave Mom penniless, he'd make sure that she couldn't keep the ranch."

The spitefulness of that threat was another blow to the loving image of her father that Megan had been clinging to despite the revelations of the past forty-eight hours. "Well, at least that's one thing that's worked out to Mom's advantage." She finally recognized the same note of bitterness in her voice that she'd heard earlier in her brother's. "Since Dad is dead, presumably Mom is going to inherit the ranch."

"I sure as hell hope so. Who knows how Dad may have written his will." Liam swung away, his body rigid with tension. "Goddammit, I'm a *lawyer* and I haven't the faintest idea what my mother's financial and legal situation is right now. For all I know, Dad left every penny he owns to Avery Fairfax."

"If he did, surely Mom has grounds to fight."

"Absolutely. But we could be in and out of court for years, and in the meantime, the ranch would go belly up. If Dad's left all his cash to Avery, it's going to be a real fight to keep sufficient operating funds for the ranch to survive."

Megan bit back the urge to scream imprecations at her dead father. She was so emotionally drained that she felt exhausted. "What a hideous mess. I'm so furious with Dad that I'm numb."

"Trust me, however angry you are with him, you're nowhere near as angry as I am with myself."

"A little while ago you told me not to blame myself for Dad's sins. Now I guess I'm saying the same thing to you. The truth is, he put you in an impossible situation and then manipulated your feelings for Mom in order to protect himself. Put the blame where it belongs, Liam. With Dad. Right slap bang with him."

Four

Sunday, May 7, 2006, Thatch, Wyoming

A prayer service for Ronald Howatch Raven's safe return was held immediately following regular Sunday services at the hundred-year-old Community Church located at the far end of Thatch's Main Street. Most people were pretty sure that Ron was dead, but the failure to find his body meant that neighbors felt obligated to at least pretend they wished for his speedy and safe return.

Meanwhile, the story of his disappearance kept perking along in the national press. Media outlets were currently salivating over the information that bloodstains from three different people, one most likely female, had been identified as present at the crime scene. Almost equally as intriguing, a boat from the Blue Lagoon Marina had been put to sea without the permission of its owner and had been returned after a trip of some forty-five miles. A cop in Miami, a fan of Fox News, had let drop to his favorite talk-show host the fascinating tidbit that a security camera from the marina showed a masked person, sex indeterminate, using a furniture-moving dolly to transport first one and then another long, black-wrapped object onto the boat. The cop commented that the objects looked mighty like body bags to him and to everyone else who'd seen the video. In light of these images, the Miami police were working on the theory that Ron Raven's dead body had been disposed of at sea, possibly along with that of a female companion, identity as yet unknown.

The fact that it now seemed likely that there had been a woman with Ron Raven at the time he died provided fodder for a multitude of cable news programs. The delicious possibility that Ron had been husband to *three* women was chewed over by talk-show hosts and social-commentary pundits with relentless bad taste. The prize for idiocy—hotly contested—went to a congressman who opined that Ron Raven's bigamy at least showed respect for the institution of marriage, in a society where too many people thought it was okay to cohabit without the formality of getting married.

There were already a half-dozen blogs, much visited, devoted to the juicy details of Ron's bigamous life and the puzzle of his death. Theories about the murder abounded, and only the fact that both Avery and Ellie had watertight alibis prevented them becoming favorite suspects. The tabloids, of course, assumed that they were guilty anyway, despite the alibis.

MSNBC and CNN, annoyed at being scooped by Fox, scrambled to generate their own catch-up revelations. Meanwhile, they kept the pot stirring by interviewing a variety of clueless witnesses, most of whom seemed to be connected to Ron's disappearance more by virtue of their vivid imaginations than because of any concrete information in their possession.

In view of the annoying reluctance of either widow to speak to reporters, high ratings had to be sustained somehow, and Ellie Raven's decision to hold a prayer service for her husband was counted as a blessing by news outlets everywhere. No less than thirty-five camera crews were on hand to record Stark County's tribute to Ron Raven and lots had to be drawn to determine who would be privileged to film the service from the two available spots in the upstairs organ loft.

The Reverend Dwight D. Gruber, pastor of Thatch Community Church for over twenty years, rose magnificently to the occasion. The choir, his personal pride and joy, performed “How Great Thou Art” and “Amazing Grace” with poignant beauty. Better yet, he achieved the remarkable feat of urging everyone to pray for Ron’s safe return without ever quite mentioning the disconcerting truth that all the evidence suggested the man was already dead and feeding the sharks somewhere off the coast of Miami.

Even this omission paled into insignificance in comparison to the astounding fact that in twenty minutes devoted to recounting the highlights of Ron’s life, Pastor Gruber made not a single reference to the truth that the guy had been a bigamist. A bigamist, moreover, who had disappeared from a hotel room occupied not only by himself, but also by an unknown female companion. Who said that small-town pastors had few oratorical skills?

In addition to the camera crews, the

church was bursting at the seams with Ellie's friends and neighbors. These folk appreciated their pastor's efforts to put the best possible gloss on the sordid reality of Ron Raven's life. Ellie was deeply respected in the community, and the residents of Stark County had spent the past week doing their best to remain aloof and dignified despite their collective moment of glory in the glow of the national-media spotlight.

The official consensus among Stark County residents was relief that The Other Wife and her daughter hadn't attempted to crash the prayer service. Still, Billy Carstairs summed up the feelings of many attendees when he admitted to his wife that he couldn't believe Ron had been dippin' his wick into two honeypots—could even be three—with nobody in Thatch any the wiser. He allowed as how it sure would have been interesting to catch a close-up view of the rival family. Sorry as he was for Ellie and her kids, Billy would really have liked to see what Ron Raven's two wives had to say to each other.

But with no rival wife on the scene, and reporters banned from the church meeting room after the service, Ellie's neighbors resigned themselves to being on their best behavior. The etiquette for a prayer vigil loomed over by the specter of an absent and bigamous wife, not to mention a possible dead mistress, had to be considered a challenge, even for people who'd known each other for a long time and liked each other pretty well.

For the most part, the men considered their duty had been done when they turned up and listened to Pastor Gruber's sermon without a single one of them bursting into guffaws of laughter. The women, however, felt obligated to do something more than merely keep straight faces while listening to the pastor's farcical eulogy. They'd risen to the occasion by preparing a quantity of casseroles, cookies and Jell-O salads that ensured the caloric requirements of everyone in Stark County could be met for several days simply by grazing the laden buffet tables in the church meeting room.

Unfortunately, the bountiful array of food didn't quite obviate the need to find something tactful to say to Ellie and her kids, but the residents of Stark County were a resilient lot, accustomed to dealing with drought, blizzards, insect plagues and the intrusive hand of the federal government.

Determined to do what was right, they formed themselves into a tidy line and slowly wound their way past Ellie, Liam and Megan, mumbling their somewhat sincere wishes for Ron's safe return—they figured it was just possible she was going to miss the bastard—and their much more sincere offerings of any sort of help they might be able to provide.

Ellie looked ravaged, showing every one of her fifty-five years, but she accepted the good wishes and thanked people for their offers of help with quiet dignity. Liam, tall and even better looking than his dead father, stood at his mother's side, his city-slicker suit and fancy striped silk tie reminding everyone that he had at least three strikes against him. First, he'd moved away and taken up residence in a big city. Second, he was a lawyer, and third, he hadn't come back to Thatch more than a handful of times in the past five years. However, his excellent memory for names and faces reassured people that he hadn't totally forgotten his roots. Despite the fact that he looked a lot like his dad, the neighbors were willing to grant him the benefit of the doubt and accept that in character and morals he took after his mother.

After half an hour of listening to her neighbors' well-intentioned lies, Megan realized that she wasn't coping with the multiple hypocrisies of the occasion anywhere near as efficiently as her brother. She wished she could imitate Liam's expression of bland and friendly courtesy, but the task was beyond her. The urge to scream became increasingly powerful with each hand she shook. Grateful as she was for the support of their neighbors, she could imagine all too vividly the pity lurking behind the polite, Sunday-go-to-church faces. She hated to be pitied—but she hated even more that she felt pitiable. As each excruciating minute slithered by, it took an increasing amount of willpower not to run from the room.

She finally gave up. "I have to get a drink," she murmured to Liam. "Would you like some punch? A cup of coffee?"

He shook his head, leaning down to speak softly in her ear. "You okay?"

"More or less. I need some breathing room. Can you stay here with Mom for a few minutes?"

“Not a problem. Take however much time you need.”

Megan helped herself to the alarmingly bright red punch, dry-mouthed enough to sip gratefully. Pastor Gruber was bearing down on her, accompanied by his wife, and she avoided them by dodging behind a mobile book cart. She was thankful for the lies of omission in the minister’s sermon, but she couldn’t take any more pretense. She’d zoomed past her cutoff level for bullshit concerning Ron Raven at least twenty-four hours ago.

There was no escaping outside, she realized. The camera crews were lined up, waiting to pounce, so she’d just have to suck it up and be polite to her neighbors for another hour. Please God, it wouldn’t be more than another hour before this preposterous prayer service was over. What would any of them do if her father actually returned? she wondered. Turn him over to the cops?

She spotted Cody Holmann, the lawyer her parents had used for years, walking purposefully toward her. Cody was probably as restful a person to talk to as anyone, she decided. He was a slow-moving but kindly man in his midsixties, who was still known in some local circles as Young Cody in order to distinguish him from his ninety-two-year-old father, Cody Holmann Senior.

There was no risk that he would want to discuss legal business with her, Megan decided. Liam had already met with Cody on Friday afternoon and the news from their meeting had been mostly positive. Ellie's financial and legal situation was complicated by the fact that Ron Raven hadn't yet been officially declared dead. However, Cody was confident he would be able to find a judge willing to authorize payments from Ron's accounts to cover living expenses for Ellie and salaries for the two full-time ranch employees. In addition, Cody had been able to confirm that the copy of their father's will in Ellie's possession was an exact duplicate of the document he had drawn up for Ron three years earlier.

Amazingly, after all the startling revelations following their father's death, it seemed that the disposition of Ron's estate was going to generate few surprises. The provisions of their father's will turned out to be more or less what Megan and Liam would have expected. Most importantly, the ranch had been left to their mother, along with an annual income that would be sufficient to subsidize the cattle operation in bad years.

Despite the basically good news, the clarity of the will didn't remove all their worries. The family in Chicago wasn't mentioned and Cody warned that Avery Fairfax and her daughter would most likely protest their exclusion. Liam agreed that a lawsuit was almost inevitable. In their professional opinions, even if the courts dismissed Avery's claims, they were likely to view Kate's situation sympathetically. She had been raised to believe she was Ron Raven's legitimate daughter, as well as his only child, and she was an innocent victim of her father's bigamy. Cody believed that a substantial award to Kate was entirely possible. Still, Liam and Cody were both confident that Ellie would eventually be left in sole possession of the ranch, and that the courts would ensure she had sufficient income to continue living comfortably while any legal challenges wound their way through the justice system.

Megan had been relieved to learn that, at least in terms of making financial provision, her father had behaved decently toward their mother. Ron's total silence regarding his Chicago family ought to have been welcome, but Megan had found herself fighting the impulse to feel sorry for them. She wasn't quite willing to admit that Ron's other wife and daughter deserved better treatment than they'd received, but she'd worked out in her own mind that if the fancy Chicago penthouse where they lived turned out to be titled in Avery's name, she wouldn't be altogether unhappy.

"Megan, how are you doing?" Cody reached up to touch a couple of fingers to the brim of his Stetson, then remembered he wasn't wearing what amounted to the uniform headgear for men in Stark County. He let his hand drop awkwardly to his side. "We don't get all the neighbors together like this nearly often enough. I'm sorry today's gathering was for such a sad occasion."

"Yes. The neighbors have been great. We're grateful for their kindness." Megan searched for something more to say and came up flat empty.

Cody abandoned his fleeting attempt to pretend the circumstances were normal. "Discovering the truth about your dad has been a hell of a shock to me," he said. "Can't begin to imagine how much of a shock it's been for you and your family."

Megan wasn't sure they *had* discovered the truth about her father. She had a depressing suspicion they'd merely lifted off the outer layer on a Chinese box of multiple deceptions.

"We're coping with a lot of unanswered questions, that's for sure," she said. "There are dozens of decisions Mom needs to make, but it isn't easy when we seem to be missing so much vital information."

"Wish I didn't have to add to your troubles." The lawyer scratched his head, visibly uncomfortable. "I guess there's no point in beating around the bush, Megan. I've got another problem to add to your list."

"The Chicago family is fighting the will already?" She drew in a quick, shallow breath. "They couldn't even wait until the weekend was over?"

Cody grimaced. "Worse than that. Fact is, I received a special-delivery package yesterday afternoon. A set of documents that came from a firm of fancy lawyers in Chicago. I thought I recognized the name of the firm, but I looked them up just to be sure. Fenwick Jaeger. They're a sixty-year-old law firm, entirely reputable. Twenty active partners, another forty associates and God knows how many paralegals. The covering letter came from somebody called Walter Daniels, senior partner. I decided not to trouble your mother with the details of his communication, at least until after today's services, but I'd like to give you a heads-up."

Megan's stomach lurched in anticipation of disaster. "What were the documents Mr. Daniels sent you?"

"A will." Cody cleared his throat. "Your father's will."

"But we already have his will." Megan's forehead wrinkled in puzzlement.

"This is another will, with completely different provisions from the one I drew up for Ron. Mr. Daniels claims it's the last will and testament written by your dad. By Ron Raven," Cody added, as if she might have lost track of who her father actually was.

She and Liam had obviously rejoiced way too early about her mother's financial security, Megan thought bleakly. From the way Cody was shuffling his feet, he clearly didn't like the provisions of this new will.

"Do the documents look authentic to you?" she asked.

"As far as I can tell, they're the real thing. Format's impeccable and it looks like Ron's signature to me. Of course, we can dispute it—"

"The signature or the will?"

"Either. Both. Don't know where that might get us. Like I said, Fenwick Jaeger aren't exactly fly-by-nights. I doubt if we're going to prove that this is a forgery. They have their reputation on the line in sending this to me. No way they'd knowingly be party to any hanky-panky."

Hanky-panky? Megan was too worried to find the lawyer's quaintly old-fashioned turn of phrase amusing. How about *total betrayal,* if he needed words to describe Ron's behavior toward his wife of thirty-six years? "What are the provisions of the Chicago will, Cody? Are we going to want to dispute them?"

"Yes," he said flatly.

Megan's hand was shaking enough that she had to put down her punch. "Give me the main points."

Cody actually winced. "From our point of view, there's only one main point. You, your mother and your brother aren't even mentioned."

Her mother wasn't mentioned? A shiver ran down Megan's spine. "If Mom isn't named as a beneficiary, what happens to the ranch?"

Cody stared down at the floor, then up to the ceiling. Apparently he found the help he was seeking in neither place. "It's not good, Meg. According to the Chicago will, your father's other daughter gets the ranch. That would be Kate Fairfax Raven. She gets the land, the breeding stock, everything."

Megan stared at the lawyer, literally incapable of speech.

"We can fight," Cody said quickly. "We'll fight those particular provisions tooth and nail, trust me."

"How *could* he?" Megan was suddenly ice cold with fury. The rage that she'd been struggling to hold at bay ever since hearing of her father's bigamy spewed out with volcanic force. "How *could* he give my mother's property away like that? He had no right!"

Cody laid his hand on her arm. "We'll certainly make that argument to the probate judge. Don't know exactly where it will get us. The fact is, none of the Flying W land ever belonged directly to Ellie—"

"What do you mean?" Megan realized her voice was rising and that they were surrounded by people who didn't need to hear this latest installment in the humiliation of Ellie Raven. She forced herself back under control. "The whole eastern third of the Flying W ranch has been owned by Mom's family since 1886!"

"Yes, but that's the problem. It was owned by her parents and her grandparents, not by your mother herself. Ron bought the land from Ellie's dad and the money he used for the purchase came from his business interests." Cody lifted his shoulders, the gesture apologetic. "It's not a slam dunk to get a probate judge to agree that Ellie has any intrinsic right to that land, Megan, let alone the remaining two-thirds of the property. Remember, the majority of the land that makes up the Flying W ranch was your father's, long before he married your mother."

"The ranch isn't just a business. It's my mother's home. It's her life."

"I realize how much the Flying W means to Ellie, but the ranch was set up years ago as a business with your mother's full consent. That makes a difference to the legal situation. I'll fight for her. I consider her a friend as well as a client and I'll fight hard. But, bottom line, the judge may well decide that the ranch should be sold and the money divided up among the claimants. I'm being honest with you, Megan. In my best judgment, we're in for a bruising fight."

"When is the Chicago will dated?" she asked, surprised she could ask such a coherent question in view of her simmering fury. "Did my father sign it before or after he signed the will in my mother's possession?"

Cody cleared his throat again. "Well, that's another of the odd things about the situation. The Chicago will is dated the precise same day as the one I drew up for your dad three years ago."

"The same day?" Megan stared at him. "How could Dad have signed a will in Chicago at the same time as he's signing one here in Wyoming? That's crazy." She experienced a flash of hope. "The Chicago will *must* be a forgery."

"I don't believe so. Like I said, your father's signature looked authentic to me, and the will was properly witnessed and notarized. Have to say, too, that Fenwick Jaeger are too experienced a firm to mess up something as important as the date on a legal document."

"Then how is it possible that both wills were signed the same day? Thatch and Chicago are fourteen hundred miles apart!"

"Well, it sure doesn't seem like it could be chance," Cody acknowledged. His expression suggested he'd prefer to be breaking stones on a chain gang rather than having this conversation. He coughed again. Constricted throat muscles seemed to be an inevitable accompaniment to people trying to discuss Ron Raven, Megan reflected bitterly.

"Guess your dad must have deliberately set out to ensure both wills got signed on the same day," Cody said. "I checked my appointment calendar and your dad didn't come in to my office until late in the afternoon—he was my last appointment. If Ron signed the Chicago will first thing in the morning he could have flown back to Jackson Hole and arrived here in Thatch just in time to sign another will in my office that same day. There's a one-hour time difference between here and Chicago, remember."

Why in the world would her father have

done something as bizarre as sign two wills on the same day? Megan wondered. To cast doubts on the legitimacy of both wills so that his estate would have to be divided up among the two branches of his family by the courts? Or merely to ensure that he caused as much trouble and inconvenience as possible? From what she'd learned over the past few days, she was almost willing to believe the latter.

Cody tried to smile. "There's one positive aspect of this situation. The will I drew up was signed later in the day than the one the Chicago lawyers have just sent me. Must have been. He couldn't have arrived back in Chicago during business hours. Totally impossible, even by private jet. That means the will I drew up—the one in your mother's possession—probably represents your father's *last* will and testament—"

"And therefore it's the one that will hold up in court?"'

"We'll make the argument." Cody lifted his shoulders in a defeated shrug. "The existence of another will signed on the same day suggests, at the very least, that your father was ambivalent about his wishes. Any probate judge is going to take the existence of the other will into account in deciding how to dispose of your father's assets. But here is one more fact that's in your mother's favor. She's your father's first and *legal* wife. You and Liam are his legitimate children. That counts for something, even today. But, to be frank, not as much as it would have thirty years ago."

"Don't tell my mother about this other will," Megan said. "Please, Cody, promise me that you won't burden her with this right now. She's still struggling to come to terms with all the other bombshells that have been lobbed at her over the past week. She doesn't need to be worrying that she might lose the Flying W as well."

"I can't make that promise, Megan. Wish I could. But I'm your mother's lawyer. I have an obligation to inform her of all legal developments in regard to her husband's estate."

"Give Liam and me a few days to decide how to proceed," she pleaded. "We'll fight the Chicago will, of course. Not for me, I don't care. At this point, I'm not even sure that I want any of Dad's money—" She broke off. "We need to fight for Mom's sake. We can't let the ranch go to…to the women in Chicago. That land's been in my mother's family for a hundred and forty years. It's insane to suddenly hand it over to the child of her husband's mistress!"

"Maybe not insane," Cody said, avoiding her eyes. "But certainly vindictive." He allowed the word to hang in the air, resonating painfully between the two of them.

It was almost as if her father had hated her mother, Megan reflected. Had he? Had he hated his Wyoming children, too? Had his bluff good cheer and seeming pride in her achievements concealed resentment? She closed her eyes, squeezing away the stupid tears that seemed determined to flow whenever and wherever it was most humiliating. She swallowed hard, forcing the tears to stop when she felt the light touch of Cody's hand on her arm.

"Are you okay, Megan? Although that's a damn-fool question under the circumstances."

"Yes, I'm fine." She dashed the back of her hand across her eyes. "Please don't tell my mother about the other will." She glanced across the room to Ellie, who was looking unspeakably weary as she attempted to keep up a conversation with Pastor Gruber and the choir director.

"I won't tell Ellie today," Cody conceded. "I can't promise more than that. Tomorrow morning I plan to call Mr. Daniels at Fenwick Jaeger and explain that we believe we have Ron's most recent will and that its terms vary substantially from the document he sent me. As soon as I've spoken to Mr. Daniels, I'll be in touch with your mother. I have an obligation to report to her on the situation."

Megan drew what comfort she could from the twenty-four-hour delay. "I'll talk to Liam tonight and explain what you've told me. I'm sure he'll call you first thing tomorrow morning."

"If not, I'll be stopping by at the ranch. Good day to you, Megan." Cody touched his fingers once more to his nonexistent hat and walked away.

Five

Megan had known that Liam would be upset when he heard about the existence of another will, but she hadn't anticipated the depth of his self-blame.

"It's not your fault that Dad wrote a will leaving everything to the Chicago family," she said when they finally managed a few moments alone on the porch. "For heaven's sake, Liam, why are you responsible for the fact that Dad seems to have been pretty much a major asshole?"

"Because I knew about Avery Fairfax," Liam said, leaning down to scratch Bruno's belly. "I knew and I still kept Dad's secrets. Dammit! I let him manipulate me precisely because I wanted to prevent this sort of thing happening—and now he's screwed Mom over anyway. The son of a bitch must be laughing in hell."

"I don't think you get to laugh in hell," Megan said. "That's kind of the point."

"He'll be the exception." Liam stared broodingly at a cloud of dust on the horizon. The dust resolved itself into a small panel truck, barreling down the driveway at a spanking pace.

"God, I hope that's a reporter." Liam got up from the swing. "I'm so in the mood to punch somebody out."

Judging by his scowl, Megan was pretty sure her brother wasn't joking. She ran down the porch steps in order to prevent him from throwing the threatened punch. Violence might soothe Liam's feelings for a couple of seconds, but she could just imagine the vicious media reports if he was hauled into court on assault-and-battery charges.

As soon as the dust cloud settled, she realized the truck was from a package-delivery company. A middle-aged man climbed out, extending a special-delivery envelope toward her. "Ms. Raven?"

"Yes, I'm Megan Raven."

"This package arrived in our Jackson Hole office yesterday and should've been brought out right away." The man's voice was high-pitched, making him sound oddly tense.

"We were shorthanded and didn't get to it. Sorry about the delay."

"That's okay. Thanks." Megan took the package and turned to go, but Liam grabbed the envelope from her and scanned the shipping label.

"This isn't designated for Saturday delivery, much less Sunday," he said.

To Megan's surprise, the driver immediately looked guilty. "I don't know anything about that," he mumbled.

Liam squinted at the corner of the label. "According to the date and time stamp, it only arrived at Jackson Hole airport four hours ago."

"Is that so?" The deliveryman shot an anxious glance in the direction of his van, feet scuffling in the dust. "I was just told to bring it out here—"

"I'll bet you were. But who told you?" Liam shoved past the deliveryman and leaned into the panel truck, hauling out a man who'd been hiding in the windowless rear compartment, camera angled to take pictures through the front side window. The photographer tumbled out, clutching his camera to his chest.

"Whoever you are, you're trespassing."

Liam's voice was lethal in its cold fury. "The sheriff has already warned members of the media about staying off our land."

The photographer apparently wasn't smart enough to realize that Liam's cool tones masked blazing anger. He held up an ID card and smiled with patent insincerity. "Hi, there. I'm Brad Stratford with Media International. No hard feelings, I hope? I have some questions for your family—just to set the public record straight, you know? I asked Kevin here to deliver this package right away so that I could—"

"You have one second to start deleting any pictures you took of me, my sister and our home." Liam's voice was quiet and without inflection, but Megan could see that he was hanging on to his control by his fingernails.

"What? Delete these great shots?" Brad made the mistake of laughing. "Be reasonable, Mr. Raven. I have a job to do—"

"And we have a right to privacy on our own property."

"No, you don't." Brad's veneer of friendliness dropped. "You and the rest of your family have become persons of public interest, which means you've lost your privacy rights—"

Liam silenced the reporter's explanation of the law by the simple method of grabbing him by the scruff of the neck and frog-marching him until he was pushed flat against the side of the truck. Then he put his arm across Brad's neck and applied pressure. Brad moaned and the delivery guy squeaked in alarm but made no attempt to rescue his illicit passenger.

"Guess I just retrieved some of our right to privacy," Liam said, grabbing the camera from the photographer's slackened hand. He moved a couple of steps backward and began deleting swiftly.

The delivery guy decided that discretion was the better part of valor. He scurried toward the rear of the van, navigating a wide berth around both Liam and the reporter. Then he sidled along the far side of the truck and hopped into the driver's seat, slamming and locking the door as if he expected Liam to dismember him given half a chance.

Abandoned by his fellow conspirator, the reporter took a few staggering steps away from the truck, making a great show of how difficult he found it to stand upright. He clutched his throat, massaging and groaning as if he'd just escaped an encounter with the Boston Strangler. In reality, Megan felt sure the guy was a lot more angry than injured.

"I'll sue," he said, trying to snatch his camera back from Liam and not succeeding. "I'll sue your arrogant ass off, you son of a bitch."

"Good luck getting anyone in this county to award you damages." Liam, satisfied that all the pictures were deleted, pitched the camera into the back of the van. "In the meantime, you're trespassing. Clear off our land and don't come back."

The reporter gave an anguished howl and dived into the van in pursuit of his camera. Bruno, most likely bitten by a mosquito since he was the world's most useless watchdog, chose this moment to give a fierce growl, lunging toward Liam in hopes of earning a few scratches. The deliveryman gave a panicked shriek, as if Bruno were an enraged pit bull instead of an elderly, overweight and mentally challenged golden retriever. Barely waiting for the reporter to climb into the rear cargo space, the delivery guy turned the truck around in a squeal of tires on gravel and tore back down the driveway.

Megan watched their retreat in silent gratification, rewarding Bruno with a vigorous back-scratching

"If I'd known that throttling a reporter was all it takes to make you smile, I'd have done it sooner," Liam said.

Megan tried to look severe, then gave up and laughed. "God, I've wanted to do something like that for the past week. But we'll probably regret it when Brad Thingummy sues us for millions of dollars."

"He won't sue. He was trespassing and he knew it. Why else did he hide in a delivery truck?"

"What about his point that we've lost our right to privacy?"

"Innocent people don't lose their right to privacy because a family member was murdered, or even because he was a bigamist. If you and I were the bigamists, it would be a different story." Liam pointed to the package Megan was still holding. "What are we going to do about that? It's addressed to Mom, I noticed."

"We should take it in to her, I suppose. It might be important."

"Yes, I'm guessing it is." Liam paused for a moment. "Did you notice the name of the shipper?"

Megan read off the information on the label. "The President's Office. The First Bank of Fairfax. The zip code is somewhere in Georgia." She sighed. "It's probably an offer to loan Mom money on the ranch or something equally useless. She's received a bunch of solicitations like that this past week—Oh my God—" She broke off and looked down again at the package. "Fairfax. The First Bank of *Fairfax.*"

"Yeah," Liam said. "It seems unlikely that the name's a coincidence, wouldn't you say?"

Megan gulped. "You think this has been sent by somebody who's related to Avery and Kate Fairfax." It was a statement, not a question.

"I'm afraid so. I told you Dad's senior business partner, Paul Fairfax, is Avery's brother. But she has another brother, too. His name is Adam and he's president of a small community bank in the town of Fairfax, which is about thirty miles south of Atlanta. How much would you like to bet this communication is from Adam?"

Megan's stomach, already sinking, took a

nosedive straight for her feet. “If you’re right, there’s a strong probability this letter is going to be bad news.”

“You think?” Liam’s question was heavy with irony. He echoed her sigh. “Unfortunately, good news or bad, we have to take it to Mom. She hasn’t given either of us permission to open her mail.”

“She’s probably still napping. She looked wiped out by the time we got back from church.” Megan stared down at the express letter with loathing.

“We’d better check.” Liam walked into the house and down the hallway that led to the master bedroom. They paused, listening until they heard the unmistakable sounds of their mother moving around inside the room.

Megan tapped on the door. “Mom, an express package arrived for you. Liam and I think you ought to open it right away.”

“Wait a moment, please.” After some scuffling sounds, Ellie poked her head around the door, wrapped in a terrycloth robe. “I was about to take a shower. Did you say there’s a package for me?”

“Here.” Megan held it out.

“Oh, it’s just a letter.” Sounding distracted,

Ellie turned away. "Put it on the dining-room table, could you? I'll get to it in a while."

"Mom, I think you should open it right away."

Ellie frowned, then shrugged and took the envelope. She ripped it open and took out a letter clipped to an attachment of four or five pages. She gave the letter a cursory read, her expression displaying neither particular interest nor concern. When she'd finished, she handed the entire package back to Megan.

"It's something about money your father supposedly owes a bank in Georgia," she said, not even glancing at the pages attached to the letter.

"Mom, it's from the Bank of *Fairfax.*" Megan felt compelled to draw her mother's attention to that unwelcome fact.

Ellie's eyes flickered for a moment, indicating—just barely—that she understood the significance of the name. "Yes, I noticed that. Will you take care of it? The claim's ridiculous, of course. Tell Cody we have no intention of settling something so obviously trumped up. Sorry, but I'm in a real rush. I need to take that shower." She closed her bedroom door with a firm thud.

Megan stared at the closed door in simmering frustration. "Well, that was helpful. Not. How much money is the bank claiming that Dad owes them?"

Liam read quickly. "Try three million dollars," he said grimly.

Megan felt her eyes bulge. "Three *million* dollars?"

"Yep, and Adam Fairfax is officially putting us on notice that the bank is calling the loan. As far as I can see on a quick reading, they have the right to force us to put the Flying W ranch up for auction if the debt isn't repaid—in full—within thirty business days."

She couldn't have understood correctly, Megan thought, rubbing her forehead. Her father was too smart a businessman to have signed such a punitive loan agreement.

She had to swallow a couple of times before she could speak again. "Run that by me one more time, Liam. Did you really say that Dad owes the Bank of Fairfax *three million dollars?*"

"Unfortunately, that's exactly what I said. And the loan is secured by a mortgage on the Flying W."

"Maybe Mom's right. Maybe the bank is

trying to scam us. The president is Avery's brother, after all."

Liam shook his head. "I doubt if Adam Fairfax would run an outright fraud. He'd be risking several years in prison."

"Dad risked prosecution every day for the past twenty-six years or so. Apparently some people like to live dangerously."

Liam thumbed through the attachment. "This is a copy of the loan agreement, executed two years ago. It looks like Dad's signature to me. And everything's notarized. If the documents are forged, Adam Fairfax would have to persuade other bank employees to lie, too. Why would they?"

"Let me see the loan agreement." Megan leaned across and squinted at the signature line. *Ronald H. Raven* and *Adam Pierce Fairfax.* The sick churning in her stomach increased. Liam was correct: her father's signature looked depressingly authentic. Plus, the notary seal, with its official date and time stamp, would be hard to forge.

"Maybe the terms of the loan are so punitive we can protest?" She scanned the pages of the agreement without managing to absorb a word of what they said. Her brain felt like overcooked oatmeal, all lumps and scorched grains, and her normally swift grasp of the written word seemed to have congealed into one of the lumps.

"Punitive terms, provided they're freely entered into by all parties, aren't usually grounds for legal protest." Liam put down the papers. "Besides, the overall terms of this loan aren't punitive. In fact they look pretty reasonable to me. The rate of interest is prime plus one percent, and Dad isn't required to pay off any of the capital until 2010, or until the completion of the Flying W Resort, whichever comes first, at which point he's required to pay off the loan in its entirety—"

"The Flying W Resort?" Megan wondered if the punch at the church had been spiked with something a lot more hallucinogenic than sugar and red dye. "What in the world is the Flying W Resort?"

"The hotel and entertainment complex that Dad apparently planned to build right here on Flying W land. According to Adam Fairfax, Dad presented him with a five-year business plan for the resort, plus a prospectus and architectural drawings for a new lodge-style hotel, to be built adjacent to the Silver River."

"A hotel near the river? But Dad never suggested building so much as an outhouse on Flying W land!" Megan felt as if her foot were poised inches above the rabbit hole, and the slightest push would toss her down into Wonderland. "Surely Mom would have mentioned if she and Dad had been planning to turn the ranch into a hotel? Or even if it was only Dad who wanted to end the cattle operation and she was resisting."

"You'd have thought, wouldn't you?" Liam sounded bleak. "Well, that's neither here nor there at the moment. The point is that Dad seems to have signed a loan agreement authorizing the First Bank of Fairfax to demand repayment of the entire debt in the event of his death. Not surprisingly, Adam Fairfax has chosen to call the loan. That wouldn't be a problem if Dad had left a single, valid will. But since he didn't, we're in big trouble. Unless you know where we can lay our hands on three million dollars, Mom is about to have the ranch sold out from under her."

Megan leaned against the wall. Her legs were so shaky she needed to feel something solid behind her spine. "But she didn't even seem worried when she read the letter. What's that about?"

"She's on overload," Liam said. "I'm guessing she's about half a step away from total breakdown. I realized at the memorial service that she was going through the motions on sheer autopilot. She was physically present, but the thinking part of her brain wasn't there."

Belatedly, Megan registered several other occasions over the past couple of days when her mother had seemed distinctly out of it. She felt a spurt of guilt as she realized that she'd been too self-absorbed to notice how badly her mother needed help. "We have to persuade her to see the doctor. He needs to prescribe some antianxiety medication."

"Good suggestion." Liam nodded. "In the meantime, what do you suggest we do about Adam Fairfax and his demand for three million dollars?"

"Write him one of your snooty lawyer-type letters and point out to him that Dad hasn't yet been declared dead, so there are no grounds for calling the loan. That should hold him for a while."

Liam shot her one of his rare smiles, the

sort that made his cool gray eyes warm up, and transformed him from merely handsome to movie-star stunning. "Hey, squirt, have I told you recently that you're a genius?"

"No, but feel free to pile on the praise. Until Dad is officially declared dead, I guess we can simply pay the interest—" She broke off as their mother emerged from the master bedroom. "Mom, you're all dressed up. Are you going out?"

"I'm going to Jackson Hole," Ellie said in the sort of conversational tone that suggested this had already been discussed several times and wasn't cause for comment. "I'll be back in a couple of days."

"I'll come with you," Megan said at once. "You can stay at my apartment—"

"No." Ellie's response was sharp and adamant. She drew in a quick breath, then spoke more softly, clearly trying to soften her earlier abruptness. "Thanks, Meg, I appreciate the offer of your company, but I'd prefer to be alone."

Liam took her hand. "Mom, I understand why you would feel that way, but I'm not sure this is a good time for you to be on your own."

Ellie drew herself up to her full height,

which meant that she just about made it to five foot one. "Thank you both for your concern. I'm grateful for all you've done over the past few days, but I have to make this trip alone."

"Where are you going to stay?" Megan asked. "Have you made a booking? I could get you an employee discount at the ski lodge—"

"Thanks, but I'd prefer to go someplace where people won't recognize me." Ellie seemed to realize that might be difficult anywhere in Jackson Hole, given the circumstances. She spoke quickly. "I'll decide which hotel when I get there. I'll call to give you the number where I can be reached." She walked past them, talking over their continuing protests. "Goodbye for now. Thanks again for everything. I'll see you by midweek at the latest."

Six

Ellie had never been a good flier at the best of times, which was part of the reason she'd been so content to stay home on the ranch while Ron traveled all over the country putting together exciting business deals. On those rare occasions when she did accompany Ron, she was happy to leave him to make all the arrangements and simply tag along, a shadow to his vibrant, larger-than-life persona.

In fact, she realized when she arrived in Jackson Hole and booked her flight to Chicago's O'Hare airport that she'd never actually traveled outside the state of Wyoming without Ron or one of her children at her side. When she was a student at the state agricultural college, she'd been accepted to spend the second semester of her sophomore year at a sheep ranch in New Zealand. Then Ron, the glamorous boy-from-the-ranch-next-door had returned from a tour of duty in Vietnam. His physical injuries were minor, his psychic ones more severe, severe enough to be visible even to a naive eighteen-year-old. He had seemed to need her so badly that she hadn't hesitated for a second when the choice came to pursue her grand New Zealand adventure or to marry him. At eighteen, sacrificing herself for her true love had seemed the obviously right thing to do. From her current perspective, it seemed incredibly stupid.

Her first solo flight turned out to be a waking nightmare. With all the real problems she had to worry about, Ellie realized it was pathetic to spend the flight curled into a fetal funk, agonizing in case an engine fell off, or lightning struck, or terrorists swarmed down the aisles, but that was what happened.

And if the panic itself wasn't silly enough, as a final humiliation Ellie knew the woman in the next seat had recognized her. The covert stares from her seatmate set her stomach churning and any dregs of willpower she could summon had to be devoted to the miserable task of making sure that she didn't throw up into her inquisitive neighbor's lap.

Not that she could blame the nausea entirely on the fact that she'd been recognized. For the past week, she'd spent so much time with her head held over the toilet bowl that it had been like revisiting the first three months of her pregnancy with Megan. Sleeplessness, nausea and incredible mood swings—she'd endured all the worst symptoms of pregnancy with no baby to make it worthwhile, she thought wryly.

Guilt was never a good companion, especially on a journey, and Ellie had moments when she decided she was only getting her just desserts. She'd flat out lied to Liam and Meg about where she was going, but her children would never have allowed her to leave the ranch if she'd told them the truth, and she'd been desperate to escape.

Her desperation had been building all week and finally trumped every other emotion. With Ron's body nowhere to be found, and the police still investigating who had killed him, it was likely to take months for him to be officially declared dead. That meant a funeral was out of the question. Ellie had hoped against hope that a prayer service would provide the closure she craved, but she'd realized as she listened to Pastor

Gruber's dreadful, well-meant sermon that lies spoken in public had even less healing power than lies whispered in private.

After the prayer service failed to provide any relief, Ellie finally faced up to the fact that an elephant had invaded her home and was busy crashing through the ruins of her life. Instead of pretending the elephant wasn't there, she needed to confront it, otherwise she was likely to get a giant load of dung dropped onto her shoes every time she tried to maneuver around the beast. If she continued pretending that Ron had been a good husband, and that everything in their lives had been normal, she would literally go mad from the pretense.

Not that going insane was such a terrible option, all things considered. During the past week there had been several occasions when the idea of climbing into bed, pulling the covers over her head and waiting for the men in white coats to carry her off had been mighty appealing. But Ron had already stolen so much—her dignity, her trust, her memories—that she wasn't willing to allow him the theft of her sanity, as well. It was mostly the determination not to surrender another single atom of her being to the power of his lies that had kept her plodding forward, somehow finding strength to put one foot in front of the other over the past seven interminable days.

Ellie disembarked from the plane, so relieved to be rid of her seatmate and on firm ground that she could almost count herself as happy, at least for a few moments. Refusing to be intimidated by O'Hare's vast concourses, she followed the signs to ground transportation and found herself a cab. Her driver, thank goodness, spoke enough English to understand where she wanted to go, but not enough to feel motivated to converse with her.

She relished the sensation of anonymity. Until her family had been the lead story on every cable news channel, she hadn't fully appreciated the joy of going about her business unrecognized. Cocooned in the driver's lack of interest, she leaned back against the cracked vinyl seat and concentrated on adjusting her senses to the overwhelming noise and bumper-to-bumper city traffic.

Ellie had loathed Chicago on her previous visits, but she hadn't given the city much of a chance to win her over. Looking back without the distorting lens of Ron's commentary to color what she saw, she had to admit her attitude had been unbearably smug, not to mention narrow-minded. It had seemed obvious to her that nobody would choose to live squashed into high-rise buildings, with ugly strip malls at every intersection, and factories belching foul smells from tall chimneys. She had viewed the city sights with quiet disdain, yearning all the time for the peace and natural beauty of Thatch. Why would anyone want to live surrounded by concrete and polluted air when they could have open range and wildflowers outside their windows?

Ron, of course, had reinforced every negative impression she expressed, for reasons that were now easy to understand. However, in her new mood of determined honesty, Ellie had to admit that her husband hadn't always been anxious to keep her away from Chicago. Once, when Liam was still a toddler, Ron had suggested they should all three move to the city and leave the Flying W in the hands of a professional manager. Ellie had refused point-blank. After a few months of gentle nagging, Ron had eventually given up asking.

When her parents heard of her repeated

refusals, they accused her of cowardice, of being afraid to make such a drastic change, even for the sake of her marriage. She had hotly denied their accusations, insisting she wanted to remain in Wyoming because it would give the whole family a better life, not because the big city intimidated her.

In her current state of self-doubt, she realized her parents might have been right. She'd never attempted to consider Ron's offer on its merits; all she'd done was invent justifications for turning him down. Most women would have questioned the wisdom of a marriage in which one spouse spent two-thirds of his nights away from home. Why hadn't she?

She could appreciate now that there would have been compensations to city living that she'd never allowed herself to consider. At the very least, a woman living in the city met a huge variety of people—more new people in a week than Ellie encountered in four or five years in rural Wyoming. A city woman might have been smarter about human nature, and so more capable of detecting Ron's multiple lies.

By all accounts, Avery Fairfax was a smart, sophisticated woman. Why hadn't she discovered the truth about her supposed husband? Maybe she had, Ellie thought painfully. Maybe Avery simply didn't care. She visualized Avery and Ron joking together about the insignificant little woman tucked away in the wilds of Wyoming and yawning with boredom at the idea of Ron even bothering to divorce her. Why waste time and energy getting rid of a nobody?

The cab drove onto North Michigan Avenue, a street that Ellie had often heard Ron mention but one that she'd never visited with him. The street had wide sidewalks and was lined with trees that shaded stores, cafés and passersby. Even through the dirty cab windows, she could see that the buildings were individually elegant and collectively magnificent. The street was nothing like any part of Chicago that Ron had shown her on their infrequent trips to the city. With a flash of bitterness, she reflected that her husband had probably spent a lot of time arranging their itinerary, selecting only those parts of the city most likely to intimidate or displease her. Once Avery entered his life, he'd never again invited Ellie to move to Chicago, of course. How relieved he must have been that she was so easy to deceive, and so content to stay tucked into her cozy little nest in faraway Thatch.

Ellie felt the stirring of intense emotion deep in the pit of her stomach. The sensation had become familiar over the past few days, but she hadn't yet managed to identify exactly what it was. Not quite anger, she thought. Certainly not anger at Ron. Perhaps disgust with herself for having been so easily manipulated?

"We here," the cabbie informed her. "Zis place what you lookin' for, ma'am?"

Ellie rolled down the window and peered out. *The Windemere.* The name of the building was emblazoned along the awning that stretched out over the sidewalk. Talk about fancy! At least there were no marauding TV vans parked anywhere in sight. Apparently even a murdered millionaire bigamist couldn't hold the fickle attention of the national media for more than a few days, especially in a big city like Chicago. Ellie wished she could feel confident that the absence of reporters meant that her family's fifteen minutes of fame were finally over. She was so ready to surrender her place in the media spotlight to the next unfortunate victim.

"Yes, this is the place I'm looking for," Ellie told the cabdriver. She wondered, as she paid him, if that was true. Was this the place she was looking for? She'd been quite certain when she made her plan to escape from the ranch that her life could never move forward until she met the other woman in Ron's life. Now she realized that finding anything appropriate to say to Avery Fairfax would be excruciatingly difficult. Not to mention that the woman would be within her rights to refuse to meet with her.

Still, she was here and there was nothing for it but to keep doing what she'd been doing for the past week: putting one foot in front of the other and inching forward. No point worrying about how she was going to say what needed to be said until she found out whether or not Avery Fairfax would meet with her.

The lobby of the Windemere struck Ellie as cold and unwelcoming, with too much marble and glass, and nothing at all to suggest that there were people in this building who called the place home. Glancing around, she caught sight of herself in a gilt-framed mirror set over a console table. She immediately turned away, but not quickly enough to avoid registering how dowdy she looked. Her gray-streaked hair was limp from the humidity and she'd left in such a rush that she'd forgotten to pack any makeup beyond the modest supply she routinely carried in her purse: a lipstick and some all-purpose moisturizer. Nothing, in other words, to conceal a week's worth of sleepless nights. As for the beige pantsuit she had chosen as smart but convenient for traveling, Ellie cringed at the sight of it. The outfit would have been considered high fashion in Thatch, Wyoming. Here in the heart of upscale, big-city Chicago, it shrieked country bumpkin.

Ellie drew to a halt in the middle of the lobby, almost prepared to turn tail and run. Except she'd endured that terrible plane flight and for the first time in her life, the Flying W felt like a prison instead of a refuge. Besides, given what was at stake, was there any outfit in the world that would make her feel more confident about meeting Avery?

"May I help you, ma'am?"

The query came from a security guard in a flashy uniform seated behind the reception desk. Ellie was quite sure he intended his question to intimidate, not to assist. Fortunately, the embarrassment of knowing her life story had been broadcast across the nation had immunized her somewhat against petty insults and snide condescension. Instead of scaring her off, the guard's snooty attitude injected a hint of steel into her backbone. Pushing aside her cowardly thoughts of running away, she squared her shoulders and met his gaze head-on.

"I'm here to see Mrs. Raven," she said.

"Is Mrs. Raven expecting you?"

"No, she isn't. Tell her Eleanor Horn would like to speak to her. It's important."

Ellie had contemplated lying about who she was, but in the end she'd decided there had been more than enough lies over the past few years and she'd take her chances with the truth, or at least the partial truth of her maiden name. She was pretty sure Avery would recognize who had come calling.

"Are you a journalist, ma'am?" He looked at her wheeled suitcase. "Or a salesperson?"

"No, I'm not." Ellie said nothing more. She knew enough after the past week not to volunteer information if she could get away with silence.

The security guard displayed no further reaction to her name or to her request to speak with Avery, although he surely must be aware of the sordid facts surrounding Ron's death. Based on the media frenzy in Wyoming, Ellie guessed the guard must have turned away dozens of journalists requesting interviews with Avery over the past week.

The guard dialed a number. Somebody must have picked up on the other end and he passed on her message. "Mrs. Raven will see you now," he said, turning back to Ellie after a brief conversation. He still showed no sign of recognizing her, but he did appear surprised that she'd been invited up. Avery probably hadn't made herself available to many visitors over the past week, Ellie reflected wryly, cutting off a sudden burst of empathy for the woman who'd stolen Ron from her.

The guard directed her to the elevator, a gilded mahogany and black-glass affair that zoomed smoothly up to the penthouse. The brief journey provided Ellie with more than enough time to stare at her reflection and consider the full wretchedness of her appearance. Good grief, what a sight she was! When had she been transformed from a petite and curvaceous woman into the dumpy has-been staring back at her from the smoked-glass mirrors? No wonder the guard had soon abandoned his suspicions. She looked too old and frumpish to be a journalist or even a door-to-door salesperson.

The elevator doors glided open into the penthouse lobby. A tall, slender woman who looked not a day over forty waited in the marble-columned foyer. Was this Avery? It had to be, Ellie decided.

Her heart pounded at the sight of her rival, and for a moment she felt light-headed. Her cheeks burned with mortification as heat flashed over her skin, leaving a sticky sheen of sweat. A few moments ago she'd been worrying about wrinkles in her pantsuit and the absence of makeup. Now she realized how laughable it was to imagine that a dab of powder or an ironed pantsuit would have made her less pitiable to this…this vision of elegance in a designer suit of dove-gray silk.

The few words Ellie had managed to plan in advance disappeared from her mind, leaving nothing except a vivid picture of Ron and Avery in bed together, quickly followed by an even more humiliating image of him leaving this woman's bed and traveling home to the Flying W. Ellie tried to shut down the images, but she couldn't blot them out, even though they made her stomach heave like a butter churn. No wonder her sex life with Ron had been so minimal for the past decade, she thought despairingly. Cringing, she visualized the flannel nightgowns that she wore in winter and the comfy, hundred-times-washed cotton T-shirts that she pulled on in summer. On those rare occasions when she and Ron had made love, had he been thinking of Avery? Fantasizing that the plump, flabby body writhing beneath his was really this slender and seductive woman? Oh God, it made her cringe with embarrassment to remember how eagerly she'd responded to Ron's advances. How…needy…he must have found her. How pathetic.

Ellie swallowed over the huge lump in her throat. She would bet large sums of money that Avery didn't even know that nightgowns could be made out of brushed-cotton flannel. She probably wore black satin to bed. Or nothing except perfumed body lotion that left her skin sleek and enticing.

"Do you feel ill?" There was an unwelcome hint of compassion in Avery's cool question.

By a monumental act of will, Ellie found her voice. "No, I'm fine, thanks. I'm sorry to intrude without warning." Despite her best efforts, the words came out sounding stiff, almost hostile. Still, that was better than sounding intimidated and shamed. "I hope this isn't a bad time?"

Avery gave a small, humorless laugh. "No worse than any other." She stepped to one side. "Will you come in?"

"Thank you." Ellie walked in, her carry-on bag rolling clumsily at her heels. The penthouse was filled with exquisite knickknacks and she was terrified of knocking into something with her suitcase. She was so busy watching where she walked that she was right into the center of the living room before she realized that the room had an entire window wall looking out over Lake Michigan.

She gave a soft, involuntary gasp. "Oh my, it's lovely. And so much water! I never realized Lake Michigan was so big."

She cringed when she heard herself. *Right, Ellie. Way to go. Make sure you demonstrate to this woman that you're an igno-*

rant rube, on the off chance she hasn't noticed already.

"It's awe-inspiring, isn't it?" Far from sounding condescending, Avery's voice actually warmed a little. "The view is the main reason we decided to buy—"

She stopped abruptly, drew in a shaky breath and started over. "This is impossibly awkward, isn't it? Everything we say to each other is likely to cause offense."

"Yes, it's awkward, all right, but I needed to see you, even so." Ellie liked the woman better for not pretending that this was a regular social visit.

"Was there some special reason why you felt it was urgent for us to meet?" Avery sounded curious, not sarcastic or condemnatory.

Ellie made sure that her suitcase was balanced on its wheels, crossing her hands in front of her as she searched for courage to ask the question that had been burning in her mind for the past week. There was no point in prolonging the agony with small talk, she decided.

"I came here because I have to ask you something. I'm sorry if it offends. Here's my question. Did you know Ron had another wife when you married him?"

"No, of course not!" Avery looked and sounded horrified. "I would *never* have agreed to a bigamous marriage!"

Ellie felt her legs turn wobbly, whether from stress or relief she wasn't sure. These days, she had a heck of a time sorting out one emotion from another. "You mean Ron lied to you, too? You were taken in by him for all these years?"

Avery didn't answer for a long time. "Yes," she said finally. "Ron lied to me, too. From the first day we met."

"And you never suspected anything was wrong with your marriage?" Ellie persisted. "Even though Ron must have been away so much?"

Avery took a while to answer. "No, I never suspected anything was wrong," she said finally. "Did you?"

Now it was Ellie's turn to hesitate. She'd suspected there was something wrong, although the truth had never once crossed her mind. "Ron always called regularly and his excuses for being away were reasonable," she said in the end. "Ron's dad had worked in Chicago, too, so nobody in Thatch really questioned why he traveled so much. Besides, in my wildest dreams I would never have thought he might be a bigamist."

"I keep telling myself that Ron must have been a master of inventing plausible lies," Avery said. "Even so, I loathe the fact that I seem to have been so gullible."

"Me, too." Ellie wasn't quite sure why the knowledge that Avery had also been deceived made her feel better, but it did. Emboldened, she asked her next question.

"I've tried not to listen to the news reports, but there's been no shortage of busybodies willing to fill me in on the details. Somebody mentioned to me that your daughter is twenty-six." She drew in a painful breath. "Megan, my daughter, is twenty-six, as well. We must have been pregnant at the same time." There, it was out in the open. The humiliating truth of two women, each carrying Ron's child. Like a harem, Ellie thought bitterly, with the wives' bellies blooming in unison to prove the lord and master's virility.

Maybe Avery had a similar image, because her cheeks took on a tinge of color. "I realized a few days ago that our daughters are almost the same age," she said. "Kate's a little younger, I think. She'll be twenty-seven in October."

"Megan turns twenty-seven in a couple of weeks from now. On June 2. That means she's just four months older than your daughter."

Avery looked distressed, but she didn't duck the obvious implication of Ellie's statement. "You must have been six or seven months pregnant with your daughter when Ron and I got married."

Pretended to get married, Ellie nearly said, then stopped herself. Before she met Avery, it had been easy to feel anger toward the other woman in Ron's life. Already, though, after only a few minutes in her company, Ellie was pretty sure that getting mad at Avery would be directing her anger at the wrong person. It seemed crystal clear that Avery hadn't known Ron kept another wife hidden in Wyoming. What's more, despite the immaculate hair and expensive outfit, she looked pale and tired. No doubt she was suffering in her own high-class way as much as Ellie. Bottom line, Avery had apparently been another of Ron's victims, not a coconspirator.

A flare of sympathy sent Ellie's thoughts

scattering again. "Your daughter...Kate... You must have been a few weeks pregnant when you got married. Was that why you and Ron...I mean...I guess it's not exactly my business...Or maybe it is...." She stumbled to a halt, not able to bring herself to ask the other question that had been spinning around inside her head for the past few days.

Avery let the silence stretch out until she broke it with a small sigh. "I was thirteen weeks pregnant when Ron and I got married. We were engaged six weeks and he never proposed to me until I told him I was expecting his child. Is that what you wanted to know?"

"It's what I thought might have happened," Ellie acknowledged. Out of appreciation for Avery's honesty, she didn't probe or try to find out if there had been any reluctance on Ron's part to offer marriage. Despite all she'd learned about Ron in the past week, Ellie still found herself putting the best possible interpretation on her husband's behavior. Given that she and Avery had both been pregnant at the same time, she could at least get a glimmering of why Ron might have found it easier to go through a second wedding ceremony rather than divorce his first wife and start over. And because she guessed that it hadn't been easy for a woman like Avery to admit that she'd been pregnant on her wedding day, she made some admissions of her own.

"There's a nine-year age gap between Liam and Megan—that's my son and my daughter. I had three miscarriages after Liam was born, so that meant Megan was my fifth pregnancy in eight years. The doctor warned me it had to be my last. Ron knew I wanted to carry the pregnancy to term real bad. When he realized you were pregnant, too, I guess he didn't want to come right out and ask me for a divorce while I was expecting."

The doctor had counseled her not to have sex with Ron and to spend as much time as possible in bed, advice that had passed for state-of-the-art obstetrical care back in those days. Between taking care of Liam, running the ranch and trying frantically to get an extra couple of hours' rest each day, there hadn't been any energy left over for being a wife.

At some level, Ellie understood why Ron had been tempted by Avery. But that sure as heck didn't mean she forgave him for straying. He'd been just loyal enough not to want to divorce her during a difficult pregnancy, but not loyal enough to remain faithful when she couldn't be an active sexual partner. And in the end, twenty-six years of bigamous marriage struck Ellie as a bigger betrayal than a clean, simple divorce.

Avery looked away, her gaze fixed on the water. "I wish Ron hadn't lied to us." She laughed. "And isn't that a silly thing to say? But he not only assured me he was single, he told me he'd never been married."

Ellie's hands curled into fists. It was bad enough for Ron to have humiliated her so completely. It hurt even worse to know he'd denied the existence of his own son. "How did Ron explain the fact that he was in his midthirties and still single? That didn't happen much back in those days."

"He told me he'd been engaged once and that his fiancée had died in the same car crash that killed his parents. He spoke about her and his dead parents so movingly that it never once crossed my mind to doubt his story. And, of course, the terrible car crash explained why he had no parents to invite to our wedding." A note of anger deepened her voice. "Of course, his sob story didn't explain why none of his cousins or aunts or uncles attended our wedding, but apparently we were all determined not to notice what was under our noses. For what it's worth...I'm sorry I was so incredibly stupid."

"Seems to me you're not the person who should be apologizing. To my mind, that would be Ron. He's the one who let both of us down. And our children, too." Ellie didn't attempt to hide her anger. "One thing we can both say for sure about Ron, he turned out to be a real good liar."

Avery looked as if she wanted to deny Ellie's statement, but honesty kept her silent. She suddenly made a small sound of distress and reached for a tissue, turning her back on Ellie. When she turned around again, the moment for confidences had obviously ended and her voice was once again blandly courteous. "I should have invited you to sit down after your long journey. Would you care for some tea?"

Ellie was parched, and she would have loved something to drink, but she wasn't about to accept the offer. She'd felt so clumsy and uncoordinated for the past week that balancing a cup and saucer, probably made of delicate bone china, was more than she was up for right now.

"No, thanks all the same. I guess I won't be keeping you any longer. I appreciate that you were willing to see me."

"I was glad of the chance. Thank you for coming. In a way, it's harder to cope now that I have a face and a personality to go with your name, but it's surprisingly comforting to know I wasn't the only woman living in a fool's paradise."

Ellie grasped the handle of her suitcase, not sure that she wanted to hear how closely Avery's feelings paralleled her own. "I wish Ron had treated both of us better, but he didn't and that's that. Now I guess we just have to learn to move on with our lives."

"I imagine that's going to prove somewhat easier said than done."

"Sure is," Ellie agreed. "That's why I needed to see you. I figured that nothing you did or said could be worse than the scenes that kept playing in my head. I was right." She once again prepared to leave.

"Don't go," said a masculine voice behind her. "I encouraged Avery to meet with you because I need to speak with you about some financial matters."

Ellie stopped, her suitcase bumping into her heels. "Who are you?" she asked, turning around.

"My name is Paul Fairfax. I'm Avery's brother. I was also Ron's business partner. A fact I assume you already know."

Strikingly good looks seemed to run in the Fairfax family, Ellie reflected. Paul was a tall, handsome man, probably in his early fifties, immaculately dressed in khaki pants and a button-down shirt, open at the neck. There was neither warmth nor kindness in his expression, and Ellie's emotions performed one of their now familiar flip-flops, reversing the sympathy she'd begun to feel for Avery and transforming it into anger that Paul should make so little effort to disguise his contempt.

"As it happens, I do know that you were my husband's partner, Mr. Fairfax. My daughter informed me of your existence a couple of days ago."

"And that was the first time you'd heard the name of your husband's senior business partner?" Paul made no attempt to hide his incredulity.

"No, of course not. But the business partners Ron mentioned to me never included you. He lied about that, same as he lied about a lot of other things." Ellie forced herself to meet the man's disapproving gaze. "I won't say I'm pleased to meet you, Mr. Fairfax. I dare say you wish I didn't exist and I definitely wish the same about you and your sister. But the circumstances are hard enough for all of us and I guess it's best if we try to remain polite."

"Politeness would be easier on my side if your husband hadn't turned out to be a lying, thieving son of a bitch." The venom of Paul's words was mild in comparison to the raw fury in his expression. "Do you know what I've just discovered—"

"Naturally, I don't." Anger at his rudeness provided Ellie with a welcome jolt of self-possession.

Paul snorted in disbelief. "Let me refresh your memory. Two years ago, Ron Raven borrowed three million dollars from the Bank of Fairfax in Georgia. He secured the loan by pretending to my brother that he was going to develop the Flying W ranch into a major resort property. Now we find out that the development was a total and complete scam.

We want that money back. And we want it now."

"I don't know what you're talking about. The Flying W is a cattle ranch. There's never been any suggestion of turning the property into a resort." Ellie spoke firmly, but in the back of her mind she had a vague suspicion she'd already heard about this missing three million. Was that why Megan and Liam had looked so worried right before she left home? Had they been trying to warn her that Ron had taken out this huge loan that was now being called?

Paul's face turned dark red. "How could Ron develop a plan to turn the ranch into a vacation resort without you knowing about it?"

Ellie gave a short, bitter laugh. "Well, I can't give you the precise details, Mr. Fairfax. But I'd guess he did it the same way it seems he did everything else—by lying and cheating."

"Goddammit, don't pretend this is the first time you heard about this three-million-dollar loan!" Paul sounded on the verge of an explosion. "You can claim to be as innocent as you please, but the bottom line is that, for once, your husband seems to have outsmarted himself. He signed an ironclad loan agreement and I can assure you, my brother is going to claim what's his. Bad enough that my sister will have to sell this condo because she has no income—" He stopped abruptly, pacing the length of the picture window in an obvious effort to control his temper.

"I'm sorry to hear that you're facing such a change in your lifestyle." Not wanting to say something she would later regret, Ellie ignored Paul and spoke directly to Avery, who had remained silent during her brother's tirade. "The shocks just keep coming, don't they?"

"Forget the butter-wouldn't-melt-in-my-mouth act," Paul snapped, whirling around to confront her again. "It doesn't work with me. Ron took the money he raised from my brother's bank and put it into one of the Flying W's development accounts. Adam and I have already traced the transaction. If you think I'm going to let you keep that money, you're mistaken. I'll sue you for every penny. Dammit, I'm not going to see my sister lose her home while you use funds stolen from my brother's bank to keep the Flying W afloat."

Ellie gulped, for the first time understanding why Ron's partner was so angry with her. "Mr. Fairfax, if there's millions of dollars lying around in any of the Flying W's bank accounts, it's sure news to me. Last time I checked the books, which was a couple of days before Ron died, we had a few thousand dollars on hand, barely enough to cover wages and operating expenses for the next six weeks or so."

"Well, I don't suppose you were stupid enough to leave the three million lying around in your checking account," Paul said. "I'm quite sure you've squirreled it away somewhere by now. But you're not going to get away with stealing—"

"Paul, stop." Avery spoke quietly, but with considerable force. "You're shouting at the wrong person. Until Ron disappeared, Ellie didn't know I existed any more than I knew about her—"

"So she claims," Paul muttered. "I know her type—"

"I'm not a type, Mr. Fairfax. I'm an individual who, as your sister just said, had no idea either of you existed until last week." Ellie finally forced herself to look straight into Paul's eyes, even though she had to tilt her head back and crane her neck to do it. "You know, this conversation isn't likely to take us anywhere good. If you've finished insulting me, I believe I'll be on my way back to Wyoming."

"Running away now that this meeting has grown a little too hot for you?"

"No, Mr. Fairfax. I'm getting out of your sister's home before I say something I'll feel bad about later. I'll repeat one more time that I don't know anything about the money Ron raised from your brother's bank and that's my final statement on the matter. In future, if you have something you want to communicate to me, it would be best if you spoke with my lawyer. I won't be picking up the phone to you. Good day, Mr. Fairfax. I can't say it's been a pleasure."

Ellie grabbed her suitcase again and headed for the door, so hurt and angry that she didn't even waste energy worrying about the knickknacks. Avery caught up with her as she waited for the elevator to complete its journey from the ground floor.

"My brother is very upset by the discovery of how Ron deceived us all," Avery said, her expression apologetic.

"Yes, well, I'm a tad upset myself. My husband seems to have been murdered, and nothing about my life is what I thought it was. It takes a bit of getting used to, if you want the truth. But I do know that hurling accusations like your brother just did isn't going to help anyone."

Avery's composure suddenly broke and tears welled in her eyes. "I thought Ron loved me," she said. "I thought we were so happy. I can't believe our life together was all a lie."

Ellie winced, forcing back her own tears. No way she was going to start blubbering in front of her rival. "I hate the lies, too. It makes me feel dirty and stupid, as if there must be something wrong with me that I didn't cotton on to what Ron was doing."

She realized she'd admitted a lot more than she intended with that final confidence. The elevator arrived and she stepped in, murmuring a hasty goodbye. When the doors closed, she slumped against the wall, closing her eyes, wishing that she hadn't been blessed with a sudden flash of insight into precisely what had been causing her so much mental anguish over the past few days.

She'd come to Chicago looking for answers and, unfortunately, she'd found them.

But it turned out that the questions she'd been tormenting herself with hadn't been directly related to Avery, or to Avery's daughter, much less the missing money that Paul seemed to be obsessed with. The questions keeping her awake at night had been for herself.

Had she known, deep down inside, that Ron wasn't faithful to her? The answer, sadly, was yes. Buried under layers and layers of denial, she had been aware for years that Ron was too dynamic a man to be content with their pallid sex life and ho-hum relationship. He must have told her literally thousands of lies over the course of the past twenty-six years. She'd never caught him out, Ellie thought acidly, because she'd been darn careful not to. If ever an ostrich needed lessons in how to bury its head really deep into the sand, it should come to her. She could deliver a master class in the rules for staying oblivious.

The next question to face was why she had refused to identify the land mines that, in retrospect, had been scattered over the entire landscape of her marriage. The answer to that was as easy to find as it was shameful. She'd kept quiet because she loved the Flying W and the life she led in Thatch. For the sake of the ranch, her friends and the comfort of familiarity, she'd not only been willing to participate in a marriage that barely deserved the name, she'd even been willing to convince herself that she was happy.

That made her not only a fool, but also a coward. Ellie wondered, after twenty-six years of deceiving herself, how she was ever going to find the courage to live with the truths she'd finally confronted.

Seven

When Ellie arrived home from Chicago, Megan was waiting for her with a worried expression hidden behind a determined smile. A dinner of meat loaf, glazed carrots and mashed potatoes, usually one of Ellie's favorites, waited in the warm oven. Unfortunately, Ellie knew there was no way she could choke down food, not with all the guilt and worry roiling around in her stomach.

"I ate at the airport," she lied. "I'm sorry you went to all that trouble for nothing, Meg. Everything looks delicious, too."

"That's okay. Meat loaf freezes." Visibly biting her tongue, Megan cleared the dishes from the carefully laid table, refusing Ellie's help and urging her mother to sit down and put her feet up. Ellie repressed a sigh and sat as she was bidden. Why did everyone assume that losing a husband turned you into a mentally defective invalid?

Megan flashed another smile. “So how was your trip, Mom? I wish you’d told us where you were going, to Chicago.”

“I left a note,” Ellie said. “And I called last night as soon as I got to the hotel.”

“Yes, you did. That still left Liam and me about five hours to get really worried about what had happened to you.” Megan pulled open the cutlery drawer with such force that a spoon dropped onto the floor. She picked it up and tossed it into the sink.

It was a good thing they didn’t have a handy-dandy truth machine to read inside each other’s heads, Ellie thought wryly. She and Megan were each as cross and tense as the other.

“Where is Liam?” Ellie was truly grateful for the love and concern her daughter showed her. At the same time, she had to fight the urge to tell her to butt out and to please, for goodness’ sake, stop *hovering.*

“Liam had to go back to Denver,” Megan explained. “He left early this morning. The judge on one of his cases wasn’t willing to postpone the court hearing any longer. The judge claimed the delay was causing unnecessary hardship to the couple petitioning for divorce. Liam is planning to call you tomorrow as soon as he gets out of court. He says to tell you that if your trip to Chicago raised any legal questions, he'll be happy to research the answers for you."

"That's real kind of him. I'm sorry I missed him." Ellie tried to sound sincere, but in fact Liam's departure was a relief. For a couple of days, having her children around had been a comfort. Now, though, she was in such a state of turmoil that having to cope with Megan's protectiveness was just one more burden that she found hard to handle.

"What about you?" Ellie asked. "Shouldn't you be getting back to the ski lodge?"

Apparently she didn't do a very good job of hiding her true feelings because Megan gave her a reproachful look, which she quickly converted into her now-standard expression of patient tolerance. "May is our slowest month. The snow's gone, mostly, but it's still too cold for summer activities like hiking and horseback riding. The lodge can cope without me for another few days."

"That's good," Ellie said, trying to sound as if she meant it. Land's sake, but she was getting tired of everyone humoring her. She might be shell-shocked and not quite as decisive as usual, but she wasn't mentally incompetent to the point that she needed constant supervision. Or was she? Was she exhibiting symptoms that she didn't even recognize in herself?

"Did you get to meet Avery Fairfax while you were in Chicago?" Megan asked abruptly.

"Yes, I did."

"How about Kate? Was she there, too?"

"No, she wasn't. I guess she was working. I'm not sure. We didn't actually talk about her too much." That wasn't a lie; they'd talked about Avery's pregnancy and the time of Kate's birth rather than anything connected to Kate's current life.

"What did you and Avery discuss, then?"

"It's complicated." Ellie would have preferred not to rehash the details of her meeting, but she realized it wasn't fair to stonewall completely. "Avery isn't what I expected," she said after a moment's hesitation.

"How was she different?" Megan was visibly frustrated by her mother's too-brief answers.

She'd expected Ron's other wife to be more crude and grasping, Ellie thought.

She'd expected somebody who didn't look quite so perfect for the role of intelligent companion and gracious hostess. "I'd pegged her as more of a bimbo," she said. "But Avery is nothing like that. She looks like the sort of upper-class woman you'd expect a rich, successful millionaire like your dad to marry."

"Was Dad rich and successful?" Megan asked, thumping on the lid of a plastic container she'd filled with meat loaf to lock out the air. "If he was, nobody seems to know where he's stashed his money."

"I expect his business partner knows where the bulk of it is. It must be somewhere and we sure haven't got it." Ellie knew she sounded placid to the point of stupidity, but she was tired right down to the marrow of her bones and wanted nothing more than to retreat into the sanctuary of her bedroom.

"Dad's business partner?" Megan murmured. "Oh, you mean Avery's brother?"

Ellie nodded. "He was there, you know. Paul Fairfax. Not all the time I was with Avery, but at the end."

"What did he have to say?" Megan wiped down the counters which, as far as Ellie could see, were already spotless. Her daughter was wound tight as a spring-loaded nail gun and seemed likely to fire off at any minute. Ellie was pretty sure that if she told Megan about Paul's accusations, she'd trigger the explosion. But at the moment, she could cope a lot more easily with Megan making a fuss about missing money than she could with Megan asking probing questions about Avery Fairfax and what sort of a relationship Ron might have had with his other family. Coward that she was, Ellie chose to direct Megan's pent-up energy to the trail of the missing money.

"Paul claims that your father took out a three-million-dollar loan with the Fairfax family bank in Georgia," she said. "Unfortunately, the money's disappeared, and Paul's very angry because he says I must have the money. He demanded that I should stop stonewalling and repay the loan."

Megan didn't look as startled as Ellie had expected. "Adam already sent us an express letter demanding repayment of that money. Remember, Mom? I showed you the letter just before you left for Chicago."

"Yes, I guess I do remember." Ellie could feel exhaustion leeching the emotion from her voice, whereas Megan was gripping the counter as if she were afraid she might zoom into orbit if she didn't hang on.

"I told Paul Fairfax that I didn't have the money, of course, but I don't think he believes me. I guess the Fairfaxes will send in accountants to comb through the Flying W books...you know, that special type of accountant. What are they called?"

"Forensic accountants?" Megan suggested.

"Yes, that's what I was trying to say." Ellie's brain was so foggy she kept losing words.

"Aren't you worried?" Megan slammed the dishwasher shut and pressed the button to start the wash cycle. "For heaven's sake, Mom, the Fairfax family is claiming that we owe them three million dollars! That's not exactly small change."

"I can't worry about it," Ellie said. "Look, the sooner the Fairfaxes send in their hotshot forensic accountants, the sooner they'll find out that the Flying W is operating barely above break even and that there's never been any suspicious infusion of cash."

"Mom, this isn't only about where the

money is now. It's where it might have been in the past. This is serious stuff. We can't just ignore the accusations that Dad paid the money into a Flying W account. I mean, you could end up in jail!"

Ellie's head was pounding and she could see that Megan was deeply worried. Ellie couldn't understand quite why. She was willing to admit that for the past few days her brain hadn't exactly functioned with stiletto-blade sharpness. Still, even if you conceded that the legal system was about technicalities, not justice, you couldn't wring blood from a stone. However many loan agreements the Fairfaxes waved in her face, she didn't have their money. She'd never had their money. Given that Ron had apparently lied approximately one in two times that he opened his mouth, why would anyone expect him to have told the truth about where he'd stashed the missing millions? She took a stab at clearing her fog of fatigue so that she could explain to Megan why they had no reason to worry.

"Look, honey, your father may have borrowed money from Adam Fairfax, but that's got nothing to do with us. Just because Ron set up fake accounts that he called the Flying W Development Account, or whatever the heck he called it…well, that doesn't mean anyone here at the ranch ever saw a penny of the money. And we can prove it, too."

"Can we? How do we prove a negative?"

"The real, legitimate Flying W accounts have never had a huge infusion of cash," Ellie explained, trying to be patient.

Megan, never good at hiding her emotions, was clearly zooming right toward frantic. "I know we didn't get the money, Mom! That's not the answer—that's the biggest part of the problem!" Megan gulped in air and lowered her voice. She leaned forward, forcing Ellie to meet her gaze across the kitchen table. "Mom, I know what a miserable few days this has been and how much bad news has been pouring in, but you need to face facts. The truth is, Dad signed a binding loan agreement with the First Bank of Fairfax and offered the ranch as security for the loan. In the event of Dad's death, there's a clause right there in the loan agreement that says the bank has every right to claim full and immediate repayment."

"But we can't pay if we don't have the money!"

Megan gritted her teeth. "Mom, listen to me, for heaven's sake! If we can't come up with the money, the bank has the right to take over possession of this entire property. You want the bottom line? Here it is. If you don't have three million dollars, *you're going to lose the ranch.* I'm not talking years from now. I'm talking like next week, or next month. You'll be ordered out of your home."

Ellie felt her legs turn so wobbly she was actually grateful to be sitting down. She'd realized the claim from the Bank of Fairfax meant trouble, but she'd avoided reading the fine print in the letter sent by Adam Fairfax. She'd been doing her damnedest to carry on as if the missing money was somebody else's problem, not hers. Clearly, it was way past time for her to stop pretending that ignoring problems was a good way to make them go away.

"I seem to remember Liam saying something about getting an injunction to stop Adam Fairfax carrying out his threat," she said. "I'm real sorry I wasn't paying more attention, Meg. Didn't Liam's legal maneuverings work out?"

Megan nodded. "Thank goodness, yes. Liam and Cody managed to get an emergency stay from a friendly judge in Cheyenne right after you left for Chicago. Otherwise I'm sure Adam Fairfax would already have put the ranch up for sale."

Talk about your pigeons coming home to roost, Ellie thought with bitter self-mockery. She'd been willfully blind about Ron and her marriage in order to protect the ranch and her life in Wyoming. Unfortunately, that blindness seemed to have led directly to the fact that the Flying W was now at risk: the very outcome she'd fudged and compromised in order to avoid was now within a hairbreadth of happening.

"The police haven't declared Ron dead," she said, fear of losing the ranch finally spurring her brain back into action. "Harry told me just a few days ago that since there was…there was no body, it might be weeks or even months before the authorities were prepared to officially declare him dead. How can the Bank of Fairfax invoke a death clause when Ron isn't legally dead?"

"I thought of that, too," Megan said. "Liam

wrote an express letter to Adam Fairfax pointing out that Dad was officially listed as missing, not dead, and therefore the bank had no right to call the loan—"

"Thank goodness. I'm so grateful to both of you for picking up the ball when I dropped it—"

Megan shook her head. "We tried to pick up the ball. We failed." She took an express envelope from the top of a pile of mail sitting on the desk in the corner of the kitchen and pulled out a single sheet of paper. "Here, read this. It arrived this morning in response to Liam's letter. As you can see, the bank is claiming that Dad defaulted on one of the loan payments. A routine loan payment was due on May 4, but it wasn't paid."

"Well, we could pay that installment now," Ellie said, hearing the shake in her voice. "There must be a grace period."

"There is. Thirty-six hours, which is long past. Naturally, Adam Fairfax was careful not to warn us in advance that the loan was about to go into default." Megan lowered her voice and muttered, "Bastard."

Ellie took the letter, rubbing her forehead in a vain attempt to banish the headache that seemed to extend from her temples to the soles of her feet. "Surely we can claim extenuating circumstances?"

"Maybe." Megan sounded as tired and drained as Ellie felt. "But I don't suppose Adam Fairfax has any interest in being generous. Why would he? If he can take his pound of flesh, he will. Avery's his sister, after all. He has no reason to be kind to us."

"I can't believe that I'm in danger of losing my home." Ellie shook her head, woozy with worry. "I have a few thousand in the bank and a few thousand more that my parents left me. That must be enough to make a loan payment and buy us another few weeks to work this out."

"Unfortunately, Adam Fairfax has to agree to accept a late payment for that solution to work. What would motivate him to agree? Not a damn thing I can think of."

"The Fairfaxes believe I have the missing money," Ellie murmured. "Or else that I squandered it. Even if they're basically decent folks, they're likely to be mad as hell at us over that."

"And Adam certainly doesn't seem to be a basically decent person," Megan interjected. "He knew the loan payment was about to fall due and he was careful not to warn us. He probably realized that we'd claim Dad wasn't officially dead, so he kept quiet to make sure he would have a backup reason to call the loan. Based on his behavior so far, I'd have to guess he'll go after the Flying W with every legal weapon he can find."

Ellie clamped her teeth together to stop them chattering. It took several moments before she trusted herself to speak. "You think I'm going to lose the Flying W, don't you?"

Megan hesitated, but then gave a curt nod. She didn't speak. She didn't need to.

Ellie's eyes stung. A moment later, she felt a huge sob well up inside her. She fought to keep it back, but the wave of anger and sadness was too great. Putting her head down onto her folded arms, she leaned over the kitchen table and cried the torrent of tears that she'd never been able to find for her dead husband. The final humiliation, she thought, reaching for a tissue but not finding one. She grabbed a paper napkin instead, mopping in a vain attempt to stanch the flow. She hadn't been able to weep for Ron, but she was crying up a storm for the loss of the Flying W. What a miserable apology for a human being she was, crying for possessions instead of for a person.

"Mom, don't cry. It's all right. I've changed my mind. I'm sure Liam and I can find a way to save the ranch." Megan's arm around her shoulders provided Ellie some comfort, but not nearly enough. What in God's name would she do with herself if she lost the ranch? Ellie wondered.

She drew in a shuddering breath and blew her nose in another napkin. "You'll find a way to save the ranch? Now there's a fine cliché if ever I heard one." Ellie wondered if her smile looked as weak and shaky as it felt. "Unfortunately, since Liam can't ride out and shoot the bad guys, I'm not too sure how he's going to save the ranch."

"He's a really good lawyer," Megan said. "He'll find something that neither of us is thinking about."

"Yes, you're right. I expect he will." Ellie appreciated the warmth of Megan's hand covering hers. The gesture was comforting and yet at the same time she couldn't quite banish the thought that however much love her children showered on her, they couldn't prevent the consequences of Ron's actions—and her own fatal inaction. It was too late to put things right. She had practiced willful blindness in her marriage for the past twenty-odd years. She shouldn't be surprised that, stumbling around in the darkness, she had fallen deep into the danger of losing everything she held most dear.

Eight

Heat shimmered above the highway leading from the Atlanta airport to the town of Fairfax, seeping into Megan's rental car even though she had the air-conditioning blasting at maximum. She shoved a piece of hair out of her eyes and wriggled her butt in a vain attempt to prevent her legs from sticking to the vinyl seat. She couldn't afford to let her attention wander, not on these roads. Three times as many people lived in greater Atlanta as inhabited the entire state of Wyoming, and it seemed to Megan that most of those people were currently traveling on the same stretch of highway she was. The traffic alternately zoomed along at miles over the speed limit or crawled forward in clouds of exhaust fumes, following a secret rhythm that all the local drivers seemed to understand but was totally mysterious to her.

Still, despite the heat, the fumes and the intimidating traffic, her situation wasn't all bad. Megan considered it close to a miracle that she'd managed to find her way onto I-75 without once going north instead of south, or east instead of west as she headed out of the airport. Driving ten or twenty miles in the wrong direction was usually the minimum price she paid for putting herself behind the wheel of a rental car in any state other than Wyoming.

It had already been a long day and the purpose for her trip still loomed ahead, weighty with the prospect of failure. She'd boarded the plane in Jackson Hole at 6:00 a.m., but with the two-hour time difference, it had been after one before they landed, and even though she hadn't checked any baggage, it was almost two before she picked up her rental car. Given that she needed to reach Fairfax before the bank closed at four-thirty, she simply couldn't afford to screw up and lose her way.

At least the long hours on the plane had provided her with plenty of time to decide how she was going to approach Adam Fairfax. An appeal to the ogre himself seemed the only hope left at this point for saving the

Flying W. Even Liam had agreed the situation was so bleak that there was nothing to lose if she wanted to try the personal touch.

Frantically playing catch-up with his clients after a week away from his office, her brother had brainstormed with Cody Holmann on various legal remedies to help their mother save the ranch. Unfortunately, the loan agreement their father had signed with the Bank of Fairfax two years earlier was a model of clarity. Even more unfortunately, it specifically included references to Ron's death and to the consequences of late payments. However much Liam tried to plead extenuating circumstances on Ellie's behalf, the unpalatable truth was that the loan was already in technical default. Therefore Adam Fairfax had every right to insist on getting paid the full three million bucks. If Ellie couldn't come up with the cash, the bank had the right to foreclose on the property.

It had broken Megan's heart to see their mother stoically pretend that she would be just fine, even if she was forced to move into a little condo in Cheyenne or Casper. After twenty-four hours of watching Ellie smile on the outside and die on the inside, Megan was willing to do anything—even swallow her pride and beg Adam Fairfax for mercy, if that's what it took to prevent her mother losing the Flying W. There was no reason to believe the Fairfaxes would be generous and a dozen reasons to believe the opposite, but Megan was an optimist to her core, and she wasn't ready to give up hope.

She had resolved as the plane flew east over the Rocky Mountains that a polite and dignified request for understanding was the best way to approach Adam Fairfax. She would point out that they both had family members who'd suffered at the hands of Ron Raven, and it was cruel to punish Ellie for her husband's sins. She would also point out that nobody in her family had known anything about the loan. Now that they were aware of Ron's debt, they would make payments to the Bank of Fairfax each month, on schedule. Liam and Cody both agreed that the probate court would sign off on such payments, so the bank wouldn't lose money if Adam agreed to be generous. Meanwhile, she and Liam and her mother would search to find out what her father had actually done with the missing three million so that the Bank of Fairfax could be repaid in full. In other words, she would appeal to Adam's better nature, despite the fact that the evidence suggested his good nature was in mighty short supply.

Luckily, begging wasn't the only weapon in Megan's arsenal. If dignified appeals failed, her backup plan was to threaten a massive media campaign. She had spent the final hour of the flight concocting a truly damning storyline in which Adam came off as a major wart on humanity's nose, while Ellie starred as the poor helpless widow who had not only suffered at the hands of her bigamous, lying husband but was now being victimized all over again by the greedy, grasping family of Ron's illicit second wife.

A lengthy article in this week's *People* magazine had tipped Megan off to the useful fact that while Adam might resist appeals to his better nature, he was quite likely to cave under the threat of a negative media campaign aimed at him and his bank. According to *People,* the Fairfaxes were an established Southern family with roots deep in the Georgia soil. The reporter had actually referred to them as *aristocrats of the Old South,* which Megan thought might not be too much of a stretch when you considered they had an entire town named after them. Bottom line, it was clear the Fairfax family placed a premium on social prestige and Megan was more than ready to play on their fears of public disgrace.

She had some useful contacts she could exploit to that end. Her official job title at the Teton Mountain Ski Lodge was events coordinator, although a more accurate job title might have been Gofer and General Dogsbody for the Incompetent CEO. Nevertheless, her job had provided plenty of experience working with the local media in pursuit of positive PR for the lodge. She not only knew all the friendly, honest and reliable journalists in Wyoming, she knew all the sleazebags, too. She would turn the sleazebags loose on the Fairfax family without a qualm if that would deter Adam from auctioning off the Flying W.

Megan reached the highway exit for Fairfax at three-thirty and was driving down Main Street five minutes later, congratulating herself on having arrived not only in time but with a few moments to spare. The town bustled with late-afternoon activity despite the broiling heat and incredible humidity.

The sidewalk outside one of the cafés was crammed with umbrella-shaded tables, and she cast an envious glance at the people sipping tall iced drinks as they watched the world pass by. A wine store and a bakery welcomed customers with flower-filled window boxes and striped awnings, and the bookstore appeared to have been designed by Disney in quaint imitation Victoriana. In fact, Fairfax looked a lot more like yuppie heaven than a bastion of the Old South.

However, as she drove farther along Main Street, Megan saw that not all the buildings were new and self-consciously charming. In contrast to its upscale neighbors, the farm-supply store and the small public library appeared almost aggressively run-down, as if flaunting their status as relics of Fairfax's past when the town had eked out a living as a commercial center for the local peanut farmers.

The First Bank of Fairfax definitely belonged to the gentrified side of town. It was the largest building on Main Street, gleaming with fresh paint and adorned with fake *Gone With the Wind* pillars. There was enough brass lettering on its heavy entrance doors to reassure clients that it took the subject of making money with appropriate solemnity. No frivolous window boxes here. A side alley leading to a rear parking lot meant that patrons didn't have to search for quarters to feed the parking meters lining Main Street, a perk Megan appreciated.

She parked her white Ford rental car beneath the spreading branches of a magnolia tree heavy with blossoms, appreciating the unexpected beauty at the edge of the asphalt lot. Despite the welcome shade, she gasped as she opened the car door and the humid, perfumed air rushed in to clog her lungs. She stood up, catching her breath as she straightened her linen miniskirt and made sure the buttons on her short-sleeved jacket were all securely fastened.

Megan had chosen her outfit with care, but she avoided glancing into the car's side mirrors since she didn't want to destroy her self-confidence. On occasions like this, she always wished she were six inches taller, at least five pounds skinnier and blessed with straight hair. Even in the dry mountain air of Jackson Hole she fought a running battle to prevent her hair from collapsing into a mass of squiggly, auburn-tinged curls. With this level of humidity, she realized there was no hope. She didn't need a mirror to know that she already looked like Little Orphan Annie on one of her less cute days.

The bank was smaller inside than she'd expected from its imposing exterior facade and it was crowded with clients. The three teller windows all had lines in front of them, which was a relief, since it enabled Megan to look around and get her bearings without anyone paying her the least attention.

Two men seated in the carpeted space near the front entrance were, according to the signs on their desks, in charge of mortgage applications and new accounts, respectively. A couple of doors with frosted-glass windows had nameplates indicating that these were offices for a vice president and a corporate loan officer. And a middle-aged woman seated at a desk in the far corner had a nameplate in front of her that read Gayle Tummins, Notary Public.

Megan recognized Tummins as the name of the person who'd witnessed her father's signature on the infamous loan documents. There was also, she noticed, a solid wooden door behind the woman's desk. Black lettering, highlighted with gold, informed the world that this was the office of Adam Fairfax,

President and CEO. In addition to being a notary public, it seemed as if Gayle might be the gatekeeper who guarded access to the president. Gayle Tummins was clearly her quarry, Megan decided.

She walked over and gave the woman a polite smile. “Good afternoon. I’d like to speak with Mr. Fairfax.”

She’d expected resistance—in her experience, presidents were almost never available to casual visitors—but Gayle Tummins returned her smile without hesitation. “If you’ll tell me your name and give me an idea of what you want to discuss, I’ll be real happy to make an appointment right away. Are you already a client of ours? I’m sorry, I should maybe recognize you, but we’re getting so many new customers, I can’t quite recall....”

“We’ve not met. I’ve never been in the bank before.”

“Oh, a new client. That’s even better!” Gayle smiled again. “Fairfax is growing so fast, some days I can hardly find my way around town. And I was born here!” She turned to her computer screen and keyed in a command. “Mr. Fairfax could see you on Monday at eleven-thirty, or on Tuesda—”

"I need to see Mr. Fairfax today. Now. It's urgent."

Gayle's smile slipped just slightly. "I'm real sorry, miss, but Mr. Fairfax is already over-scheduled today. If you could tell me what this is about, I'd be more than happy to direct you to one of our other officers."

"It's in regard to the three-million-dollar loan Ron Raven took out at this bank and I definitely need to speak with Mr. Fairfax in person."

"Oh my." Gayle's smile faded completely. "Are you a reporter?" Her voice was suddenly curt. Or at least as curt as she could manage, given that she spoke with a drawl that was thicker and slower moving than a river of chocolate syrup.

"No, I'm not a reporter." Megan hesitated before accepting that only the truth was going to get her inside Adam Fairfax's office. "My name is Megan Raven. I'm Ron Raven's daughter. I've just flown in from Wyoming specifically to speak with Mr. Fairfax."

Gayle's eyes widened in surprise, but she didn't look any friendlier than when she'd suspected Megan of being a reporter. "That's a long journey, Ms. Raven. You should have let us know you were coming."

"It was a spur-of-the-moment decision." That was true enough, although when she'd called to check that Adam Fairfax would be in the office today, she'd made a deliberate decision not to let anyone at the bank know her plans. Better, she'd thought, if her quarry didn't have time to prepare evasions and weasel excuses for not meeting with her.

Gayle gestured to the chair in front of her desk. "If you'll just take a seat, I'll let Mr. Fairfax know that you're here. Like I said, he's real busy today. I honestly don't know if he'll be able to make time for you."

She disappeared into her boss's office. "Mr. Fairfax has a meeting at four-thirty," she said when she emerged. "But he can give you fifteen minutes right now. No more than that, I'm afraid."

"Fifteen minutes is a start, at least. Thank you." Megan rose to her feet, relieved that Adam hadn't refused point-blank to see her. Maybe her plan to have a polite and dignified resolution of the loan issue was going to work after all.

Gayle held open the door to the office.

"This is Ms. Raven," she said to the man standing behind an imposing mahogany desk with a gleaming surface. "Would you like me to stay and take notes, Mr. Fairfax?"

"No thanks, Gayle. But I'd appreciate it if you'd answer any phone calls for the next few minutes."

"I'll be happy to." Gayle left the room, closing the door behind her, and Megan was left alone with Adam Fairfax.

He was not only the best-looking man Megan could remember seeing in her entire life, on the movie screen or off, he was also at least twenty years younger than she'd expected: midthirties instead of midfifties. He was tall, over six feet, with enough muscles to prove he worked out, and thick, light brown hair cut in a conservative style suitable for the president of a bank in a small southern town. His eyes were an unusual shade of silver gray and his features were so classically perfect that it was hard to avoid staring.

Unfortunately, his good looks weren't complemented by any hint of friendliness. His gaze was shuttered and his mouth was compressed into a hard, uncompromising line. Short of a judge in the process of pronouncing a death sentence, Megan couldn't imagine how anyone could manage to appear less warm and fuzzy. Her stomach gave an odd little jump—probably an instinctive reaction to his icy expression.

"There was no need for you to come in person." He held her gaze, setting her stomach to turning somersaults. His voice was deep, and unlike Gayle Tummins, retained only a trace of southern softness. "It's a long way from Thatch to Fairfax and there are several secure methods you could have used to repay the three million dollars your family owes my bank."

His bank? *What about the shareholders, you arrogant prick?* Megan recognized that Adam was being deliberately condescending in an attempt to intimidate her. Under normal circumstances that would have set her hackles rising, but she resisted the impulse to inform him he was an idiot. For her mother's sake, she was determined not to fall into the trap of scoring verbal points at the expense of achieving her goal. She reminded herself that she'd just spent three hours deciding to be courteous and dignified. Under the circumstances, it wouldn't be smart to blow her cool in the first thirty seconds.

"Thank you for agreeing to see me," she said. Given that her teeth were clenched tight, she thought she did a pretty good job of sounding pleasant. Not to mention humble, which required even more self-control. "Unfortunately, I haven't come to repay the money my father owed this bank. My mother…our family doesn't have three million dollars."

Adam lifted his shoulders in a dismissive shrug. "Then you appear to have made a long journey for no reason."

Megan drew in a deep breath and discarded the first three responses that sprang to mind, all of which involved Adam performing anatomically impossible acts and fell a long way outside the scope of polite and dignified.

"I realize the situation created by my father is awkward for both of us, and I appreciate your willingness to meet with me." By now, her teeth were positively grinding. She unlocked her jaw and even attempted a conciliatory smile. "Nevertheless, I hope we can find some way to resolve this issue without getting bogged down in personal hostility."

"I'm a businessman, Ms. Raven." Adam was clearly unimpressed by her smile. His voice remained ice-chip frosty, although his gray eyes were no longer quite so cool. Instead, they sparked with temper. "My personal conviction that your father was a lying, cheating son of a bitch doesn't enter into my calculations concerning the three-million-dollar loan you're referring to. My decision to call the loan was based on strictly financial considerations."

Ron Raven had obviously been a less than perfect human being, but he was her father and Megan's temper flared when she heard him being insulted by a mean-spirited banker with a poker up his ass. Deep breathing was no longer doing it, so she counted to ten, and then to twenty, before she spoke.

"A question, Mr. Fairfax. Did my father always pay the agreed interest on the money he owed you when he was alive?"

"Yes." The admission was visibly grudging.

"So this three-million-dollar loan wasn't in default before my father was murdered?"

"No, it wasn't."

"I fail to see, then, why you're accusing him of lying and cheating."

"Do you? Then you should take off your rose-colored glasses and look hard at the reality."

"I don't wear glasses of any color and this is reality as I see it. My father took out a loan with this bank. After that, he met all his payment obligations—"

"Having lied about his purpose for the loan," Adam interjected. "But I didn't refer to your father as a lying, cheating son of a bitch solely because of his conduct in regard to this loan. I was referring more generally to his treatment of my sister and my niece. His daughter and supposed wife are suffering because of his lies—"

"I agree that my father treated them badly—"

"A breathtaking understatement. However, I'm pressed for time, even if you aren't, and this discussion is irrelevant. The loan taken out by Ron Raven is now in default and my bank is calling for full repayment of the capital. That's the only business between the two of us, Ms. Raven. If you haven't come to pay your father's debt, we have nothing more to talk about."

"My mother needs time to raise the money. I'm requesting an extension—"

"Regrettably, she has no time. There can be no extension. I've already taken steps to have the current market value of the Flying W ranch assessed."

"Don't do this, Mr. Fairfax. Please. For you, the land is just a line item on the bank's account ledger. For my mother, the Flying W is her life. A third of the land that makes up the current property came from her family. It's land that was settled by her great-great-grandfather in the nineteenth century, before Wyoming was even a state. My father may have had the legal right to put it up as collateral for his loan, but he had no moral right. The ranch has been my mother's home for the past thirty-five years—"

"Spare me the sob story. It isn't working." Adam looked down at the single thick file folder on his desk and almost snarled. "The truth is, I'm not feeling very charitable right now."

"You were the person who told me you didn't allow personal feelings to intrude on your business decisions. And yet it seems to me you're calling the loan because you're angry with my father for his treatment of your sister."

"You're wrong."

"Then why, exactly, are you calling the loan?"

"Because your father lied about the purpose of the loan from the very beginning of our negotiations. I assumed I was investing in a real estate development project. I wasn't. In fact, because of your father's calculated plan to mislead me, I committed bank funds to aid him to do...God knows what. Something criminal seems likely."

"What are you talking about?"

Adam Fairfax opened the file and shook it so that three or four dozen photographs tumbled across the gleaming surface of his desk. "Take a look, Ms. Raven. Take a good look at these construction photos. As you can see, they show the development of a fine hotel and several peripheral buildings, such as a stable, a restaurant and a couple of guest cottages."

Megan gave the photos a cursory glance, wondering why Adam Fairfax sounded almost beside himself with fury. "I don't see what these construction pictures have to do with our discussion."

Adam laughed without a trace of humor. “You don’t recognize them?”

“No. Why would I?”

“Why would you? An excellent question. This happens to be a collection of the pictures your father has sent me over the past two years. They supposedly show the construction of a major vacation resort on Flying W land.”

“What?” Megan stared down at the photos, not even attempting to conceal her amazement. “This construction is supposed to be taking place on our family’s land in Wyoming?”

“Yes.”

She had to ask him again, still trying to take it in. “My father told you this resort was already under construction on Flying W land?”

“Yes, he did.” For a moment, a gleam of sympathy lightened Adam’s expression, but he quickly banished it. “I understand your surprise. From the panoramic views of the ranch that have been plastered all over the cable news channels for the past ten days, I already deduced that these photos your father sent me are as fraudulent as everything else about him.” Irony and anger colored Adam's voice in equal proportions. "Once I realized there was no resort being built on Flying W land, I had no choice other than to call the loan. Your father had the use of bank money for two years and he hadn't so much as brought in a bulldozer to start digging the foundation of a single building."

Megan looked again at the photos, more to give herself time to think than for any other reason. As she looked, she suddenly recognized the buildings she was seeing. The shots were of a hotel and condominium development located in Colorado, a few miles west of Vail. But the resort wasn't currently under construction as these pictures suggested; it had been finished at least four years earlier.

It was sheer chance that she recognized the pictures scattered over Adam's desk. Her father invested in so many projects, big and small, that he rarely shared details about any specific venture with her. However, he had invited her along for the grand opening of this particular resort, suggesting that she might be interested in checking out the competition since Vail was a major rival to Jackson Hole for skiing-vacation dollars.

She and her father had really enjoyed their

three days in Colorado, Megan remembered. The skiing had been fabulous after a fresh snowfall, her room had its own fireplace as well as a breathtaking view, and the restaurant had served exceptionally fine food. But then, she'd always had a great time when she was with her father. He tended to shower her with attention, praise and gifts whenever they were together. Probably because pretending to be a doting father was a very efficient way of disguising the truth, Megan thought bitterly.

A wave of grief washed over her, as intense as any she'd experienced since hearing that her father was dead. Grief because he was gone. Grief because he'd been a pathological liar. Grief because she was beginning to fear that he might have been a criminal, too. And, most painful of all, grief because yet another happy memory had been tainted by the poison of her father's multiple deceptions.

She refused to give in to the sadness, pushing it away as she considered how best to handle this latest revelation. Assuming Adam was telling the truth—and she feared he was—her father had lied over a two-year time span about his reasons for needing three million dollars. Why? What in the world had he done with the three million dollars he borrowed? Even more to the point, where was the money now? She *really* needed to find the answer to that question, since tracking down the missing money seemed the only chance there might be of saving the ranch for her mother.

Megan wasn't about to tell Adam Fairfax that she'd recognized the location in the photos. The less information she gave him, the less chance he had of twisting the information and flinging it back in her face.

"I'm sorry, but you're right about these pictures being fraudulent," she said, scooping them into a neat pile. "As you already concluded, none of this construction is taking place on our land."

"So what did your father use my money for?" Adam demanded. "Where is it now?"

"I have no idea. No clue." At least she could be a hundred percent honest about that. "Believe me, I *wish* I knew."

"Two years ago, on June eighth to be precise, we wired three million dollars to the Flying W trust account at the First Savings Bank of Casper. Here's the authorization, signed by me. What happened once the money went into the Flying W account?" Adam shoved a couple of sheets of paper in her direction, jabbing his finger to indicate Ron's signature. Then he leaned forward, his hands gripping the edge of the desk, waiting for her answer.

Megan didn't doubt that her father's signature was genuine and that he'd received the money. "As far as I know, the ranch accounts are all held by the Citizens Investment Bank in Jackson Hole. To the best of my knowledge, we don't have an account at the First Bank of Casper."

"But your father obviously did." Adam's temper was visibly fraying. "Of course, I've learned since your father died that the account was closed within a month of the initial transfer."

"None of the money from the First Bank of Casper was transferred into the regular ranch accounts, I promise you."

"I agree the money wasn't transferred directly into another Flying W account. Your father transferred the entire sum from the First Bank of Casper to an account in Bermuda. I have no way of finding out what happened after that. For all I know, it might have come straight back to your mother and the Flying W."

"It didn't."

He shrugged. "So you claim. However, my bank lived up to its part of the bargain, Ms. Raven. Now it's time for your family to live up to its end of the bargain. I want my money."

Megan leaned forward, mimicking his actions, her own temper slipping rapidly away. "You didn't have an agreement with *my family,* Mr. Fairfax, your bank had a deal with one member of it—Ron Raven. And unfortunately, he's not here to honor his obligations."

"You're right that he's not here, although it's debatable whether Ron Raven ever honored an obligation in his life. So, unluckily for you, your family ends up stuck with the consequences of Ron's actions. I'm calling the loan. You either pay, or you lose the collateral. Which happens to be the ranch."

The dickhead was making Ellie pay for the fact that he'd authorized a dumb loan. Megan seethed with rage. "It's not *our* fault that you chose to invest three million bucks in a development project that you never took the time to inspect." Her voice rose several decibels above cool and courteous, but she no longer cared. "One trip to Thatch, that's all it would have taken on your part. One trip, anytime during the past two years, and you'd have seen for yourself that there was no hotel being built on Flying W land."

"You're absolutely right. I should have traveled to Wyoming. I should have checked the project out for myself instead of trusting Ron's word. And his pictures. And his goddamn monthly faked progress reports. But you know what? I didn't expect my brother-in-law to be lying every time he opened his mouth or put pen to paper. I didn't expect my brother-in-law to have spent the past twenty-six years cheating on my sister. I didn't expect my brother-in-law to steal money from me because I was stupid enough to trust him—"

"Then don't blame my mother because you were careless with the bank's money," Megan yelled. It took about a nanosecond for her to realize that she'd hit on the precise reason why Adam Fairfax was so upset. Of course! He was furious with Ron for deceiving him, but he was even more furious with himself for having been deceived.

And he was most furious of all because it was the bank's money that he'd put at risk, not his own.

"I'm not blaming your mother," Adam said, jaw visibly clenched. His voice remained low, but that was the only vestige of control he retained. He jammed his left fist into his right hand and looked about two seconds away from sweeping the photos and loan documents onto the floor. Or punching his fist through the wall.

"You say you blame my father, but the reality is that you're punishing my mother."

"You're right. My bad." Adam shrugged. "Life's tough."

"You wouldn't be this vindictive unless you had a guilty conscience." Megan didn't stop to consider whether it was smart to point out to Adam just what psychological demons underpinned his anger. "The truth is, you blame yourself for making a stupid loan and then for not exercising more careful oversight. My father may have lied about why he needed the money, but you fell hook, line and sinker for his scam. Not just for the brief period when he applied for the loan, but for two entire years afterward."

"I followed normal bank procedure. Loan

officers don't travel to the site of every loan they make. There aren't enough hours in the day for that. Your father knew our procedures and exploited his knowledge—"

"But you wanted to believe his lies. You know that scams only work with willing victims. You forgot the first rule of investing—if an investment seems too good to be true, it almost certainly is. Now you're punishing my mother because you were greedy. Not to mention gullible."

Adam stepped back from the desk so fast that the chair behind him crashed to the floor. They both ignored the crash, but at least the noise stopped Adam in his tracks. "We have nothing more to say to each other, Ms. Raven. I'm calling the loan. That's my final word. Please leave before I have to ask the security guards to escort you out."

"If you want to pretend we have nothing more to discuss, so be it." Megan had a whole new understanding of what it meant to be hopping mad. It required physical effort on her part not to jump around Adam's office, yelling and throwing things. "But this isn't over. Since you won't deal with me in the privacy of your office, expect to see our business being conducted in the full glare of the media spotlight. You've left me no choice."

"What the hell does that mean?"

"I'm about to become your bank's worst nightmare, Mr. Fairfax. Given the number of reporters who've approached me over the past week, I shouldn't have any difficulty getting myself booked on a dozen different TV talk shows within the next forty-eight hours. I've already spent several hours working on the story of how you and your bank are harassing an innocent, grieving widow. Trust me, meeting you face-to-face has given me a gold mine of new material. By the time I've finished with you, there won't be many people left in Fairfax willing to do business with your bank."

Adam no longer looked in the least inscrutable. He looked appalled—and furious. "Even you couldn't sink so low as to take this dispute to the cable news talk-show circuit."

"Even me? What does that mean? Oh, let me guess. You mean *even the scumbag daughter of Ron Raven wouldn't dare to dis the great Adam Fairfax on national TV.* Boy, are you wrong!"

"You called yourself a scumbag, not me.

And be warned, I'll fight back. Let's see which the public finds more disgusting, your father's criminal lies or my willingness to trust him."

"I'd say they'll find you a matched pair, with my mother as the victim who deserved better from you as well as from her husband. And by the way, when you set out to blacken my father's name, you might spare a thought for the fact that your precious niece is also his daughter."

"But luckily for Katie, her mother is a wonderful woman. Thanks to my sister, Katie is blessed with at least one parent who has a clear idea of the difference between right and wrong."

The not-so-subtle suggestion that her mother was less ethical than Avery Fairfax was more than Megan could tolerate. Too angry to find words, she acted instinctively. She picked up the pile of fraudulent photos, flung them as hard as she could at Adam's head and stormed out of his office. If she stayed another second she'd probably throw her chair at him, as well, and with the small part of her brain that was still functioning rationally, she knew that getting arrested for assault wouldn't exactly advance her cause.

They must have been shouting even louder than she'd realized. Gayle Tummins stared at her in openmouthed horror as she rushed past. Megan glared right back. Adrenaline was still pouring through her system, drowning her normal inhibitions. Her legs were shaking, she was hot with frustration and she had an almost irresistible desire to poke her tongue out at the poor woman.

She managed to get outside without screaming at anyone or destroying bank property, but it was a close call. She couldn't remember a time in her life when she'd been this angry.

So much for keeping her cool and remaining dignified while she dealt with a difficult situation, Megan thought wryly. Pity she'd done such a spectacularly lousy job of following her own game plan. She really wasn't looking forward to taking her campaign to save the Flying W to the national airwaves, but Adam had left her with no other choice.

Nine

Talk about like father, like daughter. Adam glared savagely at the door that had just slammed shut behind Megan. He should have been prepared for Ron Raven's daughter to play dirty, but he'd been caught off guard and ended up losing his temper. He couldn't remember the last time he'd made the elementary mistake of losing his control in the midst of a negotiation and he still wasn't quite sure how the debacle had happened.

Whatever the reason, the truth was that he'd screwed up. Big-time. He was afraid Megan's threat to go to the media was a real one, which meant that he needed to prepare for the flood of negative PR likely to wash over the bank in the very near future. As if he didn't have enough to cope with right now.

Adam picked up his chair and slammed it

against the desk, images of Megan painfully vivid. God, she even looked like Ron. Not in body build or coloring, but in the shape of her face and the way she smiled. Fake smiles, of course, just as her father's had been, designed to soften up her quarry, but she doled them out far less often, so their impact was more powerful. She had all of Ron's charisma, too.

No wonder she'd come to see him in person. She'd probably grown up exploiting the fact that men were guaranteed to think with their dicks instead of their brains whenever she was in the vicinity. Too bad for her that his personal taste ran to tall, leggy blondes and not petite, curvy brunettes with luscious boobs.

Swearing softly, Adam collected the photos that Megan had thrown onto the floor and started to stack them into a pile. Suddenly impatient with his own obsessive neatness, he ripped the useless pictures in half and tossed them into the trash. Megan had recognized the place depicted in these photos; he was sure of it. Not that it mattered much, except as a useful reminder that she wasn't telling him everything she knew about her father's exploits, not by a long shot.

But why would she? Megan had no reason to trust him, any more than he had reason to trust her. It was flat-out stupid to suspect her of being in league with Ron Raven simply because she chose not to confide in a hostile stranger. Instead of losing his temper, he'd have been a lot smarter to go out of his way to win her over.

Adam loosened his tie and unfastened the top button of his shirt, his rage ratcheting down from boil to simmer. The more he thought about it, the less he understood why Megan had made him so angry. He was known for his icy cool when everyone else was getting heated, so why had he needled Megan to the point that she had threatened to go public with their dispute? He hated to admit that she was right and that he'd called the loan out of a juvenile need to punish Ron's legal family for the hurts inflicted on Avery and Katie. Surely to God he wasn't that petty.

He couldn't even pretend that he believed Megan and her mother were part of Ron's scam. Within minutes of Megan walking into his office he had accepted her claim that she had no idea where the missing three million bucks might be. It was dangerous to assume he understood her on the basis of a single brief meeting, but he was surprisingly confident that he'd read her correctly. She would never have risked losing the Flying W if she had the ability to pay him off. She'd tried to keep a poker face during their meeting but she hadn't succeeded worth a damn and he could tell that the potential loss of the ranch was tearing her apart. In his opinion, judging by the rest of her behavior, she'd have rammed the money down his throat if she'd been able to lay her hands on any part of it.

It was a pity he hadn't found Ron Raven equally easy to read, Adam thought bitterly, although there was some consolation in discovering that he wasn't alone in having been deceived by the son of a bitch. There had been nothing fake about Megan's claim that her mother would be devastated to lose the ranch, a property that had been in her family for over a hundred years.

He shoved aside a wave of guilt. Dammit, Ron's Wyoming family wasn't his problem. The bank was his problem, and the fact that he'd made a loan to his supposed brother-in-law based on fraudulent documents. His stomach knotted every time he contemplated next month's board meeting. He could visualize it with painful clarity. Agenda item number one: Adam Fairfax, president and CEO, had his head so far up his ass for the past two years that he didn't notice his brother-in-law wasn't actually building anything up there in Wyoming. Resolution: We only hired you because your great-uncle insisted. We told you your newfangled banking methods wouldn't work, and now we have proof. By the way, you're fired.

Some of the older members of the board had been looking for an excuse to fire him since the day they realized he wasn't the malleable patsy they'd expected and that he intended to modernize the bank. Now, idiot that he was, he'd given them the grounds they needed to get rid of him.

Adam pushed the Raven loan file back into his desk drawer and swallowed a couple of aspirin while he had the drawer open. He was scheduled to join his parents for dinner at seven-thirty and he realized he couldn't face it. Not tonight. Listening to the two of them rake over the coals of Ron Raven's treachery for the umpteenth time was more than he could tolerate in his current bleak mood.

His parents would follow their lifelong pattern and complain endlessly about Ron's past misdeeds while making no attempt to consider how they might improve the present or prepare for the future. Genteel inaction in the face of mounting problems was a three-generation Fairfax specialty and his parents had the routine down to a fine art. Right now, he simply wasn't up for sympathizing with how they were too embarrassed to show their faces at the country club for fear of what their friends might say. He'd already had this conversation several times in the past ten days and his suggestion that friends who set out to embarrass them weren't worth keeping was invariably met with blank stares.

The blankness wasn't feigned on his parents' part. He'd realized years ago that they had a curious definition of friendship. They didn't spend time with people because they liked them; they spent time with people who belonged to the right Georgia families and held the correct political, social and religious views. Their attitudes alternately bewildered and infuriated him, but at seventy-five and eighty, it was too late to expect them to change.

Chugging another painkiller, Adam dialed his parents' number. He got lucky when the answering machine picked up and he was able to leave a message apologizing for his absence without actually speaking to anyone. His four-thirty meeting had been a fiction, invented so that he would have an excuse to get rid of Megan and tackle the mound of paperwork waiting for his attention. Now that she'd gone, however, the prospect of another two or three hours at his desk crunching numbers held even less appeal than meeting with his parents.

He'd behaved badly, Adam finally admitted, pacing up and down his office. He'd not only been unnecessarily brutal to Megan, he'd allowed personal feelings to get the better of him, which was exactly what he'd sworn not to do. His desire to lash out at Ron Raven had caused him to neglect the real interests of the bank. If he made his decision purely on economic factors, foreclosing on the ranch wasn't necessarily his smartest move at this point.

The initial guesstimate he'd received from a real estate broker in Jackson Hole suggested that the Flying W land was likely to sell for no more than two point five million, not enough to pay off the full amount of Ron's loan. The low price was a reflection of how much work needed to be done before the property could successfully be converted from ranch to resort. The road leading out from town was currently dirt, not paved, and although the county had indicated willingness to upgrade the gravel to asphalt if the ranch was developed, there was still a ton of infrastructure requirements that the county wouldn't pay for. Bringing in adequate sewage, water, utilities, and cutting private roads through the property would require the outlay of at least another million bucks before construction could start on actual buildings. It was precisely because of all those up-front costs that Ron's consortium of ready-made investors had been so appealing.

Ron's consortium had never existed, of course, but that didn't change any of the basic facts about what the unimproved Flying W land was worth. From the bank's perspective, Adam had nothing to lose by granting Megan a few months' grace to come up with the missing three million dollars. If no money had been found once Ron's estate was settled, the bank could still insist on their right to sell the ranch. Far from being worse off, waiting to foreclose meant that they would actually gain a few thousand dollars of monthly income, since Megan had offered to continue paying the interest charges on the loan.

From the bank's perspective, the only real issue was whether Megan and her mother would be able to keep the loan payments current. They almost certainly would, Adam decided. Ron had left plenty of money, even if it was tied up either in Raven Enterprises, or in probate. His brother had assured him that Raven Enterprises was in rock-solid financial shape, and he had no reason to doubt Paul's judgment. However messy the legal situation might be in view of the duplicate wills Ron had signed, and the fact that the police still hadn't officially declared him deceased, the probate court would undoubtedly authorize payments to meet Ron's debts.

In other words, Adam thought resignedly, he needed to find Megan and apologize for the way he'd behaved. Eating humble pie had never been his favorite activity, but there was no point in putting off the inevitable. Grimacing, he grabbed his briefcase and took his car keys from the brass bowl sitting on top of the credenza.

"See you on Monday," he said to Gayle, speeding past her desk. "Have a good weekend."

"You're leaving?" Gayle was shocked into asking the obvious, since Adam was notorious for working extra late on Friday nights and it wasn't even five o'clock.

"Yes. Gotta dash. See you Monday." For some reason, Adam chose not to explain where he was going, and Gayle, bless her, was too well trained to inquire. He drove his BMW out of its coveted spot in the cool underground parking garage and headed for the interstate. He could only hope that Megan hadn't decided to cut her losses and fly back to Wyoming. Fortunately, it was a long journey from Atlanta to Jackson Hole and there probably weren't any more direct flights this evening. Assuming she was still in Fairfax, he shouldn't have any trouble finding her. There were only two motels in town, and they faced each other across the access road leading onto the interstate.

He tried the Fairfax Country Inn first because it was the nicer motel, and also because one of his classmates from high school worked there as the day manager. It would make his inquiries easier if LizAnne happened to be on duty. He got lucky and found her standing behind the reception desk, looking bored.

"Hi, LizAnne, how are you? And how is little Merrie doing? It's a while since I've seen her."

"She's doing fine, but she's not so little." LizAnne laughed ruefully. "She'll be starting fifth grade in the fall."

"*Fifth grade?* You're kidding me, right?"

"I wish. But she'll be eleven next month."

Adam shook his head in genuine bewilderment. "I swear it was only last week you told me she was starting preschool."

"Seems that way to me and her daddy, too."

Adam grinned. "Watch out. At this rate, before you know it, she'll be setting out on her first date."

"Bite your tongue. I've told her she can start dating when she's graduated from college. Provided she graduates with honors."

He rolled his eyes. "Real smart parenting, LizAnne. There's a deal that'll hold up well to teenage pressures."

She gave a resigned chuckle. "Well, we can try."

"Yeah. Good luck." The smile he gave her was warm, even though it was several months since he'd last seen her. Some bonds were unbreakable, he reflected in silent amusement. He and LizAnne had been enrolled in the same health class their senior year and she had been his assigned partner for a memorable week when they had been temporary "parents" to a doll programmed to cry at regular intervals. Sometimes it was possible to stop the crying by holding a bottle to the doll's mouth for ten minutes or so. Sometimes the bottle didn't work. Then you had to try changing the doll's diaper, or walking up and down, jiggling the doll and rubbing its back. If you ignored the doll, the crying got louder and louder until you paid attention and figured out what needed to be done.

The expensive program had been designed to demonstrate to hormonal high-school kids that college was a better choice than parenthood. Adam had been awestruck by LizAnne's patience as a make-believe mom and her willingness to help him out when he called her frantically one night with a wailing doll that refused to respond to his jiggles and pats. She'd even seemed sorry when the week ended, whereas he'd handed the doll back with a rush of fervent gratitude that his girlfriend wasn't pregnant. He'd made a silent vow, still unbroken, that he would never again have sex without using a condom, and never become a father except by design.

Recently, though, he'd begun to wonder if the doll might have been too successful in its mission. At thirty-six, he was finding the rituals of dating and casual sex increasingly tedious. Part of him was ready to embrace the idea of marriage and a family of his own, and yet he got cold feet every time he found himself in a relationship that looked as if it might be heading toward long-term commitment.

There were so many attractive, intelligent women out there and he enjoyed the time he spent with at least half the women he dated. How did you decide that this was the woman you wanted to be with forever? The question struck him as a lot more difficult than most people were willing to acknowledge. Several of his friends had seemed to make up their minds one day that they were ready to get married and then proposed to whatever woman they happened to be dating at the time. Given the divorce rate among those same friends, he figured there had to be a better decision-making process than that, but he didn't have a clue what it might be.

"Well, it's sure nice to see you again, Adam. It's been way too long." LizAnne returned his smile, but she carefully avoided asking him any questions about what was going on in his life. No doubt because she'd been watching pictures of his sister and Ron Raven flashing all over her TV screen. "How can I help you?" she asked. "I guess you're not looking for a room."

"No, I don't need a room, thanks. I'm looking for one of your guests. Megan Raven. Could you let her know that I'm here and that I'd like to meet her in the bar?"

He'd decided that the direct approach was best, along with the implication that he already knew Megan was checked in to this motel. After all, he had a fifty-fifty chance of being right and the fewer questions he asked the better. This was a small town and he was the bank president. Whatever tactic he used to find Megan, word was soon going to be flying all over Fairfax that he'd come calling. And if Megan refused to see him, there was no getting around the fact that the whole town would know it by tomorrow morning. LizAnne might be an old friend, but she wouldn't be able to resist spreading such delicious gossip any more than the next person.

Sure enough, LizAnne couldn't quite conceal the immediate interest in her gaze. "Megan Raven, you said? Yes, I'll give her a call right away. She only checked in a few minutes ago, so you arrived just at the right time." She waited, obviously hoping that he would say something more, but he smiled blandly and made no comment.

He noticed with resignation that LizAnne dialed the room without needing to look up the number. That might be due to the fact that Megan had just checked in. More likely it was because LizAnne had recognized the name and had been curious about what Ron Raven's daughter was doing in town. His visit to the motel would simply confirm that Megan's trip to Fairfax involved him.

Megan was in her room, apparently, and answered the phone. "Ms. Raven, this is LizAnne at the reception desk. I'm calling to let you know that Adam Fairfax is here in the lobby. He'd like to meet you in the bar, if that's all right with you." LizAnne paused for a moment. "I think he'd like to meet with you as soon as possible."

Adam held his breath while LizAnne listened again, then said goodbye and hung up. "Ms. Raven will meet you in the bar in ten minutes," she said.

"Thanks, LizAnne. I appreciate your help." Adam managed to conceal his sigh of relief. Thankfully, an elderly couple who had just driven up and were looking for a room took LizAnne's attention and allowed him to escape to the bar without any more explanations.

He ordered a bourbon on the rocks and sipped slowly while he waited for Megan to arrive. After the disaster of their last meeting, he needed to be in complete control this time around and for some reason he was having a hard time getting his act together. His pulse was racing, and he felt ridiculously nervous.

When Megan finally walked into the bar, his stomach clenched with an odd sort of anticipation. Kate was so tall and blond that he hadn't noticed the similarities between the two half sisters. Now, with his temper under control, he saw the resemblance. Neither sister had inherited Ron's coloring or body build, but they'd both inherited their father's facial features, including Ron's full mouth, his small straight nose and his high cheekbones. Perhaps the subtle physical similarity to Ron was the reason that he had this irrational feeling that he'd known Megan for a lot longer than a couple of hours.

He got to his feet, setting his glass on the bar. "Thank you for agreeing to see me. I appreciate it."

"At this point, I figured I don't have much to lose by meeting with you." Megan sounded cool. She tipped her head back so that she could hold his gaze, her spectacular green eyes clear and assessing. Adam felt a tightening in his gut and realized to his astonishment that what he was feeling at this precise moment had nothing to do with lingering anger and everything to do with sexual desire. How in hell had that happened?

"Why have you come looking for me?" Megan asked. "I thought you'd announced that we have nothing more to say to each other."

Better get straight to the point or she might

walk away. Adam drew in a deep breath. "I'm glad I found you. I came because I owe you an apology. I lost my temper just now for no better reason than that you pointed out several home truths I'd have preferred not to hear."

Her expression didn't soften. "Which home truths were those?"

"The fact that it was irrational to call Ron's loan. Before you arrived, I'd talked myself into believing that I called the loan because it was the only way for the bank to recover its money. But that wasn't true. As you pointed out, I called the loan because I was furious with your father."

"That's a very generous apology." Megan continued to hold his gaze, and Adam was delighted when he saw some of the chill finally thaw from her eyes. Considering that he'd classified her smiles as fake and strictly in the manipulative tradition of her father, it was surprising how much he wanted to see one of them again.

"Does that mean you're willing to consider extending the loan for a few months and allowing my mother to make the same monthly payments my father did?" Megan asked.

"Possibly. Look, despite what I said at the bank, there are clearly issues we need to talk about. It would be better if we could find somewhere private to have that discussion. This is a small town, and my family has lived here for a long time. There's no decent restaurant within a fifteen-mile radius where I can take you that we aren't going to be recognized. And gossiped about, quite frankly."

"So what do you suggest?"

"I live in a small house just outside of town. Would you be willing to come back to my place? I could make us dinner—"

"You cook?" Her wary expression faded to one of frank admiration.

"Kinda, sorta. I live alone and got tired of eating out all the time, so the only alternative was learning to cook. I'm really good at heating packages in the microwave. But I can also do steaks on the grill, baked potatoes and Caesar salad. No fancy desserts, but I have chocolate chip cookies in the freezer and I make great coffee."

"I'm sold," Megan said and smiled. "Not to mention impressed. Thanks for the invitation."

"You're welcome." Adam realized he was

staring at her smile. He quickly turned his back on her, sticking a ten-dollar bill under his glass on the bar. Time to snap out of whatever weird sexual thing was going on here and get back to business.

"Do you need to get anything from your room before we leave?" He was pleased at how businesslike he sounded.

"No." She held up her purse. "I have everything important in here."

"Okay, then. My car's parked out front. Let's go."

Ten

If you'd asked her to guess, Megan would have said that Adam probably lived in a brand-new town house, with a black-and-white color scheme, lots of slate and granite and a few pieces of abstract art strategically hung for dramatic effect. As for the landscaping, it would be all paved patio to cut down on tiresome yard work. Plus, of course, a fancy outdoor kitchen just to prove he was really trendy.

Her guesses couldn't have been more wrong. Adam lived in a rambling, eighty-year-old cottage that had once been owned by a peach farmer. The cottage had been updated but still had the original, smoke-stained brick fireplace and uneven wooden-plank floors. The color scheme was warm comfort rather than to make a fashion statement of any sort.

As for the backyard, far from being a sterile paved courtyard, it was full of flowers and backed up to a field where half a dozen horses grazed with the lazy indifference of the overfed. The horses, Adam told her, belonged to a local riding stable.

Megan followed him through the old-fashioned screened porch and out onto the lawn. The heady scent of roses, phlox, marigolds and carnations hit her in an almost tangible wave. The riotous color assortment and variety of heights at first suggested almost random plantings in the three flower beds. After a moment, Megan realized that a lot of care had gone into creating precisely that effect of abundant wildness and vivid, slapdash color.

But at least she'd been right about the state-of-the-art outdoor kitchen, she saw with silent amusement. Positioned under a sloping roof extension and protected by a trellis twined with morning glory vines, the built-in grill was stainless steel, the sink was set into a tumbled marble work counter, and in addition to a sleek minifridge, there was also an automatic ice maker and a fancy brick fire pit.

"I see you have everything the bachelor about town needs to impress his dates," she said, gesturing toward the gleaming kitchen equipment.

"Is that so?" Adam raised an eyebrow. "I wish I'd known all it took was an outdoor grill. I hate to think how many hours I wasted in sensitivity-training classes."

Megan realized she was smiling. "I'm taking a wild guess here, but I'd be willing to bet large sums of money you've never been anywhere near a sensitivity-training class."

"You'd lose your money." His voice remained cool, but his eyes were laughing.

With or without sensitivity training, Megan was pretty sure Adam had never experienced the slightest difficulty capturing the attention of any woman he wanted. This afternoon at the bank her anger had been strong enough to block out any other reaction. Now that she was calmer, she was dismayed to discover how sexy she found him. Getting involved with a man was about the last thing in the world she needed right now, and getting involved with Adam Fairfax would be worse than virtually any other man she could choose.

Eager to put some distance, psychic and physical, between the two of them, she walked around the flower beds that bordered three sides of the small lawn and bent down to admire a lovely pale pink rose.

"I'm envious," she said, letting the velvety petals brush against the back of her hand. "I'm so used to hothouse flowers at the ski lodge where I work that I'd forgotten how sweet roses can actually smell."

"That particular bush is a hybrid derived from China tea roses. Did you know that light-colored roses always have a stronger scent than darker ones?"

"No, I had no idea." She was intrigued by the snippet of gardening lore.

Adam picked a stem of freesias and handed it to her. "Most flowers are like roses—the pale ones have stronger scents. Freesia is one of the rare exceptions."

Megan sniffed the brightly colored freesia. "You sound very knowledgeable about flowers."

He grinned. "My college professors always used to say I was an outstanding bullshitter. The truth is, you've just heard ten percent of my total store of botanical knowledge."

His smile packed an almost lethal punch and her body responded with a hot rush of sexual awareness. "I've never had the chance to do much gardening," she said, fixing her gaze on one of the horses as a safer alternative to Adam's smile. "At the ranch we can only expect four months without frost. Mom always considers herself lucky if we can get a few tubs of geraniums to bloom by early June and hang around until September."

Adam pinched off a couple of deadheads. "I think I'd miss the color if I had to survive eight months of winter."

"Wyoming is colorful," she insisted. "We don't have flowers, of course, but even in winter, we have brilliant blue skies, lots of sun glistening on the snow and thousands of evergreens in different shades of green. In our part of the state especially it's almost never gray or bleak. You should pay a visit to Jackson Hole one of these days. It's a great resort and stunningly beautiful."

Megan couldn't believe that she was actually encouraging him to visit Wyoming. The whole point of coming out into the garden had been to establish psychological distance. That plan hadn't worked too well, she thought wryly.

Adam said something polite about hoping to visit Wyoming one day and they talked about skiing as he walked over to the kitchen area and lit the grill. Megan continued to stroll around the perimeter of the lawn. The artistry and passion she saw in the design of the garden surprised her all over again. In the bank this afternoon, Adam had struck her as one of the world's more buttoned-up human beings, and the exuberant garden didn't fit with that impression.

"Do you take care of all this yourself?" she asked, curious about the seeming inconsistency between the man and his home.

Adam shook his head, shutting the lid on the grill. "I'm not allowed."

"Oh. Are you allergic?"

"Not allergic. Intimidated." He gave a rueful laugh. "I have a gardener who used to work for my parents when I was a kid. When Joe discovered that I'd bought this cottage, he announced he was coming out of retirement to help me get the garden in shape. He's eighty years old, at least, lies to all the women he dates by pretending he's only seventy, and on top of that he's a complete tyrant. We fought for a month before he would agree to plant those freesias. For some reason he doesn't approve of freesias."

"Have you ever tried dropping a casual reminder that you're paying his wages, which gives you at least a small right to choose which flowers you'll plant?"

Adam grinned. "Joe would consider that totally irrelevant. He allows me to pull weeds on the weekend, and I can prune the roses if I ask his permission first. Other than that, he pretty much expects me to keep my pesky, interfering hands off his flower garden."

Megan laughed. Perversely, the story about Joe convinced her that the design of the garden was actually Adam's. "Well, I'm glad somebody is able to put you in your place. Three cheers for Joe." She flushed. "I'm sorry. I didn't mean to sound rude."

"You weren't. And you didn't." He walked over to the porch and opened the screen door. "It'll take a few minutes for the grill to heat, so we'd better go inside. The bugs will make a feast out of us if we stay out here at this time in the evening. What can I get you to drink? Wine? Bourbon? Something tall and cold?"

"If you have some Merlot, I would enjoy a glass. Otherwise iced tea is fine."

"I have Merlot, and I'll be right back." Adam returned with two glasses and a bottle of red wine, but minus his jacket and tie. He'd unfastened the top couple of buttons of his shirt and rolled up his sleeves, forcefully reminding Megan that he was not only the handsomest man she'd ever seen, he also had one of the more fantastic bodies that she'd come across outside the pages of a muscle magazine. At the bank this afternoon she'd been so certain that he was a pompous prick. It was really annoying of him to be turning into...something else...right before her eyes.

He opened the wine with quiet efficiency and smiled as he handed a glass to her. His smile perfected the God's-gift-to-women effect of his appearance. Megan tried to tell herself she wasn't dazzled but the attempt failed.

"This Merlot comes from a vineyard in California I visited last year." Adam turned the ket for only five years or so, but I was surprised by how much they've already accomplished. They consider this one of their best wines and I agree. I hope you like it."

She took a sip. "It's wonderful." And it was. In addition to his other skills, Adam was clearly a wine connoisseur. The man was rapidly completing his transformation from arrogant asshole to just-too-good-to-be-true. And, as she'd pointed out to him at the bank, anytime somebody appeared too good to be true, he almost certainly was. She would be smart to bear her own advice in mind and look for the flaws behind the too-handsome facade.

"I'm glad you like the wine," he said. "Stay here and relax for a few minutes. Put your feet up, literally. I'm just going to season the steaks and microwave a couple of potatoes."

"May I help?"

"Thanks, but there's almost nothing to do. Enjoy the wine and the garden."

He was right that she was tired, and the wine made a perfect partner to the peace and quiet of the garden. Besides, cooking she didn't press the issue. She sipped in appreciative silence, her muscles unknotting after days of tension. The overhead fan whirred quietly, ruffling her hair with a cool breeze. She realized this might be the most tranquil few minutes she'd experienced since the sheriff arrived ten days ago to give them the news about her father.

Adam ruptured that tranquillity as soon as he came back out to the porch. "Tell me how Ron got away with it," he said without preamble, hooking a wicker chair with his foot and pulling it closer to hers. "Every time I think I've wrapped my mind around it, the whole thing slips out of focus again."

The sensation of peace vanished in a flash. Megan sat up straighter in the chair, her stomach tying itself into a fresh knot. She reminded herself that Adam was not only a Fairfax, he was also the man who held her mother's happiness within his grasp. She couldn't afford to forget those basic facts simply because he had a sexy body and had designed a beautiful garden.

"Are you asking how my father managed to scam your bank out of three million dollars?" Megan asked. Even to her own ears, her voice sounded cool to the point of hostility.

Adam shook his head. “No. I know precisely how Ron did that. Unfortunately, I was right there every step of the way while he ripped me off. What I want to understand is how he got away with having two wives, two homes and two families. Not just for a few months but for more than twenty years. That’s the entire time you and Katie have been alive. The more I think about it, the more incredible it becomes. Why the hell wasn’t he found out?”

Adam sounded frustrated rather than accusing, but Megan wasn’t ready to trust her instincts and blurt out confidences about her family. And she certainly wasn’t about to admit that Liam had known the truth about their father’s double life for several years before Ron died. That would open a can of worms that would be wriggling out of control within seconds.

“Dad juggled brilliantly, I guess. He seems to have been really good at keeping his families separate.” She ran her finger around the rim of her wineglass, and thought for the hundredth time about her father’s multiple deceptions and how he’d pulled them off.

"The cops told us they found two of everything in the hotel-room safe. Two cell phones, two wallets, two sets of family photos, two BlackBerries with different friends listed on each one, along with different appointments and memos and phone numbers. In lots of ways, it seems as if Dad became a totally different person depending on whether he was in Thatch or Chicago."

"That's it? The secret of Ron's success was keeping two separate sets of personal items?" Adam's words were sharp with skepticism.

"And we were blind," she admitted. "The truth is, we didn't suspect anything was amiss so we never checked up on him."

"But that's precisely my point." Adam looked exasperated by her failure to provide a more satisfactory explanation. "How in the world did Ron prevent you and the rest of your family from getting suspicious?"

"I don't know what to tell you except that he lied well…." Megan knew it was an inadequate answer, but she had nothing better to offer.

"It's usually the little things that catch a person out in the big lie. Why didn't Ron fall into the same trap?" Adam scowled. "You must have called his hotel a few times and discovered he wasn't where he was supposed to be."

Megan shook her head. "No, I don't believe that ever happened. Dad had a cell phone from the first moment they were available, and with a cell phone there's no way to check up if a person is where he says he is."

"True, but that doesn't explain all the years before cell phones. And what about the days when he didn't come home on schedule? Birthdays when he wasn't there?"

"He was always there for my birthday, and for my brother's. My mother's, too, of course."

"Okay. He came home for birthdays. But that still leaves Thanksgiving. And Christmas. Good God, Christmas! How the *hell* did Ron manage Christmas?"

"There were a few Christmases when my father didn't get home until late," Megan admitted. "And then there were all the holidays when he had to leave early because of—quote—unavoidable business. And then I remember a couple of times when he claimed he was snowed in at an airport after a business trip and couldn't make it until the day after the holiday."

"And that never made you suspicious?" Adam's face displayed blank incredulity.

Megan wasn't sure whether to laugh or cry. "No, we were never suspicious. Although in retrospect I admit that sounds crazy. He was our father and he loved us. He told us so all the time. Why would we doubt him?"

Adam expelled an exasperated breath. *"Because it was Christmas and he wasn't home!"*

"But his excuses were so good!" Now that she thought about it with logic instead of emotion, it seemed beyond incredible that they had never suspected her father of lying, even though she could recall three occasions when he had pretended to be unable to get home on Christmas Day because his flight was canceled. Why had nobody in her family ever wondered why he was so unlucky?

"Dad never claimed to be snowed in at an airport unless that particular airport was genuinely shut down." She gave the explanation as much to herself as to Adam. "If he said he couldn't get a plane out of Detroit, for example, you can be sure that if you turned on the TV they were broadcasting endless pictures of the blizzard in Michigan, along with the closed-down Detroit airport and the disrupted holiday traffic. There would be nothing in the story Dad told to trigger our suspicions. On the contrary, we just felt sorry for him because he was spending Christmas Day sitting in an airport, eating an overcooked hamburger instead of Mom's delicious holiday dinner."

"Jesus, the man was a master of deception."

"Yes, I think he was." Megan nodded her agreement. "My brother and I were talking about those supposed Christmas blizzards a couple of days ago. We realize now that Dad must have waited until an airport shut down and then leaped at the excuse to explain his absence over the holidays. He was never actually at the affected airport, of course. When he claimed to be in Detroit, or Indianapolis or St. Paul, he would really have been in Chicago, celebrating Christmas with your sister and Kate."

Adam looked somewhere between disgusted and awestruck. "There must have been years when Ron worked the same scam in reverse. He would have told Avery and Kate he was stuck at some airport in Cleveland, or Boston, when really he was with you."

"I'm sure that must have happened," Megan agreed. "As it turns out, we were easy marks because we loved him, but I'm not sure how any of us would have caught Dad out even if we'd been trying. How do you discover whether somebody is really sitting out a blizzard in an airport on Christmas Eve?"

"I don't know," Adam said, frowning. "But I do know that clever juggling and brilliant lies couldn't have been enough to lull everyone's suspicions for twenty-seven years. There has to have been something more that allowed him to get away with his deceptions."

"What could there possibly be? We were free to question Dad but we never did. Our choice. Our decision. Believe me, now that we know what was really going on, everyone in my family feels extremely stupid."

"Avery feels exactly the same," Adam said. "She's devastated at having been so gullible. Kate is more angry than devastated, but that's not surprising." His cool gray eyes were suddenly warm with affection. "Kate is the best friend you could ever have as long as you're trustworthy. Betray her trust, though, and she'll cut you right out of her life without a backward glance."

It sounded as if her half sister had some personality traits in common with Liam, Megan reflected wryly. "Is it possible that at some level Avery feared something wasn't quite right and chose not to explore her worries?" she asked. "And I'm not insulting your sister. I've wondered the same thing about my mother."

Adam shook his head. "If you'd asked Avery about her marriage the day before Ron died, she'd have sworn on a stack of bibles that she and Ron were one of the happiest couples in America. Not surprisingly, she's spent the past several days kicking herself for every tiny incident that, with hindsight, should have warned her she was living with a fraud."

Megan hesitated a moment before speaking. "Maybe your sister wasn't living with a fraud."

Adam made a dismissive gesture. "I'd say that bigamy is about as big a fraud as you can get in terms of a husband and wife."

"In a way. Except the thing about con artists is that the really good ones often believe their own scams. Maybe my father truly did love both of his families. Maybe he truly did hate to be away from my mother, and from your sister, too. Otherwise I don't understand why he would have kept up the pretense. Think of how much easier it would have been to get divorced from one wife or the other. After all, that's what fifty percent of married couples do, even when they're not juggling two spouses." She shrugged, staring out into the garden to avoid Adam's gaze. "Or maybe I just can't bring myself to believe that my father didn't give a damn about any of us and had some other purpose altogether."

"You don't strike me as a very self-deceiving kind of person." Adam was silent for a moment. "In fact, you've hit on an explanation that makes more sense than anything else I've heard in the past couple of weeks. In other words, you think your father was lying about the practical details, but the emotions he expressed were basically honest."

"It's possible, isn't it?" Megan wished that she didn't sound quite so wistful. "Especially in view of how he managed to deceive so many people over such a long period. Sincerity seems the best explanation of how he pulled off that amazing trick."

"Yes, it does. If you don't mind, I'm going to pass on your theory to Avery. It might help her to put Ron's bigamy in a better perspective." Adam rose to his feet. "In the meantime, I'm going to stick a fork in the meat and pretend I know what I'm doing. How do you like your steak cooked?"

"Medium would be good."

"For me, too. But don't get excited yet. There's about a fifty-fifty chance I'll get somewhere in the ballpark."

"I'm flexible. As long as I don't see blood. Despite having grown up on a ranch, I prefer not to be reminded I'm eating something that was once part of a cow."

"Steak comes from cows? My God, who knew?" He sent her a look of such wide-eyed astonishment that it took her a moment to realize he was teasing.

They ate two perfect medium steaks at the small table in the porch and watched the sun cast a purple glow over the garden before sinking below the horizon. As they ate, Adam asked questions about Megan's job at the ski lodge in Jackson Hole.

She started off spouting platitudes about the pleasures of working at a resort, but his questions were insightful and she found herself answering with increasing honesty until she ended up confiding some of the difficulties she was experiencing working for a boss who had been promoted one time too many and was now floundering above his level of competence. Adam, not surprisingly in view of his experience as a CEO, had several useful suggestions about coping mechanisms. As they cleared off the dishes, he switched the conversation to his niece. Kate, it turned out, was a prize-winning pastry chef, who not only worked for La Lanterne, one of Chicago's most prestigious restaurants, but last year had won a place on the U.S. national team competing at the international contest for pastry chefs held in Bologna, Italy. The Americans had come in fourth, beaten by the Austrians, French and Italians. Kate's goal was to be on the first-ever American team to take home the Golden Medallion.

By the time they were sipping after-dinner coffee and eating to-die-for chocolate chip cookies—Kate routinely shipped Adam a batch of her secret recipe—Megan realized

Adam was deliberately leaving it up to her to introduce the subject of the loan and the missing three million dollars. She wished she could just kick back and listen to more stories about the sister she'd never met, but from the moment the sheriff had brought news of her father's death, it seemed there was always something unpleasant waiting to be dealt with. Tonight, unfortunately, was no exception.

"We have to talk about the money my father owes your bank," she said. She noticed with self-mocking awareness that she referred to it as *his* bank, when earlier in the afternoon Adam had irritated her intensely by saying the same thing.

"I'm sorry to put you in the awkward position of listening to me beg for favors, but you'd be giving my mother a huge gift if you could see your way clear to allowing us a few months to track down the missing money."

"Do you think there's any chance you can find it?" Adam immediately sounded more businesslike and she noticed that he pushed his chair back from the small table. Apparently he shared her instinctive need to erect a barrier of physical space between the two of them as soon as the subject of the missing money came up.

Megan was perverse enough to regret the changed atmosphere, even though she'd been telling herself for the past hour that she and Adam couldn't afford to get too friendly. The hostility between their two families made any relationship other than neutral courtesy impossible.

"The honest answer is that I don't know if we'll be able track down the money," she said. "But my brother and I are willing to do whatever it takes to pursue the trail if you'll give us some extra time."

Adam thought for a moment, and then gave an abrupt nod of his head. "If you can get a signed agreement from the executor of your father's estate, guaranteeing continued payment of the interest, then I'll hold off on calling the loan."

"Thank you." Her mother wasn't going to lose the ranch! At least not yet. "Thank you, Adam. I'm truly grateful. Really." Relief washed over her in a giant wave.

"Megan, what's the matter?" He stared at her. "Are you sick? Was it something I said?

reaction to emotional overload. Megan gritted her teeth and scrubbed at the tears with the solitary limp tissue she was able to find buried in her jacket pocket. God, in her next life she not only wanted to have straight hair and be a skinny beanpole, she was going to put in an official request to come back as an ice princess who was incapable of displaying emotion. She suspected Adam was the type of man who would prefer red-hot needles thrust under his fingernails to being confronted by a sobbing woman.

She finally managed to force a watery smile. "Sorry. I feel fine. Happier than I've felt in several days, in fact. I just seem to be overreacting to everything since my father died."

He looked at her in silence for a long moment, then got up and walked into the kitchen. He came back with a box of tissues. "Here, help yourself. You looked as if you might need these."

That must mean she was red eyed and drippy nosed, Megan thought gloomily. "Thank you," she said, reaching for another tissue and trying to sound chirpy.

was much closer to hers. "There's so much about Ron that I still don't understand. What's especially puzzling is why he chose to come to me for the loan in the first place."

She gave a wry smile. "Well, you're a banker and banks have money. That's a pretty good reason."

"But Ron didn't need to come to a small bank in Georgia to raise money. He and my brother must have access to at least twenty million dollars in venture capital investment funds. Why didn't he tap into that?"

"You would know the answer to that way better than I do. What did he tell you at the time?"

"That his plans to develop the ranch were strictly personal, nothing to do with Raven Enterprises, and that he was raising most of the development capital from investors with strong ties to the resort industry in Wyoming and Montana. Oh, and that it was a great opportunity for me to take the bank into a potentially profitable development deal. It was written into the contract that as soon as the resort was fully built, the bank had the right to convert the three-million-dollar loan into shares in the property. In other words, the Bank of Fairfax would become part owners of the resort."

The extent of her father's deception was truly mind-blowing. She sighed. "Clearly there isn't even a shred of truth to the story he told you, and that makes tracking the money even more difficult. His reasons for taking out the loan could be almost anything."

"Well, almost anything except building a resort on Flying W land." Adam once again looked furious, but by now Megan knew enough to realize that the anger was directed exclusively at himself. "I fell so completely for Ron's lies that he actually managed to make me feel grateful that he'd approached my bank for the loan. Your father is a highflier in the investment world and I was dumb enough to be *flattered* that he was willing to send some business my way."

Since her father's death, Megan had developed an entirely different concept of what had made him tick. Her father had liked living on the knife's edge, she'd decided. She had a suspicion he'd borrowed the three million from Adam not because he couldn't raise it anywhere else, but precisely because it was courting disaster to involve Avery's brother in a scheme where the Flying W was being offered as collateral.

"After we heard about Dad…about the fact that he'd most likely been murdered…did it occur to you that he might have needed the money for something illegal? Or at least for something that he couldn't reveal to his usual investment partners?"

"Of course it's occurred to me." Adam sounded grim.

Reluctantly, Megan gave voice to her worst nightmare. "Then you've probably also considered that my father may have spent the three million dollars before he died."

"Yeah, I surely have." Adam's voice went from grim to grimmer.

"With all the secrets Dad was hiding from us, there could be a dozen more waiting for us to uncover. Maybe he had a gambling problem. Maybe…" Megan swallowed over the constriction in her throat. "Maybe that's why he was killed. Because the money's gone."

"And he owed the wrong set of people more than he could repay?"

She nodded. "Compulsive gamblers start

out borrowing from a bank and end up borrowing from people who kill you if you miss a payment." She gave a smile that didn't quite make it. "At least, that's what happens in the movies."

Adam pulled a face. "Somehow, I can't see Ron with a gambling problem. For one thing, how the hell would he have found time to gamble? He had two wives, two families and a demanding business to run. Which he did very successfully, don't forget. We're talking about a man with zero spare time."

"That's true," Megan conceded. "But you don't have to run off to Vegas or Atlantic City to gamble these days. There's always the Internet. Or maybe he was playing the stock market and got caught short. You can lose an enormous amount of money in a very short time if you're buying shares on margin, can't you?"

"Yes, you can. But then we come right back to my original question. If Ron simply needed to pay off creditors, why wouldn't he have tapped into the profits he's generating with his legitimate business? Why involve me?"

"How would Paul have reacted to the

news that his partner had a gambling problem and needed to take cash out of the business? Not well, I bet."

"No, my brother doesn't have much sympathy for human weakness. On the other hand, Ron is the senior partner in Raven Enterprises and he's the one who generates at least two-thirds of their profits. Bottom line, if Ron wanted to take money out of the business, Paul would have no choice but to suck it up. On top of that, I'm sticking to my original point. I can't see Ron as a gambler so addicted that he's millions in debt."

"Why not? He gambled every day of his life for the past twenty-seven years," Megan said flatly. "Otherwise he'd have divorced one of his wives."

"That was a different sort of risk. He was gambling with his personal life, not with his money. Taking the risk of being a bigamist isn't the same thing as having a compulsive need to toss money into slot machines, or to play the stock market."

"The cops in Miami are convinced my father's death was premeditated," Megan reminded him. "And if it was premeditated, doesn't that make it more likely that the motive for his murder was something to do with money? Presumably money he owed to someone?"

"I'm not following your logic. Why would premeditation mean that money was the motive for his murder?"

"Because people plan murders when money is involved. That's almost always the nature of the crime. But they don't plan crimes of passion."

"Sure they do," Adam said swiftly. "All the time. Want me to run down a list of the people who've made news over the past year because they planned the murder of an unfaithful spouse? I hope you have another couple of hours to spare because that's how long it would take to go down the list."

Megan realized how much of a relief it was to talk about her father's murder with somebody who was willing to discuss the issues honestly, in all their sordid or unpleasant details. Friends and neighbors in Thatch had danced so tactfully around the subject of Ron Raven's demise that it had become excruciating to listen to their evasions. Although she could hardly blame her neighbors for cowardice, Megan reflected wryly, since she performed almost the same evasive dance with her mother.

"So you think my father was murdered by his mistress? Or an angry husband, maybe, since the blood splatters suggest there were three people in the Miami hotel room?"

Adam shook his head. "I'm not sure I have a favorite theory. I just don't think we can leap to the conclusion that Ron's death was precipitated by a dispute over money. We don't know enough about what was going on in his life to make that judgment. Who was the woman in the hotel room, for example? Was she really his mistress? Do you have any idea?"

"None." Megan made a small sound, somewhere between a sob and a laugh. "My mother refuses to accept that there even was a woman in the room with Dad. She says that the three different sets of blood samples only prove that there were other people in the room, not that one of them was a woman. And she's right, technically speaking. The crime lab will only say there's a strong likelihood one of the blood samples comes from a woman. They won't flat out confirm it. It's the media that's made

"For once, I'm fairly sure the media has it right, aren't you?"

"Why not? If you have two wives, why wouldn't you have a mistress?"

Adam's mouth turned down in a rueful grimace. "It isn't just the blood in the room, anyway. The police have confirmed finding a woman's cosmetics bag in the bathroom."

"Yes, that's what I heard, too."

"If it's any consolation, Avery is reacting much the same way as your mother. I had this surreal conversation with her a couple of days ago during which she tried to convince me that if the third person in the room was a woman, then she was probably a business acquaintance of Ron's, there for a meeting—"

"In Dad's hotel room in the middle of the night?" Megan was surprised into laughing. "Jeez, Adam, that's stretching the bounds of possibility, isn't it?"

"Of course, but I was so desperate to stop Avery crying that I actually pretended to agree with her! Besides, we're so short of hard facts, it didn't seem worth making an casual pickup? Or was she a long-time mistress?"

"In my worst nightmares, I've wondered if she was another wife," Megan admitted.

"God, I hadn't even considered that!" Adam frowned and then shook his head. "I don't think she could have been another wife for the same reason I can't believe Ron had a gambling problem. Your father was already juggling a jam-packed schedule with days in Chicago and days in Thatch, not to mention business trips to cities all over the country."

"Maybe the so-called business trips were really days he spent with another wife."

"No, that's not possible." Adam gave an adamant shake of his head. "Ron and Paul kept track of each other's business travel. Paul doesn't have a kind word to say about Ron these days, but he's certain Ron genuinely went where he said he was going, and met the businesspeople he claimed to be meeting."

"Why is your brother so convinced? Dad lied about everything else. Why not about that?"

"Because Ron brought home important deals as a consequence of those trips. He also left a voluminous paper trail. There were expense records to fill out for the IRS, with lots of hotel bills and airplane tickets and car rental receipts to be filed away by his office assistant. The records are detailed enough that they'd have been difficult to fudge."

"I'd hazard a guess that my father was really good at combining business and pleasure and fudging which was which." Surprisingly, Megan found the thought no longer produced anger, merely a sort of weary cynicism.

"Ron could have picked up casual dates when he was away on a business trip," Adam agreed. "But it would have been a different woman in every city, with no repeat visits. I'm willing to bet there was no third wife in Ron's life. Even a long-term mistress seems unlikely."

"You're right, the logistics are almost insurmountable. When you think about it logically, Dad couldn't have juggled three wives." Megan drew in an unsteady breath. "You've no idea what a relief it is to feel hopeful that there isn't another family lurking somewhere in the wings, waiting to introduce themselves."

Adam reached across the table and put his hand over hers. The touch startled her, but she didn't take her hand away.

"This has been really hard on you, hasn't it? Not just Ron's death, but discovering how badly he betrayed you."

She shrugged, looking at Adam's tanned fingers curved around hers. "I try not to feel too sorry for myself. When you get right down to it, I've lived a cushy life. I'm due a few problems that are more serious than why my boss is a major dick and why my mother acts as though it's my personal responsibility to get my brother married off to one of his dozens of girlfriends."

Adam's hand tightened briefly. "Saying you've led a cushy life is the rational response. It's got nothing to do with how you feel. And if your family is anything like ours, everyone's been so busy sympathizing with your mother that nobody's spared much energy worrying about what it feels like to be one of Ron's children. It was only a couple of days ago that I realized how torn up Kate is about Ron's endless lies to her."

"Not to mention that she just discovered she has a sister and brother she never knew about." Megan forced a smile, even though it was a bit shaky around the edges. "That takes some getting used to."

Adam's gaze sought hers and his gray eyes were suddenly warm. "Yeah, that, too. Although I think she may consider the existence of a brother and sister one of the few positives of the situation. Kate always wished she hadn't been an only child."

"*Be careful what you wish for.* I'm sure this wasn't the way Kate wanted to acquire siblings. I wonder why the old clichés always seem trite until you find yourself living one of them?"

"Because human beings don't know how to learn from other people's experiences. We have to slog through the problems ourselves before we get any wiser. Otherwise we'd be living in a better world by now, don't you think?"

She sighed. Until a couple of weeks ago, the world that cradled her had seemed mighty fine. Her last two boyfriends had been a little boring, maybe, and her asshole boss was a pain, but basically life had been enjoyable. And simple. God, she really wished she could go back to simple. Suppressing a sigh, Megan switched her gaze to the now-dark garden and took her hand away from

Adam's, partly because it felt much too good to leave it there.

"We were trying to work out whether or not the woman in my father's hotel room was a casual date or something more important," she said. "I guess we've just about proved that she was no more than a casual date. Would you agree?"

"Yes, I would."

"Then even if this murder was premeditated as far as my father is concerned, that poor woman was probably killed just because she was unlucky enough to have been in the room when the murderer arrived."

Adam nodded his agreement. "Unless the police can trace that cosmetics kit, we'll probably never know who she was."

"Meanwhile, her family must be frantic, wondering where she is and what's happened to her. Why does life have to be so cruel, I wonder?"

"If I knew the answer to that, I'd have been elected president of the world by now." Adam got up, stretched. "The whole situation is a mess and the cops in Miami don't seem to have a damn thing new to offer in terms of identifying who killed your father."

"They're working hard, I think. Maybe that's one good thing to come out of all the media attention. I heard they've put a rush on the lab work for the DNA identifications. Once those results come through, at least we'll know with a hundred percent certainty that the blood they've found in various places actually came from my father."

"I didn't know the cops had put a rush on the lab work." Adam frowned. "In fact, the cops have done a lousy job of keeping my sister informed about the investigation."

"Don't worry, they're not cutting your sister out of the loop, if that's what you're wondering. We haven't heard directly from anyone in Miami, either. Harry—the sheriff of Stark County—went to high school with my mother and they've been friends ever since. He's making it a personal mission to stay on top of the investigation."

"Does he have any other tidbits I could pass on to Avery and Kate?"

"Harry told Mom a couple of days ago that the Miami cops are satisfied the owner of the boat that was used to dispose of the…the bodies had nothing to do with the crime. The cops have also decided that the security on the marina is tight enough to be effective.

They're working on the theory that the killer may once have been employed there, otherwise he'd have had a really hard time stealing the boat without getting caught."

Adam seemed to mull over her answer for a few seconds. "How important is it to you that the cops find out who killed your father?" he asked eventually.

"I'm surprised at how important it is to me," she replied, her voice quiet. "I need the closure. And that's another one of those clichés I didn't understand before. Knowing who killed Dad won't bring him back, but I need to know. To have a name to pin onto the shadowy figure I've seen in those horrible security-camera videos."

"My sister and Kate feel the same. I hope like hell they can get the closure they want."

"It's going to be difficult, isn't it?"

"Probably." Adam leaned down and took her hands, tugging her to her feet. "Come on, we've analyzed enough for one night. Let's go out into the garden. It's cooled down now and the bugs have mostly gone to bed."

They walked into the garden, Megan acutely aware that Adam was still holding her hand. The full moon cast silver light from behind a veil of cloud, the horses had been corralled in their barn, and the night was blissfully quiet except for the intermittent hum of cicadas.

"When are you going back to Wyoming?" Adam asked, breaking a silence that Megan had found curiously restful given the rage she'd experienced at their first meeting.

"Tomorrow morning, around nine-thirty. I have to be back at work on Monday and I want to spend one more night with Mom out at the ranch."

"I'll bring some papers around to the hotel tomorrow morning before you leave. One of the accountants at the bank did some preliminary research last week in an attempt to find out what Ron did with the money we loaned him. We hit a wall after the first couple of transactions, but you might have more luck. Apart from anything else, your mother is Ron's legal wife and she can get court orders forcing banks to give her information. We weren't entitled to that, which made the investigation more difficult. Impossible, in fact."

"Thanks. I really appreciate that. Any leads you can provide will be a help, I'm sure." Megan was surprised by his offer, although on reflection she supposed it made sense from his point of view. She and Adam had different motives for needing to track the trail of the loan, but they both wanted the same end result: they wanted to find the money.

He shrugged away her thanks. "The quicker you succeed, the better for my bank. I don't know if this counts as a lead, but it's just occurred to me that finding out who Ron was meeting with for the last couple of months of his life might be a big help in discovering what he was up to and where the three million bucks might have gone."

"Great idea, except we don't even know where he really was most of the time, much less whom he was meeting!"

"But working together, we could put together a pretty accurate schedule of his movements. I could get his official business-travel schedule from Paul, and Avery ought to be able to provide a rough estimate of the nights he spent with her in Chicago. You could work with your mother to pin down the dates he was in Wyoming. Once we coordinate those three schedules, who knows what interesting information might turn up."

"That's a great idea." She shook her head.

"Isn't it amazing that neither family really had any idea where Dad was for more than half the year?"

"Yes, it's amazing. But remember, his deceptions only worked because nobody was checking up on him. That's changed."

"And how!"

His smile echoed her own bitter amusement. "Between the two of us, with help from our families, we should at least be able to identify the days when nobody seems to have known where Ron was."

"We need to develop an itinerary for him that stretches back two years," Megan pointed out. "That's when he came to you for the loan, after all. I'll ask my mother if she can think of anything that was going on back then that might have caused Dad to need millions of dollars. You should check with your sister, too."

"Excellent point. Whatever he needed the money for, the need stretched back two years. And the fact that he was murdered suggests the situation has grown worse since then."

"You think he was involved in something illegal, don't you?"

Adam looked down at her and whatever

he'd planned to say, he didn't. The moonlit space between them filled with a tension that pulsed with silent energy and the hard angles of his face suddenly looked even more taut and sharply defined. For a few incredible seconds, she had the impression that he was going to kiss her. For an even more incredible moment, she had the impression that if he did, she would kiss him right back.

Then Adam looked away and the space between them was just space instead of a danger zone of electric charges.

"I'm a banker," he said, belatedly responding to her question. "Where money is concerned, I tend to take a cynical view of human nature."

In other words, Adam believed her father had been involved with something criminal. Megan wished with all her heart that she wasn't becoming more and more convinced that Adam was precisely right.

Eleven

Megan had barely stepped inside the front door of the ranch house when her mother hurried into the hall to greet her. They both automatically stepped around the bounding, tail-thumping dogs to hug each other.

"Harry's here," Ellie said, her slightly plump body feeling stiff with tension. "He's brought news about Ron. You need to hear what he has to say." She abruptly turned and walked through to the kitchen, dogs sliding after her on the polished wooden floor.

The sheriff was seated at the table by the big bay window. He rose to his feet as Megan entered the room, smoothing the string tie that formed part of his uniform. An official visit, then.

"Hey, Megan, honey. Did you have a good flight? Your mother tells me the Fairfaxes have agreed not to call the loan for a month or two. That's real good news. For a while there, I was afraid your mom was going to lose her home."

"Me, too. Adam Fairfax was more willing to help than I expected, thank goodness." Megan was a little surprised that her mother had been so honest about Ron's financial dealings and the purpose of her trip to Georgia. Still, it could only be beneficial if Ellie had found someone to confide in, especially Harry, who'd been a friend for so many years. In the wake of the revelations about her father, Megan's trust meter hovered close to zero, but if anyone in the world was as honest and aboveboard as he seemed, surely that person had to be Harry Ford.

She searched the sheriff's sun-wrinkled features, relieved to detect no sign that he was the bearer of worse tidings than usual. "Mom says you have news about Dad. What's up, Harry?"

"We have a real break in the case. Remember the blood samples the Miami police found in the hotel room and in your father's rental car? And remember I took swabs from you and Liam to send to Florida so that the crime lab down there could make a DNA match?"

"Of course I remember." Megan's heart was racing and she tamped down the urge to snap. Harry was never good at getting to the point and tonight he seemed more frustratingly slow than usual. Or maybe she was just feeling extra impatient.

"The police in Florida have gotten back the DNA results." Harry switched into official sheriff mode. "I'm sorry to have to report that the lab has confirmed one set of blood samples definitely came from Ronald Howatch Raven, your father." He patted her arm, transforming back into Harry, family friend. "I guess that's pretty much what we all expected, but I know hearing the official pronouncement is never easy."

So many revelations had poured in concerning her father over the past couple of weeks that Megan was caught off guard by the shockwave of renewed grief that flooded through her. In the absence of her father's body, it seemed that some tiny part of her had been nursing the hope that it was all a terrible mistake and that some other unfortunate person had died in the hotel room. Now she had to accept there was no wiggle room for denial. She glanced toward her mother, wondering if Ellie had harbored any similar vain hopes, but her mother was preoccupied with making a pot of tea, her constant refuge in times of stress, and she didn't look up.

The sheriff gave Megan's hand a comforting squeeze. "I know it's tough, honey, but there's more to tell you. The big news from the lab is that they've given us a name to go with one of the other blood samples—"

"They've identified the woman?"

"Nope. The man. The suspected perp. The lab says that the single smear of blood the cops found near the bathroom door came from a man called Julio Castellano."

"I can't believe we have a name for the murderer. How on earth did the cops manage to identify him so quickly?"

Ellie grabbed the kettle as it started to whistle. "They had this man's DNA records in their database because he's served time for manslaughter," she said.

Megan shot another glance toward her mother. "Oh my God! He's already killed somebody else?"

"Two somebodies, apparently." Ellie's forehead wrinkled more in puzzlement than alarm. “Harry tells me there’s a note in this Julio person’s file that he doesn’t speak English.” She raised her shoulders in a bewildered shrug. “Julio doesn’t speak English. Ron doesn’t speak Spanish. What dealings could the two of them have had? It makes no sense.”

“Castellano got out of prison eighteen months ago.” Harry firmly maneuvered the conversation back to what was known rather than what was still a mystery. “The cops down in Miami are practically dancing the macarena at having found a DNA match. They think there’s a darn good chance Castellano is the guy who killed your father and his…um…female companion. Seems to me they’re right. Have to admit, the Florida cops did good work. It ain’t too shabby to have a likely name for the killer this early.”

“Have the police arrested Castellano?” Megan asked, scratching Belle’s head in an effort to persuade her to sit still.

“ ’Fraid not. But there’s a warrant out for his arrest and they’re looking for him real hard.”

“Do they have any clue where to look?”

“Not much, to be honest.” Harry lost his cheerful expression for a moment.

Megan felt chilled, perhaps because the kitchen was cool after the humid warmth of Georgia. She walked over to the stove and poured herself a cup of the hot tea her mother had just made. She held up the pot in a silent question to Harry, but he shook his head.

"Castellano wasn't on parole, then?" she asked.

"No, he was an illegal, so he was shipped back to Mexico right after he got out of prison. To Guadalajara, in fact. That's where the Florida authorities assumed he still was. Given that he left his blood in your dad's hotel room, it seems safe to conclude he's crossed the border and returned to the States."

"Using false documentation?" Megan realized her legs were shaking and she pulled out a chair to sit down. There was no logical reason why hearing the name of her father's murderer should have such an impact, but she felt as if she'd been pummeled by hard fists aiming straight for her belly.

"Most likely." Harry scowled. "Don't get me started on the subject of our borders. Otherwise known as the place where citizens get held up for hours, and illegals get through with no difficulty." He drew in a deep breath. "Anyway, the cops faxed me a copy of Castellano's mug shots. I was showing your mother the guy's pictures when you arrived home."

He turned the folder on the table around and Megan looked down at the image of a stocky, dark-haired Hispanic man with a drooping mustache and tired, angry eyes.

"Is the picture all the cops have to go on to locate him?" she asked. "Do they know who he hangs out with, if he has a job, any of that stuff?"

"They're working on that. Unfortunately, their leads date from the prior arrest and are ten years old. Plus, the guy probably learned a lot in prison about how to buy himself a nice set of false immigration papers. I don't suppose he's using the name Julio Castellano, so it's likely to take a while to track him down. Still, there's no denying that having an ID is a huge step forward."

Megan stared at the mug shot, seeking enlightenment that didn't come. "Like Mom said, why in the world would this guy want to kill my father? What's the cops' theory about his motive?"

Harry hesitated for a moment. "Well, cops

don't always look for a motive, you know. There're lots of sociopaths out there who kill for reasons the rest of us would find downright crazy. Discovering his name doesn't tell us much about his motive."

"Castellano's previous conviction was for a bar fight," Ellie said. "He got into an argument, ended up stabbing the man, and the man died."

Harry nodded an endorsement of Ellie's statement. "Castellano claimed self-defense, but he'd already killed another man and narrowly avoided jail, so this time the prosecutors were anxious to get him behind bars. He copped a plea and served a few years. Seven, I think. Obviously not near long enough." The sheriff's mouth turned down. "It's possible that Castellano had some reason to be real angry with your dad. The wrecked hotel room looks like the sort of thing he might do if he lost his temper. And we know that when this guy gets angry, he kills people. Could be that's what happened."

Megan tried to imagine what argument might have arisen between her father and an ex-convict...a two-time killer who'd entered the country illegally and who shared no language in common with his victim. Her imagination wasn't up to the task.

"It seems more likely to me that Julio Castellano had no personal grudge against my father," she said, pushing the mug shot away. The man's angry gaze was beginning to haunt her. "Have the police in Miami considered the possibility that somebody paid him to kill my father?"

"You're a step ahead of me," Harry said. "In fact, that's the theory the cops are working on right now. They're assuming that Castellano was recruited as a killer-for-hire."

"The cops have already released Castellano's name and arrest record to the press." Ellie gave a hard laugh, the harsh sound so unusual for her mother that Megan winced at the pain it revealed. "How much do you bet the media morons are right now gearing up to inform the world that I discovered Ron had been two-timing me for twenty-seven years so I hired Castellano to blow my adulterous husband to kingdom come?"

Megan exchanged a horrified glance with the sheriff. In view of the missing three million dollars, she had been thinking along the lines of a shady deal gone bad, and an angry business partner hiring Castellano to wipe out a business rival. She certainly hadn't intended to suggest that the cops should move her mother to the head of the suspect list.

"The cops can't be crazy enough to suspect Mom, can they?" She directed a silent plea for reassurance toward the sheriff. "How in the world do they think Mom would make contact with a convicted killer who's an illegal immigrant living three thousand miles from here?"

"The Miami police don't suspect your mother of having anything to do with Ron's death," Harry said quickly. "To be honest, they don't suspect Avery Fairfax, either. Look, if they had the slightest suspicion Ellie was involved, they'd have sent one of their detectives out here to interview her."

"As if that's going to stop the media from speculating." Ellie's voice was acid. "In fact, it will provide the media with an excuse to blame the cops. They'll have me tried and convicted on half a dozen TV channels before the night is out."

"And Avery will be convicted on half a dozen more," Megan pointed out. "I guess it's some consolation that the media tend to be equal-opportunity slanderers."

"The speculation will only last until the cops locate Castellano," Harry said. "Then the accusations will stop because we'll know the truth."

"Assuming Castellano is willing to talk," Ellie said.

"Trust me, that won't be a problem." Harry rocked back in his chair, balancing on the two rear legs. "You mark my words, Castellano will be falling over himself to save his hide by selling out whomever hired him."

"And how long before the Miami cops manage to find Castellano?"

"Could be real soon." Honesty compelled Harry to modify his optimism. "Worst case, it could be a month or two."

Or three or four, Megan thought gloomily.

Ellie gave an inelegant snort. "It's all very well for you, Harry. But you try living as an accused murderer for *only* a month or two. I'm here to tell you this fifteen-minutes-of-fame business is no fun. Anyone who wants my remaining minutes, they're welcome."

"There's a good side to all the media coverage." Harry took Ellie's hand and absently brushed his thumb over her knuckles. "All that publicity keeps a fire lit under the tails of the Miami cops. They're gonna be working real hard to find Castellano or they're gonna look real stupid on national TV."

Megan was relieved that her mother seemed focused on the likely irritation of a fresh burst of media attention rather than on the grisly details of Ron's murder and Julio Castellano's brutal past. For her own part, the new information raised more questions than it answered. If Castellano had been a gun for hire, he seemed to have been less than competent at his job. Once he'd gained access to her father's hotel room—surely the most difficult part of his assignment, given the heightened security these days—why hadn't he killed Ron while he slept? Why had there been so many signs of a struggle and so much splattered blood, including his own? Unless, of course, Julio had expected to find her father alone and asleep, but instead had found him awake and having sex with the unknown woman.

That seemed a likely explanation, although Megan squirmed at the mental images it evoked. She wanted to ask Harry why a killer who had been efficient enough to remove two dead bodies from a hotel room and toss them deep into the Atlantic Ocean without a single person noticing him had been too dumb to spray Clorox on the one and only smear of blood that could identify him, but she was afraid that might be too upsetting a question for her mother to hear.

The phone rang while she was still debating. Ellie, in another hopeful sign that she was starting to pick up the pieces of her life, squinted at the caller ID and gave Megan a faintly baffled look. “It says Adam Fairfax. Do you want me to answer?”

“I’ll get it. Thanks.” Megan realized that her voice sounded breathless. She decided that must be because she was hurrying to take the receiver from her mother and dodging Belle and Bruno who, judging by their rush to the phone, labored under the delusion that the call was for them.

“Hello.”

“Megan? Hey, I’m glad I reached you.”

“Hi, Adam.” A swarm of butterflies took up residence in her stomach, possibly because Harry and her mother were both staring at her as if she were talking to a certified alien life-form.

“Did you have a good journey home?” Adam asked.

"Uneventful, at least. I just arrived at the ranch a few minutes ago." Trying for a relaxed smile, probably without much success, she gave her mother and the sheriff a casual wave, edging out into the hallway in search of privacy.

"I wouldn't have called so soon after your return, but I wanted to give you a heads-up," Adam said. "Did you hear that the police in Miami have the results back from the DNA testing? They have a name to go with one of the blood spots they found in Ron's hotel room."

"Yes, I just heard. The sheriff is here right now. He was explaining that the cops identified the blood as belonging to an ex-con, an illegal immigrant named Julio Castellano. I guess my mother and I are both relieved that the cops seem to be making progress in identifying Dad's killer."

"Avery would be relieved, too, except a reporter called—on her new and supposedly unlisted phone—and told her the cops suspect her of hiring Castellano," Adam said flatly. "According to the reporters, she's officially suspect number one. I guess that means your mother is suspect number two."

Megan rubbed her forehead. "Oh, no!"

"Unfortunately, oh, yes. Avery has always been prominent on the Chicago social circuit and I guess that makes her a hot media target. It's so much more fun to smear dirt if they can make it stick to somebody whose reputation has always been impeccable."

"Which reporter called your sister?"

"Doug Deerwent from *Crime Search.* They're devoting another entire prime-time hour to the case tomorrow night."

Megan's stomach sank. The last thing her mother needed right now was a renewed bout of rabid media attention. "I wish we could find a way to stop the talk-show speculation, but my brother says it would be almost impossible to win a slander case."

"Our lawyers say the same thing. But Paul is livid, and this time he isn't willing to sit back and do nothing. He's hired a media-savvy criminal defense lawyer specifically to make the rounds of the talk shows and defend Avery. You might want to consider doing the same for your mother."

"I'll suggest it to Liam. It sounds like a very good idea." Megan sat down in the nearest chair. "I thought Mom was being morbid when she warned me that reporters were going to have a field day accusing her of hiring Castellano to murder my father."

"Not morbid at all. I'd say admirably realistic. I called Miami and spoke to Carlos Jones—"

"That's the senior detective in charge of the case, isn't it?"

"Yeah, that's the guy. Jones assured me he doesn't suspect either my sister or your mother of being involved in Ron's murder, but I'm not sure I believe him. He sounded uptight and embarrassed, so my guess is that he planted this theory with various media outlets to see if it can get any traction."

Megan's stomach gave another sickly churn. They'd only just rid themselves of the reporters who'd swarmed over the ranch in the immediate aftermath of her father's death. It would be torment for her mother if the media circus started up again after barely seventy-two hours of peace.

"I'll let Harry—the sheriff—know what you've told me, and I'll ask him to check with the Miami cops right away. Harry certainly didn't pick up on any hint that they suspect either Avery or my mother of being involved in my father's death. The opposite, in fact. But Detective Jones must know by now that Harry is our friend as well as the local sheriff. Perhaps the Miami cops aren't being as open with him as we'd assumed."

"I'd work on that premise if I were you."

"Yes, it sounds like we should. Anyway, I really appreciate the warning, Adam."

"You're welcome." His voice softened. "Sorry to dump this on you the minute you get home."

"Way better for you to dump it than for Mom to be left unprepared for a renewed attack of the media ghouls."

Adam's deep voice roughened with frustration. "I wish we could point the Miami cops away from my sister and your mother in terms of who had a motive to kill your father."

"I'm ready to point. Man, I'm ready. Unfortunately, I haven't a clue where to point them."

"We could tell them about the missing money. That might give Jones and his partners something to think about beyond angry wives. Would you mind if I told him about the loan and the fact that Ron lied about how he planned to use it?"

"Please, go ahead." She was gratified that he'd even asked her permission. "I'd much prefer to have the cops wondering if my father skipped out on a bank loan than wondering if my mother hired someone to kill her husband. But do you think three million bucks is enough to catch the attention of a big-city detective like Jones? Aren't the criminals and cops in Miami swimming around in multimillion-dollar drug deals?"

Adam gave a rueful laugh. "Hey, you're talking to a man who runs a family bank in a small town in rural Georgia. We get excited about three thousand dollars, let alone three million. But based on such highly reliable sources as TV and the movies, it's my understanding that cops are taught to follow the money."

"Maybe Detective Jones will do us all a favor and find the missing three million for us."

"We can hope. In the meantime, the two of us pooling our information still strikes me as the most likely way to unravel any trail Ron might have left. Once we know where he went and whom he met for the past couple of years, we'll be on our way to discovering why he needed the money. Then we might have a really valuable lead to hand over to Detective Jones."

Finding out the truth about her father's

schedule was definitely a starting point, Megan thought. Her father would surely have assumed that if his two wives and their families ever found out about each other they would retreat into immediate mutual hostility. Her cooperation with Adam might be the one tool strong enough—or unexpected enough—to crack the secrecy shrouding the reality of Ron's life.

"I'll talk to Mom tonight and we'll flesh out a schedule that shows every day my father was in Wyoming for as far back as she can remember."

"And I'll do the same with Avery and Paul. If we get lucky, Ron will have made some elementary mistake such as using the regular Raven Enterprises travel agent to book a plane ticket to one of his secret destinations. And then we'll have him."

"I don't think we'll get that lucky." Megan glanced over at the photo of her father in his air force pilot's uniform that rested in a place of honor on the living-room mantelpiece. Conflicting waves of love, pride and rage swept through her in a rhythm that had become depressingly familiar over the past couple of weeks. "I can't imagine that a man who was careful enough to carry duplicate sets of every document, credit card and family photo is going to slip up and do something as careless as using his company travel agent to book a flight to a destination he wanted to keep secret. It's so easy to get online these days and book a flight directly with the airline. Why would my father use *any* travel agent for business he wanted to keep private?"

"I'm afraid you're right," Adam said. "Tell me, did your father have an office at the ranch? Is there a computer you can check out?"

"We have a room here that Dad used as his office, but there's no desktop computer in there. He brought a laptop with him whenever he came to the ranch."

"Ron always brought a laptop when he came here, too," Adam said. "He joked it was his security blanket."

Megan winced. "That's another one of those statements that takes on a whole new significance with the advantage of hindsight."

"Yeah, well, hindsight is making me wonder where Ron's laptop is right now. It seems likely to be the only place where the two halves of his life were allowed to come into contact with each other. Finding it would be a big help."

Megan frowned, visualizing her father's office. "The laptop's not here, I'm sure. But then, it wouldn't be. Dad would have taken it with him to Miami." She walked down the hallway as she spoke, so that she could confirm her memory of the empty desktop surface in her father's office.

"The police mentioned finding duplicate sets of everything, including BlackBerries, in Ron's hotel room," Adam said. "But they didn't mention finding his laptop. I never picked up on the omission before."

Megan's heartbeat quickened. "You're right, the cops never mentioned word one about a laptop. And I've just checked out Dad's office. The laptop definitely isn't here."

"I guess the police assumed that with two BlackBerries in his baggage, Ron wouldn't have needed to travel with a laptop. But based on his past behavior, we'd both say they're wrong. He almost certainly had his laptop with him, so where is it?"

Megan was silent for a moment. "The killer took it?"

"That would make sense," Adam conceded. "Especially if the killer had reason to believe there was information on the laptop that it would be better the cops didn't find."

Megan sat down at her father's desk and thought about the pictures of Julio Castellano with his drooping mustache and angry eyes. "It seems likely that Castellano was capable of wrapping up two dead bodies and transporting them with nobody any the wiser. If he could do that, for sure he could slip a five-pound laptop into one of the body bags and smuggle it out of the hotel."

"The interesting question is why he would go to the trouble when he didn't steal anything else. Did Castellano know enough about your father to realize the laptop was likely to be important?"

"Maybe. More likely he took the laptop because it was in plain sight, whereas all Dad's documents, plus the two cell phones and the BlackBerries, were in the wall safe. Castellano might not have realized the safe existed, much less that it was stuffed with Dad's valuables."

"Could be. And I suppose it's just possible that Ron didn't have his laptop with him in Miami. I'll call my brother right now and see if it's in Chicago."

There seemed almost no chance her

father would have conveniently left his laptop behind in Chicago. That would be too easy, Megan thought bitterly. Too much like a normally careless human being and not like the calculating deceiver she now knew her father to have been. She drew in a deep breath and pulled another layer of protective anger over the wound of her father's lies.

"I think we can safely assume Dad's laptop is at the bottom of the Atlantic Ocean. Or tucked away in Castellano's hidey-hole."

"Yeah. Which leaves us with no choice but to reconstruct Ron's schedule the hard way. Day by day, trip by trip."

"'Fraid so. I'll get back to you before the weekend with anything I've been able to find out from Mom."

"I'll look forward to hearing from you."

He sounded as if he meant it, and an unintended softness crept into Megan's voice. "Thanks again for calling, Adam. I really appreciate the warning about the renewed media interest."

"Don't hang up," he said. "Something's bothering you. What is it?"

Megan was caught off guard by the question. Her mother and brother not only exercised rigid control over their own emotions, they tended to deal with other people's feelings by politely ignoring them whenever possible. It was astonishing that Adam, who had appeared to be coldness and rage personified at their first meeting, should prove so sensitive to her subtle changes of mood that he could even detect them at long distance.

Her first instinct was to respond with a polite evasion, but she realized she was tired of considering everyone's feelings except her own. She wanted to tell him the truth. With a lot less crispness than she would have liked, she explained the difficulty she had experienced reconfiguring her memories of her father to conform to the startling new facts about his life.

"For some reason, talking about Dad and his laptop forcefully reminded me that I spent the last twenty-seven years living with an illusion. I know it's crazy to get upset about a missing laptop, but my grief meter must be off center, because for the past two weeks it invariably seems to be the weird little things that upset me the most."

"That might be because you can wrap your mind around the little things, whereas the big things still feel as if they're happening to somebody else." Adam's voice wasn't noticeably warm and yet she sensed his sympathy. "I guess we cope with grief and loss by reacting to the little things until we're healed enough to tackle the big picture." He gave a wry laugh. "And that makes me sound like the pitch person for a very expensive and entirely useless therapy program."

"No, it doesn't." For once Megan didn't attempt to censor her instinctive reaction. "It makes you sound like a friend and I'm grateful. Thank you, Adam."

Twelve

The first time Adam ever noticed what Avery was wearing had been on the day of her wedding to Ron Raven. He had been almost ten at the time. Too old, thank God, for the ultimate humiliation of being roped in as a frilled-shirt ring bearer, but young enough to be blown away by the realization that his big sister was stunningly beautiful.

From that day onward, Adam could never remember seeing Avery look less than elegant. Today was no exception. His sister looked chic and dignified in dove-gray linen; she also looked tired and sad. It was clearly a major effort for her to pretend interest in the schedule Adam was trying to construct of her dead husband's final few months of life.

The third time she glanced at her watch in the space of ten minutes, Adam reached out and wrapped his fingers around her wrist, covering the watch face. “What’s up, Ree?” he asked, using the nickname left over from babyhood, when he hadn’t been able to pronounce her name. “Who are you expecting to arrive, or call, or whatever?”

“No one.” Avery’s smile drooped a little at the corners. “I don’t get phone calls or visitors these days, except for Kate. And occasionally Paul, when he’s not swamped trying to straighten out the chaos Ron left behind.”

“Hey, I’m here. Don’t I count as a visitor?”

Her smile warmed a little. “Yes, you do. Very much so, and I’m grateful for the company. It’s good to see you, Adam, really. I apologize for being such a wet blanket.”

“Except that I only came to Chicago when I needed your help in reconstructing Ron’s schedule.” Adam’s hand tightened around his sister’s. “I’m sorry, Ree. I should have made the trip a lot sooner, but I knew Mom and Dad had been here and I assumed you might be grateful for some breathing room without family members hanging around. The Fairfaxes en masse can be a bit much. But I shouldn’t have assumed you needed time alone. I should have asked.”

“Don’t beat up on yourself. You have a

bank to run and anyway, what could you have said or done in person that you didn't already say over the phone? The facts are what they are. Ron was a cheat and I was a fool. What can anyone do about that?"

"What I'm doing now. Hold your hand, offer hugs if you want them and remind you that being trusting isn't the same thing as being foolish."

She pulled a face. "Unfortunately, from where I'm sitting, the results appear to be the same."

Adam brushed his thumb across the pulse beating in her wrist. "Everything will work out, Ree. It will, you know."

"Oh, yes, I'm bursting with confidence about the future." Avery's voice was dark with self-mockery.

"You're smart, attractive and still young by today's standards." The simple truth, but Adam hoped his optimism didn't sound as fake to his sister as it did to him. "I'm betting you'll be surprised. Before too long things will be better than they were before."

"That I believe." Avery flashed a mordant smile. "Chiefly because I can't imagine how they could be much worse. Surely even I couldn't manage to get involved in another relationship as ridiculously phony as my so-called marriage to Ron."

"Not everything about your marriage was phony. I'm sure Ron loved you."

"Of course he did. Deeply and faithfully." Avery's voice dripped sarcasm. "It's the honesty of our marriage that I'm always going to treasure in my memories."

Much as he despised Ron, Adam had an unpleasant suspicion that plenty of legal marriages involved almost as much deception and a lot less happiness. Avery had a firsthand example of that, since their parents had stayed together for fifty-five years united, as far as Adam could tell, only by their shared prejudices and a weary reluctance to face the prospect of change.

"I think Ron really loved you," he persisted, restating Megan's theory. "Otherwise why would he have bothered to keep up the pretense of a bigamous marriage for twenty-seven years?"

"Habit strikes me as the most likely explanation."

"Or the fact that he very much wanted to be with you."

"With me, and apparently also with Ellie. I just can't get over the image of Ron leaving her bed in the morning and tucking himself into mine that same night. Not just once or twice, but routinely, week after week, year after year." Avery sounded more tired than anything else. She drew in a shaky breath, visibly struggling to overcome her depression. "Anyway, that part of my life is over and there's no point in endless rehashing. We'll never know why Ron did what he did, so there's not much point in speculating. What I need right now is to move on with my life. I've decided that I ought to find a job, and not just for the money. I need the focus. Not to mention a distraction from my self-pity."

"Getting a job sounds like a great idea, and it's an area where Paul should be able to help. He has contacts all over Chicago's business community."

"Even with Paul's help it's going to be tough. Tell me, Adam, what career opportunities do you see out there for a fifty-year-old woman whose major qualification is a degree in art history, followed by twenty-seven years of blind stupidity? Oh, and don't forget the résumé-enhancing fact that half my prospective employers probably think I'm guilty of murder."

Adam hoped to God she wasn't right about that, but feared she was. "That sort of crazy suspicion will blow over very soon. A hundred percent of the media and most of the public will have forgotten your name two days after the cops find Julio Castellano and arrest him for Ron's murder."

"God, I so hope you're right." Avery echoed his earlier thought. She pushed away from the small table where they were sitting with calendars and date books fanned out across most of the surface. "I'm sorry to sound so defeatist, Adam. You caught me on a particularly bad day. Usually I don't wallow quite this deeply in my own misery."

"You're entitled. It's less than a month since your whole life was turned upside down."

"Is that all? It feels more like half a lifetime." Avery blew her nose, trying to conceal that she was about to cry. It hurt Adam to see the effort it took for his sister to shake off her gloom. Ron Raven didn't know how lucky he was to be dead, he reflected. Jesus, he wished he could get his hands on the guy just one more time! After that, Ron wouldn't be entertaining one wife, let alone two, because he'd be missing functioning balls. Not to mention his front teeth.

Avery managed to banish her budding tears and gave him a smile that damn near broke his heart. "Thanks for being so patient, Adam. I guess I needed to let off steam more than I realized. I envy Ellie, you know. When she came here, she seemed so…resilient. So…strong. She's running an entire cattle ranch and has been for years. What have I done except look decorative at charity balls?" Avery lapsed into silence, staring at the papers spread out across the table without giving any indication that she actually saw them.

They still had a fair bit of work to do if they were going to build a clear picture of Ron's schedule during the last month of his life. Adam knew why his sister was finding the task of clarifying Ron's schedule so depressing. God knew, it depressed him to document his brother-in-law's myriad deceptions and he had never loved the guy. For Avery, it must be torture to see black-and-white evidence that her marriage had been nothing but a lie-encrusted sham.

Maybe he should ask Avery to open a bottle of wine. A glass of her favorite Chardonnay might take the rough edges off the pain she was feeling. On the other hand, he didn't want to encourage her to start drowning her troubles in a bottle. It was symptomatic of the mess Ron had left behind, Adam reflected wryly, that he was actually sitting here debating the pros and cons of something as simple as asking his sister to share a glass of wine.

His cell phone rang before he'd reached a decision. The caller ID showed a number in Jackson Hole. Megan! It had to be her, since nobody else in Wyoming knew his cell number. Adam's spirits lifted. He felt a flash of excitement, immediately doused by embarrassment. He must be in more trouble than he'd realized to be this pleased about getting a phone call from Megan. And he'd already suspected he was in pretty big trouble where she was concerned.

With a murmured apology to Avery, he flipped the phone open and spoke with deliberate coolness. "Hello. This is Adam."

"Hey, Adam! I'm so glad I reached you. I was expecting the dreaded voice mail." Megan's voice vibrated with energy and friendliness. The formality of his greeting had clearly been lost on her. Or maybe she just assumed he always sounded like a pompous dick and simply ignored it. He had a sudden vivid recollection of her standing in his office the previous week, her eyes sparkling and her whole body pulsing with suppressed anger. And why in hell he found that image arousing, he couldn't imagine. What had happened to his lifelong preference for ice princesses who were guaranteed never to burden him with either their exuberance or their messy emotions?

"I have news. At least, I think I have news." Megan laughed. "I was so excited when I found the file folder that I've leaped to about a hundred conclusions already. Probably ninety-nine of them aren't justified, but I really believe I'm on to something."

Adam made an apologetic face to his sister and walked over to the window, pretending to admire the lake view as an excuse to buy himself some privacy. Not because he didn't want Avery to hear about the investigation into Ron's past, but because he didn't want her to watch him make a horse's ass of himself over Megan. All Avery needed at this point was to learn that her younger brother was on the verge of launching a serious campaign to get Ron Raven's daughter into his bed and she'd totally lose it. And Avery was far from being the only problem in contemplating a sexual relationship between a Fairfax and a Raven. The news that the two of them had become lovers would be greeted by both families with about as much enthusiasm as an alligator at a beach picnic.

"You found a file folder containing some of your father's private papers?" he asked, forcing his attention back to the purpose of Megan's call.

"Yes. I finished reading through the contents just a few minutes ago." Megan's voice was so vibrant he could almost see her head nodding and her curls bouncing.

"Today was the first chance I'd had to get back out to the ranch and I decided to search Dad's home office from top to bottom. I figured maybe I'd get really lucky and find a safe hidden behind a picture, or a false shelf tucked into the bookcase. In my wildest flights of fancy, I hoped I might come across a concealed walk-in closet built into the wall and stuffed to the brim with millions of dollars. Or, at the very least, a journal recording all Dad's darkest secrets for the past thirty years."

"And did you? I especially like the idea of finding millions of dollars, by the way."

Her laughter turned rueful. "I didn't find even a small secret drawer in Dad's desk, much less a closetful of money, but I'm almost sure I've found the information about his travel schedule that we were looking for." Megan's voice lilted with satisfaction. "After I'd wasted far too much time tapping on wood panels and crawling around in search of loose floorboards, I realized if there's one thing we've learned about my father since he died, it's that he's a master of hiding his secrets in plain sight. It dawned on me that anything he wanted to hide was going to be stuffed into the regular file cabinet, right next to the phone bills and the warranty for the new dishwasher and all the other routine household papers."

That made perfect sense, Adam reflected. Slipping a few extra papers in amongst the household bills was the sort of gamble Ron had loved to take, and that neither family ever suspected the existence of the other proved that his gamble had paid off, until murder intervened and upset all his careful planning.

"So what did you find tucked in Ron's file cabinet?" Adam asked.

"A set of travel documents." Megan sounded pleased with herself. "The record shows Dad took a trip two years ago that fits perfectly with the dates we're interested in. He flew to Mexico City from Chicago on the morning of May 4. He returned to the States on May 8. A couple of days later, he was hitting you up for a loan. What's more, Dad paid another five visits to Mexico since then. This last trip, when he was killed, would have made the seventh. That's seven trips in barely two years. Every three months or so, despite his jam-packed schedule, Dad was flying off to Mexico. Put those trips together with the fact that he was murdered by a Mexican, when he was en route to Mexico City, and I'd say we've found a trail that could easily lead to the missing money."

"It's a starting point, that's for sure." Adam forced himself to react cautiously and not to add two and two into five. "Did your mother know Ron was making so many trips to Mexico?"

"She had no idea Dad had left the country anytime during the past two years, at least until this final trip. Neither did I. What's more, on two occasions when Dad was in Mexico City, he told my mother he was in Chicago. The other times she has no record of where he told her he was going. But that's not surprising. She didn't always have a reason to keep a note about where Dad was supposed to be."

"What about your father's schedule in the couple of weeks prior to his first trip to Mexico? Was anything unusual going on then as far as you can tell? Did Ron stay away from the ranch more than usual in April, for example?"

"The opposite," Megan admitted. "My uncle Ted paid us a visit in April two years ago and my father spent eight days at the ranch toward the end of the month, catching up on old times. As you can imagine, Dad didn't often spend that long in Wyoming at one stretch."

"Good God, I didn't realize your father had a brother—"

"No, no, he doesn't. Dad's an only child. Uncle Ted isn't Dad's brother. He's my mother's older brother. Uncle Ted is an engineer and he's worked overseas for years, so it's not as if he and my dad are close buddies. But they were in school together, so the two of them have known each other since they were little kids."

No wonder Ron had complained of feeling tired when he came to Fairfax to sign off on the loan agreement, Adam reflected. For several weeks preceding their meeting, Ron must have been juggling balls even harder and faster than usual in order to keep his two families ignorant of each other's existence. "With your uncle in town, I guess your father had no choice other than to clear his schedule and spend time in Wyoming, whatever irons he might have had heating in the fire somewhere else."

"Absolutely," Megan agreed. "If he'd blown off Uncle Ted, it would have seemed really odd as well as rude. And we've seen over and over again that Dad never did anything that might cause people to become suspicious. In fact, virtually everyone in Thatch paid a visit to the ranch while Uncle Ted was staying here. For an entire two weeks, we never sat down to dinner without half a dozen extra people at the table, all reminiscing about the good old days. And I'm here to tell you, some of those stories get mighty boring around the tenth time you listen to them!"

"It sounds as if Thatch is a lot like Fairfax," Adam said, smiling. "Until the recent wave of new building on the west side, everybody in town not only knew everybody else, their parents and grandparents all knew each other, too. It's great in some ways, and other times it can be a major pain in the ass. I've had to work really hard to keep at least a few areas of my life out of the gossip pool."

"That's exactly how I feel about Thatch." Megan gave a rueful laugh. "Depending on the day and my mood, the forced intimacy is either great or the pits. And I'm living a hundred miles away most of the time! I don't believe I could stand the feeling of being in a fishbowl on a full-time basis. Anyway, to get back to Dad's schedule, even though he was at the ranch more than usual at the end of April, there were still plenty of days earlier in the month when he was out of town. Uncle Ted's visit wouldn't have prevented him from conducting whatever business caused him to travel to Mexico."

"And Ron's initial arrangements with his contact in Mexico could have been made by phone, so he wouldn't need to leave the ranch. Or they could have been made in March, before your uncle arrived in Wyoming.

For that matter, they could have been made a year earlier. We have no clue what those arrangements were, so it's impossible to establish parameters."

"That's true." Megan sounded deflated, then perked up again. Adam had the impression that she was a person whose energy level was so high that discouragement had a hard time finding its way through her defenses.

"The important thing for us is to confirm that Dad lied to *everyone* about where he was going during those Mexico trips," she said. "That has to be our starting point. Mom has already confirmed that my father lied to her. Can you check with your brother and sister to find out where they thought Dad was in early May, two years ago? We know my father usually told at least one set of family members the truth about where he planned to be. If he lied to Paul and to Avery, as well as to Mom, that means he was determined to keep his Mexico trips secret from everyone."

"I can give you the answer a lot sooner than you would expect. I'm actually with my sister in Chicago right now. If you give me the dates of those trips to Mexico again, I can check right away."

"Oh gosh, I'm sorry to have interrupted your visit. I assumed you were in Georgia. I should have asked if this was a convenient moment for you to talk."

"If it hadn't been convenient, I'd have told you. You're not interrupting anything, I promise." Adam finally turned around from the picture window and saw that he was speaking the truth. Megan wasn't interrupting anything, because Avery had given up on waiting for him. Now that he was paying attention, the sounds filtering through from the kitchen suggested his sister was making preparations for dinner. Relieved to have a few more minutes of privacy, he took down the dates Megan reeled off and flicked quickly through the stacks of paper scattered over the table, searching for Ron's schedule for the beginning of May, two years earlier.

"It looks as if your father told both Paul and Avery that he was going to be in Boca Raton on the night of May 3," Adam said when he located the appropriate itinerary. "According to Paul's notes, Ron flew to Boca Raton and stayed there five days. He was supposedly deciding whether to buy a small beachfront hotel and convert it into luxury condos."

"Boca Raton isn't far from Miami airport," Megan pointed out. "Dad could easily have spent the night in Boca Raton and caught a flight to Mexico the next morning. The fact that he was in Boca Raton on the third would tie in with his May 4 plane ticket."

"You're right. And that means for the next three days your mother thought Ron was in Chicago and Avery and Paul thought he was in Boca Raton, but really he was in Mexico City." Adam marveled anew at the multilayered complexity of Ron's deceptions. "You know, from Ron's point of view, dealing with my brother must have been even more difficult than dealing with his two wives. Where Paul was concerned, he not only had to lie about where he was going, he had to invent reasonable business excuses to justify the trip."

"Plus, he had to give your brother progress reports on all these supposed projects when he came back." Megan sounded torn between admiration and horror. "How in the world did he pull that off?"

"It doesn't seem to have fazed him,"

Adam said. "According to Paul's notes, Ron recommended that they drop this particular project because the asking price for the hotel was too high. Who knows whether Ron pulled that judgment out of the air, or actually visited the place."

"The more I learn about my father, the more amazed I am at his capacity to remember dozens of different lies and never get his stories mixed up. Personally, I'd have been so exhausted that I'd have blown everything the first year."

"Hell, I'd have given myself away within the first couple of weeks. But then, my parents always did tell me I have no creative spark."

"You sound as if that makes you sad."

Megan could be disconcertingly insightful "I'm a banker," Adam said with deliberate lightness. "Creativity is the last thing I need."

"I'd have thought small-town banking is much more about personal relationships and creative thinking than it is about adding up columns of numbers."

"You have to keep a firm control of the numbers or you soon won't have any funds to support your creative thoughts," he said, surprised by her perceptiveness into answering with more honesty than was usual for him. He quickly brought the conversation back from territory that he tended to avoid discussing, especially with the women who flitted in and out of his orbit. For him, the First Bank of Fairfax wasn't merely a financial institution; it was the heart beating at the center of Fairfax community life. He had spent a lot of time since he became CEO defending his vision against opponents who wanted to keep the bank as an old-fashioned bulwark against change.

"If you'll hold on a minute, I can check the dates you gave me for your father's other Mexican trips." Adam put down the phone and made a quick comparison of Ron's various schedules. It turned out—no surprise—that Ron had kept his Mexican trips completely secret.

"Neither Avery nor Paul had a clue that Ron was ever in Mexico," Adam said, picking up the phone. "Your father invented different destinations for each set of travel dates you've given me. He seems to have picked major hub cities like Dallas or Atlanta, presumably to make the connection to Mexico City easier."

"And in Mexico City it seems he always

made reservations at the same hotel," Megan said. "A place called the Sierra Nevada. According to the police, they found a confirmed reservation for that same hotel along with all the other personal documents in my father's room safe. And Dad had even told Mom where he'd be staying in Mexico so that she could call him there. Your sister knew where he was going, too...." Megan's voice drifted into silence.

"What is it?" Adam asked. "What have you remembered?"

"Not exactly remembered. It's something that's been bothering me ever since I found this file folder. Doesn't it strike you as strange that my father kept five of his trips to Mexico a deep, dark secret and then—hey, presto—right before what turns out to be his last trip ever, he suddenly tells Paul, *and* my mother *and* your sister the truth about his destination? Both his families knew he was going to be at the Doral Beach Hotel in Miami, that he was leaving for Mexico City the next morning, and that he planned to stay at the Sierra Nevada Hotel. Why did he suddenly decide to clue everyone in on precisely where he would be?"

"It's a good question and I have no answer." Adam frowned in thought. "What was going to be different about this trip from Ron's point of view?"

"We don't have enough basic information even to make wild guesses. The only thing we can assume is that Dad's death is possibly linked to whatever business he was planning to conduct in Mexico."

"I agree. Apart from anything else, the murderer must have known in advance that Ron planned to spend the night in Miami, otherwise he wouldn't have had time to make such complicated arrangements for stealing a boat and disposing of the bodies. And who could have given Castellano that information—right down to the hotel-room number—other than the person your father planned to meet in Mexico City?"

"Apart from me, my mother, your sister and Paul?" Megan asked dryly. "As the cops in Miami have taken to pointing out with alarming frequency, we all knew exactly where Dad would be staying the night he was killed. And according to the police, we're the only people who could have known his precise hotel-room number."

"All the more reason to pass on this information right away. We need to get the cops moving in the right direction. Detective Jones needs to consult with the cops in Mexico City and ask for their cooperation. If Ron stayed at the Sierra Nevada six times in the past two years, there might easily be hotel employees who remember him. There's even a chance someone on staff will be able to identify some of the people Ron met with in Mexico. This could be a real lead to the missing money and from there to the person who hired Castellano."

"My thoughts exactly. Except that this is way too important to trust to the Mexican cops. We need to follow up as soon as we can, in person."

"That's a really bad idea," Adam said, shaking his head. "We should leave the police work to the professionals."

"You can't be serious! Their most likely reaction to hearing that Dad took several trips to Mexico is to blow us off. Why wouldn't it be? They'll assume it's just a diversion we've cooked up to distract them. They're focused on finding Castellano and they're confident that as soon as they have him in custody, he'll talk. Probably incriminating Avery or my mother. End of story as far as they're concerned."

"Detective Jones strikes me as a basically smart guy. Once we explain our reasoning, he'll agree with us that these trips were significant."

"Even assuming you're right—a mighty big if—the Mexican police have no motive to do anything more than go through the motions. This isn't their case. My father didn't get killed on Mexican territory. There isn't a reason in the world for them to waste hours of valuable police time questioning staff at the Sierra Nevada."

"Maybe Detective Jones will go to Mexico in person."

"Dream on. He'd be filling out paperwork for the next six months trying to get permission to go there, and we don't have six months to waste. Unless we follow up right now, you can kiss goodbye any hope of finding the missing money."

"Ron had the three million dollars from my bank at his disposal for two years before he was killed." Adam scowled as he admitted the truth. "Unfortunately, the logical conclusion is that the money's already gone."

"I don't agree. Maybe Dad had to be dead before the murderer could steal the money. Otherwise, why kill him? Come on, Adam, admit it! If we want to find out what my father did with your bank's money, we need to go to Mexico ourselves."

Adam was astonished to find himself seriously contemplating the possibility of a trip to Mexico in hot pursuit of Ron's killer and the missing three million. He shook off the moment of insanity. Bankers and other sensible people didn't go charging off south of the border on the basis of a few travel documents found in an unlocked file cabinet.

"Be realistic, Meg. You know we have to call the police. We're not qualified for this sort of investigation."

"Why not? You're a banker and we're looking for money. That seems like a darn good fit to me. Plus, we're starting our search in a hotel, which is the industry I work in. Seems like an even better fit. You know the questions to ask, and I know how to persuade the staff to answer them. It's not as if I'm planning to go *mano a mano* with Dad's killer. I just want to hand the police a few clues as to who the killer is. I want to present them with information that's concrete enough that even stodgy cops can't ignore it."

Adam couldn't believe how Megan managed to make the plan sound almost logical. "I have a board meeting next week. I can't possibly get away—"

"I understand. Of course I do." Her voice oozed fake sympathy. "You stay home and put in a call to the Miami cops. Explain that my father took several trips to Mexico City, so we think his murder may have resulted from business he conducted there. I'm sure Detective Jones will jump right on the hot lead. Unless he decides to arrest your sister or my mother instead. Meanwhile, I'm booking a plane ticket to Mexico."

Her sarcasm stoked Adam's irritation, already simmering toward a fast boil. "And what, *exactly,* are you going to do when you get there?"

"I told you already. I'll go to the Sierra Nevada Hotel and ask questions."

"Oh yeah, that's a great plan." Adam's temper was slipping away with amazing speed. "I really like the complex details you've managed to incorporate into your preparations. And if by some incredible chance you stumble across the person Ron did business with, what are you going to say? *Hey,* señor*, so glad to have run into* *you. Did you hire Julio Castellano to kill my daddy?*"

"When I know more about what's involved, I'll come up with a slightly more useful question than that."

"Has it occurred to you that it might be *dangerous* to start an investigation when we know so little? Have you remembered that your father managed to get himself *killed* by dealing with these people, whoever they are?"

"No," Megan said, her voice suddenly quiet. "I haven't forgotten that for a minute. My father is dead, brutally murdered, and his body dropped in the Atlantic Ocean. A woman died with him, probably for no better reason than that she was unlucky enough to be in his room at the wrong moment. She has no grave. She doesn't even have a name. But she sure as hell deserves to have her murderer brought to justice. So does my father. For all his faults, I loved him. When I was a little kid, he was a pretty great dad in a lot of ways and I…miss him. If I can do something to bring his killer to justice, then I intend to do it."

The pain in her voice instantly let the steam out of Adam's anger. "Jesus, Meg,

I'm sorry. I didn't mean to be so tactless." How in hell did he always manage to lose his cool around her? He drew in an unsteady breath and gave voice to what was really bothering him. "The truth is that the prospect of you flying off to Mexico City to investigate Ron's murder scares the crap out of me."

"That's okay. I understand completely. I'm scared, too. Two people are already dead. We'd be crazy if we weren't scared."

He'd grown up in a family that spent a lot of time apportioning blame and assigning guilt for every little disagreement. Megan's easy willingness to forgive and move on struck him as liberating in the extreme.

"Let's start this part of the conversation over," he said. "When are you thinking of going to Mexico?"

"The sooner the better. First, if there is a trail, I don't want it to get cold. And second, it's relatively easy for me to get off work right now. Ski season ended seven weeks ago and the summer visitors don't start arriving in Jackson Hole until mid-June, so it's low season at the ski lodge. I was planning to call and ask for another week's leave of absence as soon as I hung up from you, then get on the Internet and book a flight for tomorrow morning. I can't fly direct from here, of course, but I can probably go through Denver and connect to Mexico City."

"Fly into Chicago instead of Denver," Adam said, resigned to the fact that he'd lost his mind sometime in the five days that had elapsed since Megan erupted into his life. "If you can get here by early afternoon, we should be able to get a direct flight into Mexico. The flight's only about four hours from O'Hare, I seem to recall."

"*We?* You're coming with me?"

He wondered if he was kidding himself, or whether he really had heard pleasure as well as relief in Megan's voice. "Yes," he said. "I'm coming with you. Call me back when you have an idea of what flights are available to get you into Chicago tomorrow."

"I'll do a flight search right now. I'll call you back soon. Bye, Adam."

"Goodbye." He closed his phone and paced the room. God help him, he was as excited as a kid on the way to Walt Disney World at the prospect of spending the next several days in Megan's company. Usually, Adam was as analytical about his feelings as he was about the rest of his life, but not this time. For a man who prided himself on never getting caught off guard by his emotions, he was astonishingly reluctant to probe too deeply beneath the surface.

What the hell. He was going to Mexico. Megan was coming, too. No big deal. And if his body suddenly seemed flooded with adrenaline…well, they were searching for a brutal killer. No need to go looking for any explanation beyond that.

Thirteen

"Hey, Meg, time to wake up. We're here."

With great reluctance, Megan cracked a leaden eyelid and saw a dazzle of street-lights shimmering through a mist of rain. "Where's here?"

"At the Sierra Nevada hotel. We're in Mexico City, remember?"

Shaking off clouds of drowsiness, Megan opened both eyes and realized that she'd fallen asleep during the cab ride from the airport. To her acute embarrassment, she discovered that her head was resting on Adam's chest and her hands were nestled over his crotch. Good Lord, how in the world had that happened?

She shot upright, zooming toward the far corner of the cab, hoping Adam would understand that what a person did when she was asleep had nothing to do with what that same person might do when she was awake and in full possession of her faculties.

The zooming-across-the-seat move would have worked better if her hair—her infuriating hair—hadn't wound a hank of itself around Adam's shirt buttons. She yelped in pain, and realized she was stuck with her butt at least a foot to the left of her shoulders, unable to lift her head without sacrificing a chunk of her hair. Great. Just great. Now she was trapped with her nose buried against Adam's chest. And while his shirt might be collared, button-down and starched, underneath he wore nothing except skin. Accessorized by a cologne that smelled pretty damn good.

"Hold still." Adam ignored both the hotel doorman, who was looking at them with undisguised interest, and the driver waiting for his cab fare to be paid. He proceeded to disentangle her hair with surprising efficiency but no discernible sense of urgency. "All fixed," he said finally.

She scuttled along the seat in a futile quest for dignity. "Thank you. Sorry about that."

Still paying no attention to either the cabdriver or the doorman, Adam reached across the space she'd just established between the two of them and pulled her close again. He cradled her face in his hands and looked down at her. Even in the dim light of the cab's interior, she could see a definite gleam of amusement in his cool gray eyes. "Sorry about what?" he asked.

She cleared her throat. Better not to mention what was really bothering her, namely the previous location of her hands. "Falling asleep. Using you as a pillow."

"You're welcome. Anytime." He grinned. "Besides, there were definite side benefits to the situation."

So much for tact and discretion. Megan could feel her cheeks growing hot. Fortunately she didn't have to come up with a clever response, or even a coherent one, because Adam finally turned away to pay off the taxi driver. He then tipped the doorman with a wad of pesos thick enough to have the man beaming as he removed their suitcases from the trunk of the cab and carried them to the registration counter. The bellman ignored the built-in wheels in favor of hefting a case under each arm, presumably to demonstrate his weight-lifting machismo.

The sidewalk outside the hotel was screened by shrubs and flowers, but the night air carried the heavy smell of industrial chemicals and diesel fumes generated by the ceaseless traffic in one of the world's most populous cities. The lobby was air-conditioned and cut off some of the near-deafening street noise, but it was thronged with people heading toward the various hotel restaurants. The ricochet of at least three dozen different conversations bounced off the high ceiling and stucco walls, creating a buzz of liveliness and adding another layer to the general din.

All this place needed was a strolling mariachi band, Megan thought wryly. Having been raised in Wyoming, where the population of the entire state, including all the cows, barely equaled one average-size Mexico City suburb, the noisy crowd made her claustrophobic, although she realized that some of her reaction sprang from the fact that she was exhausted. She'd left the Flying W at four-thirty that morning and had been traveling ever since.

Still, she'd been counting heavily on the fact that the Sierra Nevada was a relatively small hotel. Its Web site boasted that it contained fewer than a hundred and thirty rooms, and promised each guest individual attention. The modest number of rooms had inspired her to hope that some of the hotel employees might remember her father. But if the on-property restaurants served as a neighborhood hub, the staff probably paid little real attention to individual guests, despite what the Web site claimed. It would be frustrating, to say the least, if it turned out that her father had stayed here six times but had gone unnoticed and unremembered.

Despite the crowd, their check-in was smooth and quick, and their rooms were next door to each other as requested. The "exquisite individual decor" proclaimed on the Web site differed from one room to the next only in the color of the wall paint and the pattern of the bedspreads. Still, both rooms had large windows overlooking the courtyard with its tiered, splashing fountain. The views were somewhat marred by the wrought iron security bars barricading the windows, but the rooms were spacious and the bathrooms sleekly contemporary, with lots of fluffy towels and brass faucets shaped like dolphins, presumably to convince guests that the hotel was worth the high rates it charged.

"I'm going to take a shower and fall directly into bed," Megan said, standing at the door that connected her room with Adam's, planning to close it as soon as she'd said good-night. They'd already agreed that they weren't going to attempt to question the hotel staff until the following morning when they'd be rested enough to do a more efficient job. The last thing they wanted was to blunder because of fatigue and cause the staff to clam up.

"Sounds like a plan." Adam unlocked his case then came and stood facing her in the doorway.

"Do you want to meet for breakfast?" Megan asked.

"I'm not sure." He sent her an assessing look. "I have a suspicion you're a morning person. A singing-in-the-shower-to-greet-the-new-day type of morning person."

"That's more my mother than me." Megan laughed. "I'm not quite that bad. But if you hate being around cheerful people before you've had coffee, you'd better avoid me. My brother's a night owl and he takes care to stay clear of my mother and me at breakfast time. He claims we're obnoxious."

"Your brother sounds like my kind of guy." Adam leaned against the doorjamb and loosened his tie. Only a banker would wear a striped navy-blue tie and button-down shirt to fly to Mexico, Megan thought amusedly, although the hours of travel seemed to have left him sartorially unscathed. Even his shirt hadn't crumpled when she'd slept on him in the cab.

"Exactly how cheerful are you in the morning?" he asked, tossing his tie onto the bed behind him.

"On a scale of one to ten, at least a seven point five. That's according to Liam."

"I can probably handle that." He sounded martyred. "Once I've showered and brushed my teeth, I can do a pretty fair imitation of a wide-awake human being."

She was sure that if Adam chose, he could be alert, cheery and anything else he wanted twenty-four hours a day, but she'd noticed before that he tended to downplay both his drive and his determination, not to mention his adaptability. Perhaps bankers in a small Southern town couldn't afford to come across as too focused and aggressive.

"What time do you want to meet and where?" she asked. "Eight o'clock? In the coffee shop?"

He frowned, calculating. "Eight o'clock here is seven in Wyoming and nine in Georgia. Yeah, sounds good to me. But let's not try the restaurants. They looked as if they get pretty crowded. I'll order room service for both of us. It'll be quieter. Easier for us to talk."

That made a lot of sense, if there were even a quarter as many people eating breakfast in the hotel as had come for dinner. She smiled at him. "Okay, that's a date. I'll just have coffee and orange juice. And hot milk to go with the coffee, please."

He shook his head, adamant. "You can't come to Mexico and not eat churros. That's the rule."

"Then I've broken the rule twice already. Possibly because I don't have a clue what churros are."

"A thin, extra-light doughnut sprinkled with cinnamon and sugar. They're often served with chocolate sauce, for dipping."

"With chocolate sauce? At breakfast time?"

"Since you've been here twice before, you may have noticed that Mexicans aren't afflicted with our rigid sense of timing."

She laughed. "As a favor to you, I guess I could manage one churro."

"I'll order several. You can thank me later."

She rolled her eyes. "Easy for you to talk. You're a man and you're over six feet tall. You can probably scarf down six churros, run around the block once and come back five pounds lighter. But in case you haven't noticed, I'm five foot two and a half if I stand up *really* straight—"

"Of course I've noticed." His voice was suddenly deeper, and when she tried to look away, she found that her gaze had locked with his.

Heat flamed in her cheeks, an alarmingly frequent occurrence when she was with Adam, but she forced herself to produce a casual smile, as if she hadn't noticed that the space between them was thick with tension. Her attraction to Adam was not only unwelcome, given the situation of their two families, it was a dangerous distraction from the purpose of their trip. She needed to remember that Adam was a Fairfax and, by definition, not pursuing the same goals as she was.

"Well, if we're agreed on our breakfast order, I guess I should take that shower." The air between the two of them seemed to have vanished, making it hard to breathe, and she could only hope her smile looked less fake than it felt. "It's way past my bedtime. Anything else we need to talk about or are we all set?"

There was a moment of electric stillness and then he spoke softly. "Not quite all set."

"What else?" She tilted her head up to look at him.

"This," he said, and leaned down to kiss her.

Ever since fourteen-year-old Jack Dublenski kissed her at the eighth-grade spring dance, Megan had considered kissing one of life's more enjoyable activities, even despite the fact that she and Jack had both been wearing braces at the time, which had made for a less than perfect kissing environment. In the years since, she'd never had any reason to change her opinion. Unless your partner was a real jerk, kissing was a fun way to pass the time.

But kissing Adam was different. Instead of feeling a pleasant glow or a mild rush of desire, the moment his lips touched hers she was swept by a torrent of sensations that were powerful enough to be disconcerting. The stubble of his beard scratched against her face, pricking her skin, but instead of repelling her, the small intimacy provoked a raw ache of longing. Within seconds, her body had dispensed with the preliminary stages of arousal and had hurtled into a state of acute desire. Her arms and legs felt heavy and she shivered when Adam pulled her closer, as if she was reacting to tiny electric shocks and not the simple pressure of his body against hers. She arched against him, locking her hands at the back of his head and opening her mouth beneath his.

Adam's arousal seemed equally swift and urgent. His hands slid down to her hips and he lifted her onto her tiptoes, pressing her spine against the narrow strip of interconnecting wall and jamming himself against her so that his erection thrust hard against her belly. He was so much taller that they didn't fit together in the way she was accustomed to with other men, but the disparity in their heights merely made her impatient to get to a bed where the difference would no longer matter and they could lie next to each other without clothes to get in the way.

It was Adam who ended the kiss, stepping back just enough that their bodies were no longer touching. He held on to the doorjamb as if he didn't trust himself to keep his hands away from her unless he gripped something solid.

"This probably isn't a smart thing for us to do," he said. His voice was husky and there was dark color on his cheekbones, but he was visibly winning the struggle to get himself back under control.

Megan felt chilled where moments before she had felt warmth. "Why not?" she asked. Her breathing was so fast and shallow it was hard to speak. She wasn't quite sure what had happened between the two of them just now, but whatever it was had been intense enough that she wasn't capable of pretending she didn't want him, however threatening the admission might be to her pride.

His eyes burned with a silvery light that bore no resemblance to his usual faintly sardonic expression, but he spoke coolly enough. "I'm ten years older than you. That's one reason."

She shrugged. "A reason maybe, but not a good one."

"Here's a better one. Your father betrayed my sister. That makes for a damn awkward history between the two of us."

"Why? I'm not my father. You're not your sister. We're also not in Sicily suffering under a blood vendetta."

"Perhaps not, but our families wouldn't approve."

She dismissed his point, although earlier it had seemed vitally important. "Personally, I'm not in the habit of asking my family to give my sexual partners their official stamp of approval."

He flashed a tight, humorless smile. "Your mother would shoot me if she knew what almost happened a few minutes ago."

Megan unzipped the cotton knit jacket she was wearing. Her nipples still tingled, and her breasts were almost unbearably sensitive. She could never remember an occasion when she'd been so thoroughly aroused as the result of a simple kiss. "Fortunately, she doesn't know and I don't see any reason to fill her in on the details. Do you?"

"None that I can think of at this precise moment." Adam's eyes narrowed as she let her jacket drop onto the floor. "But then, I haven't been thinking clearly for several days now."

If his cryptic statement meant he'd been fighting his attraction to her, Megan was delighted to hear it. She unhooked her bra and dangled it by the strap from her index finger. "Since my mother is at least three thousand miles away, you seem safe from castration by shotgun. I'm relieved."

He looked at her breasts and then closed his eyes. "I'm not."

Dropping her bra on the floor, Megan began unfastening the buttons on his shirt. "You know, Adam, I'd noticed before tonight that you have an alarming tendency to overanalyze."

He opened his eyes, and the intensity of his gaze sent heat rushing through her entire body. "You could be right."

She pitched his shirt in the direction of a chair. "You need to work on the problem. Do or not do, as Yoda would say."

"Now, there's a philosopher for the ages—

a puppet with a brain made out of Styrofoam. Can't think of a single reason why I wouldn't listen to Yoda's advice."

"There you go again. Overanalyzing and coming up with the wrong answer. Yoda is much more than a puppet."

"Sure he is. He's a puppet packing all the wisdom of Hollywood—" Adam broke off and shot her a tiny smile. "You're right, I overanalyze. I'll try to conquer my annoying habit of being rational."

"Good." She rested the palms of her hands against his chest and tilted her head to look up at him. His eyes met hers, hot with desire, but he didn't kiss her again.

She spoke softly. "Your move, Adam."

"Yes, it is." He kissed her before she could say anything more, a demanding tongue-in-the-throat kiss that made her realize just how much he'd been holding back before. His mouth still on hers, he swept her into his arms and carried her across to the bed. They tumbled together onto the dark red cover, and then he was kissing her breasts while he unzipped her cotton slacks and reached between her thighs. Her reaction was swift and overwhelming. Wherever he touched, heat shimmered on her skin, transformed by some subtle alchemy into a state that hovered on the knife edge between need and gratification. Blood pounded in her ears, a throbbing drumbeat that propelled her toward a level of sexual pleasure she had never reached before.

They hadn't spoken since Adam carried her to the bed—as far as Megan was concerned, finding her voice would have been close to impossible—but when he entered her, he stilled for a moment, looking down at her and pushing her hair out of her eyes with a touch that was gentle enough to bring a lump to her throat.

"You're incredibly beautiful, Megan. I've wanted to make love to you since the first moment I saw you."

She tried to respond, but the words she searched for kept slipping out of her grasp. In the end, she could only murmur that she wanted him, too. As he started to move inside her he picked up her hand, cradling it against his cheek. Then he turned his face and pressed his lips against her palm, the gesture tender. Adam, she realized in a flash of insight, presented a cool facade to the world in order to hide the vulnerability that was hidden quite close to the surface.

It was her last coherent thought. She arched to meet him, climbing with him to a place so perfect that when she climaxed she was sure, for a few amazing moments, that together they had finally unlocked the secrets of the universe.

Fourteen

There ought to be a law against the morning after, Megan thought gloomily. She turned the shower water as hot as it would go, letting the spray pour out of the dolphin's gaping mouth and pound down on her idiotic head. If she had set out to get involved with the man most likely to complicate her life she couldn't have done better than to pick Adam Fairfax.

However hard she scrubbed there was no erasing the fact that she had spent most of the previous night having sex with the man who held the power to foreclose on the Flying W and who only a few days earlier had accused her of stealing three million dollars. They hadn't just had ordinary sex, either. They'd had mind-blowing, incredibly wonderful sex that had left her longing for more.

Where she expected the relationship to go from here, Megan couldn't imagine. Last night, wound tight with desire, it had been all too easy to wave a nonchalant hand and dismiss the feelings of their families and the hard fact that her father had contracted a bigamous marriage with Adam's sister. This morning it didn't seem anywhere near as easy to ignore the complicated past that had woven her and Adam together. It was a no-brainer to conclude that Ellie would be distraught if she knew what had happened last night. More to the point, she'd be deeply hurt. Inconvenient as it might be, she couldn't ignore her mother's feelings. She owed Ellie some degree of loyalty. Adam undoubtedly felt the same about Avery, which brought Megan right back to the fact that there was absolutely nowhere for this relationship to go. Better to end it now, before anyone got badly hurt.

Sighing, Megan wrapped herself in the toweling robe hanging on the back of the bathroom door. It was too long, of course. The hem touched her ankles, the sleeves flapped over her knuckles and the lapels reached almost to her armpits when she crossed them over to tighten the belt around her waist. Usually she despised reminders of her lack of inches. Right at this moment, however, being covered from neck to toe didn't strike her as such a bad idea. A little excess modesty might help to obliterate the memory of how she'd behaved last night. The image of standing in the doorway to Adam's bedroom, bra dangling from her hooked finger, was mortifying enough to make her blush from scalp to toe. Where in God's name had she parked her brain during that little exercise in seductive craziness? The answer, unfortunately, seemed clear. She'd parked her brain slap bang in the middle of a cloud of lust, where it had remained blissful but otherwise nonfunctional all night long.

Much as she would like to practice avoidance where Adam was concerned, a busy schedule loomed ahead and she couldn't spend the rest of the day lurking in the bathroom. Gathering her courage, Megan reluctantly made her way into Adam's room.

His usual efficiency hadn't deserted him, she saw, despite the relatively early hour and his professed inability to function in the morning. They'd parted company less than an hour ago, but breakfast was already set out on the table in front of the window and the curtains had been drawn back to reveal a sunny morning. Already dressed in slacks and a cotton knit shirt, Adam was sitting in an armchair sipping orange juice and reading a newspaper. A Spanish-language paper, she realized as he set it aside. She hadn't known that he could speak Spanish well enough to follow a newspaper. But then, her general ignorance about Adam was a large part of their problem. She didn't know much more about him than that he was fantastic in bed and that he was furiously angry with her father. Two small bookends of information propping up a dangerous void.

He got to his feet, pulling out a chair for her and frowning slightly as his gaze met hers. "What's up? You don't look as if you were even remotely tempted to sing in the shower this morning."

"I'm suffering from a major attack of morning-after blues," she admitted. "Last night…got out of hand."

"Ah." He raised an eyebrow. "Personally, I thought what happened last night was pretty spectacular for both of us. Am I wrong?"

"No, you aren't wrong. You were… I had… It was….fabulous."

"Then help me out here, because I'm not

understanding the problem. Fabulous, consensual sex makes you miserable?"

"It's not the sex. It's...it's everything else about our situation."

"Define 'everything else.' "

She shrugged. "Those family problems you mentioned last night appear a lot more valid this morning. When I was in the shower, I tried to imagine spending a weekend with you at the ranch, and all I could see was my mother's horrified expression when I introduced you. I'm sure your sister would be equally horrified if she knew what had happened. It's not that I expect to define our relationship for the next ten years after one night of sex. But I can't help wondering where we go from here."

"We eat breakfast." Adam gestured to the basket of churros and the coffeepot. "Then you get dressed. We take the elevator down to the lobby and show the hotel staff your father's picture. We hope to acquire some useful information. If we get lucky and somebody recognizes Ron, we follow up on the leads—"

She shook her head impatiently. "You know that wasn't what I meant."

"Last night you accused me of overanalyzing," Adam said quietly. "Isn't that what you're doing now?"

Perhaps it was, Megan mused. She'd never been involved in a relationship before where her common sense was at war with her feelings, and she was lost in the unfamiliar terrain.

Adam took one of the churros and dipped it into the bowl of thick, warm chocolate sauce. "Live dangerously," he said, holding it out to Megan. "Take a bite."

She hesitated, well aware that he was offering her much more than a mouthful of cinnamon-flavored chocolate.

"'Fear is the path to the dark side,'" he murmured, his gaze holding hers. A hint of a smile lurked deep in his eyes, treacherously disarming.

She would never have expected him to quote Yoda back at her and she felt her heart squeeze tight with an emotion she chose not to acknowledge. Adam was just too damn good at playing the flirtation game and she'd regret it if she took him too seriously. Still, she had to eat breakfast. She bit into the churro, feeling as if she'd just done something momentous.

He watched her, his gaze intent. “Is it good?”

“It’s heavenly.”

“You see how easy that was?”

She looked at him, not attempting to hide the turmoil of her feelings. “I never thought it would be difficult, only unwise. There’s a difference.”

He leaned forward and kissed her. It was a casual kiss, almost as much that of a friend as of a lover. Megan felt a response all the way from her asinine head down to her overexcitable toes.

“We’ll take it one step at a time,” he said softly. “One day at a time.”

She shook off the sensual spell he was already weaving around her. “You’re making our relationship sound like a twelve-step program.” She spoke caustically, for her own benefit as much as his.

He laughed and stood up, stretching. “Maybe a twelve-step program is what I need. As far as I’m concerned, you’re definitely addictive.” He ruffled her hair. “While you stoke up on coffee, I’m going to find those pictures of your father that we packed. For some reason, this morning I’m bursting with optimism.”

“Sex seems to have that effect on most men,” she said dryly.

He took her hand, kissing her palm and closing her fingers over the kiss. “Only if it’s great sex,” he said. Humming beneath his breath, he went in search of her suitcase.

They’d devised their plan of action for questioning the hotel staff during the long plane ride from Chicago. Based on everything they’d learned about Ron over the past couple of weeks, they agreed that he would probably have kept his interactions with hotel staff to a minimum. After a quarter century of deception, he would have become adept at shielding the details of his life from inquisitive bystanders. Still, it was more difficult to fly beneath the radar than most people realized. Megan had been working in Jackson Hole’s tourist industry since before she graduated from college and she knew just how much information hotel employees could pick up about guests if they set their minds to it. Her father had stayed at the Sierra Nevada six times and Megan was hopeful that he’d done something—at least once—that had triggered the curiosity of the staff.

The hotel worked on a two-shift system during the day, with a skeleton night shift. In addition, there were two sets of cleaning crews: the maids who took care of the rooms and were usually gone by three, and the janitors who polished floors and maintained the public areas, mostly during the predawn hours.

It seemed unlikely that the cleaning crews would remember Ron, so there was no point in questioning them until every other lead had fizzled out. In fact, their entire interview process was going to be hit or miss, since Megan guessed there would be several employees who'd quit or been fired in the three months since her father's last visit. Still, she calculated that in a hotel this size, they would be able to question almost three-quarters of current employees within a forty-eight-hour period, which gave them decent odds of finding someone who remembered her father.

They started their inquiries with the bellmen and the clerks at the registration desk, since Ron would have found it difficult to avoid them, however reclusive he tried to be. Megan had been afraid that the wall-to-wall news coverage of her father's death would have seeped down into Mexico, especially since the likely killer had been identified as a Mexican national, but Adam had downplayed that worry. Crime was essentially a local news item, he insisted, and it was very rare that homicide provoked international attention unless there was either a celebrity victim or a celebrity killer. As a businessman, albeit successful, Ron Raven didn't rise to that level of celebrity.

In the event, Adam proved correct. As far as Megan could tell, not a single hotel employee recognized that they were being shown pictures of a man who'd been brutally murdered, and whose image had been plastered over media outlets in the States for more than two weeks. The staff all seemed to accept her story that she was looking for her father who had early-stage Alzheimer's disease and had gone missing somewhere in Mexico City. A couple of clerks at the reception desk even remembered him as a guest who'd stayed several times at their hotel. Unfortunately, they had no recollection of anything special about those stays except that Señor Raven had been very charming. They all professed astonishment to learn that he was suffering from mental problems. Señor Raven had always seemed so healthy and alert, they said, shaking their heads.

Moving on to the restaurants during the midmorning lull between the end of breakfast and the start of lunch, Adam and Megan repeated their story and asked the same questions. The waiters were all polite but none of them recognized the pictures of Señor Raven, which made it pointless to inquire if they'd ever seen him share a meal with anyone. Megan didn't realize how much she'd been counting on gleaning information from an observant waiter until their restaurant interviews came up totally empty.

"Are we discouraged enough to consider approaching hotel management?" Adam asked as they regrouped in the lobby. "Management could pull invoices and tell us precisely when and where Ron ate, for example, even if it turned out that he always used room service."

Megan pulled a face. "I know the law here is different from the States. Even so, I can't imagine that anyone in senior management is going to provide us with information about a guest's meals and room charges.

They'd need some sort of police order to do that, surely?"

"I don't know. You're very convincing when you talk about Ron's Alzheimer's. If I stayed in the background, you don't think you could find a young and susceptible assistant manager who might relent?"

"I might," Megan conceded. "But that's a risky tactic. If the manager resists my amazing charms, we'll be screwed. He'll instruct all staff members that they're not to answer any of our questions, and then we might as well pack up and go home, because nobody will talk to us. They're not going to risk their jobs for us."

"I'm afraid you're right." Adam frowned and then brightened when his gaze was caught by the cluster of guests around the concierge desk. "We haven't checked with him," he said, tipping his head toward the middle-aged man behind the brochure-laden desk.

Megan looked doubtful. "I can't imagine my father calling attention to himself by asking for help getting tickets to a bullfight or flamenco dancing or whatever."

"True, but we might as well give it a shot, since we have no better alternative. We've exhausted everyone else until the shift change this evening."

They had to wait ten minutes while the concierge arranged a minivan for a group of tourists who wanted to tour the National Anthropological Museum, but then he turned his attention to them with a pleasant smile.

"Good morning. You have a fine day for exploring our city." The concierge flashed an expert and almost imperceptible glance toward Megan's left hand and deduced her nonmarried status. "How may I help you, *señorita? Señor?*"

Megan produced the two photos of her father and launched yet again into her story about the onset of Alzheimer's disease and her father's tragic refusal to acknowledge his problem. The result was that he had been missing for two weeks and the only clue his distraught family had concerning his whereabouts was that this hotel had been on his itinerary.

"And how do you hope that I may be able to help you, *señorita?*" The concierge remained polite, but Megan sensed that somehow she'd lost him, that either he hadn't believed her story, or he had some other reason for withholding whatever he knew.

"We have no intention of causing trouble for your hotel," Adam said smoothly, reaching into his wallet to find a business card and handing it to the concierge. "If you are worried about any possible…unpleasantness…for Mr. Raven's family or for your hotel, you can be sure that his daughter and I plan to be entirely discreet. That's why we're here in person. Anything we may discover about Mr. Raven's friends or companions will, of course, remain entirely confidential."

Of course! Megan thought. *If Dad was here with a woman, the concierge would be reluctant to pass on that information.*

"You misunderstand me, *señor.* Regrettably, I have no memory of assisting Mr. Raven with any arrangements of any sort. And I definitely never saw him in the company of a—companion."

If the concierge didn't remember her father, how could he be so sure that he'd never seen him with a companion? Megan wondered. Adam obviously picked up on the same contradiction and realized belatedly what it was going to take to get the concierge to talk.

Flashing the concierge a man-to-man

smile, he pointed to the photos. “Please look again more closely and see if you can refresh your memory. We simply want to find out if Mr. Raven might have some friends or acquaintances here who can provide us with a clue as to his current whereabouts.” He paused for a weighted moment before placing a hundred-dollar bill on top of the photo. “I’m sure you agree with me that it would be unfortunate if we were forced to turn this investigation over to the police. It would be so much better for me and his daughter to handle…whatever needs to be handled.”

The concierge hesitated for a moment and then shrugged, scruples succumbing to temptation. He scooped up the hundred-dollar bill and slipped it into his pocket in a single slick movement. “I have just remembered an occasion when I believe I may have assisted Señor Raven in making some travel arrangements.” He fell silent, staring into space.

Adam put another fifty on the table. “Are the details of those travel arrangements now coming back to you, by any chance?”

The fifty followed the hundred into the concierge’s pocket. “Yes, indeed. By good fortune, my memory is now clear. Señor Raven only asked for my assistance on one occasion, and it was some time ago…more than a year." He frowned for a moment. "I honestly can't remember the time more precisely than that. In fact, I only remember Señor Raven because he was so angry."

"Why was he angry?" Megan asked. "What about?"

"Señor Raven felt that he was wasting time," the concierge replied. "He was more than angry. He was furious. He complained that he was being forced to waste an entire day—perhaps more—in getting to his destination. In fact, he appeared so enraged, I was afraid he might have a…I have forgotten the word in English. Not a heart attack—"

"A stroke?" Megan suggested.

The concierge nodded. "Yes, that is what I feared for Señor Raven, your father. The blood vein throbbed here." He tapped his forehead and then shrugged. "I have seen the same thing many times with American businessmen. For you who live north of the border, to spend one day more than you have planned is a big disaster. For us, it is simply the chance to relax and enjoy life in an unexpected way." He fell silent for a moment, presumably contemplating the strangeness of the American obsession with not wasting time.

"Why was my father forced to waste a day?" Megan prompted him, thinking that for her father with his double life, a wasted day might be more troublesome than for a lot of other people. "Did he tell you what had happened to mess up his plans?"

"Because of too many planes at Mexico City's International Airport, it is no longer permitted for private jets to take off or land there. Señor Raven had arranged for a private plane to pick him up at our airport in Toluca. I had ordered a limousine to take him to the airport and that part of the trip was good, as it should be. But the plane Señor Raven was expecting at Toluca airport did not arrive, although he told me he had paid a big amount of money in advance." The concierge's hands stretched wide to emphasize how much money had been expended.

"Unfortunately, Señor Raven could not find anyone else available to fly him to his destination so he was…how do you say? He had no choice. He returned to the hotel.

He asked for my help in arranging for another plane."

"Did my father tell you where he wanted to go?" Megan asked.

The concierge looked vague. "I believe he may have mentioned Acapulco."

Adam and Megan exchanged puzzled glances. There were plenty of scheduled flights from various U.S. cities that went directly to Acapulco. Megan wondered why her father would have gone to all the trouble of coming to Mexico City and then hiring a private plane to get to Acapulco when he could have flown directly from the States.

"Why would he need a private plane to get to Acapulco?" Adam asked.

"Perhaps he didn't mention Acapulco. Perhaps he meant to visit the archaeological ruins at Oaxaca." The concierge lifted his shoulders in a dismissive shrug. Clearly he had found Ron's destination of little interest. Megan wouldn't be surprised to discover that he'd pulled both Acapulco and Oaxaca out of the air, rather than out of his memory.

"Do you remember the name of the aviation company you recommended to Mr. Raven?" Adam asked.

"Certainly, *señor*. We have recommended them on several occasions and our guests are always pleased with the service they provide. The name of the company is *Navgación Águila.* In English that means Eagle Navigation. I have their brochure here, I believe." The concierge searched in the desk file drawer. "Yes, here it is. You will see that their office is located right at Toluca airport."

"Could you arrange transportation for us to the airport?" Adam asked.

"For tomorrow, *señor?* If you wish, there is a minivan that can be ordered a day in advance."

"No, we would like to go today," Adam said.

"I can arrange a car rental for you, but you will have to return to the International Airport to pick up the car. Or we can order a limousine for you. The rates are quite reasonable and then there would be no danger of you getting lost. Traffic in Mexico City is not easy for newcomers to navigate."

"We'll take the limo," Megan said quickly, afraid that Adam might consider his manhood was being insulted if he didn't proclaim that Mexico City traffic held no fears for him. "How soon can you get the limo here?"

The concierge arranged for a limo to be at the door in thirty minutes, giving them barely time to return to their rooms and snag a chilled soda from the minibar.

For Megan, accustomed to driving on Wyoming roads where a dozen cars traveling in the same direction was considered a traffic jam, their journey west to Toluca was a nightmare revelation of what heavy traffic and congested highways could mean. Even the roads around Atlanta seemed easy driving by comparison, chiefly because the Atlantans she'd encountered had all assumed that a red traffic light required them to stop, whereas drivers in Mexico City simply treated stoplights as challenges to be overcome.

Their driver considered every vehicle that attempted to overtake the limo as a direct threat to his family honor, so they arrived at the airport offices of *Navigación Águila* in little more than an hour. Megan's stomach had swooped in panic so many times that by now it felt as if it were lodged permanently in her throat.

"Are you okay?" Adam asked, putting his arm around her shoulders and drawing her close against his chest. "You were turning pretty green during the last ten kilometers or so."

"Give me a minute to absorb the happy fact that I've arrived with all my limbs still attached and no pieces of automobile through my skull." Megan drew in a couple of shaky breaths and her stomach gradually sank back to where it belonged. "Okay, I'm functional again. Well, semifunctional at least."

"Good girl." He gave her a comforting squeeze. "Ready with the new and improved version of our story?"

She nodded. "Ready. But you'd better do the talking. Your Spanish is a million times better than mine."

"They're almost certain to speak English since they're in the tourist business."

The *Navigación Águila* offices were less distinguished than their glossy brochure would have suggested. The brown linoleum floor looked as if it had been several days since it had been swept and several months since it had been polished. Faded posters of Mexican resorts were stuck onto cinder block walls painted a virulent shade of turquoise, and the only visible employee was a fortysomething woman seated at a cluttered metal desk.

She looked up from her computer monitor and gave them a pleasant enough smile, although her makeup was applied so thickly that it seemed in danger of cracking with any facial movement.

"Buenos días, señor y señorita. Como puedo ayudearle?"

"*Buenos días.* We need some information if you can help us." Adam flashed one of his high-wattage smiles. "Do you speak English, *señorita?*"

The woman blossomed under the impact of his smile. She picked up a pen and pulled a pad toward her, ready to take notes. "Yes, I speak some leetle English. You wish to hire one of our planes, *señor?*"

"No, thank you. At least not right now. We're hoping you might be able to help us trace a relative of ours who's missing from home." Adam gestured to Megan. "My friend is searching for her father. Sadly, he's suffering from Alzheimer's disease and we're afraid that he may have forgotten his home address and phone number. He hasn't been in touch with anyone in his family for almost two weeks now. We're all very worried."

The receptionist tilted her head to look at Megan. Her expression was genuinely sympathetic. “That is terrible, *señorita,* but I do not know how can I help you.”

“I believe my father has hired one of your company’s planes on several occasions over the past two years.” Megan risked an assertion that she didn’t know to be true. “He was scheduled to fly with you again just before he disappeared.”

“When was that, *señorita?* He is missing since two weeks, did you say?”

“Yes.” Megan pulled the photographs out of her purse. “This is my father. Do you recognize him, by any chance?”

The receptionist glanced down at the pictures and her expression transformed instantly from warmth to cold anger. “Who are you?” she demanded, half rising from her chair, generous breasts thrusting against her too-tight blouse. “What do you want? Why do you ask questions about Señor Raven? Are you from the American newspapers? If so, I have nothing to say to you.”

“No, I’m not a journalist. I’m Megan Raven, Ron Raven’s daughter—”

“I do not believe you. If you were truly the daughter of Señor Raven, then you must know that he is dead. He is killed in most horrible way in the United States. And now, I must ask for you to leave this office—"

"Cual es el problema, Esmerelda?" A chubby man burst through an interior door, a silver Saint Christopher medallion bouncing against his open shirt buttons, and his long hair slicked back in a style that might have been considered sexy around 1983. The receptionist must have summoned him with a silent emergency signal, Megan thought ruefully, listening as Esmerelda launched into a tirade of passionate Spanish that was much too rapid for her to understand.

The man silenced the receptionist with an angry frown and a curt hand signal. Then he turned to greet them. "Sorry about all the excitement," he said, his attitude a lot friendlier than Megan would have expected, given Esmerelda's near meltdown. "My name is Eric Connolly and I'm the owner of Eagle Navigation. The senior pilot, too." His smile broadened. "As you probably guessed from the accent, I'm a fellow American."

"How did you end up owning a company in Mexico City?" Adam asked, leaning casually against the corner of Esmerelda's desk. "I thought you had to be a Mexican citizen to do that."

Eric put his arm around the receptionist's shoulders, a gesture that struck Megan as more controlling than affectionate. "I got lucky and married the lovely Mexican *señorita* you see here five years ago. I bought the business from her cousin when he wanted to retire, and I've been living down here ever since."

"A great city, and a great place to live except for the pollution," Adam said.

"Yep, that about sums it up." Eric's smile didn't fade, but his voice hardened. "Esmerelda tells me you're making inquiries about Ron Raven. Since we all know he's dead, murdered in Miami, maybe you could show me some ID and explain why you came in here with a cock-and-bull story about him having Alzheimer's and you trying to find him."

Megan exchanged a quick glance with Adam. He nodded almost imperceptibly and she pulled out her passport. "As you can see, Mr. Connolly, I'm exactly who I claimed to be. I'm Megan Raven, Ron Raven's daughter, and this is my friend Adam." She didn't mention Adam's last name, wanting to avoid questions about why a member of Ron's legal family had joined forces with the enemy Fairfaxes.

"We know my father hired your planes on several occasions and we just want to know where he was flying." She flashed a smile as wide and insincere as Eric's own. "We're trying to trace his movements in the final couple of months before he was killed, that's all."

Eric wasn't in the least distracted by her smile. He took her passport and examined it carefully. He snapped it closed before returning it, holding out his hand to shake hers. "I'm pleased to meet you, Megan, even if the circumstances aren't the best. You, too, Adam. I'd like to offer my condolences and say how sorry I was to hear of your father's tragic passing. That was a terrible way for Mr. Raven to go. And then to find out he had two wives and two families—" Eric stopped abruptly, as if embarrassed by his own lack of tact. "Well, sorry to have brought up such a sore point. Enough said on that subject. I'm sure you've been living with reporters harassing you for the last couple of weeks, Ms. Raven, so you'll understand why my wife here was so concerned."

"I didn't realize Mr. Raven's death was reported in Mexico," Adam said, ending his sentence in a slight question. "I'm surprised it was considered newsworthy this far south."

Megan noticed that Eric's fingers tightened on his wife's shoulder, but his demeanor remained friendly. "In fact, you're right, nothing was reported in the papers here. But it so happens I made a vacation trip to Boston ten days ago. Once I realized that the Ron Raven everyone was talking about on TV was the same man I'd had in the back of my plane on a few occasions, well, you'd better believe I paid attention. That was some story—"

He broke off again. "In view of the media circus in the States, I warned Esmerelda that it wouldn't be smart to speak to any reporters who might come sniffing around." He spread his hands. "That's why she reacted the way she did to your inquiries. I'm sure you understand my reasons for advising her to be careful."

"Completely," Adam said blandly. "But I'm still a bit puzzled. Why did you imagine that reporters might be interested enough in Mr. Raven's travel schedule to come and talk with you? It's his murder and bigamous lifestyle they're investigating, not his vacation trips."

"You're here," Eric pointed out, his smile finally fading. "Why are you so interested?"

"I'm his daughter," Megan said, drawing Eric's attention back to her. "I want to know what really happened to him. The police in Miami have named a suspect in the crime, but they aren't suggesting any motive for what happened. I'd like to find out why he died."

"I can surely appreciate that you need to know how your father's sad…passing…came about. But what does it matter where he flew months and months ago? I don't understand the connection between his flight schedule and his…passing."

"Perhaps there isn't one, but there's another reason we're making inquiries," Adam said. "I had business dealings with Megan's father. His unexpected death resulted in a significant financial loss for my organization—"

"Well, talking to me sure isn't going to help you recover any financial losses." Eric gave a woeful chuckle. "I'm just a pilot, trying to keep my planes in the air and hoping not to get eaten alive by rising fuel prices."

"I realize you can't give us any direct

leads," Adam said. "That goes without saying. But I'm trying to find out who Ron Raven was doing business with here in Mexico. If we knew where you took him, that might provide a starting point for our inquiries."

"I very much doubt it." Eric shrugged. "I'm sorry if you've lost money, but I can pretty much guarantee business was the last thing on Ron Raven's mind when he hired my plane."

"Even so, we'd appreciate hearing where he went."

"I guess there's no harm in telling you. At this point, it's not exactly a secret."

Esmerelda made a small sound of protest, but her husband silenced her with a single fierce glare. Then he swung back to look at Adam, ignoring Megan. His smile returned, toothier than before. Megan, used to picking up on the body language of guests at the ski lodge, concluded that the wider Eric's smile, the more he was hiding.

"Our flight plans are all on file, anyway, so Mr. Raven's destination is basically a matter of public record."

"Yes, I'd thought of that," Adam said, still blandly courteous. "It would be illegal to fly any of your passengers to their destinations without filing the details of exactly where you were going."

Eric nodded. "Since 9/11, the authorities have really cracked down and enforced the rules, even here where rules aren't exactly their thing. Guess the American feds are keeping on their tails." He gave another shrug. "Look, since you're insisting, I'll tell you where I flew Ron Raven, but don't blame me if you don't like what you hear. Unfortunately, there's no way to be tactful about this. That's why I didn't want to talk about it. The truth is, I'm pretty sure Ron was having an affair. I flew him to the Yucatán peninsula several times. Chichén Itzá, to be precise. I guess he had a...how shall I put this? He had a lady friend living there. Amazing, isn't it, given that he was already stuck with trying to keep two wives happy."

Megan smothered a small sound of protest. "How do you know that my father went to visit a woman?"

"Because the same woman was always waiting to meet him when we landed. Chichén Itzá isn't a big airport with a ton of fancy buildings. It's a single strip of tarmac and cars can drive right up alongside the planes. Each time we arrived in Chichén Itzá a car was waiting for Mr. Raven. The driver was a pretty young lady—dark hair, maybe in her thirties, and slim. Almost too slim, but she wore great clothes. Short skirts, tight fit, but classy, you know? I'm sorry, but that's all I can tell you about her. I have no idea where Mr. Raven went with her, or what her name was. I don't even know if they stayed in a private home, or in a hotel. All I know is that Mr. Raven usually remained in Chichén Itzá forty-eight hours or so, and then I flew back to pick him up."

"The woman who met the plane might have been a business associate," Adam suggested.

Eric snorted with laughter. "You're kidding, right?" He remembered that Ron Raven's daughter was present and he sent Megan an apologetic glance, softening his conclusion. "You're right, of course. The meeting could've been business related. I've no idea what went on once Mr. Raven left the landing strip, but it sure didn't look to me as if he and this woman had business on their minds. They were all over each other the moment he got off the plane. Anyway, sorry I can't be more help."

"Oh, I think you could be a lot more help if you tried." Adam took off his sunglasses, his gaze locking with Eric's as he leaned forward, hands braced on the edge of Esmerelda's desk. "It's a convincing story you've just told us—I really liked the bit about the woman's classy clothes. That was a clever touch. I'm impressed that you can come up with such a good lie on such short notice. You must have a lot of practice. However, I'd be more inclined to believe your fairy tale if I didn't happen to speak Spanish rather fluently."

Eric's brows drew together in a ferocious frown. "I have no clue what you're talking about."

"If you took Ron Raven to Chichén Itzá to meet his girlfriend, how come Esmerelda was yelling at you about how she'd warned you not to get involved with flying Ron to Belize? How come she was yelling that she'd told you all along it was trouble? That no good could come out of it, especially filing inaccurate flight plans. There's a detail that's going to get you in really big trouble, Mr. Connolly."

The color drained out of Eric's cheeks but he rallied quickly. "You must have misunderstood Esmerelda—"

"No, Mr. Connolly. I understood perfectly. I worked in Peru with the Peace Corps for two years after I graduated from college, and I had no difficulty following what your wife was yelling at you. Esmerelda wanted to know what the hell was going to happen if we found out that you'd flown Ron Raven half a dozen times to Belize. Under the circumstances, would you like to reconsider your story about Ron having a lover in the Yucatán peninsula?"

"Esmerelda has made a mistake—"

"Maybe. But not about flying Ron to Belize. Give it up, Eric. I'm not buying what you have on offer. I want to know precisely where in Belize you took Ron, and what the hell he did when he got there. And this time, try telling the truth, or I'm going straight to the aviation authorities with a recommendation that they pull your license."

Fifteen

Whatever Eric answered, Megan didn't hear his reply. She could see his mouth moving but the roaring in her ears was so loud she could make no sense of his words.

Her father had hired Eric's plane to fly to Belize.

Adam didn't understand the significance of that particular destination, but unfortunately Megan did. Belize was a tiny country, with less than half a million inhabitants. One of those inhabitants was Uncle Ted, her mother's brother. He'd been living there for almost three years now.

A dozen separate images jostled inside her head, swirling around so fast that she was mentally panting to catch up with them. She saw her uncle Ted two years ago, seated at the Flying W dinner table. An engineer who had worked in South and Central America all his adult life, her uncle was a great storyteller. He had kept everyone in Thatch spellbound as he spun humorous tales about his important new job working for a mining consortium in Belize. Platinum deposits, he said, had been found near a sleepy Mayan village called Las Criandas. Platinum was difficult to mine, he explained, but the complex process was worth it because platinum sold for about a thousand dollars an ounce. Its uses were as diverse as settings for diamond jewelry and coatings for the nose cones of missiles.

Ellie had deadpanned that she was real grateful Ted had brought her a gift of a platinum lapel pin and not a surface-to-air missile. It was the sort of affectionate, silly comment that caused the dinner guests, gathered to catch up on old times, to chuckle with appreciative laughter.

Belize, a former British colony, wasn't known for its deposits of precious metals. According to Uncle Ted, the tiny country was chiefly renowned as the location of some of the most important Mayan archaeological sites on the American continent. Tourism to ancient ruins was almost the only existing industry, and once the Las Criandas platinum mine was fully operational, her uncle had jokingly claimed that he and his partners would be responsible for five percent of the total gross national product of Belize. The country might not be an economic powerhouse, but that still meant there was a hell of a lot of money and potential profit tied up in the Las Criandas platinum mine.

Snippets of information about Belize weren't Megan's only memories of her uncle's visit. She had noticed an undercurrent of tension between her father and uncle, despite the fact that on the surface they had maintained their usual facade of hearty friendship. She remembered seeing the two of them standing outside the tractor storage shed at the Flying W, deep in conversation. They had appeared to be arguing and their conversation had ended abruptly when Ellie and one of the ranch hands rode in from a distant pasture and Uncle Ted strode off, leaving Ron to greet his wife alone.

At the time, Megan had assumed the two men were arguing about Uncle Ted's tactless suggestion that Ellie needed to stop burying herself at the ranch and see more of the world before it was too late. Now Megan wondered if the tension between her father and uncle might have had a more ominous basis.

In retrospect, she marveled again that her family dynamics were so dysfunctional that it had never crossed her mind that she ought to delve behind the superficial good humor to try to discover why her uncle and her father weren't seeing eye to eye. Her habit of not questioning the apparent calm of family relationships was so deeply ingrained—instilled by her parents?—that she'd simply never made a connection between Uncle Ted's presence at the ranch and her father's sudden decision to take out a three-million-dollar loan. Even when she'd discussed her father's itinerary with Adam, she had dismissed Uncle Ted's presence as irrelevant to the missing money.

The fact that her father had been flying regularly to Belize changed everything, as if a distorting overlay had been ripped off her memories, revealing them for what they truly were. Nausea roiled in her stomach as she struggled to piece the disconnected images into a coherent story line. Before her father died she would automatically have assumed there was an innocent reason for him to have paid multiple secret visits to Uncle Ted in Las

Criandas. Now Megan found herself formulating one criminal explanation after another. And all of her explanations, every single damn one, had Adam's missing three million dollars right at the heart.

It seemed clear that her father had borrowed the money from Adam's bank and invested it in Uncle Ted's platinum mine. The two questions for which she could imagine no answers were why the investment had been kept so secret and where the money was now.

The last question was the one that troubled her most. She was already more or less resigned to discovering that her father had been up to no good and that the three million dollars had been put to dubious use. But why had her uncle never discussed the loan with Ellie? Even if there had been some reason to keep quiet while Ron was alive—if Ron had pressured him, for example—there was no excuse for Uncle Ted failing to notify his sister now that Ron was dead. Megan really hoped that she didn't need to add Uncle Ted, her mother's much-loved brother, to the list of her relatives who were hiding criminal secrets.

"What do you think, Megan?" Adam slipped

his arm around her waist, propelling her back to awareness of the fact that they were still in the offices of *Navigación Águila,* and that the three other people in the room were all looking at her, clearly waiting for an answer to some important question.

"I'm not sure." That was entirely true, since she hadn't heard the question. She forced herself to look up and meet Adam's gaze, trying to appear as if she knew exactly what they were talking about. "What do *you* think we should do?" she asked brightly.

Fortunately, her question seemed to fit into the conversation she hadn't heard. "In my opinion we need to go to Belmopan," Adam said at once.

Where the heck was Belmopan? Megan wondered. *What* the heck was Belmopan? Thank goodness Adam answered her silent question. Apparently it was the capital of Belize, located more or less in the center of the country. As far as she recalled, Uncle Ted had never once mentioned the place.

Adam pointed to a map of Central America as he expanded his answer. "As Eric just pointed out, the total population of Belmopan is only seven thousand. There's just one hotel where Ron is likely to have stayed and it should be pretty easy to track down staff members who remember him. How big did you say the hotel is, Eric?"

"Twenty-five rooms. Like I told you, it's real tiny." Eric was back to smiling again, a fact that Megan considered cause for alarm. "Given that Mr. Raven stayed there half a dozen times, I'm sure the folks at the hotel will remember a lot about him."

"But why would my father go to Belmopan?" Megan asked, wishing she'd listened to whatever Eric had been saying instead of letting her attention get lost in the maze of Uncle Ted's last visit to Wyoming.

Adam shot her a slightly puzzled look. "Well, you heard what Eric said. Your father implied he was negotiating with the Belizean government for an important development project on behalf of a big U.S. corporation."

She rubbed her forehead, which was beginning to throb painfully. "But Dad didn't work for big corporations. He invested in small- and medium-size projects and did all the building and development himself." Eric's explanation sounded so plausible, though, that Megan wondered if she'd jumped too soon to the conclusion that her father had invested in Uncle Ted's platinum mine. Maybe her uncle hadn't been involved in the disappearance of Adam's three million dollars, after all. That would certainly be wonderful, but she dismissed the hope almost as soon as it formed. The long arm of coincidence would be stretched far beyond the breaking point if her father had suddenly decided to fly to Belize on a secret mission for some unnamed U.S. corporation only days after Uncle Ted had returned to Las Criandas.

"I realize the story your father told Eric doesn't tie in well with what we know about his normal business dealings," Adam said patiently. "That's why we need to make a trip there. Most of the people living in Belmopan are diplomats or civil servants, so it could be that your father was trying to get government approval for some new investment plan he had, just like he said."

Judging by Adam's remarks, Megan concluded that neither Eric nor Esmerelda had made any mention of the Las Criandas platinum mine while she'd been busy tripping down memory lane. Were the two of them holding back information, or had they been genuinely unaware of her father's true destination? It was possible that her father had flown to Belmopan just to avoid telling Eric the truth about where he was going, but that would have left Ron with hours of driving along dangerous roads to reach Las Criandas. His desire for secrecy would surely have clashed with his even more compelling desire to take care of business in the shortest possible time.

Megan wished she could have a few moments alone to sort through the turmoil of her thoughts. An internal alarm bell was clanging, warning that she shouldn't share what she knew about Uncle Ted and the platinum mine with Eric, certainly not now when she had no plan. The odds were that Eric knew about Las Criandas and was deliberately lying about where he'd taken her father. However, she wasn't likely to achieve much by outing him on the lie. Better to let him believe that she had no clue why Ron Raven would want to fly to Belize.

"Bearing in mind how tiny Belmopan is, I guess it's definitely worth going there," she said, hoping she didn't sound as distracted as she felt. "You're right, Adam, there must be some employees at the hotel who'll remember my dad. I mean, with only twenty-five rooms, how could the staff forget any guest who stayed there six times within the space of a couple of years?"

Adam nodded his agreement. "My thoughts precisely. We may as well go tomorrow, right? No point in waiting." He turned to Eric. "How long is the flight?"

Eric pointed to the map on the desk and used the tip of a ruler to draw a line between Mexico City and Belmopan. "It's about seven hundred miles, give or take. I have a Beechcraft King Air twin turbine that's available for hire tomorrow. The King Air needs only one pilot, seats up to four, and it cruises at a top speed of two hundred and seventy knots—that's more than three hundred miles an hour. So the travel time will be about three hours once you've factored in takeoff and landing. Maybe a bit less if we get lucky with tailwinds. Since you have valid U.S. passports, you don't need entry visas. With a commercial flight, you have to change planes in San Salvador or Guatemala, or both, and it takes eighteen hours, with a twelve-hour layover in one country or the other to make your connections."

"Good God, that's a huge difference," Adam said. "It would be quicker to take the bus!"

"Not really. The roads are lousy," Eric said. "And there are so many rumors of bandits and kidnappings that you have to figure some of them must be true. So if you need to get to Belmopan in a hurry, private charter is the only way to go."

Esmerelda had just taken a brochure out of the desk drawer and Eric spread it open on top of the map. "Here's information about the Beechcraft King Air that we fly. You can keep the brochure and read it at your leisure. You won't be sorry that you decided to spring for the extra cost of chartering with our company. It's comfortable, its quick and it's safe. That's why Ron always hired our services. He used to say you could grow roots hanging around waiting for commercial flights." Eric was superfriendly again, probably relieved that neither Adam nor Megan was casting doubt on his latest story.

Adam handed the brochure to Megan and turned his own attention back to the map. "Belize City looks much bigger than Belmopan. Why isn't that the capital?"

"It used to be, until half of it got blown away by a hurricane back in the seventies, or maybe the eighties. The government decided to rebuild the capital inland, where it was safer. Smart of them, really, but they can't persuade most of the citizens to move away from the coast. That's why Belmopan is still so tiny." Eric pulled a face. "There's not much to do there, to be honest."

"Well, if there isn't much in the way of entertainment, that's all the more reason for people to remember Ron." Adam seemed to be going out of his way to be chatty with Eric, presumably because he didn't want to alienate the guy who was going to be flying their plane. He turned back to Megan. "Since the flight's only three hours or so, I suggest we leave around ten tomorrow morning. Does that work for you? That means we can get up at a reasonable hour and still get to Belmopan with time to make some preliminary inquiries about your father before dinner."

"Ten tomorrow morning sounds great," she replied, wondering if anybody else in the room was suffering from the same sense of unreality that she was. Eric must be wondering if she and Adam were really as clueless as they seemed, while she was wondering at what point she needed to break the news to Eric that he was going to be flying to Las Criandas tomorrow, not to Belmopan.

As soon as they were alone, she would tell Adam about Las Criandas and the platinum mine, Megan decided. Against all the odds, Adam trusted her and it would be a real betrayal if she didn't share such vital information. The prospect of telling him the truth left her feeling sick to her stomach, but that wasn't surprising. The probability that her father had been involved in something illegal was growing exponentially. Try as she might to find innocent explanations for his behavior, she wasn't having much luck. If his investment was aboveboard, why had it been so secret? Then there was the fact of Uncle Ted's involvement. Confessing to a straight arrow like Adam that her uncle might also be involved in the disappearance of his three million dollars wouldn't be easy or pleasant, but it had to be faced.

She was still debating how best to break the news when their limo arrived to transport them back to the Sierra Nevada. As soon as they were inside, Adam stretched out his arm and pulled her head down against his chest, sheltering her against his body. After a few silent moments, he pushed the inevitable mop of curls behind her ear and tilted her face up so that he could look straight into her eyes.

She'd never known until now that a man could look incredibly sexy and heartbreakingly caring all at the same time. For some reason she didn't fully grasp, her stomach knotted with regret.

"What happened to you in there?" Adam asked. "As soon as Eric admitted that he'd flown your father to Belize, you seemed to freeze."

Now was the time to tell him what she knew. Megan opened her mouth to explain about Uncle Ted. "You're right, I freaked out," she heard herself say. "I don't know quite why. It just seemed beyond weird that Dad would have been flying to Mexico City as a cover for the fact that really he was going to Belize. I mean, why did he need to be so secretive? And why Belize? It makes no sense."

She sounded convincingly puzzled and was ashamed at the skill with which she was able to lie. Perhaps the ability to deceive was one of the genes she'd inherited from her father, she thought despairingly, right along with the shape of her mouth and her small, straight nose.

"It makes no sense to us right now, but Ron always had a reason for what he did, even if his logic might seem twisted to us." Adam stroked her cheek with the back of his hand, the caress tender enough to make her ache inside. "Let's just hope that Belmopan turns out to be the end of the trail."

Megan shivered. "Yes, let's hope."

"This is really hard on you, isn't it?" Adam's gray eyes, which she'd once considered so cool and judgmental, were warm with sympathy. He tucked her head back against his chest and Megan could feel his heart beating beneath her cheek. The rhythm was strong and steady. She discovered to her dismay that she was fighting tears. Her stupid sensitivity button still hadn't managed to develop an off switch.

"I'm afraid of what we might find out tomorrow." That, at least, was the absolute truth.

He didn't reassure her by pretending that their discoveries were likely to be pleasant. Adam, she thought miserably, was not a man who manipulated the truth even in an attempt to be kind.

"Let's make a pact to enjoy dinner tonight without once mentioning your father's name," he said. “We could both use the break and I feel in the mood to eat chiles rellenos, drink tequila, listen to a mariachi band and pretend we’re tourists. How about you?”

“Sounds like a plan.” Megan was delighted at the prospect of another few hours without the need to talk about Uncle Ted and the platinum mine. Perhaps she could even hold off revealing what she knew until they were en route for the airport tomorrow. Telling Adam what she suspected about her father’s investment in the platinum mine would make no practical difference to their plans at this point. On the other hand, explaining to Adam about her uncle and Las Criandas was likely to make a great deal of difference in his attitude toward her, so why spoil their evening? From Adam’s perspective, one lying, cheating relative might be considered bad luck. Two lying, cheating relatives made for an unpleasant pattern. Add that to all the complicated baggage from their past and she couldn’t think of a reason in the world why he would decide to maintain their relationship once this trip was over.

They were heading deeper into the traffic jungle of Mexico City’s core, and Megan’s stomach started to swoop in a now-familiar pattern as their limo driver played chicken with his fellow road warriors. Megan was almost glad for the distraction from her gloomy thoughts. The driver suddenly stomped the heel of his hand on the horn and dodged between two trucks, a bus and assorted, horn-screeching taxicabs. She gasped and gripped the nearest solid object, which happened to be Adam's arm.

When they'd made it through, a true miracle if ever she'd witnessed one, Adam laughed and hugged her. "You've no idea how cute you look when you're scared."

"That's a blatantly sexist remark." She met his eyes, trying to appear severe, which was difficult given that her heart was pretty much melting. "I disapprove of sexism. If I didn't still need to borrow your arm as a safety blanket, I'd move to the far corner of the limo."

"Don't move," he said softly. "I like having you close to me." As he spoke, he leaned down and kissed her, one of those bewildering kisses that seemed equal parts passion and tenderness and left her feeling disoriented. Except that this time, when the disorientation passed, she felt a rush of new certainty about her own feelings. She realized, with a sense of recognition rather than surprise, that she'd fallen in love with Adam. Her reluctance to tell him the truth about Las Criandas and Uncle Ted suddenly made perfect sense: their relationship was too new and too weighted with baggage to survive any more sordid revelations about members of her family. She had instinctively protected her chance to develop something meaningful with Adam by keeping silent. Unfortunately, whatever the consequences, the amount of time left for her to avoid talking about Uncle Ted was measured in hours, not even days.

Sometimes, she thought gloomily, life really sucked.

They ate dinner in one of the hotel restaurants so that they wouldn't have to brave the traffic yet again. The restaurant was crowded, but the maître d' led them to a table by the window with a view of the courtyard, and he presented Megan with a red rose as he seated her, bowing with a flourish and ordering her to enjoy her dinner.

Megan was in a reckless mood—the condemned woman ate and drank heartily, she thought ironically. The chiles rellenos were delicious, the drinks were free-flowing, the mariachi band was loud and Adam's company was outstanding. The more time she spent with him, the more fascinating she found him. It wasn't merely that he was so handsome, looking at him made her weak; he was also the most interesting person she had ever met. She was deeply attracted to his rock-solid honesty, an honesty she had missed in the moral ambiguities and compromises that inevitably flourished around her father. Of course, she was responding to Adam's honesty by withholding the truth about her uncle and Las Criandas, Megan reflected ruefully. Still, she was only holding out for a little while longer, so perhaps that didn't count as hard-core dishonesty.

As they waited for their desserts to arrive, despite having sworn not to talk about Ron, their conversation drifted back to the ranch and the resort he had pretended to be developing there.

Megan drained her third oversize margarita, which was at least two and a half more than she could safely consume if she wanted to be sure of guarding her tongue. "The most frustrating part of Dad's scam is that I've been begging my parents for the past four years to consider developing the Flying W just the way he proposed to you. Cattle ranching makes for a hard life, and even though Mom has a full-time manager, she still works long hours for very little reward. Last year, according to my brother, the entire ranching operation barely broke even after expenses and there's almost no prospect of an improvement in profits anytime soon. I have a ton of ideas about how the property could be developed without ruining the natural beauty of the land down by the Silver River. We wouldn't even need to tear down the existing ranch house. It could easily be screened from the rest of the property with evergreens, so Mom could carry on living right in her own house. It burns me up that Dad listened to my ideas enough to parrot them back to you, but he wasn't prepared to invest any time or energy to persuade Mom to let him start building."

"I take it that it's your mother who's opposed to the idea of development?" Adam asked.

Megan nodded. "She's so accustomed to thinking of the Flying W as a cattle ranch that she's fixated on the ranching operations as the heart and soul of the property. But I think she loves the Flying W for reasons that have diddly-squat to do with how the land is utilized. She loves the place because it's been in her family for generations, end of story. I've tried to convince Mom that it makes almost no difference whether there are cattle or tourists roaming over the pastures. The land is still the land and she'd still wake up to see the Grand Tetons in the distance every morning." Megan gave a thin smile. "So far, though, she shows no signs of agreeing with me."

Adam grinned. "I've never considered tourists and cows as interchangeable commodities before. It's an interesting new perspective. Maybe we just have to convince your mother that we can make more money per tourist than we can per cow."

"I don't think it's that simple." Megan sighed. "Money isn't high on the list of things that motivate my mother."

Adam drained his tequila. "What we need is to bring in some experts who've developed other resort areas successfully, with genuine respect for the environment. They might be able to convince your mother that development doesn't always mean destruction of everything that makes a place special. If she agreed to the concept of developing the land, we should be able to raise the capital. Ron provided me with a slew of numbers about the potential profitability of the project, and the figures were impressive. Raising the investment funds shouldn't be a problem."

"But weren't the numbers Dad provided fake?"

"Only in the sense that he didn't plan to go ahead with the project. As regards costs and potential returns, Ron's numbers were carefully worked out, and on the conservative side." Adam gave a short laugh. "Nobody can accuse your father of not being willing to work hard in order to pull off his scams. It must have taken him hours and hours to get those numbers together, not to mention that he genuinely consulted with dozens of land-use experts. I know those reports were genuine because I checked them out personally."

Megan drew wistfully in the frost on the side of her glass. "It would be a dream come true for me if we could persuade my mother to go along with the idea of putting a lodge down by the river." She broke off as one of the waiters approached their table.

"*Señorita,* there is a phone call for you. You can take it at the table of the maître d'."

"For me?" she asked, puzzled. "For Megan Raven?"

"Yes, *señorita.* The call is for you. It is a man," he said helpfully.

Megan stood up and the waiter pulled out her chair. "Will you excuse me? I'll be right back," she told Adam.

"I'll be here." He toasted her with his tequila glass. "If I get too bored, I'll eat your dessert."

"Don't you dare." She followed the waiter back to the maître d's desk and he handed her the phone before hurrying toward the kitchen.

"This is Megan Raven," she said. "Who's calling, please?"

The male voice was impossible to identify over the crackle of a bad phone connection. "I need to be sure you're who you claim to be. Tell me the name of your mother's favorite mare."

Megan's breathing quickened. The caller was definitely American, and probably from the middle part of the country, judging by his accent, although the bad connection made it hard to narrow the identification any further. “Who is this?” she demanded again.

“Tell me the name of your mother’s mare,” the voice repeated.

She hesitated for a moment. “Her name was Pretty Woman. Who are you? What do you want?”

“I have a message for you from your uncle Ted. Las Criandas is a dangerous place for you and for your boyfriend. Be a smart girl, Megan. Keep yourself and everyone else safe. Go back to Thatch and stop interfering. Go home now.”

Sixteen

Adam watched Megan wind her way back to the table, hips swaying as she edged past bustling waiters and strolling mariachi players. God, she was sexy! She was also smart, pretty and totally not his type. He had no idea how or why he'd fallen in love with her. He only knew that his throat tightened and his heart raced like a high school kid's every time he looked at her. More astonishing still, he wanted to comfort and protect her almost as much as he wanted to take her to bed. *Almost,* he thought with a wry grin.

She slipped back into the chair opposite his and although she smiled brightly, he saw at once that she was upset. She was good at putting on a cheerful facade, but there were signs of strain around her eyes and mouth that hadn't been there earlier.

"I hope the phone call wasn't bad news," he said.

"Not exactly." She hesitated for a moment. "It was Eric, from Eagle Navigation."

"What on earth did he want? And why did he ask for you, not me, I wonder?"

"I think you intimidate him." Her smile relaxed a little. "He was completely caught off guard this afternoon when he realized you speak fluent Spanish."

"I have to admit, it was *really* satisfying to point out that I knew he was lying. Almost makes those months sleeping in a mud hut in Peru worth it. Eric was so damn smug with his story about your father having a mistress in Chichén Itzá. If I hadn't understood what Esmerelda yelled at him, I'd have believed every word of his story. The details he came up with were so persuasive."

"Not to mention his frequent apologetic glances to let me know how sorry he was to be forced to reveal my father's indiscretions." Megan's nose wrinkled. "Jeez, he's such a slimeball. In reality, he was enjoying every minute."

"And did you notice that he gave us just enough description of the supposed mistress that she didn't seem generic, but there was absolutely no way for us to attempt to trace her?"

"I did notice." Megan paused for a moment. "In fact, the lies were so good I wondered if my father had coached Eric in the story."

"That possibility had occurred to me, too," Adam said. "Given that Eric doesn't appear to be the brightest light on the Christmas tree, his story was a bit too pat. Anyway, back to the phone call. What did he want?"

"He claims there's been a scheduling problem with another flight and that we can't take off from Toluca until eleven tomorrow morning. He said he didn't want us to be inconvenienced by hanging around at the airport, waiting."

Adam raised an eyebrow. "Eric certainly hasn't adapted to the Mexican concept of time management, has he? I'm amazed that he bothered to call just for an hour's delay."

"Yes, it's surprising. To be honest, it makes me wonder if he's telling the truth."

"I'm sure he isn't. Truth seemed to be in pretty short supply at the Eagle Navigation offices this afternoon."

Megan stared at him, eyes wide. Adam

had the oddest impression that his throw-away comment had really frightened her. "What do you mean?" she asked at last. "Did Eric… Did Esmerelda say anything else when she was yelling at him?"

"Nothing important." He grinned. "Unless you're referring to the bit where she called her husband a stupid dickhead. I think that's more or less how to translate the phrase."

Megan didn't smile. "To be honest, Adam, I don't have a good feeling about this trip to Belize." She poked her spoon through the caramel custard that had been delivered while she was answering the phone call, but she didn't eat anything. "Maybe we've bitten off more than we can chew here."

Adam looked at her long and hard. "Did Eric threaten you just now?" he asked.

Her spoon clattered onto her dessert plate. "No, of course not! I told you exactly what he said. But there's something about him that sets my teeth on edge…."

Adam shrugged. "Like you said, he's a slimeball."

"It's more than his general excess of sliminess. Why did he insist on speaking to me personally instead of just leaving a message for us on the hotel voice mail system? After all, you're right, his message was trivial. It occurred to me while he was talking… What if he gets us up in the air and then kidnaps us, or something?"

"Why would he risk the entire future of Eagle Navigation to do that? Leaving aside the fact that there's a huge difference between being a slimeball and being a criminal, he'd lose his livelihood forever and there's almost no chance he'd be able to ransom us for enough money to compensate."

"I don't know what his motive could be. That's what's so frustrating. I can't even identify exactly what he said that's making me uneasy. But *why* did he spin that story about taking my father to Chichén Itzá? Why would he lie unless he's involved in something he doesn't want discovered?"

"Except for embarrassment, there were no real consequences for Eric if we caught him lying," Adam pointed out. "And he didn't strike me as man who suffers from an excess of embarrassment. It's not as if he's going to lose his operating license. There's no law that says pilots have to give accurate reports to members of the public wandering in off the street. My guess is that Eric lied to us because your father paid him to, and it was no skin off his nose to go along with Ron's request. In other words, it's your father who was keeping secrets, not Eric."

Adam could see that his answer didn't satisfy Megan. The phone call really seemed to have shaken her up, he reflected. There was a slight tremor in her hand and she gave up on the pretense of eating dessert, pushing the plate away with a moue of distaste.

"That doesn't explain Esmerelda's outburst," she said. "According to you, she yelled at Eric that she'd *warned* him not to get involved in flying my father to Belize. That sounds as if she knew there was something dangerous waiting at the end of the journey."

Adam frowned. "You're right, it does. That subtlety slipped right past me. Although it's hard for me to believe that Eric would attempt to harm us when he'd be the first person law enforcement would suspect."

"When we're paddling through the jungle swamps with piranhas snapping at our inflatable life raft, I'm not sure how much relief I'll get from knowing that the police are sure to suspect Eric." Megan's voice was dry.

Adam laughed. "At least we'll be paddling

together. And in the interests of accuracy, I don't believe there are any piranhas in Mexico. They're limited to slow-moving rivers in the Amazon basin."

"I'll be sure to inform the fish that bites off your hand that he's exceeded his habitat limitations." Megan's response was lighthearted but her eyes were still dark with fear.

"Tell me what you want us to do," he said, putting his hand over hers. Her fingers, he realized, were ice cold. "Look, there's nothing forcing us to go to Belize. We can cancel tomorrow's flight if that's what you'd prefer."

She closed her eyes for a moment. "You've no idea how much I want to cancel…."

Despite Megan's evident attack of nerves, Adam hadn't expected her to back off from the idea of going to Belize. "I understand why you're worried. But the downside of canceling is that we're never going to find out what your father was up to—"

"Or what happened to your three million dollars," she said bleakly.

"Forget the money for a moment." If the money had been his and not the bank's, Adam would have written it off days ago. "There are more important reasons to go to

Belize. Don't you get the feeling that we're closing in on the motive for your father's murder?"

Megan dropped her gaze. When she looked up again, her eyes were bright with tears. "I do have that feeling," she admitted, but she said nothing more.

He tightened his grip on her hand. "We can cancel the trip, Megan, but I'm guessing you'd spend the rest of your life wondering what your father had been involved in. Yes, if we go to Belize, we risk learning things about your father that you may not like, but at least you'll have definite answers." He paused for a moment. "However, it's your choice, sweetheart."

The endearment slipped out with no warning. He discovered to his surprise that he had no wish to call it back. Megan looked up, clearly startled. Her gaze locked with his and he saw a flood of conflicting emotions jostle for supremacy. In the end, she tried for a jaunty smile and only managed to look heartbreakingly vulnerable.

"Your choice," he said again softly.

"Do you really mean that, Adam?"

"Yes. No recriminations either way."

Color ran along her cheekbones. "I guess

I'm a wimp, but I don't want us to go to Belize." Her smile was wan. "I have this gut suspicion that we stirred up something dangerous when we questioned Eric this afternoon. I think we should go back to the police in Miami and tell them what we've found out. Leave them to do the investigating."

"Then we'll call Eric tomorrow and cancel the flight." He chose not to remind her that she was the one who'd originally insisted they come to Mexico because the police would do nothing useful.

"Adam, I'm so sorry—"

"Shh." He pressed his fingers against her lips. "Don't apologize. The decision's made. And every member of both our families would undoubtedly consider that you made a wise choice."

"But not you," she said and he heard desolation where before music and laughter had filled her voice.

"You made the sensible decision," he repeated. And it probably had been sensible, even though it surprised him. Shocked him, almost. It was an indication of how deep his feelings for Megan ran that he felt no irritation at her change of mind, only concern because she was so clearly unhappy.

He lifted her hand and kissed the tips of her cold fingers, deliberately changing the subject. “If you’ve finished massacring that poor flan caramelisado, we could walk around the courtyard and admire the stars. The ones we can see through the pollution haze, that is.”

“I’d like that.”

He signed the check and she reached for his hand as they walked outside. The simple gesture made his heart beat faster. The night air wrapped them in the scent of gardenias and the water fountain splashed soothingly enough to counteract the roar of not-so-distant traffic.

Adam walked over to the fountain and let the tepid water trickle over his wrists. He could have used something icier, he thought, silently amused by his own hopelessly infatuated state.

“One day I’d like to come back to Mexico with you,” he said as she came to stand beside him, the water splashing across her wrists and onto his. “Not here to Mexico City, but to one of the lovely old towns in the Yucatán. Izamal, perhaps. Have you ever been there?”

“No, I’ve only been to Acapulco and Cancún, staying in big hotels on each occasion. I try to use my vacation time to visit major tourist resorts. That way I can check out if they have any good ideas we could utilize in Jackson Hole." She looked up at him, her usually expressive features pale in the moonlight. "I'd love to visit the Yucatán with you, Adam. Thank you for suggesting it."

Her response struck him as oddly formal and entirely sweet. He'd been wanting to kiss her ever since they sat down to dinner. He finally abandoned the delusion that he could hold out any longer. He shook the water from his hands and took her into his arms, holding her close. Her skin felt hot beneath his damp fingers and he was aware of a tension in both of them that hadn't been present when they'd made love the night before.

He heard her sigh when she finally let go of her conflicted emotions and surrendered to the simplicity of straightforward physical need. She flowed against him, offering him a promise of gratification that he was only too eager to accept. Heat surged in his blood, pulsing in time with his racing heartbeat. Logic disappeared, drowned in the wild rush of desire, but a muddled thought surfaced through the morass of sensation, a recognition that he had waited a lifetime for a woman like this. Megan was vital and interesting enough to penetrate his carefully honed facade and expose the truth of the man he really was. With her, he could be himself, not merely Adam Fairfax IV, the great-grandson of U.S. Senator Adam Fairfax, bastion of the Old South. He hadn't realized until he met Megan just how tired he was of being permanently on display as the designated savior of the First Bank of Fairfax and polisher of the tarnished Fairfax family honor.

It was Megan who broke off the kiss. "Come upstairs," she murmured, her mouth still close to his, her body flattened against his chest. Her voice was husky, almost rough. He found it entirely seductive. "Please, Adam. I want you so much."

They almost ran out of the elevator when they arrived upstairs, choosing his room for the simple reason that he managed to find his key card first. The maid had already turned down the bed and Adam brushed the foil-wrapped chocolates from his pillow with fingers made clumsy by desire. Megan looked especially tiny and defenseless as she tumbled onto the king-size bed, her hair spread out on the big square Mexican pillows, her nipples showing through her silk blouse where he had made it damp with water from the fountain. Even though the cynical part of him mocked the surge of protectiveness that swept over him, another part of him was overwhelmed with tenderness. Then cynicism and tenderness both disappeared in a rush of all-consuming need.

Megan held out her hands, pulling him down onto the bed. Her breath was sharp and unsteady and she gave a little moan of anticipation when he lay down beside her. He took her mouth in a deep, savoring kiss and the magic of the night before rushed back in a giant shock wave.

Neither of them had chosen to switch out the light left on by the maid and he watched the emotions chasing across her face as they made love, relishing every quiver of pleasure and every tremor of delight. He saw the need that was almost pain tighten her features as she raced toward climax, and the moment of aching regret when she realized that she couldn't hold back any longer. He thought he said her name, but he wasn't sure because he was racked by his own climax, a torrent of release and gratification that left him lying panting, exhausted and replete in Megan's arms.

It was, he thought drowsily, the perfect place to be.

Seventeen

The sound that woke him was muffled, but Adam had spent two years living in a Peruvian village that was located in territory disputed between the Shining Path rebel army and the government in Lima. He'd quickly learned that people who slept too soundly ran the risk of never waking up. At the very least, deep sleepers could expect to find themselves barricaded in a makeshift camp at the mercy of soldiers who might trade you, ransom you or slit your throat, depending on their mood.

His stint in Peru had been over twelve years ago, but since then he'd never lost the habit of sleeping with a thin thread of consciousness alert for trouble. He woke up often, but fortunately he usually fell asleep again the minute he reassured his subconscious that he wasn't about to become slashing practice for a rebel soldier.

He turned his head on the pillow, expecting to find Megan next to him. Instead, he realized that the bed was empty and that she must have been the source of the sound that had woken him.

In the dim light filtering through the crack in the draperies, he watched her creep toward the door connecting their two rooms. His mouth curved into a smile as he quietly raised himself on his elbow, not speaking, just watching. She was picking up her clothes that were scattered randomly across the floor, her movements careful and silent. Her naked body bending and lifting was a rewarding sight, definitely worth waking up for, and he spent a pleasant thirty seconds debating precisely which part of her anatomy was the most enticing. In the end he decided it was impossible to choose from such a surfeit of perfection.

The red figures of the bedside clock flicked to a new number: 5:00 a.m. He frowned, mildly puzzled. Why was Megan awake so early? And why was she picking up her clothes? They had made love to the point of mutual exhaustion and it had been almost three in the morning by the time she fell asleep. He knew, because he'd been holding her when she finally dozed off. It was strange that she would be awake already, let alone that she would feel motivated to start organizing her laundry.

He continued to observe Megan, his attention suddenly more focused on her actions and less on the jiggle of her breasts. Each step was slow and calculated as she crept to the doors that separated their two rooms. They'd left the doors ajar ever since breakfast yesterday morning and she slipped her fingers into the little gap, pulling the door on his side open. She was exercising the sort of care that might have been appropriate for detonating the fuse of an unexploded bomb.

What the *hell* was going on?

Despite all Megan's precautions, the second door made a tiny creaking noise as she pushed it open. Adam barely had time to drop his head back onto the pillow before she whipped around to check if he was still sleeping.

He lay still, his breathing regular, his eyes closed, and eventually he heard the almost imperceptible sound of her pushing open the second door. His failure to let Megan know he was awake added another mystery to the already existing one of what she was up to. His behavior, he thought bleakly, was almost as strange as hers. Why hadn't he spoken to her? Why was he watching her as if she were a criminal intruder instead of his lover?

Adam came up with no answer to his own questions, but he still didn't move, much less say anything. A lead weight lodged itself in the pit of his stomach. He squinted from his prone position, watching Megan slip through the second door and into her room. He waited for her to lock the door on her side, but apparently she was afraid the clicking sound would wake him.

If he wanted to, he could follow her into her room and she would be none the wiser.

It seemed that he wanted. He got up, his movements as noiseless as Megan's. The linen slacks he'd worn for dinner lay in a crumpled heap on the floor next to the bed. He pulled them on, his mind determinedly empty as he tugged the zipper upward.

Adam crossed to the connecting doors, opening the one on his side and flattening himself against it. By craning forward, he could see a section of Megan's room that included one side of the bed and the nightstand. She'd switched on the lamp but draped a towel over the shade. The resulting glow provided just enough light to prevent her bumping into furniture but not enough to seep through the connecting doors.

Megan herself was nowhere in his line of sight. He wondered for a moment if he'd totally overreacted. He'd feel pretty dumb if it turned out he'd been acting like a commando on a night raid because she needed to use the bathroom and hadn't wanted to disturb him.

But after a couple of minutes, he saw that he hadn't misjudged the situation. Megan walked back to the bed from the direction of the bathroom. She was now dressed in cotton slacks and a summery jacket and her hair was brushed and tugged into a ponytail, although she was still shoeless. She was taking no chances of waking him, Adam thought grimly.

She was packing, he realized. Not her big suitcase, but the flight bag she'd carried onto the plane for their trip to Mexico City from the States. As he watched, she disappeared from view again and returned carrying her toilet articles. She stashed the travel pack in the bottom of the flight bag, followed by what looked like underclothes and a couple of T-shirts. The light was dim enough that it was hard to be sure, but he could make a damn good guess that it was her passport she took out of the wall safe and slipped into her purse.

The weight in the pit of his stomach turned into a ball of fire, the flames roaring through his veins with furious speed. First Ron Raven had scammed him and now Ron Raven's daughter was doing the same thing! He couldn't believe he'd been so fucking stupid. Megan was obviously preparing to run. She'd let him tag along until they picked up a good lead to the missing millions and now she was ditching him. What was he, for Christ's sake? Candidate-in-chief for the role of village idiot? He'd sat there last night at dinner and practically invited her to screw him over.

Megan, sweetheart, we don't have to go to Belize if you're feeling nervous. He winced at the memory of his own sentimental behavior. What a goddamn fool he'd been.

He slammed open the connecting door and walked into her room. "What the hell are you doing?"

Megan's head jerked up. She looked

panic-stricken, which might indicate something about the true state of her feelings. Or not. Clearly she was capable of faking just about any emotion or expression she chose. Up to and including some pretty damn spectacular orgasms.

"Adam—I thought you were asleep." Her voice sounded breathless.

"Your first mistake." The ball of fire in his gut was congealing into familiar ice as he reasserted control over his idiotic, lovesick emotions. "I repeat, what the hell are you doing?"

"I couldn't sleep." Her hands fluttered. "I…I'm so sorry I disturbed you. I'm just organizing some…stuff."

He cast a pointed glance at her outfit and she blushed. She was dressed to go out and they both knew it. He grabbed her travel bag and upended it over the bed. Clothes, sneakers and toilet articles landed in a heap on the cover.

"Like to try a do-over on that answer, sweetheart?"

She didn't mistake his endearment for anything other than the insult it was. "Adam, don't be angry." Her voice thinned. "I know this looks bad, but I tried to do what I thought was best—"

"I'm sure you did. As in, what's best for you. Since you seem to be experiencing more trouble than usual in speaking the truth, I'll cut to the chase. Where were you planning to go? Belmopan?"

"Not Belmopan." Her voice was suddenly weary, leeched of all emotion, and he could see tears in her eyes. He ignored them as the trick of the trade they undoubtedly were.

"If you're not going to Belmopan, then where?"

She shook her head and looked away from him. He grabbed her by the shoulders, forcing her to face him. "I asked you a question. If not Belmopan, then where?"

"You don't want to know. Honestly, Adam, just let me leave. It's better that way." Her voice dropped. "Safer."

He laughed, a marginally better alternative than screaming insults at the top of his lungs. His protective ice kept melting under the heat of his anger and until he could get the ice back in place, he was hurting. Right at this moment, the hurt kept stoking the fire of his anger in a splendidly effective vicious circle.

"We'll move faster if you accept that whatever you're selling this morning, I'm not buying. Let's get a couple of things straight here. I'm not sure if your passionate plea to save the Flying W for your poor old mom was any more genuine than the rest of the garbage you've served up to me over the past couple of weeks. That being the case, I won't threaten you with foreclosing on the ranch because the threat might not be effective. Let's just say that if you don't tell me in the next ten seconds where you were planning to go this morning, I'll lay charges of attempted grand theft against you as soon as I get back to the States. I'll make the charges stick, too." His threat sounded credible because he meant it.

Megan lost color. "Attempted grand theft? What are you talking about? I haven't stolen anything."

"Except three million dollars of my bank's money. Clearly, you know where it is."

"I don't know where the money is, Adam. I wish to God I did! My greatest fear is that it's already gone beyond any hope of reclaiming."

He didn't respond, just walked toward the phone and started counting. "Ten, nine, eight, seven—"

"Las Criandas," she said in a rush. "I was going to ask Eric to fly me to Las Criandas. It's a small Mayan village in the west of Belize, only a few miles from the Mexican border."

He turned around and leaned against the nightstand, feigning a casualness he was about a million years away from feeling. He managed to make his voice sound coolly mocking. "I assume you aren't going in search of Mayan antiquities, so what in hell interests you about the small village of Las Criandas?"

She hesitated. "There's a platinum mine located close to the village."

"Ah. A platinum mine. How enlightening. No doubt a platinum mine in which Ron Raven invested my money."

"It's not your money. It's the bank's and we've paid the interest—"

He cut across her justification as if she hadn't spoken. "You expect to retrieve *my* three million dollars from somebody working at the platinum mine in Las Criandas—"

"Not expect. Hope."

He ignored her again. "Since you were anxious to avoid having me along for the ride, you obviously weren't intending to hand the money over to me. That's theft. Where were you planning to go with the loot, sweetheart? To Brazil, maybe? Or how about the Cayman Islands? They have an interesting banking system over there. Of course, you probably know that already from your daddy." Acid choked his throat. "God, I'll bet you were Ron's star pupil in his Art of Deception class."

"I wasn't planning to run away," she said woodenly. "I didn't try to con you. If you'd only stop insulting me for a moment and think back over everything that's happened between the two of us, you'd realize I never intended to set you up. For heaven's sake, Adam, be rational! If I'd planned to steal the bank's money, I'd never have invited you to come to Mexico with me in the first place."

"Of course you would, honey. The best con artists always bring their mark along as far as they possibly can. That's part of the fun."

"Maybe it's fun if you're a con artist. I'm not." She bit out each word. "I don't consider scamming people even remotely amusing."

"Your virtue is awe-inspiring. Forgive me if I'm not quite ready to nominate you for sainthood."

"I had reasons for not telling you that I was leaving this morning." She drew in a shaky breath. "I swear that if I managed to find the money, I was planning to return it to you. Every damn penny."

Adam made the harsh, abrupt sound that was all he could currently summon in place of laughter. "Of course." He straightened. "You know what? This conversation is getting tedious. I'm declaring it over." He gestured to indicate she should go back into his room and she shook her head.

"No."

"You can walk yourself in there, or I'll carry you." He hoped, he really hoped, that she would refuse to move. That would provide him with the excuse he needed to get his hands on her. God, it would feel so great to grab her shoulders and shake her until she cried. She would plead with him to forgive her. He wouldn't. Then, if her tears got too intense, he'd throw her on the bed and kiss her senseless. No, not kiss her, that implied too much intimacy.

Adam drew in a long, slow breath, forcing

his thoughts away from the precipice. Once he was capable of rational functioning again, he decided he needed to get dressed and that he needed Megan under his eye while he did it.

He gestured again to indicate that she should go into his bedroom. She didn't move and he reached toward her.

"Don't touch me!" She jumped away from him, looking as if so much as his finger on her skin would be enough to contaminate her.

Astonishingly, her repugnance hurt. Adam felt his mouth curl into a sneer. "Why don't you want me to touch you, babe? Last night I seem to recall several occasions when you were begging me to touch you. And not just on your arm, either."

"Last night was different."

"You bet it was." He could hear the cold fury in his own voice. "Last night I didn't realize you were willing to exchange sex for money. Unfortunately for you, you overpriced yourself, sweetheart. You're good, but nowhere near in the three-million-bucks-a-bang class."

She looked at him in silence, her features no longer mobile and expressive but seemingly carved out of granite. Even her eyes were blank. Without speaking, her shoulder turned to avoid any possible contact with him, she stalked into his room. Once there, she stood with her back to the windows but her gaze pointedly averted from him.

Well, screw her. He could play the ignoring game as well as she could. Adam went into the bathroom and turned on the shower, sticking his head and shoulders under the cold spray. He supposed it helped. At least his heart no longer felt as if it might burst out of his chest. He draped a towel around his neck and returned to the bedroom just in time to see Megan disappearing through the connecting door back to her room.

This time he didn't bother to rationalize; he just grabbed her. She felt fragile as she struggled in his grasp. The ten-inch gap in their heights had never felt so enormous and he'd never in his life felt so brutal. Once he had her subdued, he was angry with her all over again because she made him feel ashamed. Of what, he wasn't quite sure.

Neither of them spoke a word as he shoved her into the bathroom, slamming the door and wedging it shut with a chair. He pushed away his feelings of guilt. Hell, Megan had betrayed *him,* not the other way around. In fact, what she'd done couldn't even be considered a betrayal because that presupposed at least some level of genuine commitment and trust. He doubted if that had ever been present in their relationship. Megan had simply played him for a sucker, and he'd sucked her game right up.

With a vicious tug, he took a clean shirt from the closet, found socks and loafers, and tossed miscellaneous clean clothes into his flight bag, adding money, credit cards and his passport from the wall safe. He called down to the front desk and requested a limo for the trip to Toluca airport, then went into Megan's room to collect her purse and luggage. He wrote a brief message on hotel stationery explaining that he and Megan planned to fly to Las Criandas in Belize with Eagle Navigation, Eric Connolly as pilot, and addressed the envelope to the manager before shoving the note into his pocket, ready to hand over to the desk clerk. Finally, he pushed aside the chair and jerked open the bathroom door.

Megan had been crying, but she scrubbed her hand across her face, dashing away the tears. The look she gave him was hard-eyed and defiant. He ignored both the tears and the defiance and held out her bag.

"Are you ready to leave?" His gaze glided away from her tear-stained face. He was nicely frozen right now and he didn't want the fire in his gut to come back.

"Where are we going?" She slung the purse over her shoulder.

"To Las Criandas. Where else?"

"That could be a dangerous decision," she said.

"Is that a threat, sweetheart?"

"No, simply a warning."

Adam bared his teeth in what might pass for a smile in the dim light. "Considering the source of the warning, I see no reason to change my plans."

She didn't reply beyond a single rebellious glance, just stormed out of the room. She didn't bother to check if he was following.

Eighteen

She supposed it would have been possible to screw up the situation a bit more than she had. Right now, however, Megan wasn't quite sure how. The limo Adam had ordered was waiting for them when they came downstairs and she got in, sliding across the seat to the far corner and putting her flight bag on the seat next to her. A totally unnecessary barrier between her and Adam, since he looked as if he'd just as soon curl up with a rabid skunk as sit anywhere close to her.

Five minutes elapsed before Adam joined her, but she was too tired to speculate on what he'd been doing. She leaned back against the upholstery and closed her eyes, wondering how her father had survived his life of lies and deception for so many years. Had his stomach churned with sickness when one of his scams went awry? Had his head throbbed with the pain of knowing he'd made the wrong choice but that his options had closed off and there was no way to put things right? Probably not, she thought. As far as she could tell, her father had relished the thrill of deceiving people. She was apparently made of different stuff. She was exhausted, right down to her bones. It was a kind of fatigue that was new to her, caused more by despair than the fact that she was short of sleep.

"We have some business matters that need to be discussed," Adam said once their driver reached the highway. It was the first time he'd spoken since they left the hotel. "You might want to take into account that my temper is currently on a short leash and the consequences aren't likely to be good if you lie."

"I haven't lied to you. Except last night at dinner."

He ignored her, of course. Not surprising, since it wasn't exactly a ringing defense of her integrity.

"What did Eric really say to you when he called? Was it even Eric who called?" His mouth twisted ironically. "In fact, did you actually receive a phone call, or did you bribe the waiter so that you'd have an excuse to perform your masterful little riff about being too scared to fly to Belmopan?"

At this point, she might as well tell him the whole truth and nothing but the truth, although she had a depressing suspicion that Adam was going to put the worst possible interpretation on everything she'd done and not done over the past twelve hours. It was tempting to tell him to go to hell, but for the sake of their mutual safety, he needed to know just what they were getting into if they flew to Las Criandas.

"I received a phone call," she said. "I wasn't expecting it, and I certainly didn't bribe the waiter." She drew in a fortifying breath. "It wasn't from Eric, though. It was from somebody who claimed to be delivering a message from my uncle. From my mother's brother, Ted Horn."

Nobody could accuse Adam of being slow on the uptake. "Ah. Presumably that would be the same Uncle Ted who came to stay at the Flying W two years ago, right before your father approached my bank and scammed me out of three million dollars."

"Yes."

"And this would be the same uncle who's an engineer and works in South America."

The limo screeched to a juddering halt behind a giant semi but Megan barely noticed. There was nothing like being called a three-million-dollar whore to take your mind off the problems of Mexico City's traffic.

"It's not strictly true to say that Uncle Ted works in South America. He actually works in Central America." She swallowed. "In Belize."

Adam's eyes narrowed, but that was his only sign of surprise. "At the platinum mine in Las Criandas, I assume."

Megan nodded miserably. "He's the senior operations manager there." She looked out of the car window, seeing nothing of the early-morning rush hour beyond a blur of undifferentiated vehicles. "You won't believe me, but it never crossed my mind to link my father's mystery trips to Mexico City with the fact that Uncle Ted works in Belize. At least not until you translated what Esmerelda had yelled at her husband. It's embarrassing to admit, but before Eric showed us that map yesterday, I had no idea that Belize and Mexico shared a border, much less that

Las Criandas is only about twenty miles inside Belize."

Adam's face expressed not only disbelief but boredom, as if her confession was so obviously untruthful that it was tedious. "You're even better with the convincing details than Eric," he said with sardonic admiration. "Unfortunately, even the dumbest mark eventually wises up. Your story would be more likely to fool me if you'd mentioned one word about Uncle Ted sometime in the fifteen hours between yesterday afternoon and the time this morning when I caught you creeping out of the hotel."

"I was going to tell you about Uncle Ted." She stopped abruptly.

"Right, I'm sure you were."

His sarcasm ate into Megan's small remaining stock of self-respect. "I planned to tell you as soon as we left the Eagle Navigation offices."

He sent her a satirical glance. "You were going to tell me all about your uncle but in the end you neglected to mention him because...?"

She was sick and tired of being bludgeoned by Adam's scorn, so she gave him a crooked smile and told the simple truth. "I didn't tell you because I was crazy enough to imagine I'd fallen in love with you. I wanted us to spend another night together without the shadow of Uncle Ted coming between us."

Adam looked at her with bleak silver eyes. "Don't," he said. "Just—don't go there."

She shrugged. "You asked me to explain something. I did." Adam's rejection hurt less than she would have expected. Right now she was so numb that it was difficult to remember what it had felt like yesterday, when he had seemed to be the man she'd spent the past several years searching for.

"Tell me what your uncle said." Adam's words were clipped. "And do us both a favor, leave out any embellishments about your irresistible passion for me."

This lifetime was unlikely to last long enough for her to make any further reference to the fact that she'd been stupid enough to fall in love with Adam Fairfax. "It wasn't my uncle himself who called," she said flatly. "It was somebody who claimed to have a message from my uncle. The person warned me that it was dangerous for us to come to Belize. He told me to be a smart girl—his words—and go home to Thatch."

"And yet, judging by your actions this morning, you had no intention of taking his advice. If that's really what was said, of course."

"It's exactly what was said—"

"My guess would be more along the lines that good ole Uncle Ted called in person and suggested you fly to Las Criandas without your annoying tagalong and the two of you could then do a deal to split the three million."

Is that what Adam really thought of her? Megan realized that she felt empty all the way to her core. It was a novel sensation for a woman who had spent most of her life praying that her emotions would one day become less exuberant. What a pity people only learned to be careful what they wished for when it was too late, she thought wearily.

She didn't bother to deny his accusation; there was a limit to how much energy she was willing to waste. "Here's what happened yesterday, Adam, starting with our visit to Eagle Navigation. You can believe me, or not. I'm past caring. When Eric said that he'd flown my father to Belize, it was as if he'd handed me the missing piece of the puzzle. I realized Dad must have struck some sort of a deal with Uncle Ted two years ago. I have no idea what their deal was, but clearly it involved the three million dollars from your bank. I also understood, finally, why Dad hadn't chosen to raise the money he needed through his usual sources at Raven Enterprises. He couldn't, of course, because there was no way for him to justify Ted's existence to Paul. How could my father explain having a brother-in-law who wasn't part of your family?"

Adam's brows drew together in an incredulous line. "So Ron came to me because Paul would have been too difficult to deceive? He went to his *other* supposed brother-in-law? Why the *hell* would he do that?"

Megan gave a wan smile. "Why do bank robbers rob banks? Because that's where the money is. Dad came to you because you're a banker with access to funds and because he needed somebody who wasn't going to check into his lies about the Flying W too closely. Sure, it was a risk, but you weren't as close to him as Paul, you're rarely in Chicago and never in Wyoming, and we're talking about my father—a man who seems to have eaten risk for breakfast."

For a moment, despite everything, she actually felt a spurt of sympathy for Adam. Popular wisdom claimed that it was impossible to con an honest man. Megan didn't agree. It seemed to her that cheating an honest man who trusted you would be rather easy. "You'd heard Dad talk about his family home in Wyoming for twenty-five years, which must have made the scam simpler for him to pull off. And then he no doubt developed a pitch that was just about guaranteed to draw you in. Dad knew you well enough to be aware of your vulnerabilities and I'm sure he played every one of them."

She saw Adam wince before he turned away. He might not believe much of what she had to say this morning, but she'd obviously touched an exposed nerve with that particular piece of analysis, especially its unstated implication that he'd been easier to fool than his older brother. She was tempted to take a cheap shot and repay him for some of the terrible accusations he'd hurled at her earlier, but she hung on to the few shreds of integrity she had left and made no comment when he chose to change the subject.

"If Ron was flying into Belize to meet with your uncle in Las Criandas, it makes no sense for him to have gone to Belmopan first." The sarcastic edge was temporarily gone from Adam's voice, replaced by perplexity. "The flight path from Mexico City would take them directly over the village, and then Ron would have to turn around and drive for hours over lousy roads to get back to Las Criandas. Why in hell would he waste almost an entire day in unnecessary travel?"

"It's possible that Dad and Uncle Ted made arrangements to meet up in Belmopan, but I don't think that's what happened. Dad was a hands-on investor. If he had three million bucks riding on the success of the platinum mine in Las Criandas, you can bet he went on-site as often as possible and checked every detail of what was happening there."

"Then why did Eric claim to have flown Ron into Belmopan? What did he hope to gain by the lie?"

She shrugged. "Eric had to say something to pacify us. Given that you'd understood

Esmerelda's flood of Spanish, he had no choice but to indicate a specific destination inside Belize. He chose Belmopan because it's the capital, the sort of place where my father might have gone to negotiate a business deal. Eric probably hoped we'd waste a few days questioning a bunch of people in Belmopan, none of whom had ever heard of Ron Raven. At which point, we'd be stymied. We'd fly back to Mexico City, and the trail linking Eric to Las Criandas would be dead. Unluckily for Eric, it seems he didn't know about my uncle. Or, more likely, he knew that Ted Horn is my uncle, but had no idea that my uncle had visited us in Wyoming and talked at length about his job."

Adam actually gave a brief nod of acknowledgment. "That makes sense. But the only logical reason for Eric to avoid telling us about Las Criandas is because he's involved in something that won't stand up to scrutiny."

"I agree. And it can't be just that he was flying my father in and out of the village. There's nothing illegal about that."

Adam's eyes gleamed with sudden inspiration. "When you have a platinum mine in a remote location and a private plane making regular trips in and out, it's not exactly a giant leap to wonder if some of the platinum found its way onto the plane."

"Smuggling, you mean?" As soon as Adam made the suggestion, Megan was struck by its obviousness. "I guess at thirty thousand dollars for a single bar, the motive is there. Ounce for ounce, platinum must be as valuable as cocaine."

"The interesting question is, who was doing the smuggling? Your father? Eric? Someone else entirely? And whoever it was, were the other owners of the mine aware of the smuggling?"

Megan tried not to dwell on the depressing image of her father as platinum smuggler. "Why would my father or the other mine owners smuggle out their own platinum?"

Adam shrugged. "To avoid government taxes. To understate the profits to their shareholders. To avoid delivering an honest return to the investors who paid for the construction of the mine."

Megan felt a tightening in the pit of her stomach. "The shareholders or the investors who helped pay for construction of the mine might well include my father. Perhaps my father wasn't in on the smuggling. Perhaps the people on the spot were trying to cheat him. And, knowing him, if he discovered he was being cheated, he's likely to have been very angry."

"Angry enough to make rash threats?" Adam answered his own question. "Yes, I can see Ron lashing out with threats that had enough bite to give the smugglers reasons to want him dead."

A sordid falling-out among thieves. Was that what had precipitated her father's murder? The wave of sadness that washed over Megan warned her that she wasn't quite as numb as she'd imagined only a few moments ago. "What an incredible waste of two human lives, if that's what happened."

She hadn't meant to speak out loud. She certainly hadn't intended to let her feelings of loss invade her voice. Apparently she did both. For a moment, the harshness of Adam's expression softened and he leaned toward her, instinctively offering comfort.

As soon as he realized what he was doing, however, he drew back, his face shuttering once again into remoteness. "Excuse me," he said coolly. He dropped her hand and retreated to his own corner of the limo.

Megan refused to waste time mourning their lost intimacy. Realistically, her relationship with Adam had always been impossible. If it hadn't ruptured this morning, it would have eroded slowly and painfully under the strain of reconciling that he was a Fairfax and she was Ron Raven's daughter. She needed to wrap her mind around the depressing truth that her affair with Adam had been magical for the short while it lasted but it was over. Now her goal had to be to restore a minimum level of trust. That might be hard to do, but they still had mutual interests that would be much more effectively pursued if they could find a way to work together.

"We're almost at the airport and there are still several things we need to clear up," Adam said. "We seem to have concluded in the last fifteen minutes or so that your father and the woman in his hotel room may have been murdered because somebody is smuggling platinum out of Belize and your father got in their way. Under the circumstances, we'd be crazy to fly to Las Criandas without taking some precautions."

"We can only take realistic safety precautions if we're in agreement about the facts."

Megan was pleased to hear that she sounded brisk and businesslike, rather than pleading. “It’s a fact that somebody called me last night. It’s a fact that he claimed to be speaking on behalf of my uncle. It’s a fact that he warned me not to travel to Belize. Whether you believe me or not, it’s also a fact that I never told my uncle Ted that we were coming to Mexico. I certainly didn’t tell him where we were staying and I didn’t tell him we had plans to fly to Belize. But the person talking to me knew all those things. Where did he get the information? My mother could have told Uncle Ted we were in Mexico, I guess, and given him the name of our hotel, although she and my uncle don’t talk all that often. However, she couldn’t have informed him we were flying to Belize, because she didn’t know. The only logical person to suspect is Eric. He talked to somebody in Las Criandas. Maybe my uncle, but maybe not. It’s possible that my uncle knows nothing at all about the phone call and that somebody used his name just to be sure I’d pay attention.”

Adam was silent for a long moment. “If we’re right and somebody in Las Criandas is smuggling platinum, then we’re about to fly into a remote village where the people who own 99.9 percent of the local wealth are also the people who may have put out a contract on your father's life."

When she heard their plans expressed in those terms, Megan wondered precisely how crazy she'd been this morning to contemplate flying into Las Criandas alone. "Perhaps we should reconsider our itinerary," she said. "In fact, leaving the rest of this investigation up to the police in Miami is beginning to look like a really smart move on our part."

"You suggested the same thing last night."

"This time I really mean it."

"We can take precautions to increase our safety. I've left a note with the hotel manager telling him that Eric Connolly, the senior pilot at Eagle Navigation, is flying us to the airstrip in the village of Las Criandas, and that if we're not back within forty-eight hours, the police should be notified."

"We had this conversation at dinner last night, too," Megan pointed out. "It seems to console you much more than it consoles me to know that Eric is likely to be arrested if he tosses us out of his airplane. I keep picturing this remote village where absolutely every police officer and government official is in the pay of the mine owners. That seems to leave a lot of scope for a—quote—tragic accident."

"So what was *your* plan?" Adam asked. "If it's dangerous for the two of us to fly into Las Criandas, why would it have been less dangerous for you to fly there alone?"

"I intended to call my brother from the airport both to let him know where I was and also to ask him to contact Uncle Ted and Eric Connolly right away. Once it's clear to people in Las Criandas that everyone in my family knows about my father's investment in the platinum mine, there isn't much point in silencing me. In fact, if I disappeared, it would just be more likely to bring unwelcome attention to the mining operation. As for the missing millions, I figured it would help some that Liam was a criminal defense attorney for several years, and he would know how to trot out reams of intimidating lawyerspeak to persuade Eric and Uncle Ted that it's in their best interests to cooperate." She shrugged. "I don't know if that's going to shake any of the three million loose, but it seemed worth a shot."

"That provides a much better safety net for us than simply telling the hotel manager where we've gone," Adam agreed. "Do you still plan to call your brother?"

Megan sent an ironic glance in his direction. "I assumed you'd forbid me to get anywhere near a phone on the grounds that my brother and I undoubtedly had some secret code worked out between the two of us that would guarantee we cheated you out of your precious three million dollars."

"I don't give a flying flip about the three million," Adam snarled.

"You sure fooled me. You've given an excellent impression these past few days of a man who's positively *obsessed* with his missing millions."

The limo drew to a halt in front of the Eagle Navigation offices, and Adam indulged in a bout of muttered profanity before breaking off and speaking rapidly to the driver in Spanish. Megan managed to grasp that he was asking the man to wait for a few minutes more and to keep the air-conditioning on.

For a while it was eerily quiet inside the limo except for the hum of the car engine. "Could you bring yourself to share the reason that we're sitting outside the entrance to Eagle Navigation, twiddling our thumbs?" she said finally.

Adam turned to her, his expression still shuttered, although his voice had lost its edge. "I overreacted this morning," he said abruptly. "It's the second time I owe you an apology for losing my temper. You might be surprised to hear that it's not something I'm in the habit of doing."

She studied him consideringly. "You're sorry you lost your temper, but you still don't trust me."

Adam closed his eyes for a moment. When he opened them again, they were the flat, endless gray of a lake in winter. "I'm not sure whether I trust you or not. The person I *know* I don't trust is me."

"I don't do cryptic very well, Adam. What does that mean, exactly?"

He pulled out his billfold and searched for pesos to tip the driver, a good excuse for avoiding looking at her. "I find you incredibly attractive." He managed to deliver the compliment in a voice entirely devoid of inflection. "When I'm with you, it's hard to stop thinking about how much I want to have sex with you."

"I thought that was the standard male condition," she said caustically.

He gave a grim smile of acknowledgment. "With you it's much more than the standard male wanting. In fact, everything about our relationship is…more. More attraction, more sexual desire, more pleasure, more doubts. And a ton more baggage from the past."

"You're wrong," she said quietly. "We have no baggage from the past. You and my father have baggage. Not you and me."

He shook his head. "That's not true. You should understand what I'm talking about because you have exactly the same sort of baggage. Why else did you work so hard to hide the truth about your uncle from me? It wasn't rational for you to keep quiet about the phone call last night and it sure as hell wasn't logical for you to try to sneak out of our hotel room and fly to Belize without me. But you did."

He was right, Megan thought resignedly. Both about the baggage and the lack of rationality. "I kept quiet because I was ashamed," she admitted. "It was bad enough to discover that my father was a bigamist. Discovering that Uncle Ted was quite likely a thief seemed like one despicable relative too many. I wanted to retrieve the damn money and come back and throw it in your face." And she hadn't realized how strong the urge had been until she spoke it out loud.

"We have to get rid of the baggage," Adam said. "To do that, we need to find out why your father invested three million dollars in a platinum mine in Belize. When it's just you and me, with no more strings trailing, maybe we'll be able to look at each other without the past distorting what we see."

"I'm not sure if we'll ever manage to see each other without the giant shadow of my father's bigamy hovering over us."

"Maybe not." Adam's voice was controlled and his expression was so carefully neutral they might as well have been discussing the likelihood of rain tomorrow in New York City. "But I'd like to try."

She felt the squeeze of dangerous emotions in the region of her heart. She had only known Adam for a short time if you counted the days, but there were aspects of his personality that she already understood with absolute certainty. Chief among those was that the more controlled Adam appeared, the deeper the feelings he was suppressing. His admission that he still wanted to explore the possibility of a relationship with her was huge, despite his efforts to make the confession sound trivial.

If they continued as lovers, Megan was afraid that circumstances would keep throwing them into situations like the one this morning where they almost couldn't avoid hurting each other. On the other hand, the night before had been so wonderful, she was almost ready to pay the price of the morning after.

In the end, she sighed and resigned herself to the inevitable. The attraction between her and Adam had been instantaneous. Apparently it was also intense enough to survive her lies and his explosions of temper.

"I'd like to try that, too," she said. "But perhaps we need to back off for a couple of days. It's impossible to get a realistic sense of how we really feel about each other until we've been to Belize and found out what my father did with your damn money."

He smiled slightly, the first touch of genuine humor she'd seen so far that morning. "It's not my money, remember? It's the bank's." He touched her lightly on the arm, but before she could even react, he leaned forward to hand the bundle of pesos over to their driver.

"Come on," he said. "Let's go and tell Eric he's flying us to Las Criandas."

Nineteen

"This is your captain speaking. We're now approaching the landing strip at Las Criandas. Our flight path brings us in from the northwest, and we should have wheels on the ground in approximately five minutes."

Megan glanced at Adam, rolling her eyes at Eric's grandiose announcement. Then she remembered the two of them were in a state of wary truce, not exactly on eye-rolling terms. It was all very well to have laid down ground rules for the next couple of days that allowed for no physical intimacy, but she was discovering it was something else entirely to stick to the rules.

Smothering a sigh, she looked out the small window as the plane skimmed over clusters of scraggy trees and touched down with impeccable smoothness on the narrow landing strip. Eric might be a liar, possibly a smuggler, and definitely a pain in the ass, but he also seemed to be an excellent pilot.

Her relief that Eric hadn't chosen to ditch them in a swamp was mitigated somewhat when she realized that the two men waving the plane to a halt beside a ramshackle hangar were brandishing assault rifles instead of reflective paddles. She pointed the men out to Adam.

"They're wearing uniforms," he said, squinting into the sun.

"Oh, well, that's just fine, then. I wouldn't have wanted to be shot at by men in their undershorts."

"It's a platinum mine," he said patiently. "There's bound to be some heavy-duty security around."

Eric cut the engines and came back into the cabin, crouching to accommodate the low ceiling. He unbarred the exit and swung the door open, waving to the two gunmen who were now standing guard on either side of a rickety set of metal steps.

"We're here to see Mr. Ted Horn," he called out in English, which was the official language in Belize, courtesy of its colonial past. "Can you bring the Jeep?"

"Sure thing. Be right back." One of the

guards jogged off to the hangar. The other one pushed the steps up against the side of the small plane and waved with his assault rifle to invite Adam and Megan to disembark.

"Welcome to Las Criandas," the gunman said when they were on the ground. He was Mayan, and his English was heavily accented, but he smiled cheerily enough, displaying a mouthful of gold teeth. A badge pinned above his pocket announced that he was Gaspar Tzina of the Department of Customs and Excise. He apparently didn't consider the three of them much of a threat to Belize's national security, or even to the platinum mine. He took the entry cards Adam and Megan had filled out during the flight and stuck them into his hip pocket without even pretending to read them.

Gaspar's colleague returned with the Jeep and invited Adam and Megan to get into the rear while Eric climbed into the front seat. "Seat belts fastened, please," he said, sticking his assault rifle on the floor, where it rolled gently from side to side as soon as he set the vehicle in motion. Loose bullets were apparently considered less of a safety hazard than unsecured bodies, Megan concluded.

The single-lane paved road led from the tarmac toward a huge cluster of buildings. "You know anything about platinum mining?" Eric asked as they swerved to avoid a pair of iguanas sunbathing in the middle of the road.

"Mostly that platinum's difficult to extract and therefore expensive to mine," Adam said.

"Expensive is right," Eric replied, nodding for emphasis. The discovery that Megan and Adam knew all about Ron's trips to Las Criandas, plus the phone call from Liam confirming that several other people in the States also knew, seemed to have caused him little shame. His manner remained over-friendly, like a smile that was all teeth and no warmth. He had assured them when confronted that he'd only lied because Ron paid him to do so. It hadn't seemed right, he said soulfully, to betray a bargain he'd made with a man who was now tragically dead.

It was a believable story. Adam and Megan had agreed that it might even be true.

"There's an international consortium of

owners for this mine, at least that's what I heard from Mr. Raven," Eric told them, apparently anxious to make up for past omissions by sharing any information he had. "As you can see, it's an integrated plant, not just a mine. They've got a mill, a concentrator, a smelter and converter, as well as the base-metal refinery. It's too expensive to ship out the ore, so they do everything right here on-site."

"How do they extract the ore from the ground?" Adam asked. "Is it a mechanized process?"

Eric shook his head. "The dip and narrowness of the ore body means they can't utilize much machinery underground, not like the big mines off the coast of Africa. Anyway, here they're using a lot of manual labor, which is good for the locals. The farming around here is hardscrabble at best and people had no work until the mine opened. Now the villagers are eating three square meals a day and they're calling their cousins from all over to come join them working in the mines. The population's doubled in the last couple of years. That building over there to your left is the school. It only goes through eighth grade. Still, that's three grades higher than they used to have before the mine opened up. The company doctor has his offices right there in the school building."

"I had no idea it would be such a big complex," Megan said. "I realized the mine was going to be more than a bunch of men digging with shovels, but I wasn't prepared for so much heavy-duty construction."

Their driver beamed, as if he were personally responsible for the impressive size of the development. "The ore vein is very rich."

He was interrupted by a crackle on the radio fixed to his dashboard. A brief conversation ensued in the local Mayan dialect before he turned around to pass on the message he'd received.

"Mr. Ted Horn has been notified of your arrival and he's waiting for you. I'll take you to his office." The driver swung the Jeep in a narrow semicircle, making the turn with an abandon that would have caused envy among even the most daring of Mexico City's drivers. Then he floored the accelerator and sped a quarter of a mile to the double-wide trailer that was signposted as the headquarters for the Operations Division.

Ted Horn must have seen them coming. He threw open the door and bounded down the trailer steps. He was short, like his sister, and shared the same thick, curly hair that had also been passed down to Megan. Unlike Ellie, though, he was solidly built and barrel chested, and the well-developed muscles in his upper arms showed to advantage in the short-sleeved shirt he wore.

"Megan, honey!" He greeted her with a hug. "I couldn't believe it when Liam said you were coming to visit! But it's good to see you. You're looking well. Really well."

"You are, too." Megan didn't break free of her uncle's embrace, but she didn't return it, either. "Uncle Ted, this is a friend of mine, Adam Fairfax."

"Fairfax?" Her uncle obviously recognized the name and didn't attempt to conceal his surprise. "Liam told me that Megan was bringing a friend, but he didn't mention your name. Are you…um…are you related to Avery Fairfax?"

"I'm Avery's younger brother." Arms crossed, Adam leaned against the Jeep, providing no further explanation of his presence.

Ted didn't seem quite sure what to say next. "What do you think of the place we have here?" he asked finally.

"We only got a few glimpses of the mine as we drove by," Adam said. "It looks to be an impressive facility."

"I'll give you a tour tomorrow morning, if you like." Ted beamed with the same sort of proprietary pride shown a few moments earlier by their driver. "We've still got a ways to go to take advantage of the full potential of the deposits, but we're getting more efficient every week."

He nodded to Eric, who had remained in the Jeep. "Are you planning to stay overnight, Eric? If so, I'll call through to the guesthouse and let them know you're coming."

"Thanks for the offer," Eric said. "I'll take you up on it. Megan and Adam need to be back in Mexico City by tomorrow night, so it's not worth my making the round trip, the cost of fuel being what it is these days."

"Great. I'll warn the housekeeper, then." Ted turned back to Megan and chuckled as he saw her wipe her forehead with a tissue. "I see the afternoon heat's getting to you. It's something else, isn't it? It cools off some toward nightfall, but at this stage of the afternoon, we can count on the high nineties."

"Only the nineties?" Megan gave up on

her attempts to prevent sweat rolling into her eyes. "I'd have guessed a hundred at least."

"Could be. The truth is, I don't notice the heat anymore. It's thirty years since I lived in Wyoming and I've adapted. My blood's thinned, or something. Anyway, my Jeep's in the carport over there." Ted indicated an awning extending from the side of the trailer. "I'll take you home to my place, and you can cool off with a dip in the pool."

"A swim sounds heavenly. Thank you." Megan felt as if she'd stepped into an alternate universe. Far from displaying resentment that she'd arrived in defiance of his phone call, her uncle's attitude suggested that he was delighted she'd chosen to pay him a visit.

"Hop into the Jeep. It's not locked. We have excellent security around here." Ted gave Adam a friendly thump on the shoulder. "I'll just let Marisella know I'm leaving for the day. Once you two have cooled off with a swim, I'll throw a few hamburgers on the outdoor grill, add some corn, and we'll have us a good old Yankee cookout." Ted took the steps back up to the trailer entrance two at a time and stuck his head around the door, his voice floating down to them.

"Marisella! My niece has arrived from the States. I'm going home to spend some time with her. Get last week's production figures ready for me to look at first thing tomorrow, okay? Oh, and arrange for a room at the guesthouse for Mr. Connolly, will you? He's the pilot from Eagle Navigation, remember? Thanks a lot. See you tomorrow.

"My bungalow's about a mile down the road," he said, joining Megan and Adam in the shade of the carport. "It won't take us a minute to get there."

"What about Eric?" she asked. "Can we drop him at the guesthouse?"

Ted turned to the pilot. "You want to ride with us?"

Eric shook his head. "Thanks, but I'll get Gaspar to shuttle me over. He'll be glad of something to do. He told me last time I was here that sometimes days pass by without anyone flying in or out. He gets real bored."

"If there are so few flights, why does Customs keep two agents stationed here?" Megan asked.

Her uncle gave a crack of wry laughter. "We're talking about the government, honey.

A Central American government, at that. What do you expect? Besides, they're determined to make sure none of our platinum leaves the country via the back door, so to speak."

"I wouldn't have thought two customs agents made for a very sturdy barrier against smuggling," Adam commented neutrally. "Even if they are armed with assault rifles."

"You'd be surprised," Ted replied. "This was a British colony until thirty years ago and the civil service has a tradition of attracting some of the smartest people in the country. They're proud of their government here, and it certainly seems less corrupt than most. Besides, the customs agents are just the frosting on the cake. We have our own security. A ton of it. Anyway, let's get going. Bye, Eric. See you around."

Megan decided not to point out that having a basically honest central government didn't mean that two lone customs officials, posted way out in the boonies, couldn't be bought off or just plain deceived by determined smugglers. The two men worked without supervision, and there was a lot to tempt them. Still, nothing about the mine, the physical plant or the people working here were what she'd anticipated, and she realized she needed a lot more information before she started to form any theories about what might have been going on. However, her earlier vision of her father stuffing nuggets of platinum into Eric's pockets was clearly ridiculous. A plant this sophisticated would have metal detectors and security cameras at every entrance and exit, and the miners probably wore special clothing that was left at the mine head to be processed for the retrieval of every last gram of platinum. Any smuggling going on was a sophisticated endeavor with complicity from insiders. Her father didn't qualify as that sort of insider.

"My bungalow is about another mile down the road," Ted explained, driving past a dazzlingly white village church that looked as if it had been sunbathing in the same spot for the past three hundred years. "There's a dozen senior managers on the project and we have a little housing compound built around a central swimming pool. My place isn't big, but it's comfortable for a bachelor like me." He jerked his head toward Adam. "Are you married, Adam?"

"No, I'm not."

"Me, neither." Ted chuckled. "I tried it three times. It definitely didn't take. My wives weren't perfect, but I admit to being a lousy husband." He drew his hand in a sweeping arc that took in the narrow strip of road, the scraggy trees and the mine buildings that dominated the horizon. "This is my definition of a great place to live. Unfortunately, most women don't agree. The nearest store is thirty miles southeast of here and once you're there, you have more choice of chili peppers than you do of shoes or clothes. That doesn't go down well with most women. Nowadays, at least we can get satellite-dish TV, so you don't feel quite so isolated. Last time I was married, we were living in Ecuador, a hundred miles south of Quito, and if we got to read a week-old newspaper, my wife thought she'd died and gone to heaven."

They arrived at a cluster of adobe cottages, the exteriors stained an eye-catching but oddly restful ochre. "Home sweet home," Ted said cheerfully. "Jump out and I'll show you around."

He conducted them up a white gravel path and unlocked the front door, ushering them into the bliss of the air-conditioned interior.

"We're standing in the living area," he said, allowing them time to register the tile floor, the comfortable leather furniture and the heavy, dark oak table, along with an antique, cast-iron charcoal stove that would have been the envy of many interior designers back in the States.

"The kitchen's over to your left," he continued. "The master bedroom's to your right, and I have my home office right next door, but there's a bed in there, too." He pushed open the door to demonstrate, revealing a sparsely furnished but functional room. "There's also a guest room with its own bathroom next to the kitchen."

"You take the guest room," Adam said to Megan. "I'll do fine in the office."

"It's a comfortable bed," Ted assured him. If it had crossed his mind to wonder if the two of them were sleeping together, he gave no sign of it. "Now, are you ready for a swim?"

"We didn't bring suits," Megan said. "At least I didn't. Adam?"

He shook his head. "Nor I."

"No problem." Ted couldn't have been a more genial host if their visit had been looked forward to for months. "I know there's a supply in the pool house, along with a stack of towels. The maids keep everything laundered. That's one of the major advantages of living in a place like this—you can afford all the household help you can use. Even my ex-wives would have appreciated the maid service!"

The small backyards of the managers' houses all backed up to a central swimming pool surrounded by a brick-paved patio. Clay pots of flowers decorated the edge of the patio, and several defiantly nonnative palm trees shaded the loungers set out at one end of the pool.

The water was almost too warm to be refreshing, but after swimming fifteen fast laps, Megan's sense of physical disorientation began to dissipate. Her mental disorientation was another matter.

Her uncle was puttering between the kitchen and his backyard grill, calling out the occasional comment.

"Have we fallen down the rabbit hole, or does Uncle Ted really think this is a social visit?" Megan asked Adam as they sat in the shade of the palm trees sipping cold sodas.

"We haven't fallen down the rabbit hole

and I'm sure your uncle doesn't think this is a social visit." Adam kept his voice low. "Let's ask him a few tough questions and see what he has to say for himself."

"I'm ready. More than ready." Megan drained her soda and walked over to the grill, where her uncle was busy brushing seasoning onto ears of fresh corn. "Those look delicious," she said. "Is there something I can do to help?"

"Nothing, thanks." Ted grinned. "You're watching a master chef at work." He deftly wrapped one ear in foil, making a neat enough package to validate his statement. "You and Adam should just sit down, put your feet up and relax. You've had a tiring journey, after all."

"Uncle Ted, I appreciate your hospitality, but this isn't a social visit and I'm sure you know that. Adam and I came here to talk to you about the three million dollars my father invested in the Las Criandas platinum mine."

"The money was a loan from my bank," Adam said. "Under the terms of Ron's contract with our institution, the loan fell due immediately after he died. I'm here to find out how I should set about claiming repayment of the three million dollars now owed to my bank."

Ted said nothing for a long while. His hands stilled on the aluminum foil. Megan saw guilt, defiance and finally resignation flash across his weather-beaten face. He sighed, adding a final piece of corn to the neat stack on the side of the grill. "I guess we'd better go inside," he said. "This is going to take a while and we might as well stay cool."

"Would you like something to drink?" he asked when they were settled in the living room.

"No, thanks," Megan said, trying to contain her impatience. "I just finished my Coke."

"Adam?"

"No, not for me, thank you."

"Well, I sure as hell need a drink." Ted walked to the bar and poured himself a bourbon, not bothering to add ice or anything else before tossing it back in a single, long gulp.

"Look, what I'm going to say doesn't make me look good. Makes me look like a pretty miserable human being, in fact, and I wish I didn't have to 'fess up. In my defense, I'll just point out that I've had seven hours to think about this since Liam called this morning, and by now I could have invented a lot of lies that would have painted my actions in a more decent light. I decided not to do that. What I'm about to tell you is the straight skinny." Ted broke off. "Hell, I need another drink."

He poured himself a second bourbon, then came and stood in front of the unlit charcoal stove, his expression brooding. "Okay, here goes. You'll recall, Megan, that I came to Wyoming two years ago. The main reason for the trip was to see you and Ellie and the rest of the family, but there was another reason, as well. I'd been offered the chance to make an investment in this mine, and I wanted to seize it. Hell, it was a once-in-a-lifetime opportunity. The chief investor in Las Criandas is a multimillionaire called Rafael Williamson. Rafe came by most of his money the old-fashioned way—he inherited it. One of Rafe's ancestors was governor of Belize for seven years when it was a British colony. When a new governor was appointed, Rafe's ancestor never left. He turned to international trade and just stayed here, raking in the money. On top of that,

Rafe's mother comes from a wealthy Bolivian family that made a fortune mining tin, so he ended up inheriting millions from both sides. Anyway, given his family heritage and all, it's no surprise that Rafe got interested in mining and went to study at the Colorado School of Mines. He ended up there right at the same time as me. We've kept in touch on and off over the years and when Rafe needed somebody he trusted to run the mining operations here, he offered me the job."

"Rafe has an interesting background," Megan said. "I never heard this part of the story when you were in Wyoming."

Her uncle shrugged. "It wasn't a secret. I told your father. In fact, I told your father everything about the project." Ted's voice took on a bitter note. "Like I said, Rafe had offered me the chance to buy shares in the mine. Not just to have a job here, earning a decent salary, but a chance to buy into the profits. I didn't have any money to invest, but I knew Ron did. I asked him for five million dollars, and told him we'd split the profits and capital gains fifty-fifty. Of course, the shares would be in my name, but I offered to give him a note for the loan, so he'd get back his original investment."

"That sounds like an excellent deal for you," Adam said, swirling the dregs of ice in his glass. "You don't take any of the investment risk and you earn half the profit. Nice deal if you can get it."

Color stained Ted's already ruddy cheeks. "I knew this place was going to be making money hand over fist. It was an investment opportunity Ron would never have known about if not for me. I figured I deserved to make a decent profit."

"And that's the sum of your involvement with Ron and his three-million-dollar loan from my bank?" Adam asked with scrupulous courtesy. "You borrowed five million and Ron raised some of the money with me?"

"No, that's not all. I wish it was. Hell, this is even more difficult than I expected." Ted cast a longing glance toward the bar and the bottle of bourbon, but he didn't pour another drink.

"Was your reluctance to talk about this the reason you told someone to call me last night at our hotel in Mexico City?" Megan asked. "You arranged for somebody to warn me to stay away from Las Criandas. How did you know where I was staying? And how did you know that we planned to come to Belize?"

Uncle Ted stared at her, jaw literally dropping. "Somebody called you last night and told you not to come to Belize? They pretended the message was from me?"

"Yes. And they asked me questions about Mom's favorite mare just to be sure that I was really Meg Raven."

"I have no idea what you're talking about, honey, I swear! I never called you last night. For one thing, like you just said, I didn't know you were in Mexico. For another, I sure as heck didn't know you were planning to come here."

Her uncle sounded genuinely shocked, and his disclaimer entirely sincere. Megan looked quickly toward Adam, wondering if he would start suspecting once again that she'd bribed the waiter to invent a nonexistent phone call. He met her gaze and gave an almost imperceptible shake of his head. She wasn't sure precisely what that meant, but she somehow knew it was intended to be reassuring.

"How did the caller know to ask about

your sister's mare if he wasn't calling on your behalf?" Adam asked Ted. Megan had no idea how he managed to make his questions sound so intimidating when he kept his voice low and his manner mild as green tea.

Ted gestured to a framed photograph sitting in a place of honor on the buffet bar, and then brought it over for Megan to examine more closely. It was, she realized, a picture of her mother taken in Wyoming some ten years earlier. Ellie was riding Pretty Woman, laughing into the camera. The frame was hand-painted with a scattering of horseshoes, spurs and riding boots. Across the bottom, the artisan who'd decorated the frame had lettered the inscription Ellie and Pretty Woman.

"Lots of people ask me about that picture and who painted the frame," Ted said. "I guess ninety percent of the folks who've ever walked into my house could have asked you something about my sister and her mare. Always provided they knew you were Ellie's daughter, of course."

He gave up on his efforts to resist taking another drink, and poured himself a couple of fingers' more bourbon. This time, however, he took no more than a sip. "I have my own ideas about who might have made that call," he said. "But let's leave that aside for now. I need to tell you what happened between Ron and me during my visit to the ranch two years ago. If I don't get it off my chest now, I'll probably never find the courage again."

He was interrupted by the chimes of his cell phone. He set his drink down on the bar, pulled the phone from his belt clip and read the ID. "Damn! It's my shift manager. I have to take this. Excuse me a moment. I'll be right back."

He returned five minutes later and immediately picked up his drink. Megan didn't remember her uncle as having any particular need for alcohol during his visits to Wyoming, so she could only conclude that he was under considerable stress.

"Okay, I can't think of a single way to make what I have to say sound any better than it is, so I'm going to stop trying." Ted closed his eyes and pinched the bridge of his nose as if trying to relieve a headache. "When I asked Ron to invest five million dollars in Las Criandas, he flat out refused. Didn't ask to look at the details of the survey reports or the profit projections, just flat out said he wasn't interested. He said he had more business than he could handle in the U.S., and didn't need to take on the hassle of investing overseas. I tried to persuade him to change his mind. He wasn't budging. The fact is, Ron was as charming and easygoing and friendly as anyone you'd ever meet, so long as you didn't start to talk business. Talk business, though, and he turned into this hard-nosed son of a bitch who wouldn't have bailed his own mother out of a financial jam."

Ted cast an apologetic glance toward Megan. "Sorry, honey, but it's true. Your father was a different man in a business setting from what he was when he was at home."

"I understand. And I'm not surprised to hear he turned you down. Dad was quite patriotic in his own way and he thought small entrepreneurs were the backbone of American prosperity. He often said he wasn't interested in making hundred-million-dollar deals. He'd much prefer to make a hundred deals worth a million bucks each. He thought it was a better way to build a strong economy—and a better way to guarantee his own profits."

"You've just given me a rerun of your father's spiel to me," Ted said wryly.

Adam, who had been unusually silent, finally spoke up. "So far, you've explained your proposition and explained why Ron refused to go along with it. I'm still waiting to hear how he ended up investing three million bucks from my bank in a project you say he flatly rejected."

Ted stared at his glass of bourbon then put it down on the bar with a slight thump. "I blackmailed him into investing," he said, his gaze fixed on the tile floor. "First of all I told him I'd keep quiet in exchange for the full five million. That didn't work. Ron told me to go to hell. We negotiated for a couple of days and in the end we compromised on three million."

Megan stared at her uncle, too miserable to speak. It was left to Adam to ask the inevitable question. "What did you blackmail Ron about?"

"The fact that he was a bigamist, of course. What else?"

Megan sprang to her feet, impelled by anger. "Good grief, Uncle Ted! You're my mother's brother! Didn't it occur to you that instead of blackmailing my father, you needed to tell your sister the truth?"

Ted slowly shook his head. "There are a dozen reasons to regret the choices I made two years ago. Not telling Ellie the truth about Ron isn't one of them."

"For heaven's sake, why not?"

Ted shrugged. "Ellie was happy in her marriage and in her life. Ron was a good husband—"

"To two women! Leaving aside the legal issues, my father was consistently unfaithful to two women!" Megan was back to feeling that she'd stumbled into Wonderland.

Ted had the grace to look shamefaced, but he didn't back down. "Megan, honey, you need to take a step or two into the real world. How many husbands do you think exist who are always one hundred percent faithful to their wives? Or wives who are faithful to their husbands, for that matter?"

Did her uncle really not see the difference between an extramarital affair and a quarter century of bigamous marriage? Both might be betrayals, but for Avery and her mother, their entire lives had been built on the deepest and most hurtful type of fraud.

Apparently Adam realized that steam was

about to start pouring forth from Megan's ears. "We seem to be straying down a side road here," he said. "Let's get back to basics. I'd like to be sure I've understood the finances of all this, Ted. You blackmailed Ron because he was a bigamist. Ron agreed, under duress, to invest three million dollars in the development of Las Criandas. Ron then came to me for a loan because he didn't have three million bucks lying around, at least not that he could tap into without raising questions on the part of his business partner—who happened to be older brother to one of Ron's wives. Have I got things straight so far?"

Ted nodded.

"And that's why Ron had to keep all his trips down here so secret," Adam continued. "He couldn't possibly have explained investing in a Belizean platinum mine to my brother without raising a ton of suspicions in Paul's mind."

"I guess so," Ted acknowledged, shifting uncomfortably in his chair. "I mean, that's the point about blackmail, isn't it? One party has a secret and the other gets money. Neither party wants the secret to be revealed. That's why blackmail works." He looked as if he felt sick. "I'm sorry. I'm ashamed of what happened. I told you there was no way for me to come out of this without looking like a total rat."

"I really think you should avoid insulting the rats of the world," Adam said. His voice remained quiet, and his manner perfectly pleasant, but Megan would have curled into a fetal ball and stayed there if she'd been on the receiving end of the arctic gaze Adam directed at her uncle.

"By the way, there's one other thing to clear up," he said. "At what point after Ron's death did you decide that you were going to keep quiet about your blackmailing endeavors and steal my three million dollars?"

Twenty

Far from being a cheerful all-American cookout, dinner that night was among the more unpleasant meals Megan could remember eating. Under relentless questioning from Adam, her uncle finally admitted that he'd hoped Ron's investment in the platinum mine would never be discovered, an omission that would have left Ted richer by three million dollars. At first her uncle tried to pretend that it was shame over his own blackmail that had kept him silent, but Adam demolished that excuse. Ted, he pointed out, could easily have told his sister about the three million dollars without ever mentioning the blackmail that prompted the investment.

"I'll make amends," Ted promised. "I'll sign over three million dollars' worth of my shares in Las Criandas to your bank right away. I have the forms at the office. We'll complete the transaction tomorrow morning before the two of you fly back to Mexico City."

"I'm the president of the bank that helped Ron pay your extortion demands," Adam said grimly. "I have a legal responsibility to report what's happened to the authorities."

Ted leaned across the table, his body tense with supplication. "Adam, take back the money and keep quiet about the rest of it. Please, for Ellie's sake. And Megan's, too, for that matter. Does it help anyone for me to be disgraced and in prison?"

Adam pushed aside his half-eaten hamburger, looking as if it would choke him to swallow another mouthful. "You're trying to bribe me," he said. "In exchange for three million dollars, you're expecting me to become an accessory after the fact to the crimes you've committed."

"I'm not *expecting* you to keep quiet," Ted said, his own meal sitting untouched in front of him. "I'm *begging* you not to say anything. I made mistakes. I got greedy, I admit that." Tears gathered in his eyes. "You have to believe me, Meg. Despite how badly I wanted that money, I swear I'd have spoken up about Ron's bigamy if I'd thought your mother would be better off knowing the truth."

"Don't try to justify what you did. My mother deserved to make her own decisions. Instead, you made them for her—and treated yourself to a three-million-dollar bonus as a windfall." Megan pushed her chair back from the table, unable to bear sitting across from Ted any longer. She recognized that her anger involved more than just outrage at her uncle's blackmail. Hurt from a dozen other wounds inflicted since her father's death was all mixed in with the revulsion she felt at Ted's behavior.

A fresh awareness of her own inadequacy added salt to the wounds. It wasn't only Ted who'd known about her father's bigamy; Liam had known, too. Why had she been so blind? What lack in her own character prevented her from seeing through the smoke screens other people apparently found easy to penetrate?

At least there was some consolation to be derived from the knowledge that her brother had been devastated by the discovery of Ron's double life. Ted, on the other hand, showed no real remorse. As far as Megan could tell, he had simply seen Ron's bigamy as a quick route to some easy money, and he'd told the truth only when pushed to the wall. She wasn't even sure she believed his denials about making the phone call to her last night. Who else, other than her uncle, had a motive to keep her away from Las Criandas? Ethically challenged was far too gentle a description of Ted's attitudes and behavior over the past couple of years. The bottom line seemed to be that she had a lying, cheating father and a lying, cheating, blackmailing maternal uncle. As gene pools went, hers could only be considered polluted on both sides, Megan thought miserably.

Adam finally agreed not to press formal charges against her uncle, but Megan could see that he wasn't happy with his own decision. It didn't help her gloomy mood to realize that Adam was compromising his own high standards chiefly because he felt sorry for her and her mother.

They helped Ted clear away the dishes of barely touched food, but he insisted there was no need to do anything more; the maid would take care of cleaning up the kitchen in the morning. Not surprisingly, he seemed relieved when they refused after-dinner coffee. "If you don't mind, then, I'm going to catch an early night. If you can be ready to drive with me to the office tomorrow at seven-thirty, I'll see about signing those shares over to you, Adam."

Adam gave a curt nod of acknowledgment and waited in unyielding silence until Ted shut himself in his room.

"Are you all right?" Megan asked softly.

Adam drew in a short, unsteady breath. "No. Not yet. Give me a few minutes."

"Let's go out by the pool. This house feels much too full of Uncle Ted and his sickening rationalizations."

By mutual consent, they didn't stay on the patio but ventured out onto the gravel road, walking carefully to avoid snakes and other unfriendly critters.

"Saving the ranch for Mom and getting back your three million dollars doesn't feel anywhere near as good as I'd hoped it would," Megan said.

Adam made a frustrated sound. "That's because it's such a messy resolution. Part of me wants to call the FBI the minute I get back to the States. The rest of me reluctantly agrees with Ted. There's nothing useful to be gained from having him sit in federal prison for the next five years or so."

"How did my uncle Ted end up being such a pathetic excuse for a human being?"

Megan asked. "My mother had the same parents, went to the same high school, lived in the same community. And yet I can't begin to imagine the set of circumstances that would have her behaving like her brother."

Adam shook his head. "If I could answer your question, I'd be considered the Socrates of our generation."

Megan gave a wry smile. "Well, I guess Uncle Ted's confession does clear up a bunch of minor mysteries. It looks as if Eric may have been telling the truth. He really did spin all those lies just because my father had paid him off to keep quiet."

"I don't know, Megan. I seriously doubt Eric was that loyal to a dead man. Eric and his wife were much too nervous about our inquiries for the explanation to be something that innocent. Did you notice how friendly he is with the customs officials? I'd be willing to bet he's working some sort of smuggling deal and they're taking a cut."

Megan scuffed at the gravel. "I was so hoping my father wasn't a smuggler as well as everything else."

Adam took her hand and tucked it under his arm. She didn't even pretend to protest, although they were supposed to be keeping a safe distance from each other. Then she realized that the missing three million dollars had been found and their agreement to put their relationship on hold no longer applied. It was the first happy thought she'd had in a while.

"Just because Eric may be smuggling stuff in and out of Las Criandas, that doesn't mean your father was in on the deal," Adam said. "In fact, I'd guess Ron wasn't involved. Smuggling doesn't strike me as his style."

Megan felt unable to judge what her father had and had not been capable of doing. She hadn't known the real man, and how could she assess the character flaws of an illusion? Still, she was glad to accept Adam's reassurance that he didn't consider her father the type of man to smuggle and hoped he wasn't simply being kind.

They walked back to the house, hands linked, and Megan gradually felt her spirits lifting. True, there was nothing in her uncle's story that helped to explain how or why her father had been murdered, but at least they now had the three million dollars back and the ranch was saved. That had to count for something.

By the time they reached the patio, Adam's

arm was around her waist and her head was on his shoulder. They went inside, not talking since the lights in her uncle's bedroom were already turned off. Outside the guest room he stopped and turned her within the circle of his arms, kissing her slowly and stroking her hair, murmuring soft words that had no meaning except that he cared for her.

He reached behind her, opening the door, and walked inside the guest room, still holding her. "I don't want to sleep apart from you," he said.

"Then stay." She smiled faintly. "Although I'm so tired that we may only be sleeping."

Astonishingly, it seemed that she wasn't quite as exhausted as she had believed. When she felt Adam's naked body lying next to hers, desire changed her weariness into languid sensuality. Eyes closed, relaxing against the pillows, she held him close and sighed with pleasure as his mouth trailed over her breasts and his hand reached between her thighs.

Gradually, she became aware that her lethargy had transformed into the deepest and most intense arousal she had ever experienced. Her body wasn't simply responding to Adam's expert technique. It was more, even, than feeling harmony between her needs and his. With Adam, she recognized that for the first time in her adult life she no longer felt alone.

She was almost asleep when she heard Adam getting out of bed. She reached out a limp, uncoordinated arm to stop him. "Don't leave," she mumbled. "Stay."

He sat on the edge of the bed. "You don't mind if your uncle realizes tomorrow morning that we're lovers?"

She couldn't imagine why Ted's opinion would ever matter to her again. "Stay," she said sleepily. "Please stay."

He climbed back into bed, tucking himself around her. The fit was perfect. Megan fell asleep, sure that she must be smiling.

She was in Uncle Ted's swimming pool and she couldn't breathe. Megan thrashed out, trying to swim to the surface, but a dead weight held her deep under the water.

"Stop struggling," a man's voice murmured in her ear. "And in the name of Jesus, make no sound. If we wake your uncle, you and Adam Fairfax will both die."

Megan opened her eyes. A man, dressed in a black sweat suit, leaned over her. He had just finished taping her mouth shut, she realized. He had an assault rifle slung over his shoulder and she reached instinctively to grab it. He cut off her attempt with a swift, silent blow to her wrist. He quickly slapped his hand over her mouth, muffling even the small sounds she could produce behind the duct tape.

"We have weapons and you were asleep," he said. "If we wanted to kill you, you would already be dead. We're here to help you. For God's sake, don't make a sound. You and your lover must come with us now or you *will* be dead by morning." Her captor deliberately pushed her head sideways on the pillow and she realized that Adam was pinned to the bed next to her by another man, also dressed in black, who had his hand over Adam's taped mouth. The barrel of his assault rifle was pressed hard against Adam's throat.

"Get up," her captor ordered. He pointed to the slacks and cotton shirt she'd worn for dinner, lying on the floor. "Put on your clothes," he said. "Trust me, if you scream, we will all four of us deeply regret it."

There was something about the man that seemed familiar. Not his voice, but his features. Where had she seen him before? And should she scream? Or stamp her feet since the duct tape prevented her from making more than a mewling sound. Could it possibly be true that she and Adam were in danger from her *uncle?* That seemed to be what the man was implying.

"Get up." The intruder prodded her none too gently with his assault rifle. "We need to get out of here."

Megan slid out of bed, tugging on clothes as fast as she could. The intruder watched her with sad, dark eyes, his mustache drooping as if to emphasize the many injustices that had been heaped on his head.

Sad eyes. Drooping mustache. Where in hell had she seen this man before? Recognition suddenly exploded in Megan's consciousness. Holy God! She was looking into the face of her father's murderer. Julio Castellano was standing two feet away from her. And he was pointing his assault rifle straight at her head.

Twenty-one

She had to be mistaken, Megan thought feverishly. Fear was causing her to make connections that didn't exist. The police reports identifying one of the bloodstains in her father's hotel room as belonging to Julio Castellano had made it clear that the man who killed her father was a Mexican immigrant who spoke no English. This man, on the other hand, sounded almost as if English was his native language. And why would Julio Castellano be here in Belize? That was stretching the long arm of coincidence way too far.

She realized that she'd been staring at her assailant and quickly dropped her gaze, afraid he would take violent offense at her scrutiny. He stepped threateningly close but didn't hit her, just dragged her hands behind her back, binding them with more duct tape. She heard a muffled sound from across the room, followed by an ominous thud. She swung around just in time to see Adam tumble backward onto the bed, knocked off his feet by a blow from the second assailant's rifle. Apparently he'd resisted having his hands bound.

It was instinctive to run toward Adam but her assailant grabbed her, shoving his hand across her mouth and nose. "He's not badly hurt. He'll come to in a minute." The man spoke in such a low voice that she wouldn't have been able to make out the words if he hadn't leaned down and spoken into her ear. She watched, seething in silent frustration as Adam's inert body was rolled facedown by his captor, and his hands taped behind his back.

Megan tugged at the bindings around her wrists, filled with anger powerful enough to momentarily block out fear. What in God's name was happening to her life? She yearned to go back to the humdrum existence she'd led just a few weeks ago. The life where her family had seemed normal, her roots secure and her future open to possibilities of her own choosing.

"If you're here to help us, why are you tying us up? How does knocking Adam unconscious fit into your rescue plan?" She tried to ask the questions out loud, but she should have saved her breath. Her words emerged in a stifled, broken hum, impossible to understand.

"Don't try to talk. I've covered your mouth for your own protection." Her captor's voice remained almost inaudible. "You have to trust us. Your uncle has made arrangements for you to be killed as soon as you get back to Mexico City. You need to get out of Belize by a different route, one that your uncle doesn't know about and can't control. We will take you to safety."

Her kidnapper's expression remained impassive as he made his extraordinary assertions. He bent down and picked up her small overnight bag from the floor near the closet. Megan noticed that her purse was sticking out of the top. Presumably the kidnapper was robbing her. Or was there even a remote chance that he was making sure she had the documentation and money she needed to get out of the country?

The kidnapper slung her travel bag over his shoulder, which made a bizarre contrast to the assault rifle balanced on his other side. "Move silently toward the door. Don't scream. Make no sound at all. Your life may depend on your silence."

Trusting a rifle-toting kidnapper who looked ominously like the man who'd killed her father struck Megan as one of the less smart options currently available to her. It was a giant step from accepting that her uncle was a thief and a blackmailer to believing that he planned to have her and Adam killed, a step that she wasn't ready to take.

Even if Ted wanted them dead—and why would he?—how could he expect to get away with murder? Several people in the States, including her brother, knew where she was. On top of that, Adam had left word at the hotel in Mexico City that the two of them were flying to Belize with Eagle Navigation. If any harm came to her and Adam, surely suspicion would focus on her uncle?

Perhaps not, Megan reflected grimly, especially if their death occurred in Mexico City. Before her father died and her world somersaulted into a new dimension, she wouldn't have believed any accusations against her uncle for an instant. Even now, she couldn't assimilate the possibility that Ted might want her dead. No, she wouldn't accept it. The logical conclusion was that the kidnapper was lying; he'd simply invented a ruse to keep her docile and easier to abduct.

Well, they'd picked the wrong woman if they hoped for passive obedience, Megan thought bleakly. If she was going to die, she would at least go out kicking and screaming. She'd watched enough movies to know that the fact that neither of her kidnappers wore masks wasn't a good sign. Presumably they didn't expect her and Adam to remain alive long enough to identify them.

Megan tried to think logically above the clamor of her fear. If she ran, the kidnappers would soon catch up with her. Or shoot her in the back. The sound of a shot would wake her uncle, but she would already be dead. Which certainly defeated the purpose of waking him.

How to alert her uncle without getting shot first? With duct tape gagging her mouth she could barely moan, let alone scream. If she stamped her feet and created a scuffle outside Ted's room, would she wake him? Almost certainly, Megan decided. But even if Ted heard the sounds and woke up, the kidnappers would have time to kill her and Adam long before her uncle could get out of bed and run to her aid. Reluctantly, she faced the fact that she seemed to be looking at a choice between the faint hope of ransom or the certainty of instant death. Dammit, she *would* find a way to escape. But maybe she needed to accept that this wasn't the right time and place to make her attempt.

The second assailant tugged Adam to his feet and prodded him toward the hallway. Adam swayed, apparently still groggy from the blow to his head. He seemed almost incapable of standing, which suggested he'd been hit harder than the kidnapper claimed.

"Move," Megan's captor murmured in her ear, poking his gun into her spine for emphasis.

The poke didn't hurt all that much, but it pushed her frustration to a new level. She wasn't about to walk out of here as if she'd been invited to a church picnic. The risk of waking her uncle had to be less than the risk of trusting armed assailants, Megan decided. She would create a disturbance outside her uncle's bedroom door and hope like hell that the kidnappers would run, not stand and fight. With luck, they would be smart enough to realize when it was time to cut their losses.

Her escape plan, risky as it was, never had a chance of being implemented. Instead of walking past her uncle's bedroom toward the front door, the kidnapper pushed her in the opposite direction toward the kitchen and the rear of the house. *Oh hell.* She'd forgotten about the back door. The kidnappers were obviously familiar with the layout of the house and had chosen an exit route that led into the service alleyway, a much safer choice from their point of view than the lighted swimming pool area.

She was right at the entrance to the kitchen, with Adam and his guard trailing behind, when she heard the sound of running footsteps followed by an angry exclamation, abruptly cut off. Almost at once, she heard a heavy thumping noise and she glanced over her shoulder to see Adam kicking her uncle's door, making a racket that surely couldn't avoid waking Ted. Way to go, she thought with a glimmer of hope. Adam must have been faking wooziness in order to throw his assailant off guard. His scheme had worked—at least to the extent that he'd managed to create a disturbance outside Ted's bedroom door.

Megan held her breath, recognizing the

full risks of her escape plan only now that she saw Adam executing his own version of it. She expected one or the other of the gunmen to fire at any moment. Instead, no shots were fired and her kidnapper shoved her behind him, almost as if he were protecting her. Adam didn't fare so well. Peering over the kidnapper's shoulder, she saw the other gunman grab Adam by the hair and bang his head against the wall, silencing him with swift, brutal efficiency.

With a curt order to move, her kidnapper started to drag her into the kitchen, but it was too late, at least from his perspective. The door to her uncle's bedroom was flung open. Ted loomed in the entryway, the gun he carried a surreal contrast to his pajamas, which had images of Mickey Mouse stamped all over them.

Ted's gaze flicked from Adam's bleeding nose to the gunmen and finally to Megan. He seemed to be angry at the sight of the kidnappers, rather than surprised or fearful. Megan's stomach knotted with instant dread. Ted's reaction was all wrong for the situation.

"What are you doing here?" Ted asked curtly, looking straight at the kidnapper still positioned in front of Megan. He allowed the hand holding his weapon to drop to his side.

"I changed the plans some," the kidnapper said. "I decided it was better for everyone if we acted tonight."

"You're not paid to change my plans." Ted's face suffused with hot, angry color. "You're paid to carry out my orders. Now you've fucked everything up."

The kidnapper didn't appear intimidated. "No, the opposite. I've saved your ass."

"How's that?"

"Eric. He's not reliable. Worse, he's stupid."

"Maybe." Ted shrugged. "But he can sure fly a plane, and that's all he was told to do."

"And keep his mouth shut afterward. I've warned you before that Eric freaked out after Ron Raven died. The proof of that is standing right here in your hallway. If Eric had been more reliable, your niece and her lover would never have come to Las Criandas in the first place."

"I agree with that. And since Eric caused the mess, all the more reason for him to share in the cleanup."

"It takes three hours to fly into Mexico

City. That's three long hours for Eric to totally lose his cool. Plus, he'd be the first person the police would question if they died in Mexico. This way—*my way*—Eric's out of the loop. Nobody will ask him any questions and he sure as hell isn't going to volunteer any opinions about what might have happened to your niece and lover boy here." The kidnapper jerked his head in the direction of Adam.

"The cops will want to know why the two of them were kidnapped from my house when I wasn't." Ted glared at Adam, but his gaze slid away from Megan's.

"Tell them these two have more money. Tell them there's no way to understand the motives of kidnappers. God knows, that's true enough."

Ted's mouth contorted into a snarl. "Easy for you to talk. You won't be facing the police inquiries. Nobody would have questioned me if they'd died in Mexico!" He banged his clenched fist into the wall. "You've fucked everything up."

"Go back to bed, Mr. Horn. Tell the cops you drank too much and didn't hear a thing. Just keep telling them that and you'll be fine."

Ted scratched furiously at his mane of hair. "Dump their bodies in the ocean. The cops can't make a case if they don't have any bodies."

"In the ocean again?" The kidnapper shook his head. "That's a lousy idea. We sure as hell don't want to do anything that would have the police seeing similarities between the death of Ron Raven and the disappearance of his daughter. We'll find a nice patch of jungle and tuck them into the undergrowth. This needs to look like a kidnapping gone wrong, pure and simple." His voice took on a hint of irony. "After all, kidnapping is a Central American specialty. We should give their deaths the local touch."

The second kidnapper spoke in a language Megan didn't understand, presumably Mayan, gesturing to Adam and pointing to the kitchen. He seemed to be saying that they needed to go. In fact, though, the foreign words he spoke didn't sound any more alien and incomprehensible to Megan than her uncle's. She felt as if she'd lost her ability to grasp the meaning of simple English. She stared at Ted, with his tousled hair and chubby face, creased with fifty-five years of laughter and squinting into the sun. How could this man, her mother's brother, possibly have spent the past five minutes arguing about the best way to kill her and Adam?

The kidnapper spoke again. "Oscar insists that it's time for us to go, Mr. Horn, and he's right. My sister will let you know when the job is complete. You can give her the rest of my money. No need to tell you I want U.S. dollar bills, none of that Belizean shit, and nothing bigger than a fifty."

"You don't deserve to get paid. You've fucked up."

The kidnapper's voice roughened with menace. "No, Mr. Horn, I haven't fucked up. I'm just doing the job you hired me for. Don't think about double-crossing me, not even in your darkest, most secret moments. I'm one of those people with a real fine sense of justice, and I don't deal well with people who backtrack on their bargains, if you know what I mean." He fingered his assault rifle.

"Get out of here." Ted turned to go back into his bedroom. At the last moment, he turned and looked straight at Megan. "I wish it didn't have to be this way," he said. "You were always a nice kid. But you shouldn't have come looking for the money. I killed your father to keep that three million, and I'm sure as hell not handing it over to you and Adam Fairfax. Adam Fairfax! My God, how can you insult your mother by hooking up with him?" Oblivious to the irony of his reproach, he turned away, speaking to the kidnapper over his shoulder. "Get them out of here, okay? I can't stand long-winded goodbyes."

Megan nearly choked behind her gag. Her uncle's parting remark when he left the Flying W at the end of his visits was always that he couldn't stand long-winded goodbyes. It was mind-blowing to hear him make the same comment in the context of ordering the death of two human beings. Her stomach roiled with such intense nausea that she was afraid she would vomit, a disaster, given the gag. She walked through the kitchen under her own steam, partly because resistance had zero chance of succeeding and partly because she feared she really would throw up if she had to be dragged out of the house.

There was no getaway car in the pitch-dark alley behind the kitchen. As soon as they were outside, Megan's captor grabbed her arm, urging her to walk quickly. He chivvied her along at ever-increasing speed, so that she was forced into a run by the time they reached the deserted main road where transport finally waited in the shape of a dilapidated Jeep, parked on the verge with its engine running and a black-clad woman seated behind the wheel.

Megan was pushed into the front passenger seat and trussed behind the seat belt with her hands still taped behind her. The two kidnappers crowded into the rear seat with Adam held between them. The woman drove away, accelerating gradually enough that the engine barely revved up. Apparently, despite the encounter with Ted Horn, the kidnappers still wanted to avoid attracting attention.

"Okay, listen carefully, you two, because we don't want any mishaps before we leave Las Criandas." The kidnapper spoke from the backseat and, for the first time, he pitched his voice at a normal level. "It's trouble enough that Ted Horn has seen us. There are only two ways out of town, and if he gets to mulling over what happened just now, he's more than capable of setting up roadblocks with security personnel from the mine. And, trust me on this, he'll make damn sure none of us survive the stop. My original plan was to drive you to Belize City tonight. I've changed my mind. We all need to get out of the country as soon as possible, and by separate routes, so my sister's going to drive you instead. The two of you will be able to catch a regular commercial flight from Belize to Guatemala City, and from Guatemala you can get back to the States easily enough."

For the first time in her life, Megan began to doubt her own sanity. Had stress sent her over the top? Incredible as it was to absorb that her uncle had admitted responsibility for her father's murder, and was willing to kill her and Adam for the sake of three million dollars, it was even more crazy to accept that the men hired to do the job—the same men who'd killed her father—were apparently intent on rescuing her at considerable risk to their own safety. What was she missing here? Clearly, there had to be something. Something big.

The driver turned the Jeep into the driveway of a small adobe cottage located on the eastern outskirts of Las Criandas, at the opposite side of town from the airport and the platinum mine. The driver and the two men bundled them inside the simple, stone-floored cottage, clearly anxious to get them inside, although there was nobody in sight and no other cottages anywhere near. A single oil lamp illuminated rough, whitewashed walls and the bare minimum of furniture, none of it upholstered. The woman disappeared through an arch into what looked to be a rudimentary kitchen with a stone sink and a pump to provide water. She returned carrying a cloth soaking in a small enamel bowl of water, a plastic bottle of baby oil and a vicious-looking knife. After a brief exchange with the men, she pressed her hand on Megan's shoulder to indicate that she should sit. Then she poured oil onto Megan's mouth, massaging it around the duct tape until she could pry one of the corners loose.

She looked straight into Megan's eyes, speaking at length, presumably in Mayan.

Megan's captor translated. "My sister says the only way to remove the tape is to rip it off. That will hurt. She asks you not to scream. There is nobody near enough to this cottage to hear you, but we need to know that you can be trusted to keep your word. If you agree that you won't scream or call out for help once the tape is removed, nod your head."

Megan had seen for herself that the cottage was set at least a quarter mile from its closest neighbor, so she was well aware that screaming wouldn't bring rescuers rushing to her aid. That being the case, she was much more interested in getting the gag removed than she was in symbolic defiance, so she inclined her head in brief acknowledgment of her captor's instructions.

The woman grabbed the corner of the duct tape and ripped. Megan swallowed a scream that had nothing to do with a desire for rescue and everything to do with pain. Gaze seemingly sympathetic, the woman held out the damp wash rag and murmured a few words.

Her captor translated again. "My sister apologizes for the discomfort you are suffering. The skin around your mouth has not been torn. She will now cut the tape binding your wrists and she asks you not to react with violence to your freedom."

Megan acknowledged the instruction with another curt nod. Her hands free, she rubbed the cool cloth over her face before returning it to the enamel bowl. The woman made her way to Adam's side and washed the dried blood from his face. "Nothing is broken," she said in English, gently squeezing water over his nose before repeating the process of swabbing his mouth with baby oil and ripping off the duct tape in return for a promise that he wouldn't scream. She hesitated and conferred with both men before cutting the duct-tape handcuffs, but eventually they seemed to agree that Adam could also have free hands.

"Why have you brought us here?" Adam demanded as soon as he could speak. "If you're rescuing us from Ted Horn as you claim, why don't you take us to the nearest police station and report that he plans to kill us?"

The kidnapper looked briefly amused. "I don't share your faith in the officers of the law, Mr. Fairfax. A Mayan peasant lodging an accusation of attempted murder against an American mining engineer is soon likely to find himself on the wrong side of a set of prison bars."

"You know my name."

"Of course. And much more about you." The kidnapper reached inside his pocket and pulled out a couple of sheets of paper, folded small. "As soon as Eric told Ted Horn that you were coming to Belize, Ted did a quick Internet search to see what he could learn about you. He found several interesting articles about the work you've done revitalizing the economy in your hometown. He passed them on to me."

"So that you would know the life history of the man you were paid to kill? That's a new twist for a hired killer, isn't it?"

"Something like that. Except, of course, that I have no intention of killing you. Murder isn't my style." The kidnapper stood up. "The drive to Belize City will take several hours. The difficulties of the journey will be great if you and Ms. Raven are constantly trying to escape. It will be easier for everyone if you believe that we intend neither of you any harm. This was once the home of Oscar's parents." He gestured briefly to the other kidnapper. "We brought you here because the cottage is isolated and we don't have to worry that our conversation will be overheard by neighbors. Ask whatever questions you need in order to reassure yourselves that you can safely trust us."

He sounded so rational, so honest, and yet Megan was becoming more certain by the moment that the man they were dealing with was Julio Castellano, her father's killer.

The juxtaposition of soothing words and frightening biography added to her growing sense of unreality. They were no longer in Wonderland, she thought with a touch of hysteria. They'd stepped through the looking glass and ended up somewhere a great deal scarier than that.

She was sick of the lies, the deceptions, the half truths and the endless revelations that only seemed to bring more pain. Letting this smooth-talking kidnapper know that she guessed his name might be dangerous, but it was probably the fastest way to the truth. Since her father died, she'd been living in a shape-shifting world of smoke and mirrors. It was past time, she decided, to blow away the smoke, shatter the mirrors and confront reality.

She looked straight into her kidnapper's eyes and held his gaze without flinching. "Are you Julio Castellano?" she asked. "Did you murder my father?"

Twenty-two

Sweet Jesus, she was going to get herself killed! Adam surged to his feet, reaching Megan's side before she'd even finished speaking. He'd been asking himself the same question ever since the confrontation in the hallway with Ted Horn but he'd avoided speaking it out loud. If this man really was Julio Castellano, Adam couldn't think of a single way that it would be safe for their kidnappers to let them out of their custody alive.

He stood in front of Megan, cutting off her view of the kidnapper. He gripped her hands, squeezing them in warning. "Hey, Meg, honey, I'm sure you've made a mistake. I saw Castellano's mug shot, and he looked quite different from this man." He hoped like hell that she'd understand the need to back off.

Megan stared at him blankly and he realized that events had pushed her so close to the edge that she was having a hard time climbing back. Which was hardly surprising, he thought bleakly. She had gone through a series of emotional and practical upheavals over the past three weeks that would have left almost anyone reeling. Unfortunately, she couldn't afford to give in to the luxury of an emotional breakdown. Not now.

"This isn't the man who killed your father," he said quickly, urging her with his eyes to agree with him. He cupped her cheek with his hand, hoping that physical contact would reach her if reason failed. "Remember, Julio Castellano speaks no English. It was in his police files that he was a Mexican immigrant who spoke only Spanish."

"Just another example of how wrong your American police can be," the kidnapper said coolly, interposing himself between Megan and Adam. "I am Julio Castellano. I was born in Mexico and I have a Mexican passport, but I spent my childhood right here in Belize. My mother worked as a maid in Rafael Williamson's home in Belize City, and I grew up in a trilingual household. My father was Spanish-speaking by birth, my mother was Mayan, and I went to a school where we were taught in English. Several of our teachers were Brits, on assignment to one of the last colonies in their empire, so you could say that I'm a true native English speaker."

"Then how did the police come to make such a major mistake in your records?" Adam asked, curiosity overcoming caution.

Julio Castellano gave a short laugh. "Ask instead how come the police made such a major mistake in arresting me for a murder I didn't commit."

"Which murder didn't you commit?" Megan asked quickly. "My father's murder, or the man killed in a bar fight ten years ago?"

Julio went and stood at the room's single, tiny window, peering out to the dark road. "I was referring to Steve Opporto, the man killed in the bar fight," he said, swinging back to face them, apparently reassured that nobody was coming in pursuit. "Steve happened to be the brother of a cop. He was also a drug addict who got himself killed during a cocaine deal gone wrong. A deal, by the way, that involved two members of the local police force. I was in the bar by chance, and I made the mistake of trying to break up the fight. The police found it much more convenient to pin all the blame on me than to bring out in court the fact that Steve was a drug addict and that local cops were involved in selling cocaine. The first cop on the scene happened to speak to me in Spanish. I replied in the same language. After that, it quickly became apparent that letting the cops think I was a Mexican illegal who spoke no English was to my advantage. Not enough of an advantage, sadly, to keep me out of jail since I had no money to pay for a lawyer. The public defender met me for the first time thirty minutes before we were due in court."

Julio's story had the ring of truth, Adam reflected. Did that mean there was a glimmer of hope that he and Megan might emerge from this ordeal alive?

Not if tact was a requirement for survival, he thought ruefully. Megan seemed to have passed well beyond worrying about the impact her questions might have on their chances of survival. Adam felt torn between admiration, affection and the urge to throttle her. She plunged ahead with her questions for Julio as if this were an academic exercise in truth-finding, as opposed to an interrogation that could easily end up with two dead people as the final answer.

"The police reports I read also claimed that you'd been involved in another bar fight where a man was killed," Megan said, not attempting to disguise her doubts about Julio's honesty. "Was that a police setup, too?"

"No." Julio's expression became tinged with sadness. "I killed that man, although not intentionally. He tripped and fell backward onto a tiled floor. We were both drunk, we were both young and stupid, and I fought him to the death over some ridiculous insult. I don't remember exactly what insult, but I think he referred to me as short."

His mouth twisted in bitter self-mockery. "There's nothing like hearing the truth to get a drunk fighting mad. And you notice that I didn't learn my lesson even after killing that poor man. My drinking was still out of control. I was in a bar again, on the way to being falling-down drunk, when I got arrested for Steve Opporto's murder. Life is strange, though. I didn't deserve to go to prison for murder, but the fact that I was wrongly arrested may have saved my life. I got sober while I was incarcerated, and I haven't taken a drink since. I've discovered that the world's a much more interesting place when you're seeing its real colors, with no alcoholic haze to filter out the intensity."

Oscar interrupted with a stream of impassioned Mayan and Julio nodded, putting his hand in a brief, calming gesture on the other man's arm. "My brother-in-law reminds me that we don't have all night to stand here chatting. We need to leave. You for Belize City with my sister, and Oscar with me for…another destination."

"But you still haven't answered my most important question!" Megan protested. "I need to know the truth. Did you murder my father or not?"

Adam held his breath while Julio looked at her assessingly for a long, silent moment. "No," he said finally. "No, Ms. Raven, I didn't kill your father."

"Then who did? Please tell me."

"I can't answer that question."

"Because you don't know the answer? Or because you won't tell me?"

"Because it would be unwise for me to answer that question." Julio's words were flat, but his expression was sympathetic. "If I tell you that the woman in the hotel room with Ron Raven was called Consuela Mackenzie, and that she was the daughter of my father's sister, will you believe that I would have done everything in my power to ensure that she remained alive?"

Megan's eyes widened in shock. "The woman in the hotel room with my father was your *cousin*?"

Julio nodded. "Yes, she was my cousin—and at one time, the fiancée of your uncle, Ted Horn. She was, however, a very smart woman and she fell out of love with your uncle as soon as she moved into his house and began to know him better. Ted Horn, a man whose jealousy is easily aroused, saw that his fiancée was attracted to Ron Raven and accused your father of stealing Consuela's affections from him."

"Was Ted right?" Megan asked. "Were Consuela and my father lovers?"

"I can't answer that," Julio said. He held up his hand, forestalling Megan's inevitable follow-up. "No, Ms. Raven, leave it at that. I can't answer your question, in part because we have other, much more important things to talk about in the few minutes that remain to us."

"I can't think of anything much more important to me than the events leading up to my father's murder," Megan said. "Are you suggesting that Ted Horn arranged to have my father and Consuela killed simply because he was annoyed that Consuela preferred my dad?"

"You're using the wrong words," Julio said. "For Ted Horn, there was nothing *simple* about the fact that Consuela fell out of love with him and into love with Ron Raven. All his life, from what I've heard, he's been watching Ron succeed where he failed, starting with high school, where Ron was captain of the football team and Ted couldn't even make the marching band. Then while Ted was in college, his father ran into such hopeless debt that he had to sell their land to Ron, losing a ranch that had been handed down in the Horn family through four generations. Ron had made a million bucks by the time he was forty, while Ted was scrambling around in various hellholes in South America, spending his salary as fast as he earned it, with three failed marriages and no kids. Do you wonder that when Ted discovered your father was a bigamist that he was tempted to indulge in a little blackmail?"

"Forgive me if I don't find my heart bleeding for my uncle," Megan said acidly. "Despite my dad's flaws, and however much

Ted loved Consuela, that doesn't begin to explain why he felt justified in arranging to have her and my father killed."

"You're right," Julio acknowledged. "And ultimately it wasn't only jealousy that caused Ted to plan a murderous solution to his problems. Your father was a very smart businessman. On top of that, he and Consuela were close enough that she decided to trust him with a lot of her own suspicions. Between Ron's own insights into the mining operation and Consuela's practical observations inside Ted's home, Ron soon realized that his brother-in-law was smuggling platinum out of the country, using Eric and Eagle Navigation to do the actual transportation."

"We thought that Eric might be involved in smuggling," Megan said, exchanging glances with Adam. "He was just too anxious to steer us away from Las Criandas."

"Yes, Eric came up with a clever way to hide the platinum in plain sight. If you remember the table separating the two seats in the plane, you might recall that there are four decorative metal inserts right under the Plexiglas. On inbound flights to Las Criandas, those inserts are stainless steel. On outbound flights, they're platinum. Mexican customs officials don't search Eric's plane very often. When they do, they have dogs sniffing for drugs, not metal experts pointing out stainless steel that's really platinum. It's a neat scheme, and Eric's transporting close to a couple of kilos of platinum a trip."

Adam made a quick calculation. "That means he's taking in approximately sixty thousand dollars a round trip."

"Well, Eric only gets paid about fifteen thousand of that, but he manages to shuttle passengers in or out at least once a month, so it's a profitable scheme for everyone involved. Even when you factor in all the payoffs to mine workers and Belizean customs, as well, Ted is still looking at extra income of close to half a million a year. When your father threatened to inform Rafael Williamson exactly how he was being ripped off unless Ted stopped the smuggling immediately and returned Ron's three-million-dollar investment, he was undercutting the financial arrangements of a lot of people. And his threats had bite. Rafe Williamson is like any other child of privilege—he feels entitled and he resents being ripped off. He would have shown Ted no mercy. Your uncle was looking at serious jail time, and he knew it.

So was everyone else involved in the operation."

"I guess there was only one mistake in my father's calculations," Megan said bitterly. "He didn't realize his brother-in-law was willing to commit murder in order to hang on to the three million and avoid jail."

"You're correct. And Ted had plenty of potential willing helpers because of the number of people involved in the smuggling operation one way or another. But we know now what Ted is capable of and we also know that threats won't coerce him into behaving with decency. That means we have to stop threatening and act." Julio turned to his sister. "Arabela, would you bring the key to Consuela's safety-deposit box?"

Arabela, who presumably understood just as much English as her brother, responded in Mayan before leaving for the kitchen.

"Consuela wrote a full account of everything she knew about Ted's smuggling activities," Julio said. "We also know that when Consuela left to meet your father in Miami, she took documents with her that would prove her accusations against her former fiancé. She must have secured the documents in a safety-deposit box near the hotel where she stayed with Ron—" He broke off as his sister returned to the living room. "Ah, there you have it."

Arabela held out a small, flat box, her expression difficult to read. "This is from Consuela," she said to Megan, finally condescending to speak English instead of forcing her brother to translate. "Inside you will find a key to a safety-deposit box, along with the address of a bank. Consuela also gave us the number of her account and her password. The note is in here." She tapped the box.

"How did you get the key?" Adam demanded, trying not to let his renewed suspicions sound in his voice. If this was truly the key to a safety-deposit box Consuela had rented in Miami, only somebody who had access to her belongings after her death could have obtained possession of it.

Arabela smiled faintly, apparently well aware of what his question implied. "Consuela mailed me the key the day before she died," she said. "You don't have to worry, Mr. Fairfax. My brother didn't steal it from Consuela's dead body after he killed her." She opened the lid of the box and showed him an envelope addressed to Arabela Tikal, with American stamps and a Miami postmark.

"As I already mentioned, Rafe Williamson is not a man who reacts well to the knowledge that he's been cheated," Julio said. "When he sees the information Consuela and Ron Raven accumulated about the smuggling activities at his mine, he will launch a full-scale investigation. At that point, Ted Horn, Eric Connolly and several corrupt government officials will be toast."

Arabela pushed the box of Consuela's belongings into Megan's hands. "Ted Horn sitting in a Belizean prison for a few years is not adequate punishment for a man who planned the murder of four people merely to hide his own criminal behavior. It is, however, some small balance on the scales of justice."

"You two need to go to Miami as soon as you leave here and open the safety-deposit box," Julio said. "For obvious reasons, I can't go to the States and reclaim Consuela's papers myself. First you must make copies of everything you find in the safety-deposit box. Then you must express one set of the documents to Rafe Williamson. If you wish, you can deliver another set of the documents to the police in Miami. It would provide them with a motive for Ron Raven's murder, which they don't have at the moment."

"We have to do that," Adam said, inwardly cringing at the prospect of inflicting yet more hurt and humiliating publicity on Megan's family. He put his arm around her, drawing her close to his side, wishing he could think of some honorable way to keep quiet about what they'd learned. "We owe it to you, Julio. We need to tell the police that you didn't kill Ron Raven."

"How can you tell the police any such thing?" Julio asked. "You have only my word to stand against the forensic evidence of my blood splashed on the hotel room wall. Informing the Miami police that Ted Horn ordered Ron Raven's murder wouldn't help me at all. On the contrary, I would still be the chief suspect, and the police in Miami for the first time would have an idea of where they might need to direct their search for me."

Megan's face was pale and drawn with anxiety. "I wish we could keep silent," she said. "It's bad enough that my mother has to learn that her brother is a thief only weeks after she discovered that her husband was a bigamist, but she'll be totally devastated to learn that her own brother was the man behind my father's murder."

"Then keep silent," Julio said. "Tell no one what you know."

Adam could see how badly Megan wanted to do just that. "But we owe it to Consuela to give her an identity," she said. She drew in a shaky breath and looked at Adam. "Don't we owe Avery and Kate the truth? How can we protect my mother's feelings toward her brother at the expense of lying to my dad's other family? Kate is my dad's daughter, after all." Her voice lowered. "She's my sister, too."

Julio shrugged. "I can't tell you what you must do about Ron Raven's families, and how you must weigh the needs of one family member against another. However, as far as Consuela is concerned, be assured that everyone in her family already knows the truth. There is no body to be buried, and no grave site to be named. We consider it no dishonor to my cousin if the police and media in America remain ignorant of her name. On the contrary, we would prefer her to remain anonymous."

Oscar banged his rifle against the wall, then burst into rapid-fire speech, gesticulating toward the tiny window. Then he stomped to the front door and stood there, his hand on the heavy wooden bar that held the door closed.

Julio gave a small, wry smile. “My brother-in-law points out that in less than thirty minutes, dawn will be breaking. He says that whatever we are discussing is about to become irrelevant because we will all be dead if we don’t leave here at once. He is correct.” Julio kissed his sister on each cheek. “Go with God, Arabela.”

“And you.” Arabela walked over to Oscar and they exchanged the same sort of semiformal embrace that she’d shared with her brother. They spoke briefly in Mayan, their body language so constrained that Adam would never have guessed they were experiencing deep emotion if he hadn’t seen their tears, not only in Arabela’s eyes, but also in Oscar’s.

The two men slipped out into the darkness. Silence fell, all the more complete because Adam was straining to hear the sounds of their departure.

“Do they have a car?” Megan asked.

"Surely to God they're not going to escape on foot?"

"Don't worry about them. They can take care of themselves." Arabela led them out of the tiny cottage and around to the back where the Jeep was parked.

"Get in," she said. "Buckle your seat belts. We have a long journey ahead of us and the road is rough."

Adam reached for Megan's hand. Her fingers curled tightly around his. The journey would be easy to bear, he thought, as long as they were traveling together.

Twenty-three

June 8, 2006, the Flying W Ranch, Wyoming

Megan shifted the gear stick into Park and turned off the ignition, but she didn't get out of the car. It was going to take another few moments to work up sufficient courage to walk into her mother's home.

Adam put his hand over her fingers, which she hadn't even realized were drumming on the steering wheel. She loved his hands, with their strong, square palms that contrasted with his long, slender fingers. His touch was enough to calm some of the butterflies making a combat zone out of her stomach and she turned to him, drawing courage from his steady gaze.

He lifted her hand and brushed a kiss across her knuckles, the gesture at once erotic and comforting. Until Adam, she had never met a man who could make her senses quicken and her heart race with such a simple caress and she smiled at him, cherishing the way his cool gray eyes warmed as they looked at her.

She drew in a final calming breath. "Okay, I'm ready."

They walked up the steps and rang the doorbell. Megan heard the dogs bound into the hallway, their barking almost drowning out the sound of her mother's footsteps.

Ellie opened the door, welcoming her daughter with a smile and a hug. The dogs put on their usual performance of canine ecstasy, pushing their muzzles into Megan's hands and demanding to be petted, tails thumping on the floor hard enough to rattle the pewter vase on the side table.

"Come on in, honey. You're a few minutes earlier than you said, but at least I combed my hair and put on some lipstick." Ellie smiled and turned toward Adam, holding out her hand. "Megan said she was bringing a good friend with her today, but she neglected to tell me your name. I'm Ellie Raven."

Her mother looked more relaxed than Megan had seen her in the past few weeks and she hated that she was about to destroy such hard-won peace of mind.

"I'm Adam Fairfax," Adam said, shaking Ellie's hand. Scrupulously, he identified himself, on the remote chance that Ellie had missed the connection. "I'm Avery's younger brother, from Fairfax in Georgia."

Ellie's smile vanished and she dropped Adam's hand as if it burned her. Instinctive good manners prevented her from delivering out loud any of the cutting remarks she was undoubtedly nursing inside, but she looked at Megan with an expression that hovered somewhere between astonishment and outrage.

Megan swallowed over the lump in her throat. "May we come in, Mom? We have a lot to tell you."

Ellie's gaze flicked from her daughter to Adam and back again. Whatever she saw in their expressions leeched color from her cheeks. "Come into the living room," she said abruptly and turned without looking to see if they followed her.

Ellie usually took friends and family straight into the kitchen, where she almost always had something baking in the oven, or a stew simmering in a pot on the stove. The living room was reserved for overflow crowds at parties, and entertaining people she didn't much like. Megan was perfectly well aware that she was being rebuked for bringing Adam here without proper warning.

"Would you care for something to drink?" Ellie asked when they were all three perched uncomfortably on the edge of the pristine living room chairs.

Megan shook her head. "Not for me, thanks. Adam?"

"No, I'm fine, thank you." Adam sounded determinedly friendly, but Ellie failed to respond to his overture with even a hint of warmth. Megan could see from the way she sat ramrod straight and held her hands clasped with white-knuckle firmness in her lap that she was steeling herself for the worst.

There was no point in dragging out what had to be said, Megan decided. She turned toward Adam and he nodded almost imperceptibly, silently urging her to speak. "Mom, I think you've guessed that we have some bad news to share with you."

"I assume Mr. Fairfax is here because he's about to foreclose on the ranch." Ellie spoke with quiet dignity.

Adam spoke quickly. "No, that's not it, Mrs. Raven. In fact, I had a chat this morning with your lawyer, Cody Holmann, and he believes the probate judge administering Ron's estate will agree to continue paying the interest due on the loan for several more months. That should give us plenty of time to explore…options…in regard to the ranch."

Ellie allowed her gaze to rest briefly on Adam. "And you're willing to accept interest payments even though you have the legal right to demand repayment of the loan in full?"

"Yes. I'm convinced that there are more profitable options for the First Bank of Fairfax than selling this land at fire-sale prices." Adam said no more. He and Megan had already agreed that this wasn't the day to start persuading Ellie that Flying W land could only be saved if she was prepared to use it for something more profitable than cattle ranching.

"I'm sure you know how pleased I am to hear that." Ellie visibly relaxed, until another horrifying thought occurred to her. "Oh my God! Nothing's happened to Liam, has it?" Her hand went to her throat. "Please tell me you haven't come here because something's happened to Liam."

"Liam's fine." Megan hurried to provide reassurance. "I spoke to him early this morning. He's snowed under with work, that's all. He's planning to call you over the weekend." She rushed on before she lost her nerve. "This isn't about Liam, Mom. It's about Uncle Ted."

"What's Ted done now?" Ellie answered her own question. "I suppose he's come up with a new excuse as to why he can't return the three million dollars of Ron's money that he owes the First Bank of Fairfax. Why else would you and Mr. Fairfax need to go before the probate judge and get permission to continue payments on the loan?" Embarrassed color stained Ellie's cheeks. "I hope you know, Mr. Fairfax, that I'm really sorry—no, I'm not even sorry, I'm humiliated. I was appalled when Megan called after she got back from Belize and explained that the three million dollars we were looking for had been invested in my brother's platinum mine." She shook her head. "I still can hardly believe that Ted took advantage of my husband's death to keep quiet about the three million he owed to Ron's estate."

Her mother felt this badly knowing only a fraction of Ted's sins, so Megan couldn't imagine how Ellie would feel if she knew her brother had masterminded Ron's murder and ordered the death of his niece. After hours of discussion as they waited in Guatemala City for their flight back to the States, she and Adam had decided there was nothing to be gained by telling Ellie and Avery the truth about how and why Ron Raven had died. The documentation Consuela Mackenzie had stored in the Miami safety-deposit box provided overwhelming evidence of Ted's smuggling operation, and there seemed little doubt that he would end up in one of Belize's more miserable prisons as soon as Rafael Williamson learned how he'd been ripped off by his operations manager and old college buddy.

As for the fact that she and Adam now knew the identity of the woman in the hotel room with Ron, they'd decided to downplay the seriousness of the relationship. There was no way that either of Ron's wives would feel better for knowing that Consuela Mackenzie had not been a one-night stand but a woman who'd loved him. Adam had been tactful enough not to point out the obvious, but Megan realized the fact that her father and Consuela had been together in Miami suggested their affair was far from over.

In the end, her only real objection to keeping quiet about Ted Horn's criminal behavior had been her dislike of lying. Her father's life had been wrapped in too many lies, involving too many people, and she hated that she was allowing the circumstances of his death to become obscured under yet another layer of deceit and half truths. She resented that people who were close to her had kept quiet about Ron's bigamy, arrogantly claiming for themselves the right to decide what was best for her and Ellie. Now she was doing something that struck her as alarmingly similar.

Adam had eventually persuaded her that keeping quiet about Ted's activities was different. Revealing Ron's bigamy, he pointed out, would have enabled Avery and Ellie to make decisions and choices that would have changed their lives. Revealing the truth about Ted's past sins would add greatly to Ellie's unhappiness, and possibly Avery's, without providing anyone with a single opportunity to change anything.

In view of what had happened today, and the news they'd received from Rafael Williamson, Megan was really glad that she hadn't insisted on telling her mother that

Ted was a murderer as well as a smuggler and a thief. She crossed the room and knelt beside her mother's chair.

"This isn't about the missing money, Mom. I'm afraid it's worse than that. I'm sorry, but we just had a phone call this morning from Rafael Williamson, Uncle Ted's boss down in Belize."

She paused for no more than a second, but Ellie spoke into the silence. "My brother's dead, isn't he? I can tell from your face."

Megan gripped her mother's hand. "Yes, he's dead. I'm sorry, Mom."

When she learned that her husband was dead, Ellie hadn't cried. Megan was relieved to see that today tears welled immediately in her mother's eyes and she reached into her pocket for a tissue, blowing her nose firmly before she asked, "How did Ted die?"

"He…shot himself."

"Oh my God! Why? What in the world was going on with him?"

Megan hesitated, but only for a moment. "He seems to have owed Rafael Williamson a lot of money. It's complicated. I'm not sure we'll ever understand exactly what their dealings were." And she hoped like hell that her mother would never inquire, so that she wouldn't have to explain about the smuggling.

"The bottom line is that when Ted's estate is cleared up, it seems likely he's going to owe more than a million dollars to Mr. Williamson. But he left a copy of his will right on the table in his living room and everything goes to you, Mom. So in the end, when his debts are settled, maybe you'll get back at least half of the money he borrowed from Dad."

"I don't care about the money," Ellie said. "Except for paying back Mr. Fairfax and his bank." Tears rolled down her cheeks. "Poor Ted. He always did run away from his problems instead of facing up to them, but I never, ever thought he'd end up stealing Ron's money. My money, really, since Ron's dead. And now this." She got up and walked over to the window, speaking with her back turned to them.

"Is that why you brought Adam Fairfax with you today, Megan? I'd been wondering, I must admit. I guess he needed to issue a reminder that any money I get from Ted's estate really belongs to his bank."

Megan winced at the implicit hostility in

her mother's question. She moved instinctively to Adam's side, her hand slipping into his. She was relieved when Adam not only responded to her mother but tackled the hostility head-on. She'd had about as much evasion and denial as she could handle for one day, Megan reflected.

"I understand why you don't like me, Mrs. Raven. Although of course you don't really know me, so what you dislike actually has nothing to do with me and everything to do with your late husband and the fact that he was married to my sister."

Ellie didn't turn around. "Pretended to be married to your sister," she corrected.

Adam's hand tightened around Megan's and she leaned closer to him, as if physical closeness could cushion the hurt of Ellie's barb. "Pretended to be married to her," Adam agreed. "But, I repeat, Ron's bigamy has nothing to do with who I am. Even the fact that your husband has a three-million-dollar debt owing to my bank tells you nothing about the kind of man I am. Except that I'm a banker by profession."

"You're probably right," Ellie agreed, still talking to the cow barns rather than turning around to face the two of them. "My dislike of you is irrational and most likely unfair. Life's often unfair, I've been realizing recently. The bottom line is that I have no idea how I'm supposed to separate my personal feelings from the fact that you're a Fairfax and your bank can turn me out of my home anytime you decide you're tired of waiting for Ron's estate to get settled." She drew in a breath that was audibly shaky. "I guess it's fortunate for all of us that there's no reason for us to see each other again, is there?"

Megan spoke quietly. "There's every reason, Mom."

Ellie slowly swung around. Her eyes, still red from crying over her dead brother, slowly absorbed the fact that Adam Fairfax had his arm around her daughter's shoulders, and that Megan was leaning close against his side, her hand clasped in his.

"I've asked Megan to move to Georgia," Adam told her.

"Why?" Ellie demanded.

Adam looked down at Megan, his gaze inexpressibly tender. "I wish I could say it's because we're getting married. Unfortunately, Megan hasn't agreed to that yet, but she's agreed to move in with me. It's a start, at least."

Ellie's eyes, wide with disbelief, fixed on her daughter. "You're leaving Wyoming to move in with Adam *Fairfax?*" She struggled, with total lack of success, to hide her dismay. "But what about your job?"

"I was planning to leave the ski lodge anyway," Megan said. "You know I wasn't happy there, Mom."

"But there are plenty of other good opportunities in Jackson Hole. More than there are in Fairfax, Georgia, I'm betting."

"You're right, of course. But there are two motels right in Fairfax, and another eight within two highway exits in either direction. I should be able to find a position as an assistant manager without any trouble. It's not perfect, but it's an acceptable stopgap."

"But all your friends are here." Ellie's voice died away without speaking the most hurtful fact of all. *Your widowed mother is here, too. And she's alone, betrayed by her husband and her brother.*

This was worse than she'd anticipated, Megan thought painfully. There was absolutely nothing for it but to tell her mother the stark truth, even though she was barely comfortable with it herself. "You're right, most of my friends are here. More important, you're here, and I'm going to miss you terribly. But Adam is in Fairfax, Georgia," she said. "And I'm in love with Adam."

It was the first time she'd said the words out loud since that disastrous morning in Mexico City and she was aware of a sudden rush of pure happiness. She turned to him, tilting her head back so that she could look straight into his eyes. "I do love you, Adam."

"You can't imagine how happy it makes me to hear you say that." Adam leaned down and kissed her with a tenderness that was all the more compelling because, out of deference to her mother, he deliberately doused the passion that was usually an inevitable accompaniment to any physical contact between the two of them.

He broke off the kiss but kept his arm tightly around Megan as he spoke again to Ellie. "Your husband betrayed two good women, and shortchanged all three of his children. He may have been a decent man in some ways, and he was certainly a very smart man, but he also caused a lot of grief and destruction. Megan already loves me, so it's too late to hope that I'll just slink away and be forgotten. Believe me when I say I'm going to do everything in my power to persuade your daughter to marry me. But you're her mother and she loves you a lot. We'll never be truly happy if her relationship with me is bought at the expense of her relationship with you."

Ellie was unmoved by his rhetoric. Her expression and voice both remained frosty. "Megan has been my daughter for almost twenty-seven years. How long has she known you? Is it twenty-seven days yet? Excuse me if I find it a tad hard to compare the two relationships."

Megan winced. "Mom, I know this is difficult for you. It's difficult for all of us. But the fact is, Adam and I were attracted from the moment we first met—"

"You're young. Young people are attracted to each other all the time."

"Not like this. Not like us. We've both dated other people. We both know that what we feel for each other is different and more important than what we've experienced before."

"Falling madly in love is a lot of fun, but it's not enough to make a marriage." Ellie gave a contemptuous sniff, the contempt directed at herself. "I fell madly in love with Ron and look where that got me."

"If you didn't reach your destination it was because of him," Megan said quietly. "Not because of you. He wasn't worthy of you."

"And in the few days you and Adam have been together, how do you know he's worthy of you?"

"Sometimes you meet a person and you know right away how you feel," Megan said. "Time isn't everything in getting to know a person. After all, you grew up on the ranch right next door to my father. In one way, you knew him literally from the moment you were born. In another way, you didn't know him at all. None of us did."

"That's as may be," Ellie said. "I still think you need more than a few weeks to decide that you're going to spend the rest of your life with a person."

"I agree and that's exactly why I'm planning to move to Georgia before I make any rash decisions about the rest of my life.

"So why are you the one who's doing all the moving?"

"Because it's easier for me to find a job in a hotel near Fairfax than it is for Adam to become president of a bank in Wyoming."

Adam broke a moment of silence. "Please don't allow Ron's bad behavior to destroy

Megan's happiness. He doesn't deserve that much power in her life, or in yours."

Ellie didn't respond immediately. Then she finally looked up and although she still didn't smile, her previous hostility was visibly diminished. "You're right, Adam," she said, using his given name for the first time. "I can't allow the fact of Ron's bigamy to dominate my life and to ruin my relationship with Megan. I don't have to forgive him, but I do need to move on. Thank you for making me realize that I need to put his betrayals behind me. I already understood that in my head. Now I understand it in my gut, too."

"Then you don't mind if I go to Georgia?" Megan could scarcely believe that she stood a chance of winning her mother's blessing.

"Of course I mind." Ellie gave a faint smile. "But I wish you every possible joy all the same. If Adam Fairfax is the right man for you, then he's the man you should have."

"Thank you. Oh, Mom, thank you."

Ellie returned her daughter's rapturous hug. "I'll go and start working on dinner. Adam looks as if he's going to pop if he doesn't get the chance to kiss you properly in the next twenty seconds or so."

"Your mother was right," Adam said as soon as they were alone. "I'm about to pop." He scooped her into his arms and kissed her long and hard.

"I love you, Megan Raven," he said when they came up for air. "I really love you."

* * * * *

Turn the page to read an exciting excerpt from
SUSPECT
The second book in the Ravens Trilogy

One

Denver, Colorado
Monday, August 7

Liam Raven looked at the woman sleeping in the bed next to him and tried to remember her name. He vaguely recalled that she enjoyed snowboarding. He remembered that she was studying to be a nurse. Her name, however, escaped him.

He stared at the light filtering through the broken slats of the mini-blinds and wondered how it came about that at thirty-five years of age, pushing thirty-six, he hadn't found a better way to spend his nights than by sleeping with a woman he never planned to see again and whose name he couldn't remember.

His cell phone rang—his work number—saving him from delving too deeply into the murky depths of his psyche. He was grateful for the interruption. Self-analysis was guaranteed to give you nightmares, but work, thank God, usually proved a reliable anesthetic.

He eased out of bed, flipping open his phone. Out of deference to the still-sleeping No-Name, he waited until he was in the living room before he responded. “This is Liam Raven.”

“Thank God I reached you. This is Chloe Hamilton.” The woman on the other end of the phone drew in an audible gulp of air but her voice still didn’t steady. “Do you remember me? I came to see you a few months ago. I asked for your help in filing for a divorce—”

“I remember you well, Mrs. Hamilton.” Even among Liam’s client roster of rich and famous Coloradans, it would be hard to forget a woman who’d won medals in four Olympic skiing events and was married to the mayor of Denver. Not to mention the fact that Chloe Hamilton had the sort of lithe, athletic body guaranteed to provoke a major case of lust in any straight guy still breathing.

“We discussed ways to keep the proceedings confidential until the decree was granted," Liam said, letting Chloe know that he genuinely recalled their past dealings. "In the end, though, you decided to stay with your husband for the sake of your daughter. How can I help you, Mrs. Hamilton?"

"Jason's dead," she blurted out, her voice catching on a suppressed sob. "He's been…murdered."

The mayor of Denver had been *murdered?* Holy shit! Liam smothered the exclamation. "I'm very sorry to hear of your loss—"

"I was the person who found him. I came downstairs and he was lying on the floor in our basement media room. There was blood everywhere. All over the wall. All over the floor. God, it was terrible." Chloe's explanation erupted in short, staccato bursts and it sounded to Liam as if her teeth were chattering.

"There was so much blood." Chloe's voice faded to a whisper. "My God, there was so much blood."

Liam spoke swiftly. "Have you notified the police? Called a doctor?" A doctor might be able to help Chloe even if there was nothing he could do for her husband.

"The police think I killed him." The words tumbled out, harsh with fear. "I'm sure they're going to arrest me. I need a lawyer right away. I can't let them take me to jail, even for a couple of nights. Sophie's just lost...she's just lost her father. She can't lose me, too. She simply can't."

Sophie must be the name of Chloe's daughter, but Liam had never seen the child and couldn't remember how old she was. A preschooler, he thought. Maybe three or four? He spoke quickly. "Are the police with you now?"

"Just a couple of uniformed officers guarding the crime scene and holding the reporters at bay. They've already taken away—" She broke off and started again. "They've already taken away Jason's body."

"Whatever you do, Mrs. Hamilton, don't say anything to the cops. Nothing, do you hear me? If they ask your name, you're obligated to identify yourself, but that's it. It doesn't matter how innocuous the police questions seem, don't answer them. In a murder case, the spouse and immediate family of the victim are often considered suspects. Unless you have a rock-solid alibi—"

"I was here all night," Chloe said. "It must

have happened... Jason must have been killed while I was sleeping."

She'd been sleeping—unless she'd killed him, Liam reflected cynically, but he kept any trace of skepticism out of his voice. "Under the circumstances, you should assume you're currently the prime suspect, Mrs. Hamilton. It's nothing personal on the part of the authorities. Just routine police procedure in the early stages of an investigation."

"Their suspicions seem a lot more than routine to me."

Yeah, well, most likely because the evidence pointed straight to her, Liam thought. However, that was beside the point. Guilty or innocent, his advice to Chloe Hamilton would remain the same: get a competent criminal lawyer and say nothing.

He spoke briskly. "In view of the fact that we're talking about the murder of a very prominent citizen, the police department will almost certainly send one or more of their senior detectives to question you sometime soon. Whatever these detectives ask—even if it's something as simple as the date, or the time of day—tell them you need to consult with your lawyer before responding. Got that?"

"Yes, I understand. But I guess it's too late for that piece of advice. I already answered a ton of questions about what happened last night."

Liam shook his head, groaning inwardly. He was constantly amazed at the way even sophisticated and well-educated people failed to take advantage of their right to remain silent in the wake of a crime. He attempted to reassure her anyway. Right now it wouldn't help to add to Chloe's stress level by telling her she'd screwed up, bigtime.

"There's probably no real harm done." For her daughter's sake, he hoped that wasn't a complete lie. If you really wanted to mess up a kid, he couldn't think of a much better way than having one parent murder the other. Growing up with your mom in prison wasn't exactly the model for a picture-perfect childhood, either.

"Make sure you don't answer any more questions until you have legal counsel right there with you, okay?"

"Okay. I understand."

"Do you have a pencil and paper?"

"I must have, I guess." Her voice trailed off and he could visualize her staring vaguely around the room, still too much in shock to register her surroundings with any degree of clarity. He felt an odd wish to be there with her, to offer comfort where none, realistically, was available. He was surprised at how sharp his mental images of Chloe were. Apparently she'd made even more of an impression on him three months ago than he'd realized.

"There must be a pencil somewhere," she muttered.

"You definitely need to find something to write with. I'll hold while you look."

It was a full minute before Chloe picked up the phone again. "Thank you for waiting, Mr. Raven. I'm sorry. I'm not usually this disorganized. I have a pen now."

"Write down this phone number and office address. It's for a friend of mine, Bill Schuller. Bill is an outstanding criminal defense attorney and you need to call him before the police question you again—"

"But I don't want Bill Schuller to be my lawyer!" Chloe protested. "I want you to represent me. That's why I called. Mr. Raven. Please, you have to help me."

"I *am* helping you. Trust me on this. Bill Schuller is the best criminal trial lawyer in Denver—"

"No, you're the best. Everyone says so. You won an acquittal for Sherri Norquist when the experts all predicted you were going to lose."

Liam's stomach knotted at the mention of Sherri's name. He was angry with himself for reacting to a case—and a woman—that were now more than three years in his past. Yeah, he'd been a complete idiot over Sherri Norquist. He'd allowed himself to be manipulated into falling in love with a murdering bitch and he'd hurt a good friend in the process. But hey, shit happens. It was time to move on. God knew Sherri certainly had, and seemingly without the smallest trace of guilt or regret.

He spoke crisply, skilled by now at keeping a barrier between his outward demeanor and what he was really feeling. "I appreciate the compliment, Mrs. Hamilton, but it's undeserved. The bottom line is that I just happened to make a big splash with a couple of my early cases. I haven't practiced as a criminal defense attorney in several years. These days, I deal only with divorce cases."

Which not only kept him away from an unsavory assortment of accused murderers, drug dealers and armed robbers, but provided him with the added pleasure of saying a mental *fuck you* to his bigamist father every time he took on a new case or signed off on a completed one. Liam understood that many worse things could happen to a kid than discovering his father had two wives and two separate families. Still, his disdain for his father ran deep; even the fact that the man had recently been murdered hadn't put an end to his anger.

He brought his attention back to Chloe. "You need to call Bill Schuller right away, before the police come back to question you again, Mrs. Hamilton. And keep in mind that the cops aren't joking around when they warn you that anything and everything you say can be used as evidence against you. Here's Bill's office phone number. Call him right now before you do anything else. It's important." He reeled off the number, repeated his condolences on Jason Hamilton's death and hung up before Chloe could protest any further.

Just as he finished the conversation with Chloe, No-Name came out of the bedroom, wrapped in a towel. She looked sleepy-eyed, cute and appallingly young. Jesus, what had he been thinking last night? Or not thinking, more like it, Liam reflected grimly.

"Oh, you're still here," she said, smiling in relief. "I was afraid you'd left already."

"No, I'm still here, but only just. I was answering the phone and didn't want to disturb you." He returned her smile with all the warmth he could muster. No-Name couldn't be much more than twenty-one, which would make her almost fifteen years his junior. There was still an appealing hint of hopeful innocence in her expression, and he felt a sharp twinge of remorse for having exploited her naiveté. He had years of experience in developing pick-up lines that worked, and she'd fallen for them all. True, he'd met her in a LoDo bar notorious as Casual Sex Central. Still, even for a one-night stand she deserved somebody a hell of a lot less cynical about relationships than he was. Three months ago he would almost certainly have dismissed her as off-limits, but since his father died at the beginning of May, it seemed as if the small store of human kindness left to him in the wake of the Sherri Norquist fiasco had vanished, rotting deep in the Atlantic Ocean alongside the bodies of his father and his father's mistress.

"I wish I could stay." Liam aimed another smile in No-Name's direction, a rueful one that suggested if only his job were not so demanding he'd be thrilled to spend the rest of the day with her. He wanted to let her down lightly. Or perhaps he wanted to convince himself that he hadn't been a total asshole to have slept with her in the first place.

He tapped his cell phone. "I'm sorry. I just answered an urgent call from my office and I have to leave right away. There's a family crisis involving one of my clients and they need me to catch the fallout."

"Now?" she asked, pouting. "So early? It's not even six-thirty!"

"I know. Wild, isn't it? I swear lawyers get more emergency calls than doctors."

"But you're a *divorce* lawyer. I wouldn't have expected divorce lawyers to get any emergency calls."

"Oh boy, are you wrong." He chucked her under the chin, feeling a hundred years old as he coaxed a smile. "I sometimes think divorce lawyers get more emergency calls than anyone else. Especially on a Monday morning. Weekends are tough on couples who are splitting up. That's when all the custody battles erupt and sometimes they erupt into battles that aren't just with words."

"Tell me about it." No-Name's eyes turned sad. "My parents divorced when I was fifteen. As far as I'm concerned, they'd have done us kids a huge favor if they'd split ten years earlier. They weren't physically violent, but the shouting was horrible."

"Failing marriages are rough on the kids whether you hang tough and stick it out or cut through the pain and file for divorce." Liam really didn't want to get into a discussion of the problems associated with couples who weren't willing to admit their marriage was over. That was a subject that cut too close to far too many bones.

He walked back into the bedroom, wondering if it was a custody battle between Jason and Chloe that had precipitated the mayor's murder. People killed their spouses over custody issues almost as often as they killed them over money and a lot more often than they killed them because of unfaithfulness. He'd barely been fifteen minutes into his first consultation with Chloe Hamilton when he realized that her daughter was the central focus of her life. She might well be capable of killing in defense of her daughter, Liam reflected, even if such an act would be impossible for her in other circumstances.

His professional instincts had shouted there was more going on when Chloe came to see him than a simple desire to get divorced. Equally, there had seemed to be something more behind her decision to stay with the mayor than a straightforward decision to reconcile. Despite his efforts to persuade Chloe to confide in him, she'd insisted she was the one who'd changed her mind and now wanted to give her marriage a second chance. He wasn't sure he believed her, then or now. At the time, he'd suspected that Jason Hamilton had used some sort of blackmail to prevent her from walking away from their marriage. If the mayor had threatened to fight her for custody of their daughter, Chloe might have decided to end the emotional blackmail by getting rid of her husband.

No-Name followed Liam into the bedroom, forcing his attention back to her. She leaned against the doorjamb, her towel slipping provocatively as she watched him dress. "Don't you want to take a shower before you leave? Or at least have some coffee?"

Liam tucked his shirt into his pants, zipping his fly as an excuse to pretend he hadn't noticed No-Name's bare breasts. "Thanks for the offer but I need to go home and get some clean clothes. I'm scheduled to appear in court today, and my client is paying big bucks for the privilege of having me turn up wearing a starched shirt and a silk tie."

No-Name protested some more, but not too forcefully, as if she didn't quite believe his excuses but didn't want to push too hard in case he told her something she didn't want to hear. He managed to get out of her apartment in less than five minutes. It would have been easy to lie, to promise to be in touch, but a final flare of conscience kept him silent, so that he left her standing at her front door, looking crestfallen. Truth, Liam thought wryly, was vastly overrated as an ingredient in sexual relationships.

By the time he made it to his car, his gut was twisted into a hard coil of tension. He chugged a handful of antacids, his usual breakfast, and drove with fierce concentration through the already dense traffic. Denver was a city that started early and 7:00 a.m. was well into the Monday morning rush hour.

It was a relief to enter the soothing austerity of his newly purchased condo overlooking Confluence Park. Liam had selected the white walls, slate floors and sleek contemporary furniture as a deliberate contrast to the cluttered, homey comfort of the Flying W, his parents' ranch in Wyoming.

He recognized that his almost compulsive desire for orderliness in his surroundings was a direct reflection of the chaos of his inner life and sometimes he wondered if he was ever going to reach the point where he would be able to let down his guard without risking an emotional meltdown. Still, whatever the psychological underpinnings of his decorating choices, the immaculate neatness and careful functionality of each room offered balm to his soul.

He tossed his car keys into the wooden bowl set on the chrome-and-glass side table in the entrance and made his way through the master bedroom to the shower, stopping en route to check his voice mail. There were four messages, all of them work related. It looked, thank God, as if it was going to be another frantic workweek. Just the sort of heavy-duty schedule he liked, with no time to stop and reflect.

He switched on the TV as he dressed and discovered that the murder of Jason Hamilton was making headlines on virtually every channel, not just locally but nationally, as well. Not surprising, he supposed, given that Jason had been the mayor of a major city and Chloe had worn the crown as America's Sweetheart for several months after the 1998 winter Olympics.

To make Jason's death even more tabloid-worthy, he was not only mayor, he was also a successful, multimillionaire real estate developer, and the son of a U.S. Army general who was a minor celebrity in his own right, having won the Medal of Honor for his bravery during combat service in Vietnam. The mayor's violent death represented an irresistible combination of wealth, fame and mystery for the ravenous maw of the 24-hour news machines. Flipping from one breathless report to the next, Liam decided that the cable news networks must all be praying that Chloe didn't get arrested too soon and spoil the potential for weeks of rabid speculation about the crime.

Facts about the murder were sparse, but it seemed that Jason's dead body had been discovered in the basement of their family home in Park Hill by his wife at approximately 3:30 a.m., Denver time. Death was apparently due to a stab wound, or possibly multiple stab wounds—the reports weren't clear.

Chloe Hamilton had discovered the body and tried to revive her husband. The newscasters—discreetly noncommittal at this stage of a developing story—refrained from speculating as to whether Chloe might possibly have gotten there before Jason died rather than after.

News editors were making up for lack of hard data about the crime by filling in with copious backstory. They reminded everyone that Jason Hamilton had been one of Denver's most popular mayors with approval ratings consistently hovering in the high seventies. He'd even managed to clear snow from obscure city side streets after last year's biggest blizzard—a feat that far exceeded the abilities of most of his predecessors and had won him the heartfelt gratitude of his constituents.

In between lectures on the political and civic consequences of Jason's death, the news shows ran footage of Chloe during her record-breaking gold medal run in the downhill race at the 1998 Winter Olympics. It was the first ever U.S. gold medal in this particular event, and in the wake of her win, Chloe had briefly been the recipient of wall-to-wall media attention, so there was plenty of film footage to be trotted out. The close-up shot of Chloe on the victory podium, teary-eyed but joyful, seemed to be the special favorite of news producers this morning. Liam could understand why. She was a stunning woman and her radiant smile made for a fantastic TV visual.

Having endured two weeks in the full glare of the media spotlight when his father was murdered back in May, Liam sympathized with what Chloe Hamilton must be going through right now. His sympathies were tempered, however, by the strong likelihood that she had, in fact, killed her husband. Spouses were always the first suspect in a murder case, and Liam's experience as a criminal lawyer had given him no reason to doubt the statistics. He figured that any Olympic gold medalist who chose to stab their spouse multiple times had to be prepared to face a little negative publicity.

Whatever the facts, whether she was the murderer or an innocent bystander, Chloe would be wise to steel herself for a continuing onslaught from the media ghouls. If the cops didn't identify her husband's killer within forty-eight hours, she was going to find herself soaring into the stratosphere of national attention. A miserable place to be, when the attention wasn't favorable.

Fortunately, none of the problems resulting from Jason Hamilton's murder were his to deal with. Liam shoved aside a twinge of irrational regret for his previous career as a criminal defense attorney. Yes, he'd relished the cut and thrust of courtroom battle, and he savored the memory of the innocent clients he'd help to set free, but his current work provided more income, more predictable hours and a lot less stress. He'd have to be crazy to consider switching back to the high-pressure work of defending criminals, especially with a famous client like Chloe Hamilton as his means for reentry. That would generate the sort of public scrutiny nobody in his family needed right now.

He drove to the office, mentally reviewing his schedule for the day. Jenny, the young woman who kept watch over the reception area, met him as soon as he arrived.

"Chloe Hamilton is waiting to see you." Jenny had clearly watched the morning news. She spoke in hushed tones, dazzled by Chloe's celebrity and the aura of criminal scandal surrounding her. "She realizes she doesn't have an appointment, but she says she really needs to see you as soon as you can spare a moment."

"Tell her I have no openings in my schedule this morning." Liam was in no mood to pander to Chloe Hamilton's strange fixation on hiring him as her defense attorney.

"You have almost half an hour before your next client is due to arrive," Jenny pointed out.

"If you watched the news this morning, you know Mrs. Hamilton needs a criminal lawyer," Liam said curtly.

"You were a criminal lawyer until a few years ago."

Liam glanced up, startled by Jenny's comment. She'd been with him eighteen months and never before indicated that she knew anything at all about his professional history.

"You're correct," he said coolly. "I *used* to be a criminal lawyer. Mrs. Hamilton is almost three years too late to hire me."

"Okay, you're the boss. I guess I'll tell her you're not avail— Oops." Jenny stood aside as Chloe walked into Liam's office.

"Mr. Raven, I'm sorry to force my way in, but I'm desperate—"

Chloe gave every appearance of speaking the truth. She looked nothing like the self-possessed, elegant woman who'd visited Liam's offices back in early April. Her hands visibly shook and her blue eyes had huge dark circles under them, all the more visible because her face was so pale beneath its golden tan. Her outfit passed beyond casual and well into ratty. She was wearing a misshapen lime green T-shirt that didn't match the formality of her tailored beige slacks and her hair was haphazardly tied back with a black scrunchie. Oddly, Liam still found her attractive, a fact that did nothing to improve his mood. Sherri Norquist had taught him everything he needed to know about the idiocy of defense lawyers who took on clients to whom they felt sexually attracted. He didn't need Chloe to provide a brush-up course in stupidity.

He spoke curtly. "As I informed you earlier this morning, Mrs. Hamilton, you should make an appointment to see Bill Schuller. I can assure you that Bill will provide outstanding counsel."

"I tried to hire Mr. Schuller. It can't be done. He's fishing in the Alaskan wilderness. Nobody can reach him until he gets back to the base camp on the Alagnak River, and that's going to be another forty-eight hours at least. I can't wait forty-eight hours, Mr. Raven. I need a lawyer now. This minute."

"Why the urgency?"

"Because I think the police will arrest me as soon as I go back to either my home or the official mayoral residence. My sister called me a few minutes ago. The cops have even been out to her house to see if she knew where I was."

Liam looked at her assessingly. If Chloe was right about the fact that she was on the verge of being arrested, she definitely needed immediate legal help. "I can give you fifteen minutes," he said, although he wasn't sure why he made the concession. He gestured to indicate that she should take a chair.

"Do you want me to take notes?" Jenny asked hopefully.

Liam inclined his head. "Yes, thank you."

"No," Chloe said abruptly. "I prefer to speak to you alone, Mr. Raven. No notes."

Jenny looked at him inquiringly, and Liam shrugged, then nodded to indicate that she should leave. As soon as they were alone, Chloe sat down, although she perched on the edge of her seat as if she might take flight at the slightest provocation.

"Tell me why you think the police are going to arrest you," Liam said. Since he only had a narrow time window before his next client arrived, he figured they might as well cut to the chase.

Chloe's hand fluttered; then she clenched her fists and shoved both hands into her lap as if despising the helpless gesture. "They have a witness who claims to have seen me stab Jason."

"Who's the witness?"

"Sophie's nanny."

"Does the nanny dislike you?"

"I don't think so. Trudi's from Finland and

came over here to improve her English. She's reliable and honest and she's never given the slightest sign of having a grudge against me. I like her and I think she likes me. Or she used to, until this morning. Now I daresay she thinks I'm a vicious killer."

"Is she right?" Liam asked mildly. "Did you stab your husband?"

She looked straight at him. "No, Mr. Raven, I didn't stab Jason. I didn't harm him in any way. When Trudi saw me, I was trying to unbutton Jason's shirt and look at his injuries. I know it was a crazy thing to do, but when you see somebody you love lying in a pool of blood, you don't think, you just react. I thought that if I could only pad the wound, then maybe I could give him CPR and he'd start breathing again."

Her explanation was ridiculous coming from a woman as smart as Chloe Hamilton, especially in view of the knowledge she must have of human anatomy after her years of intensive athletic training. However, that didn't mean her account was a lie. Liam's training and professional instincts all suggested to him that Chloe was the most likely murderer, but he also knew that innocent people occasionally ended up in the wrong place at the wrong time—and not only on television crime shows.

Jenny buzzed the intercom. He picked up the phone, so that Chloe wouldn't hear whatever Jenny had to say. "Liam, Tony Johnston has arrived."

"Thanks, Jenny. I'll be right with him."

Liam glanced at his watch. Tony Johnston was ten minutes early but he was a man with a high regard for his own importance. Not a good client to keep waiting and a man who couldn't be shunted aside for a preliminary meeting with Helen, Liam's highly competent paralegal. Tony Johnston's self-importance meter would explode from righteous indignation at the prospect of discussing his failed marriage with a mere paralegal.

Liam started scribbling a list of names onto the notepad on his desk. "Mrs. Hamilton, I'm sorry but my next client has already arrived." He tore off the sheet and handed it to her. "These are for you. In my opinion, those are the half-dozen best criminal attorneys currently practicing in the Denver area. As I mentioned earlier, Bill Schuller is the best, but any of these six would be more than competent. I've included Robyn Johnson's name on the list. She's outstanding, but she's approaching sixty, and these days she's spending most of her time on pro bono work for people who've already been convicted."

Chloe ripped the list in two and tossed the crumpled pieces onto Liam's desk. "I don't want Bill Schuller, or the great Robyn Johnson, who probably isn't available anyway. I don't want any of these other attorneys. I want you."

She really was beginning to sound somewhere close to obsessive. What the hell was her problem? There was something going on here that he was missing, Liam decided.

"I'm a good lawyer, Mrs. Hamilton, but I'm not *that* good, and it certainly isn't to your advantage right now to have a lawyer whose courtroom skills have been rusting for almost three years. You ought to be begging Robyn Johnson to put aside her pro bono work and take you on if you want truly brilliant representation. Why are you so determined to hire me?"

She looked at him in silence and for a moment he was sure she wouldn't answer.

Then she gave a tiny shrug, as if clearing some final mental hurdle.

"Because you're Sophie's father," she said. "I thought that might give you a vested interest in keeping me out of prison."